STOCKHAUSEN: A BIOGRAPHY

Stockhausen: A BIOGRAPHY
Michael Kurtz
TRANSLATED BY RICHARD TOOP

faber and faber
LONDON · BOSTON

First published in Great Britain in 1992
by Faber and Faber Limited
3 Queen Square London WC1N 3AU

Originally published in German in 1988
by Bärenreiter Kassel, Basel

Phototypeset by Intype, London
Printed in England by Clays Ltd, St Ives plc

© Michael Kurtz, 1988, 1992
English translation © Richard Toop, 1992

Michael Kurtz is hereby identified as author of this book
in accordance with Section 77 of the Copyright, Designs and Patents Act 1988

The publishers thank Jonathan Cott, New York,
for permission to quote passages from his book
Stockhausen: Conversations with the Composer
(Simon and Schuster, New York, 1973).
Quotations from the volumes of Stockhausen's
Texte zur Musik appear by kind permission
of the composer and DuMont Verlag, Cologne.

Translation of 'The String Man'
by Suzanne Stephens

A CIP record for this book
is available from the British Library

ISBN 0-571-14323-7

10 9 8 7 6 5 4 3 2 1

For Manfred, Ritva and my children

Contents

List of Illustrations viii
Preface xi
Preface to the German Edition xiii
Introduction: A Sirius Centre in France 1
1 Childhood and Youth 1928–47 7
2 Writer or Composer 1947–51 21
3 Awakening after a Musical 'Zero Hour' 1951–3 32
4 Electronic Music: A Musical Homunculus 1953–5 58
5 Spatial and Aleatory Music 1955–60 79
6 From Moment Form to Live Electronics 1961–5 110
7 'A Music of All Countries and Races' 1966–8 141
8 *Aus den sieben Tagen* 1968–70 160
9 Music as Gateway to the Spiritual 1970–74 182
10 New Interpreters, New Instrumental Techniques 1974–7 200
11 *Licht* 1977–91 210
Notes 237
Select Bibliography 248
List of Works 250
Index 263

Illustrations

1 Stockhausen at the start of the seventies (Klaus Barisch, Cologne)
2 Extract from the first sketch for *Licht* (Stockhausen-Verlag, Kürten)
3 Stockhausen's mother
4 Stockhausen's father (Michael Kurtz Archive, Bochum)
5 Stockhausen around 1929
6 Stockhausen in Engelsbruch with his grandmother and sister, 1936
7 Cousins' communion at Hoppengarten, Easter 1937 (Michael Kurtz Archive, Bochum)
8 Performance of *Burleska*, 1950 (Detmar Seuthe, Cologne)
9 Stockhausen, Doris Stockhausen and Karel Goeyvaerts in Cologne, 1956 (Karel Goeyvaerts, Antwerp)
10 Extract from *Kreuzspiel* (© 1960 Universal Edition AG, Vienna)
11 Messiaen's analysis class at the Paris Conservatoire, 1952
12 Gerth-Wolfgang Baruch, Stockhausen and Heinrich Strobel, 1952 (Hella Steinecke, Bildarchiv Internationales Musikinstitut, Darmstadt)
13 Luigi Nono and Stockhausen at Donaueschingen, 1952 (Archiv Universal Edition, Vienna)
14 Herbert Eimert and Stockhausen in the electronic studio at WDR Cologne, 1953–4 (WDR-Bildarchiv, Cologne)
15 Extract from *Studie II* (© 1956 Universal Edition AG, Vienna)
16 Extract from *Klavierstück V* (© 1965 Universal Edition AG, Vienna)
17 Werner Meyer-Eppler lecturing at Bonn University, 1959 (Thomas Meyer-Eppler, Cologne)
18 Ton de Leeuw, Stockhausen, Edgard Varèse and Walter Maas in Bilthoven, 1957 (Walter Maas, Bilthoven)

19 Stockhausen and John Cage in Munich, 1972 (Felicitas Timpe, Munich)
20 Fundamental spectra over seven durations (mountain panorama at Paspels) (Stockhausen-Verlag, Kürten)
21 Extract from *Zeitmasse* (© 1957 Universal Edition AG, Vienna)
22 Poster advertising the première of *Klavierstück XI*, 1957 (David Tudor, Stony Point)
23 Pierre Boulez, Bruno Maderna and Stockhausen (WDR-Bildarchiv, Cologne)
24 Extract from *Zyklus* (© 1960 Universal Edition AG, Vienna)
25 Extract from *Carré* (© 1971 Universal Edition AG, Vienna)
26 Extract from *Carré* (© 1971 Universal Edition AG, Vienna)
27 Stockhausen in the WDR electronic studio, 1959 (WDR-Bildarchiv, Cologne)
28 Extract from *Kontakte* (© 1966 Universal Edition AG, Vienna)
29 Mary Bauermeister's *Sand-Stein-Kugelgruppe* (Peter Moore, New York)
30 Mary Bauermeister in the Lintgasse studio around 1960 (Mary Bauermeister, Cologne)
31 Stockhausen, Kurt Schwertsik and David Tudor in Rome, 1962 (Leopold von Knobelsdorff, Cologne)
32 Pierre Boulez, Stockhausen and Theodor W. Adorno at Darmstadt, 1961 (Harald Bojé, Wuppertal)
33 Transformation of the Diodon and Orthagoriscus (from W. Thompson, *Growth and Form*, 2nd edn, Cambridge University Press, 1952)
34 Stockhausen rehearsing at WDR Cologne, 1965 (WDR-Bildarchiv, Cologne)
35 Stockhausen with students at the Cologne New Music Courses, 1966–7 (Leni Schmidt, Cologne)
36 Extract from *Mixtur* (© 1966 Universal Edition AG, Vienna)
37 Extract from *Mikrophonie I* (© 1974 Universal Edition AG, Vienna)
38 Stockhausen at Kürten, 1965 (Albert Günther, Cologne)
39 Stockhausen in Japan, 1966 (Ogami, Tokyo)
40 Performance of *Ensemble*, 1967 (Pit Ludwig, Bildarchiv Internationales Musikinstitut, Darmstadt)
41 The Stockhausen Group in Amsterdam, 1968 (Harald Bojé, Wuppertal)
42 Extract from *Stimmung* (© 1969 Universal Edition AG, Vienna)
43 Extract from *Stimmung* (© 1969 Universal Edition AG, Vienna)

44 Extract from *Kurzwellen* (© 1969 Universal Edition AG, Vienna)
45 Stockhausen and Rolf Gehlhaar at Darmstadt, 1968 (Pit Ludwig, Bildarchiv Internationales Musikinstitut, Darmstadt)
46 Extract from *Fresco* (© 1969 Universal Edition AG, Vienna)
47 Performance of *Hymnen* at Jeita, 1969 (Harald Bojé, Wuppertal)
48 Stockhausen in the German Pavilion at Osaka, 1970 (WDR-Bildarchiv, Cologne)
49 Formula for *Mantra* (Stockhausen-Verlag, Kürten)
50 Poster advertising the première of *Hymnen* with orchestra, 1971 (WDR-Bildarchiv, Cologne)
51 Stockhausen in the early seventies (Bernard Perrine, Paris)
52 Stockhausen and his children in the early seventies
53 Formula and prayer gestures for *Inori* (Stockhausen-Verlag, Kürten)
54 'Sei wieder fröhlich' from *Amour* (Stockhausen-Verlag, Kürten)
55 Kathinka Pasveer performing in Odense, 1987 (Henning Lohner, Cologne)
56 Suzanne Stephens performing in Odense, 1987 (Henning Lohner, Cologne)
57 Extract from *Tierkreis* (Stockhausen-Verlag, Kürten)
58 Super-formula for *Donnerstag* from *Licht* (Stockhausen-Verlag, Kürten)
59 Extract from 'Vision' (Stockhausen-Verlag, Kürten)
60 Scene from the première of *Samsag* from *Licht*, 1984 (Lelli and Masotti, Teatro alla Scala, Milan)
61 Extract from 'Luzifers Abschied' (Stockhausen-Verlag, Kürten)
62 Drawing of IRCAM, Paris (IRCAM, Paris)
63 Stockhausen and Kathinka Pasveer with children from the Chorus of Radio Budapest, 1986 (Henning Lohner, Cologne)
64 Scene from *Montag* from *Licht* (Lelli and Masotti, Teatro alla Scala, Milan)
65 Extract from 'Ave' (Stockhausen-Verlag, Kürten)
66 Stockhausen in the WDR electronic studio, 1988 (Henning Lohner, Cologne)
67 Stockhausen's autograph instructions for 'Ave' (Stockhausen-Verlag, Kürten)

Preface

The biographer of Stockhausen could have no better fortune than to find himself in the hands of a translator who is himself a Stockhausen expert. Richard Toop's credentials are impressive. He worked as Stockhausen's assistant in Cologne in the early seventies, and after that published several articles on the composer which are simply a 'must' if dealing with him. So I naturally had to meet and interview him when doing research for this book. He turned out to be a cooperative and helpful partner, and even let me make use of his own unpublished manuscript on Stockhausen.

For the English translation the book has been revised and enlarged with some new material. There is an extended passage on Stockhausen and the conjuror Adrion, as well as recent information on the years 1988 to 1991 and further quotations from letters published here for the first time – to Karel Goeyvaerts (about his first experiences in the electronic studio), to Doris Stockhausen (on the compositional process) and to Kurt Schwertsik (about pop art in New York in the early sixties). Cage's commentary on *Klavierstück XI* has been added to the section 'Darmstadt 1958': this formed part of the lecture Cage delivered there that year. And finally, there are two brief texts by the composer on his encounters with Hindemith and Shostakovich.

I would like to express my thanks to Hugh Davies, who pointed out some errors in the book. My grateful thanks are due to Karlheinz Stockhausen himself, who generously checked the typescript and was able to add a few more details.

Michael Kurtz
Bochum, May 1991

Preface to the German Edition

Perhaps the best way to gauge Stockhausen's significance for the music of the second half of the twentieth century is to try to imagine this musical era without him. From his beginnings as a student in Cologne in 1949, writing like Hindemith, to the composition of *Licht*, his *Gesamtkunstwerk*, which has occupied him since 1977, Stockhausen's work has undergone many changes. He is always setting himself new tasks, taking up 'hot themes that were in the air', as he once put it, and evolving striking musical responses to them. His works, like his whole thinking, have constantly challenged the music world and have met with much acclaim, but they have also aroused much opposition. Ever since Stockhausen began to bring the 'spiritual dimension' of music to the fore at the end of the sixties, he has attracted many critics; indeed, it would be easy to compile a 'Dictionary of Invective' for Stockhausen, just as Wilhelm Tappert did in 1876 as an apologia for Wagner. Many people imagine that it was his travels in Asia or his reading of Aurobindo that revealed this spiritual dimension to Stockhausen, but in fact, as this biography will show, it was evident during the composer's student years, and even in his childhood.

Stockhausen's musical output is well documented, and the composer himself has published six volumes of *Texte zur Musik*, but what has been lacking is a broad coverage of the composer's life and work. In 1980 I began to research this biography, interviewing and talking to many people. (The conversations with Alfred Alings and a preliminary one with Johannes Fritsch took place in the early seventies.) Clearly it is still too soon for a critical evaluation of Stockhausen, so on the whole personal judgements and interpretations have been avoided in favour of allowing Stockhausen and the people interviewed to speak for themselves. I could easily have written a book twice as long, but the publisher's brief sensibly placed a limit on the length. As a result I have not dealt with Stockhausen's work as a writer on music, and as a rule have confined myself to the outstanding events from his concerts and lectures.

This book is the first to give a detailed description of Stockhausen's early life – the period from 1928 to 1951 – and to consider his early efforts as an author; it has also thrown up some new facts. (A few dates given in earlier publications could be corrected; for example, Stockhausen's first Webern lecture was given in Darmstadt in 1953, and not, as the composer and many others after him have claimed, 1952. Similarly, Stockhausen spent the first half of 1964 in Philadelphia and New York, not, as asserted previously, 1965. Even the score of *Originale* gives 1965 as the date for the New York première, which actually took place in 1964.)

My thanks are due to all those who contributed to this book, and above all to the composer. He made himself available for five interviews between 1980 and 1986, gave me copies of his writings, including letters, essays and interviews, and answered many further questions by letter and telephone. He took an active interest in research into his ancestors and childhood, and found that it shed new light on many aspects of those years. Heartfelt thanks are due to Suzanne Stephens, Doris Stockhausen and Mary Bauermeister, whose memories lent particular weight to the book.

For thorough ancestral research in various church records I thank Josef Schäfer and Doris Schönen. Josef Schäfer's last work before his death in 1981 was his essay 'Der Rittersitz Stockhausen'. Thanks to Luzia Stockhausen, the composer's stepmother; to his sister Katharina Ernst; to relatives on his father's side – his aunt Anna Stockhausen, his cousins Anna Thiel and Willi Heiden, and his boyhood friend Josef Jost; and to relatives on his mother's side – his aunt Agnes Kieven, his uncle Wilhelm Stupp, his cousins Gerda Heinen and Christian Stupp.

In covering every stage of Stockhausen's childhood and youth, I got a feeling for each landscape and location, and talked to his father's former fellow teachers, friends and pupils. Special thanks are due to Otto Müller from Bedburg and Christoph Buchen from the Morsbach town hall, who helped with my research in all kinds of ways. I met Anton Luig, who taught Stockhausen in Altenberg; the son and daughter-in-law (a fellow pupil of Stockhausen) of the cathedral organist Franz-Josef Kloth; and Annette Bökmann, whose father, Clemens Spürck, owned the farm where

Stockhausen worked in 1945. At a school reunion, Ernest Resken and his class-mates talked about Stockhausen and the Xanten teacher training college; his class teacher Hans Komorowski reported on Stockhausen as a pupil in Xanten, and Willi Brosseder (a member of the Blecher Theatrical Society) on Stockhausen's period as an operetta conductor and actor.

Concerning Stockhausen's student days, I learned much from Esther and Hermann Braun, Peter Lachmund, Detmar Seuthe, Gerhard Wasmuth and Klaus Weiler. Dorothea Eimert reported on Herbert Eimert, Marion Rothärmel and Helmut Kirchmeyer on the Stockhausen-Eimert relationship. The beginnings of the electronic studio were described in detail by Robert Beyer and Heinz Schütz, and Leopold von Knobelsdorff dealt with a later phase in the studio's existence. Information about Werner Meyer-Eppler came from his widow Hiltrud Meyer-Eppler and his son Thomas. Elena Ungeheuer shed light on Meyer-Eppler's origins in terms of scientific history. Georg Heike and Hans G. Tillmann told of studies with Meyer-Eppler, and Darmstadt in the fifties. For talking about Stockhausen around the fifties I am grateful to Pär Ahlbom, Konrad Boehmer, Ernst Brücher, Karel Goeyvaerts, Paul Gredinger, Hans G. Helms, Gottfried Michael Koenig, Heinz-Klaus Metzger, Pierre Schaeffer and Alfred Schlee – thanks here to Universal Edition, who gave access to their correspondence with Stockhausen and made scores available – Kurt Schwertsik, Otto Tomek and Martti Vuorenjuuri; among those who reported on the sixties were Irena Häyry, Leni Schmidt, the widow of Hugo Wolfram Schmidt, and Erich Schneider-Wessling; on the seventies and eighties I was assisted by James Ingram, Saara Leiviskä, Jayne Obst, Robert H. P. Platz, Jill Purce and Richard Toop. Richard Toop kindly made available the manuscript of his unpublished book on Stockhausen (1928–1959), from which I took facts and dates concerning the period 1953 to 1959.

I am also indebted to Stockhausen's assistants and the following composers and musicians who have worked with him – they helped in all kinds of ways and patiently answered every question: Alfred Alings, Harald Bojé, Christoph Caskel, Hugh Davies, Peter Eötvös, Johannes Fritsch, Rolf Gehlhaar, Herbert Henck, Joachim Krist, Wilhelm Meyer, Tim Souster and David Tudor. (In a cordial letter Aloys Kontarsky apologized, explaining that, because of his illness, his speech was still too poor for him to give information.)

I asked Ernst Thomas and Wilhelm Schlüter about the Darmstadt Summer Courses, and Reinhard Oelschlägel spoke about them from a

participant's point of view. My gratitude also to Rudolf Kaehr, who has
custody of Gotthard Günther's estate and is working on the further
development of his ideas; to Arthur Larnka from the Cologne Stadt-
Anzeiger, who applied his influence most helpfully; to Helmut Hopf, who
was very encouraging in the early stages of the book and paved the
way for first contacts with publishers; and to Norbert Visser for two
conversations about 'spatial music' that clarified certain things but also
raised new questions. Particularly warm thanks go to Jürgen Schriefer,
whose lectures afforded important insights into music history. From the
late sixties onwards I was always able to talk to him about Stockhausen
and present-day music, and this provided essential stimuli.

For providing information by mail or on the telephone I should like
to thank the conjuror Alexander Adrion, Valentina and Marc Chagall,
Bernhard Hansen from North German Radio, Anno Hecker, Josefa and
Eugen Heinen, Irmela Himmelmann (née Sandt), Horst Egon Kalinow-
ski, Harry Kramer, Helmut Lachenmann, Hans Ulrich Lehmann, Wolf-
gang Marschner, Adalbert Martin, Jona Meese, Marcelle Mercenier,
Volker Michels of Suhrkamp Verlag, Frankfurt, the editor and custodian
of Hermann Hesse's work, Abraham Moles, Wolfgang Pelzer, Christian
Petrescu, Jean Reuge, Georg W. Schmidt, Markus Stockhausen, Ulrich
Süsse, Viktor Suslin on Stockhausen in Moscow, Erik Tawaststjerna,
John Tilbury, who is writing a biography of Cornelius Cardew, Bernhard
Weyer, director emeritus of the Nicolaus Cusanus grammar school, and
Ernst Otto Wölper.

I am very grateful to the authors of the written contributions to this
book: Olivier Messiaen, Kurt Schwertsik and Allen Ginsberg. Particular
thanks are due to Peter Eötvös and James Ingram, who read major
parts of the manuscript and made critical remarks, to the Internationales
Musikinstitut, Darmstadt, in whose archives I was allowed to work, and
to Wilhelm Schlüter, who dealt promptly with all questions concerning
the dates of concerts, etc. I am also indebted to the city of Darmstadt,
which contributed to printing costs. Friendliest thanks to Rudolf Frisius,
who made his archive available, helped with many questions of musical
analysis, read the manuscript and commented on it.

At a private level, my particular gratitude goes to Ulrich, who got
involved in many enterprises, was a stimulating partner in conversations
about Stockhausen and offered encouragement at critical phases in writing
the book, as well as to Ritva, who looked after my well-being, listened to
each new chapter with angelic patience and made many valuable obser-

vations. Last but not least, my hearty thanks to the Cultural Foundation of the Cologne Kreissparkasse, without whose generous financial support this book would not have been possible.

Michael Kurtz
Bochum, May 1988

Introduction: A Sirius Centre in France

> Every seven years the works group
> into cycles, the tree-rings of my
> life, so to speak.
> Stockhausen

In the summer of 1977 what twenty-five years of musical activity in Germany had failed to achieve had become possible in France: Karlheinz Stockhausen was looking for a suitable building for his own music centre, which the French minister of culture had offered him for life. The Sirius Centre, named after Stockhausen's work *Sirius*, was to be 'a centre to foster the music of Karlheinz Stockhausen'. The old monastic building of Ville-neuve-les-Avignon in southern France seemed suitable, but renovation and rebuilding would take some time, so Stockhausen held his Sirius Centre courses that summer, from 22 July to 8 August, at the Darius Milhaud Conservatoire in Aix-en-Provence.

Only a few weeks earlier Stockhausen had had the idea of composing a vast musico-dramatic cycle, *Licht*: seven full-length operas, one for each day of the week – a gigantic work for which there was no precedent in music history. It was not to be a literary opera, nor a historical work. Stockhausen was seeking to write 'cosmological opera', which 'accords with the truth of the Now and the Eternal'.[1] For some years he had been working closely with a group of instrumentalists, singers and dancers, and he now saw the possibility of spending a long period each year at the Sirius Centre, where he would rehearse parts of the work and, where possible, perform them.

When Stockhausen returned from Aix-en-Provence to his house in Kürten, near Cologne, he found a letter from the Cologne Musikhochschule. He had directed the composition class there since 1971, but relations between Stockhausen and the Hochschule had reached crisis point more than once. For the forthcoming term he was being asked to teach an extra thirteen hours a week; in his brief reply he wrote: 'Great new tasks in various countries make it impossible that in future I should be as closely tied to the Hochschule as you and the ministry imagine.'[2]

I

He resigned from his teaching post and immediately began to compose a work commissioned some years earlier by the National Theatre of Tokyo – *Der Jahreslauf* for dancers and orchestra. It was an honour, as it was the first time the theatre had commissioned a foreigner. The work was to use only the instruments of the ancient imperial court music – gagaku – and no sound was to be modified electronically.

Stockhausen had been to Japan several times, and the country's ancient court culture had deeply impressed him. In 1966, at the electronic studio of Japanese Radio in Tokyo, he had composed the piece *Telemusik* and dedicated it to the people of Japan. In early autumn 1977 he flew to Tokyo and then stayed in the old imperial city of Kyoto, where he completed *Der Jahreslauf*. In the mornings, he would visit the temples of the imperial city. Many of them lie in beautiful ornamental gardens. One morning Stockhausen was sitting on the wooden terrace of a temple building, sketching a few musical ideas. In the background, from within one of the temple halls, he could hear the priests singing and praying. Stockhausen was familiar with such ceremonies from earlier visits to Japan. The idea suddenly came to him of composing a seven-part work on the basis of a single, multi-layered musical 'formula'. *Der Jahreslauf*, instead of being a self-contained composition, became a part of *Licht*.

Listening to the priests, who were singing so softly in the other building of the temple – only once did I see one of them pass by – I began to focus on what they were singing . . . and a sort of enlightenment came to me when I listened more closely to the intervals, and discovered relationships to Gregorian chant; what is it that really distinguishes European music and Indian music and this Japanese music? The intervals are more or less the same, even if here and there a second or a third or a fourth may be somewhat higher or lower. And you hear the same melodies in the Arab countries. So what makes the difference? And at a stroke I became aware that all the differences in cultures and languages, and in the compositions of individual composers, are *dialects*, and that the fundamental measure of them all is the same: the intervals.[3]

On 31 October 1977 *Der Jahreslauf* was premièred at the Tokyo National Theatre. To the sound of the gagaku instruments, a millenium dancer, a century dancer, a decade dancer and a year dancer moved to and fro across the large figures 1977 on a slightly raked stage; they moved at markedly different tempos. The course of the years is interrupted four times by the 'temptations' of Lucifer, the spirit of seduction, and each time an angel appears to give fresh courage, and the course of the years is resumed.

At the beginning of November Stockhausen went back to Germany.

1 Stockhausen at the start of the seventies

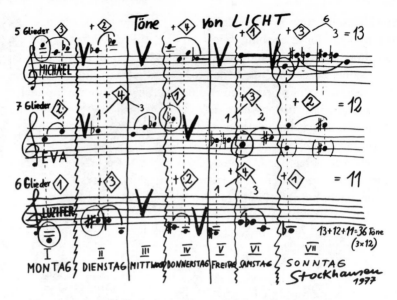

2 From the first sketch for *Licht* (Kyoto, October 1977)

He became preoccupied with the significance of the seven days of the week in various cultures and esoteric traditions – the Cabbala, the Tarot, Helena Blavatsky, Alice Bailey and many others – and began working out an overall plan for *Licht*. *Donnerstag* was the first to be composed; *Der Jahreslauf* became a scene from *Dienstag*.

The period July to November 1977 saw a concentration of important events in Stockhausen's life: the idea of composing *Licht*, the end of the Cologne professorship and the beginnings of his own Sirius Centre, as well as the experience in Japan that made *Der Jahreslauf* a part of *Licht*. Stockhausen has said that since 1949, when he was twenty-one, his work has developed in seven-year cycles – 'the tree-rings of my life'.[4] These seven-year cycles may even be discerned in Stockhausen's childhood. Now he was forty-nine years old, and beginning his *magnum opus, Licht*.[5]

Stockhausen had not been composing *Donnerstag* for long when he received the surprising news from France that for nationalist and political reasons his Sirius Centre would only be funded for three years: a clear breach of faith with Stockhausen, who had already expended much time and money in planning the centre. Stockhausen, not prepared to go along with such a short-term project, abandoned the Sirius Centre, and his hope of evolving and rehearsing the operatic cycle *Licht* there.

It was not the first time that formidable obstacles had been placed in

Stockhausen's way. From childhood on, nothing had come easily – he had to fight for everything himself. The radical nature of his works had always scandalized audiences and kindled heated discussions among professional musicians, but he looked on difficulties and resistance as a challenge, a test of whether he could nevertheless achieve his goal. Not infrequently, obstructions have actually unleashed new forces and ideas within him. Stockhausen decided, despite everything, to realize his *Licht* project. The composition commissions he constantly receives from music festivals and other organizations allow him to give preliminary concert performances of single scenes from his full-length operas, until a major, famous opera house is found to stage a whole 'day' from *Licht*.

A few months after Stockhausen had begun *Donnerstag*, his former pupil Johannes Fritsch greeted him on the occasion of his fiftieth birthday:

Anyone who has had to deal with him for any length of time has received indelible impressions; anyone who has had to part from him – and there are quite a few who have been struck off his list of friends – will never forget this parting. However much he may regard himself as a transit station for cosmic and divine forces, which he makes audible, the work and the person really are one in the most human sense. Anyone who has seen the *Momente* film remembers the 'flower'-fermata, and that perspiring face, with its utter love for the melody, for the singer, for everything it sees and hears, dividing the reality of this music between tension and resolution. In this moment of moments, as in many in other works, there is something that radiates a utopia of all-embracing unity, of the identity of the powers of myth and Eros, of the secret goal of all art . . . His current self-assurance does not make it any easier to accept his persona and work. Yet his concern to make a world music, reaching across cultures and even between planets, could always be understood as a striving for illumination, but also for power and recognition, that comes straight out of the middle European, German, Rhineland traditions of cultural history. A twentieth-century Faust, whose 'Tragedy, Part II' we are now experiencing.[6]

A twentieth-century Faust, always in search of the laws, of the active forces within all that is musical, of what it is in music that 'binds together the inmost world'. In the fifties Stockhausen penetrated the acoustic microworld of sounds, assembling the first artificial, 'electronic' timbres from the sounds of generators. Thereafter, aleatory music, spatial music and moment form were all inseparably associated with his name. At the end of the sixties his 'intuitive music' was directed towards expanding and transcending the boundaries of consciousness, towards opening oneself up fully to the realm of creative ideas, to intuition. From the very start music and religion were, for Stockhausen, closely linked; in later years, he

5

dubbed himself a 'searcher for God' and a 'child of God'. Let us turn now to Part I of this Faustian drama: Stockhausen's childhood and youth.

1 Childhood and Youth 1928–47

> I was lucky to have experienced
> so much in my childhood, to have
> learned so much.
> Stockhausen

Landscapes and Ancestors

Not far from Cologne, at the point where the Rhine leaves the landscape of vineyards and winds between subalpine peaks, its previously narrow valley broadens out into the fertile 'Cologne bight'. Here, to the left of the Rhine, and as an offshoot of the Eifel, there extends what was once a gently hilly, woodland mountain ridge, the Ville, also known locally as 'the foothills'. There are probably few landscapes in Europe that have had to change as much as that of the Ville. Huge lignite deposits lay underground, and ever since the first excavator arrived at the end of the last century, open-cast lignite mines have destroyed the landscape, leaving it unrecognizable. Numerous monasteries and churches, fortresses and castles have fallen victim to the mines, and villages, hamlets and country manors have disappeared completely or been rebuilt elsewhere. New hills, lakes and villages sprang up bit by bit – vast sums were spent in an attempt to close the wounds of the lignite mine constructions. Driving through the Ville today, it is easy to admire the technical facilities that have been introduced. And yet a certain unease may be sensed: for all its external perfection, the artificial landscape and its villages have a sterile, lifeless effect. As the lignite ran out, huge electricity power stations came into being. Today the tiny area of the Ville generates a large part of the whole of Germany's electricity supply.

At three in the morning on 22 August 1928 Karlheinz Stockhausen, weighing a handsome twelve and a quarter pounds, was born in Mödrath, a little village in the lignite district. (Since then, Mödrath too has fallen victim to open-cast mining and been rebuilt elsewhere. But 'Burg Mödrath', an early nineteenth-century manor house, which served as the local maternity home, remains unscathed.) In October 1927, less than a year before Stockhausen's birth, the primary school teacher Simon Stockhausen had married Gertrud Stupp, daughter of a well-off farming family.

7

Stockhausen's parents were both Catholics. In the political and social confusion of the Weimar Republic budget cuts led to many teaching positions being axed, to salaries being cut and to teachers being shunted from one job to another. In May 1928 Simon Stockhausen was moved to Caster. He and his young wife had found lodgings at her parents' farm in Neurath, a village at the northern edge of the fertile loess landscape of the Cologne bight, which at this point slowly changes into the plains of the Netherlands. The Stupps were the most prosperous and oldest farming family in the district, and had many employees. It was here that Stockhausen spent the first four weeks of his life, not far away from the Frimmersdorf electricity works (which thirty-five years later became the biggest heating factory in the world), and then his father was transferred once again.

Gertrud Stockhausen could be described as a beautiful woman; she was calm and orderly, had learned to play the piano and later often accompanied her own mellifluous singing. Stockhausen's father was an idealistic, dutiful man, at the same time sanguine and fervently enthusiastic. He was always busy, actively involved in many clubs (the singing club, the shooting club and the ex-servicemen's club), had been a soldier in the First World War – Stockhausen once described his father as a 'fanatical front-line man' – and had a passionate love of hunting. As an elementary school teacher he had had to learn the piano and violin, though he did not play too well. The world of theatre was in his blood, and whenever possible he would direct theatrical performances with his pupils, the Kolping family or the dramatic society. When he was only three, Karlheinz sat on the edge of the stage while his father rehearsed Ludwig Anzengruber's *Der Meineidbauer* in Morsbach and, soon after, Harald Bunje's *Der Etappenhase* in Bärbroich. Later, in Altenberg, he arranged a scene from Engelbert Humperdinck's *Hänsel und Gretel* for a Christmas festivity in the neighbouring village, and Karlheinz and his sister sang 'Abends will ich schlafen gehn, vierzehn Engel um mich stehn' ('This evening I shall go to sleep, and fourteen angels watch will keep').

His father's parents' house was on the east bank of the Rhine, in the Oberbergisch region. It was a scanty, isolated farm on the sterile heights known as Engelsbruch, above the Sieg valley where Herchen lay. The Stockhausens may be traced back to the Thirty Years War in the Dattenfelder church records: mostly they were 'field folk'. Simon Stockausen claimed he knew that his ancestors came from 'impoverished nobility', and it is possible that the Stockhausens once dwelt in the Rittersitz Stockhausen, near Asbach in the Westerwald. The Stockhausens in

3 Stockhausen's mother, Gertrud (née Stupp; 1900–1941)

4 Stockhausen's father, Simon (1899–1945)

Engelsbruch were pioneers; they left their little half-timbered home early each morning with picks slung over their shoulders and a slice of bread in their pockets to clear out a new parcel of land. They were said to have coarse, blunt dispositions that could flare up into fury. Reports of the composer's grandfather and his brother suggest they were a couple of roughnecks. At a tavern in Herchen there was a brawl with other guests that left some broken furniture, which the two gentlemen had to replace. The life of these people was stamped by the harsh Oberbergisch surroundings and hard daily toil. It would probably not be wrong to suggest that Stockhausen draws his vibrant health and vast strength from this reservoir.

Playing the Piano and Guarding Cows in the Village

The first seven years of Stockhausen's life were spent on the move; his father had four new postings and the rapidly growing family had to be rehoused six times. A sister Katherina, was born in 1929, a brother, Hermann-Josef ('Hermännchen'), in 1932. In January 1930 the family was sent to the east side of the Rhine, and Simon Stockhausen became a teacher at Morsbach. Karlheinz's earliest childhood memories stem from this period, among them the forced landing of a small sports plane on the Monday before Lent in 1932. It was decidedly cold and mist hung over the lightly snowy peaks. He heard children shouting, and he too ran up the slope. A strange vehicle was standing on the frozen soil, and amid a cluster of gesticulating men and howling children the pilot was trying to repair minor damage to the motor. Then the men clung on to the plane's wings until the motor was revved up; the bird rolled downhill, took off and disappeared into the mist. It was an exciting event for the inhabitants of the tiny locality – but a profound experience for the three-and-a-half-year-old child. Birds and their mechanical likenesses, aeroplanes, constantly crop up throughout Stockhausen's life. Whenever he went to the zoo, Stockhausen wanted to go straight to the aviary; at boarding school when he was sixteen he dreamed of becoming a pilot; the young composer on his first American tour, flying every day, had the feeling that his home was not on the ground but in the plane; the composer of the late sixties repeatedly had a dream in which he was a huge bird gliding through the air. Flying: an image of the spirit moving freely and masterfully through the realms of imagination.

The Stockhausen family was extremely poor, and Karlheinz got used to duties and hard work at an early age. Yet he knew of the paradise of

5 Around 1929

children's games. He always carried a little wooden hammer – a present from his father – which hung on a loop from his apron. Everything that stood or lay in his path was tapped, everything was made to sound, and when the hammer broke, a new one had to be fetched. Whether he was watching elephants with men dressed in Indian clothing, trotting through the village in a travelling circus, or playing adventurous games of being a hunter or a soldier, the world was a marvellous theatre, and everything unknown was explored. But the main theatrical presentations were staged by his father, who let Stockhausen play the little clown in front of friends or at school.

My theatrical life began when at the age of three I took a live frog out of my apron pocket and held it out to the people who all shrieked, 'Eek!' Then I firmly banged once on the ground with my wooden hammer, stretched up on my feet, opened my mouth and stuck out my tongue on which there was a live garden worm. Everyone yelled, 'Ugh!' – and my father gave me ten pfennigs for this.[1]

In December 1932 (by which time the family had moved to Bärbroich, in the Bergisch region not far from Cologne) a shadow was cast over Stockhausen's childhood. Unable to cope with the quick succession of births and the heavy demands of daily life, his mother became acutely depressed and had to be taken to a mental home. Stockhausen was later to portray this tragic event in the first act of his opera *Donnerstag* from *Licht*.

I can still see my father bringing her downstairs, holding her tightly because my mother kept wanting to go to the window and shouted, 'Just let me die!' . . . My little sister and I were standing next to each other in the bedroom, we were trembling, and the two grown-ups were down there, she in her nightgown and he in his nightshirt . . . And then we ran down after them, even though we weren't allowed to, and we were standing down there next to my mother. Suddenly she pointed to the cellar door, which was just next to the bottom of the stairs, and shouted, 'Down there is Hell!' . . . and then she pointed up the stairs and cried, 'Up there is Heaven! I want to go up to the loft!' . . . And suddenly a man comes in with a red cross and a white cockade on his cap, he was from the mental home . . . and takes my mother away. We children were crying, and then my father calmed us down and said, 'Just quieten down, Mummy's going to come back home!'[2]

A few months later Karlheinz's younger brother died. In the following years his father employed housekeepers or looked after the house himself.

When Simon Stockhausen was transferred to Altenberg as a secondary school teacher in January 1935, life entered a new phase. The flat in the village school looked down on to the west window of Altenberg Cathedral. The old Cistercian abbey on the floor of the Dhünn valley was surrounded by a handful of houses, and that was the whole village. The beauty and clarity of the cathedral's architecture and the simplicity of its bright interior are impressive. The Cistercians prohibited coloured pictures in the glass windows. 'Make the windows without cross or colours,' they used to say, so that, up until the later west window, the windows were made in gentle natural hues. The changing play of light inside thus reflects the passing phases of the day more than in other cathedrals. Karlheinz often watched as the whole church was bathed in gold when the sun set and the evening light flooded in through the golden west window. The medieval cathedral, the woods and the surrounding peaks form the backcloth for the next years of Stockhausen's life.

In Altenberg Karlheinz received his first piano lessons from the Protestant cathedral organist Franz-Josef Kloth. (When he was only four he would often clamber on to the piano stool and play, taking his musical mother as a model, though what he played is not known). Karlheinz made such rapid progress that by 1936, after just one year, he had to perform at village and social festivities; his was always the 'top part'. The programme included the 'Petersburg Sleighride', the 'Blue Danube' and similar showpieces. Karlheinz practised assiduously every day, and his sister remembers how he liked to sit at the piano in the 'great master' pose. He built up a repertoire of hit-songs and tunes from opera and operetta by listening to the radio. He only needed to hear a piece once to be able to play it. Stockhausen belongs to the first generation of composers who grew up with the radio and the gramophone, listening to music and human voices from the unreal world of a box or a gramophone horn. Sometimes in Bärbroich Gertrud Stockhausen would sing the second part to a song on the radio. There was a huge dispute between Karlheinz's parents when his mother tried to talk to the voices on the radio and was terribly agitated and disappointed when they did not answer back.

Then my father tried to prevent her from doing it, or corrected her, and got very angry about it. He just had a logical sense, as we would call it, of what this equipment's possibilities were. That has been of significance to me all my life, especially since I have worked a lot in radio, and have thought about radio, and about the whole kind of music one makes for radio. And it wasn't until much later, during compositions like . . . *Gesang der Jünglinge* and *Kontakte* and *Hymnen* and *Sirius* that this scene came back into my head and I got the feeling, which I still have today, that my mother was absolutely right: it is utter nonsense to invent an apparatus for people that is one-sided, and acts as if it were making contact with others, yet is incapable of involving the people sitting in front of it and reacting to them. So I felt that she was fantastically lucid in her assumption that a thing is worthwhile only if it sets minds free and does not force them into something.[3]

Stockhausen found it fascinating to put his ear next to the casing of transformers, listening to the humming sounds. Whether this was a child's natural curiosity or the first stirrings of the later electronic compositions is an open question. He developed a middle-ear infection that was to have unfortunate consequences. Since his father had no money to pay for the doctor, he sent for the district nurse. She dripped hydrogen peroxide into the infected ear once or twice a week, with the unexpected result that the ear gradually became cartilaginous. Since then Stockhausen's right ear has been only 30 per cent effective for the very high frequencies. Later, watching Stockhausen at concerts as he listened with utmost concentration at the filters and potentiometers, it was clear that his head was slightly tilted to the left so as to hear better on the right.

Karlheinz Stockhausen began going to the two-class village school at Easter 1935. He could do everything much more quickly than the others so his teacher, Anton Luig, would send him into the village each morning to fetch the post for him. Karlheinz would fasten his jacket, put on his hunter's hat and make his 'district rounds'. Luig described Stockhausen as the most gifted student he had ever had. As a secondary school teacher, Karlheinz's father was soon urged to join the Nazi Party and he became block leader in Altenberg. When the NSDAP came to power in 1933, he saw Germany recovering and was soon enthusiastic about the party's ideas. He had to collect various contributions – the party contribution, the 'Winter Aid', 'Mother and Child' and VDA (Germans Abroad) – and he always sent Karlheinz, who had to cover several kilometres in Altenberg and the surrounding villages of Holz, Glöbusch, Erberich and Blecher. 'The first four years of school in Altenberg were like an odyssey,' Stockhausen once said in an interview. His peregrination through the landscape was endlessly filled with adventure, for he knew all the people in the area and they all knew him. There were many 'originals' among them: the corpulent but severe village policeman, Mosel, who was not well disposed to Stockhausen's father and denounced him to the party; the eminent Jewish lawyer in Blecher, Dr Bein, who always gave handsome tips; the arch-communist Simon Hansen, a woodman from Bülsberg, who wanted to blow up Altenberg Cathedral.

In 1939 Karlheinz went to the Pastor Löhr grammar school in Burscheid. Not only did he learn all things intellectual with great ease, but he also soon showed an aptitude for practical handiwork. During his spare time he liked to watch the clockmaker in the neighbouring village. Even the grisly atmosphere of the abattoir attracted him. Having gained the cobbler's confidence, he was allowed to make minor repairs himself. He looked over many craftsmen's shoulders and was able to display his own skills.

The years in this closed-off village world were rich in experiences of nature. 'I still remember how, as a mere child, I used to lie in the snow

6 Summer holidays in Engelsbruch, 1936; Stockhausen with his
grandmother Katharina Stockhausen and his sister Katharina

on winter nights, gazing up at the stars.'⁴ In late summer Karlheinz was
often sent to guard the cows in the meadows, either in Bärbroich or for
relatives in Engelsbruch. There he was immersed in a mood of calm and
spaciousness. Potatoes were baking, and there was nothing to do. He cut
reed-pipes, or lay for hours on his back, watching the clouds. In such
hours he was taken right out of himself by the long time-spans of the
drifting clouds – he forgot about time, and dreamed along, with the vast
limitless sky above. Some of the sounds in Stockhausen's first works in
'moment form', *Carré*, *Kontakte* and *Momente*, are reminiscences of these
hours.

Karlheinz had attended his First Communion in Altenberg Cathedral
at Easter in 1938, an important experience for the already religious boy.

The whole teaching of confession marked a new phase of my life. That had such
a deep effect on me. To be at confession is like being at a musical rehearsal.
The confession is rehearsed many times in advance ... Even then I had such
unbelievably deep experiences that it is hard to put them into words, because
they are also experiences of temperature: for example, I have never felt so cold
– the chill I felt in my spine after I had confessed ... an absolutely incorporeal
sense of soaring within the icy coldness of the body. Of course, that is partly to
do with the fact that Altenberg Cathedral is so cold, whatever the time ... And
then I still know for certain that during the whole celebration of the first Holy

7 Cousins' Communion at Hoppengarten (Sieg), Easter 1937. *Front row, second from the right:* Stockhausen; *behind him, to the right:* his father

Communion I was in a trance . . . We had had to learn certain texts in advance: the renewed confirmation of faith, the creed, a game of question and answer between the priest and the new communicant. One learns the answers by heart, and I went through them mechanically because I had so often said them from the bottom of my heart, and God had long since known that I really meant it, that I was utterly immersed in it . . . I have never forgotten this pure state of trance.[5]

In the same year the crucifix in the classroom was taken down, prayer was forbidden by the state and morning school began with 'Heil Hitler'. This caused an inner conflict in Karlheinz's father. At school he had to discourage prayer, yet at home he himself prayed. Karlheinz observed these changes in the adult world with consternation. In the following years he would learn how, even in the religious world, it is possible to be left completely alone. When he prayed, he always saw himself as being in a daydream, kneeling on the lowest step of an infinitely long stairway of white stone that led steeply upwards. 'I knew for certain that God was shining up there, and looking at me. And he gave so much light, and was so warming and so radiant that I was blinded when I raised my head a bit and glanced upwards for even a moment . . . up there it is blinding golden-white.'[6]

Wartime Years in Xanten and Bedburg

Simon Stockhausen remarried in 1938, and he and his new wife, Luzia, had two daughters, Waltraud and Gert. Karlheinz's relations with his stepmother were not always harmonious, so in January 1942 he became a boarder at the LBA (teaching training college) in Xanten. In any case, Simon Stockhausen expected that his son would enter his own profession. The LBA had been set up in a former Carthusian monastery in the market-place at Xanten. The best school-leavers from the Rhineland and the Ruhr district were gathered here and trained as teachers in a five-year programme. Karlheinz Stockhausen was easily the youngest. He did not care for the barrack-room organization, waking and going to bed to the sound of the bugle and wearing uniforms with swastika armbands. Praying was forbidden at school: he could only do it at night, when he was on his own. His fellow pupils only bothered with people who could do something, and Karlheinz could certainly play the piano. In the 'small music room' he performed German hits with an American beat for his comrades. Jean Opel, a local musician who taught everything from piccolo to double bass, gave him oboe lessons, and every student had to learn violin. Stockhausen was second oboist in the symphony orchestra; his playing was very ordinary, but there was not much time to practise. They gave performances of easy Haydn and Mozart symphonies when parents came visiting and at little concerts in the surrounding areas. He played piano in the salon orchestra and in a small dance-music group that also performed 'tame' jazz. Then there was the band. One hundred and fifty 'cadets' in immaculate uniforms paraded through Xanten on Sunday mornings, the band at the front (with Stockhausen on the oboe) and the singers at the back. At the LBA piano was taught by the cathedral organist Theo Thernierssen. After a while he said he could teach Stockhausen nothing more.

Once his father had gone to the front as an officer in 1943, Stockhausen only rarely went home. He preferred to spend the brief holidays in Xanten, earning pocket-money at night as a 'fire-guard'. Squadrons of English planes passed over Xanten, flying in the direction of the Ruhr. When the bombs had fallen, there was a red glow on the horizon.

In the autumn of 1944 nearly all his fellow students were drafted. The three youngest were transferred to the LBA at Schloss Bedburg in Bedburg on the Erft, but there was no more instruction, and soon after it was turned into a military hospital. The western front was not far away, and Stockhausen became a stretcher-bearer; he had to help the soldiers to tend and bandage the wounded. The Allies had begun to use phosphorus bombs, and the heads of the injured men were like balls of foam rubber.

I often tried to find a hole going to the mouth with a straw to pour some liquid down it, so that someone who was still moving could be nourished – but there was just this yellow spherical mass, with no sign of a face. That was everyday life. There was no longer time to bury the dead. They were lying in a little shot-up chapel, and every day we threw thirty or forty corpses on top of the rest . . . Sometimes five hundred would arrive in a single afternoon . . . Death became something completely relative for me. Once I was carrying two buckets of steaming potatoes across the wide courtyard from the field kitchen to the main building of the hospital when suddenly there was this screaming howl of a fighter-bomber; everything was crackling, spattering and exploding around me. I just shut my eyes tight and stood stock still till I heard the hornets whistling off, opened my eyes and looked at the criss-cross of bullet-holes all around me – and nothing had happened to me.[7]

During these months Stockhausen was also forced to witness numerous atrocities committed by German soldiers.

In February 1945 he fled with his school certificate from Bedburg to meet his father, who was on leave from the front, in Altenberg. As block leader amidst the petty quarrels of village life, his father had become more and more ensnared in the service of the party; he had even been denounced twice, and knew what to expect after the war. He bade his son farewell with the words, 'I'm not coming back. Look after things.'

Farmer's Boy, Operetta Theatre and Matriculation

At the end of the war the sixteen-year-old Stockhausen was an orphan in Altenberg. His father was regarded as missing, probably killed in Hungary, and in 1941 his mother had been a victim of the Hitler regime's 'euthanasia policy'. During the first weeks after the war Stockhausen helped with salvage work. At the last moment the German soldiers had blown up all the bridges in Altenberg and the surrounding area, and they were being rebuilt as a matter of urgency; in the woods, timber was chopped for fuel rations. Then Stockhausen worked for several months for a farmer in Blecher to support Luzia Stockhausen and his little sisters. He practised the piano assiduously, and studied Latin far into the night in order to be accepted into the sixth form at the Bergisch-Gladbach grammar school (now the Nicolaus Cusanus). His wartime certificate from the LBA was not recognized, and life was not made easy for the block leader's son in other respects: later he had to struggle to get his orphan's allowance.

When Stockhausen's former piano teacher, Franz-Josef Kloth, was rehearsing Georg Mielke's *Winzerliesel* for the theatrical society in Blecher, he let Stockhausen take the chorus rehearsals. The operetta's première took place in the hall of the Hemmelrath Hotel on the last day of 1945. Stockhausen maintained connections with the theatrical society for the next three years. He was now entrusted with directing the music for Edmund Eysler's operetta *Die fromme Helene* and for a revival of *Winzerliesel*. Whenever the theatrical society put on a play, Stockhausen was there. One of his fellow artists reports that he was an astonishingly gifted actor. In the surrounding villages he earned some money as a pianist for dancing lessons, and occasionally he met up with the cathedral choirmaster, his wife Josefa, the painter Rita Hecker and the carpenter Josef Richertz in Altenberg. They sang four-part works by Heinrich Isaac and Ludwig Senfl, as well as madrigals, with Stockhausen conducting. He was sometimes allowed to play the organ in Altenberg Cathedral.

In February 1946 Stockhausen started attending the grammar school in Bergisch-Gladbach. He took the same route to school as his friend Anno Hecker. They talked only of nature, the woods and animals. Stockhausen considered becoming a forester. In November 1946 they participated in the first hunting trial to be held in the area since the war. They had practised thoroughly together and both came out on top.

The matriculation class held a colourful assortment of people, who had all kinds of wartime backgrounds. Some of them were still in uniform, with all the stripes torn off. Ewald Pees, the German teacher, knew how to dissolve the trauma of the preceding years, the struggle for survival, the bombings and the endless talk about 'foes and fatherlands'. Stockhausen's essays were often read out. His final essay, 'Is Power Immoral?', was marked 'good' by Pees, but the second examiner lowered the mark and Pees acquiesced; Stockhausen was deeply offended. As a protest, he stayed away from the graduation ceremony.

By Easter 1947 his school years were over. Many towns had been destroyed, and it would not be easy to gain a place for further training. Stockhausen wanted to study school-music in Cologne.

2 Writer or Composer 1947–51

> I realized that the highest calling
> of mankind can only be to become a
> musician in the profoundest sense:
> to conceive and shape the world musically.
> Stockhausen

Studies in Post-war Cologne

When Stockhausen went to Cologne in April 1947, large areas of the city still lay in ruins. The Second World War had struck the city particularly hard – in the old part, from the Rhine to the Ring, there was not an electric light to be seen; and in the first years after the war hunger and homelessness were everyday problems. Yet Stockhausen was happy to have left the village seclusion of Altenberg. His school music studies represented the start of an autonomous existence. For the next eighteen years Stockhausen lived in Cologne, an ancient city rich in history, which intellectually likes to look towards France yet also contains the last residues of the medieval 'Sancta Colonia', Holy Cologne; the inhabitants know how to combine this with crafty business sense.

Stockhausen was completely penniless. He owned only the clothes he was wearing and a satchel. In the following years he took countless student jobs to pay for his studies and daily needs. He was an attendant in car parks and in garrisons of the occupying forces, and night-watchman for a fashion store. He was always playing the piano – in restaurants, in cafés, for carnival entertainments – and, along with a percussionist, he often played jazz and hits right through the night at the Vater Rhein bar, which was patronized by occupation troops. At closing time Stockhausen would gather up the soldiers' cigarette ends, mix them with home-grown tobacco from Altenberg, which he had flavoured with liquorice and honey, and roll fresh cigarettes that he sold on the black market or exchanged for food.

In the desolate Cologne landscape of 1947 it was hardly possible to rent a room. If Stockhausen could not get back to Altenberg at night, he slept with fellow students who had found somewhere to stay, always conscious of the need to be at the Musikhochschule by seven o'clock so as to get a practice room with a piano. It was not until late in 1948 that

Stockhausen found a room of his own in Gottesweg (just off the Zollstock ringway). Stockhausen's landlady was troublesome; whenever a coal train pulled up at a signal on the nearby embankment, she forced Stockhausen to 'organize' a sack of coal. If he tried to refuse, she threatened to evict him.

School-music studies presupposed knowledge of harmony and figured bass. One of the curiosities of music history is that Stockhausen failed the entrance exam at Easter 1947, though as he had never had any theory lessons it is not so surprising. He passed the exam for the piano class of Hans Otto Schmidt-Neuhaus, a former pupil of Erdmann, and studied piano and theory for a year before gaining entrance to the Musikhoch-schule at Easter 1948. He took German philology, philosophy and musicol-ogy as subsidiary subjects at Cologne University. The intellectual climate of the Musikhochschule was conservative; Walter Braunfels, the director, had made a name for himself with a handful of operas in the late Romantic style, and his attitude to everything new was generally hostile. Other figures of some influence were Heinrich Lemacher and his pupil Herm-ann Schroeder. Their classes basically followed the lines of the books they later wrote together on harmony, form and figured bass. The school-music department was headed by Paul Mies, whose subject had been mathematics. He published a book entitled *Der Charakter der Tonarten* in 1948, made editions of old carnival songs and had some of the traits of a typical Cologne eccentric. When Hans Mersmann came to Cologne in 1947 and assumed the directorship of the Hochschule (for a few years Braunfels remained as president), he revitalized the teaching curriculum. Mersmann was well known as co-editor of the periodical *Melos;* a cham-pion of new music, he had been outlawed in the Third Reich. He gave analysis classes and fostered a New Music Union in which Stockhausen participated from the start. Mersmann was particularly enthusiastic about the early music of Hindemith, Stravinsky and Bartók.

In June 1948 currency reforms brought an economic buoyancy to the three zones occupied by the western powers. Gradually everything began to appear in the shops again and life became more bearable. Soon after the currency reform Stockhausen, along with Peter Lachmund and Rolf Müller-Blagovitsch, rented shop premises with a little flat at the back at 248 Alteburger Strasse. The flat became a rendezvous for a group of school-music students, a place for all-night disputes and conversations, to which even Schmidt-Neuhaus sometimes came. During the Nazi era people had been cut off from any contemporary development in the arts, so now everything new in literature, music and painting was seized upon.

If something was preoccupying Stockhausen – analysis or writing – he would withdraw. Even at that time all else was subjugated to his almost proverbial work ethic. He and his flatmates evolved a plan to give evening recitations of Rilke's *Sonnets to Orpheus* in the countryside – Stockhausen was going to read and Lachmund was to give an introduction – but it came to nothing. At the time Stockhausen was the favourite of the old Cologne actor Paul Senden, who taught elocution at the Musikhochschule (a compulsory subject for school-music students). They worked on poems, and Stockhausen impressed Senden because he could declaim in a particularly expressive way. At the end of each class Senden – a typically venerable, grey-haired court actor with a diamond pin in his tie – would say, 'If Mr Stockhausen would care to read the poem once more!'

From 1948 Stockhausen was friendly with a group of piano students from Schmidt-Neuhaus's class. He took part in their intermittent literary evenings, at which they read Shakespeare and others, sharing out the roles. It was in this circle that he met a young woman from Hamburg, Doris Andreae. The daughter of a prosperous, long-respected family that could be traced back to Johann Valentin Andreae (author of *Die Chymischen Hochzeit des Christian Rosenkreutz*), she later became his first wife. In the winter of 1948–9 the group took a trip to the Black Forest: for the first time they could have a holiday, could ski and dance. They had just one dance record ('Jalousie'), which they played over and over again. After the deprivations of the recent past, such trifles were a source of great joy: they simply wanted to live.

Poems, Short Stories and a Novelette

The first three years in Cologne produced no evidence to suggest that Stockhausen would one day become a composer of world-wide renown. His path seemed to lie in a quite different direction: the first poems and short stories were written in the summer of 1948, and within a year it appeared that music would be merely a way of earning money. An uncommonly rich inner life and a world of strong emotions were looking for a means of expression. The nightmare of the war was still within him; so were certain experiences from his childhood and youth, which he was then trying to work through in artistic terms. In one of his first poems Stockhausen calls God the 'great spirit of torment'.

Reading Hermann Hesse's *Glass Bead Game* in 1948 proved to be the key experience of those years. Stockhausen felt a deep affinity with the mental world of Hesse's novel, which takes place in the future, a few centuries after our era, and depicts the life of a boy with exceptional musical gifts, Josef Knecht. He probably grew up as an orphan, and is selected at the age of twelve for the élite school in Castalia. Castalia is a pedagogic province in which a sort of secular order dedicates itself to the fostering of musicology, mathematics and philosophy yet renounces creative artistic activity. The focal point of the order is the 'glass bead game', an exercise which the book never describes in precise detail, but which unifies the three principles of 'science, reverence for the beautiful and meditation'. Hesse names the Musikhochschule in Cologne as the place where the glass bead game was 'invented', although it was previously widespread among students in England and Germany. After a few years of studying, Josef Knecht enters the order and rises to the highest status: 'Magister Ludi'. At the end of the novel Knecht leaves the order, having realized that everything one has achieved in life petrifies and dies if one disregards transformation and renewal. Shortly afterwards, he dies. In an interview, Stockhausen said that *The Glass Bead Game* had been an essential book for him, 'because it connects the musician with the spiritual servant. I found it prophetic, for I realized that the highest calling of mankind can only be to become a musician in the profoundest sense; to conceive and shape the world musically.'[1]

In the few hours that were left to Stockhausen between study and earning a living he produced more poems, short stories and even a play, *Die Liebe der Anderen* (Love of others), in which a man killed in battle appears to his wife as a voice from the beyond; it was actually conceived as a work for radio. In May 1949 Stockhausen had an idea for a longer story, and that summer he went back to Blecher, where Luzia Stockhausen was living with his little sisters. In August and September (the weeks around his twenty-first birthday) he produced the tale 'Geburt im Tod' (Birth in death) as if in a trance. It is about the Indian Mogul emperor Humayun (1508–56), whom Stockhausen had come across when he became interested in the Indian spiritual world. At the beginning of the story Humayun has been mortally injured by a snake-bite. He revives when his father Babur suddenly dies: the father's death seems like a sacrifice for his son, hence 'Birth in death'. Humayun is driven out by rivals for his throne, but after long exile and endless battles, having grown inwardly through his deprivations and sufferings, he wins back his kingdom a year before he dies. His death is rather strange: while descending the spiral staircase of his library he plunges over the edge, strikes his head and dies. At the time Stockhausen did not know that the historical Humayun dressed in the colours of the planets associated with the seven days of the week (sun: gold, moon: silver, mars: red, etc.), that he had organized his government officials according to the four classical elements of earth, water, air and fire, that he had a passion for astronomy and mathematics, loved the arts and was the author of numerous ghazals and a divan.

Although elements of 'Geburt im Tod' may be traced back to Hesse, the work is an original creation. It is not a continuous story, but a succession of scenes, like a film script: a cohesive sequence of events, important biographical moments, conversations and symbolic images in twenty-four chapters, all of them 'variations' (as the subtitle puts it) of a single theme, birth and death. In Chapter 21, 'A Pupil's Avowal', the narrator speaks for himself, as an 'unknown pupil'; what is new can come only from death, and order only from chaos. It is the eternal 'dying and becoming', which he also describes in terms of music: the theme of a cheerful, perfect music, a group of notes as the musical kernel of a composition, which carries within itself mutation and combination, inversion and mirror, in logical order and rigour. Autobiographical experiences emerge in other chapters; the horrors of war in 'Human Animals' are a memory of Bedburg; in 'Night of Dreams and Morning' a Hindu woman in one of Humayun's dreams cries out, 'Down there is Hell, up there is Heaven.' When Humayun's Grand Vizier tells the emperor in 'Conversation on Art' that art reveals the world and uncovers the mysterious, that it portrays emotions in the face of the miraculous as a message received as if in a dream or a state of enlightenment, it could be the Stockhausen of the seventies and eighties speaking. Humayun asks whether secular and religious art should be distinguished, but the Grand Vizier says no. People observing a work of art always experience as much of its profundity as their own powers of deeper insight and their capacity to modify their perceptions permit. Stockhausen dedicated the book to Doris Andreae, now his girlfriend. Around the time of 'Geburt im Tod' Stockhausen wrote to the author of *The Glass Bead Game*, requesting a personal judgement of his (own) art; he enclosed a few poems and an incidental fairy tale, taken from the story. He received an answer shortly after, which is all the more remarkable since, on being awarded the Nobel Prize in 1946, Hesse had been inundated with mail and had placed a sign on his house in Montagnola in Switzerland turning away visitors. Hesse sent Stockhausen some small privately printed pieces and encouraged the young student to treat music as a way of making money: he had the talent to be a poet.[2]

New Music and First Compositions

After the prohibition of New Music during the Third Reich, Paul Hindemith was the first of the 'modern classics' to be performed again; Bartók
soon followed and a little later came Stravinsky. Arnold Schoenberg was
only rarely heard in the immediate post-war years, and almost no one
talked about Anton Webern. Stockhausen's acquaintance with Modernity
came about in typical fashion: no cautious approach, no circumspect
'familiarizing'. Once his interest is aroused, his enthusiasm and joy at
mastering the new is limitless. Whatever is new is worked through and
made his own, only to be set aside when something else appears. At the
beginning, even for Stockhausen, this meant studying Hindemith. During
teaching practice in the winter of 1949–50 he played Hindemith's Piano
Sonata no. 2 and analysed it in front of Paul Mies and the music-
education students. He then turned to Stravinsky, prompted by a radio
broadcast of 'Dumbarton Oaks' and Mersmann's impressive analysis of
the *Duo concertant*. He asked a friend in Freiburg to buy him some
Stravinsky scores in Switzerland since very few were available in Germany.[3]

At the beginning of December 1949 Else C. Krauss played Schoenberg's complete piano works to a full audience in the Musikhochschule.
Stockhausen was among the listeners. After the publication of Theodor
Wiesengrund Adorno's *Philosophie der neuen Musik* earlier that year some
music students in Cologne became greatly interested in Schoenberg and
ran with banners raised from Mersmann to Adorno. Stockhausen had a
more detached attitude to Adorno, but displayed much enthusiasm for
Schoenberg and twelve-note music. He later got to know the theorist and
music critic Herbert Eimert, who lived in Cologne and who gave him a
copy of his *Atonale Musiklehre*, a slim volume of barely forty pages on
twelve-note music that had been published in 1924. Schoenberg's *Herzge-
wächse* op. 20 was the library's single work from the Second Viennese
School. (The only Webern score Stockhausen knew during his studies
was the early string quartet pieces op. 5. A student friend, Detmar Seuthe,
had found it in a second-hand bookshop and given it to Stockhausen,
perhaps (in 1951) as a birthday present.) Within the Institut für Schul-
musik Schoenberg was *persona non grata*.

When I came into the main hall for a teaching-practice session [the Hindemith
analysis referred to earlier] the head of department at that time asked me what
score I was carrying under my arm. I answered that I had discovered Schoenberg's
op. 20 in the archives. Loudly, so that all the would-be music teachers could

hear him, he responded, 'Schoenberg and Hitler should'a bin drarned as kids; that would'a spared us lots.'[4]

Stockhausen's first substantial acquaintance with the compositional technique of twelve-note music was an evening with Hermann Heiss. On 1 February 1950, after a concert of his own works, the former pupil of Josef Matthias Hauer gave an extensive lecture on twelve-note technique. A little later Stockhausen presented a talk on this topic in a seminar with Hermann Schroeder, his theory teacher. Schroeder probably scratched his head in perplexity. At the performance of Olivier Messiaen's *Trois petites liturgies* at the university in October 1950, where Stockhausen heard a work by Messiaen for the first time. Schroeder ostentatiously walked out of the concert.

Free stylistic exercises in various traditions made up part of the training towards the end of the course in 1950: Stockhausen wrote chorale preludes, fugues and a scherzo in the style of Hindemith as well as song arrangements and chorale pieces. Among these were the *Chöre für Doris* on poems by Paul Verlaine and a chorale with a twelve-note melodic line, both of which were later published. (The latter piece was sung by the Hochschule choir and recorded for Cologne Radio.) Fritz Schieri, who took the second theory class for school-music students, had worked out a technique for composing twelve-note melodies with alternating chromatic and diatonic interval formations. Stockhausen too was interested in this technique.

In August 1950 Stockhausen wanted to attempt a larger work for the first time. In Blecher he wrote the three 'Lieder der Abtrünnigen' (Songs of a renegade) for contralto and chamber orchestra, setting his own poems: 'Mitten im Leben' (Midway through life), 'Frei' (Free) and 'Der Saitenmann' (The string man). In the seventies he remarked that as far as he was concerned, the last of these songs was the most moving thing he had ever written. After two weeks of intense work, 'drunk with victory', he took the score to Doris Andreae in Cologne and dedicated the *Drei Lieder* to her.

> The String Man
> The string man has torn his hands.
> Small drops of blood
> Spring over the wood of the fiddle
> Down onto the filthy cobblestones.
>
> Has already sat for a long time in the rain.

27

All the people have forgotten,
Buying a new world,
And no ear understands in the clamour,
When the old man screams his pain
Into the streets for pennies.

In his agony cried too wildly,
Plucked too hard, the string player –
And tore the hands.

Now he leans into the mute loaf
Of his fiddle
And listens to himself.

Tenderly his hand strokes the board
Like a fresh child.

And his ear perceives –
Before becoming deaf –
The never played.

It is to Hermann Schroeder's credit that he recognized Stockhausen's gift and advised him to study composition. In the autumn of 1950 Stockhausen played his *Drei Lieder* to the Swiss composer Frank Martin. Martin was in charge of the composition class at the Cologne Musikhochschule, and Stockhausen was accepted. As he later reported, he had only a few hours of tuition, during which Martin presented his own works. It seemed that Stockhausen the composer was subduing Stockhausen the author. He stopped going to the German and philosophy seminars and now devoted himself wholly to music.

Stockhausen had been living at the students' hostel at 57 Kerpener Strasse since 1949. To help his fellow residents to approach contemporary music, he began giving evening lectures at the grand piano on such pieces as Bartók's *Mikrokosmos*. In Düsseldorf in December 1950 he heard a performance of Bartók's sonata for two pianos and percussion, which became the subject of his thesis.[5] He experimented in some piano pieces, all of which he destroyed in 1954. Among them was the sonata that he probably composed at the beginning of 1951, just before starting the thesis: 'Here a note, and now a second, and the first goes away and settles back in, then along comes yet another, and then all three go away, etc.'[6]

Stockhausen had composed a piece about the process by which a theme is created. He played the piece, which lasted about twelve minutes, to Hermann Schroeder, who reckoned that the whole history of the theme's creation belonged in the seclusion of Stockhausen's closet: he should start with the theme itself. 'I accepted that and went out thinking, "The piece is rubbish, the Master ought to know!" If only I could have told him that at the moment when it appears as a new-born little piece the genesis of a phenomenon can be much more instructive than the phenomenon itself!'[7] This shows, for the first time, that in music too it is the 'dying and becoming' that is significant for Stockhausen: not something that is finished and closed off, but the processes of becoming and passing away.

Burleska, a Musical Pantomime, and Acquaintance with Herbert Eimert

At the end of each summer term the students and teachers of music education in Cologne went to Steinbach, in the Eifel region for a study week during which student compositions could be rehearsed and performed. It was known that Stockhausen wrote poetry, and a fellow student, Klaus Weiler, had asked him to write a text for a cantata for the study week in 1950. Stockhausen had agreed, but nothing more was heard from him for some while. Just before Steinbach he came up with the text and plot for a musical pantomine called *Burleska*, a play about love that is repudiated out of pride, and conversion. Since there was little time, Weiler shared out the composing of the work with two others, Detmar Seuthe and Stockhausen. Stockhausen's recollection is that, in terms of style, they agreed on a mixture of Hindemith, Stravinsky and Orff. Weiler and Seuthe stuck consistently to the agreement, but Stockhausen produced something more personal. The performance of *Burleska* became the high point of the week. To the right were the singers and a small female 'mocking chorus' in front of whom the plot unfolded in pantomime, and to the left were the instruments: string quartet, percussion and Stockhausen at the piano. After a second performance on 31 January 1951 in the main hall of the Musikhochschule, the press had this to say:

The charm of this modern play . . . whose content is presented twice over, so to speak – in song and in mime – seems to us to lie in the highly original music, which works with quite unfamiliar rhythmic and instrumental effects. Sitting in the packed hall of the Hochschule, one had the firm impression that this was an unusual contribution to the operatic art of our day.[8]

When it is remembered that thirty years later, in *Licht*, Stockhausen made

29

8 *Burleska*, a musical pantomime at Steinbach (Eifel), July 1950. Behind the curtain is a 'mocking chorus', in front of it are three of the singers and the pantomimes, with masks. *Left at the back:* Detmar Seuthe (with triangle)

each principal character appear simultaneously in three forms (as singer, instrumentalist and dancer-mime), the reviewer's last sentence seems to have renewed validity today.

It was probably early in the spring of 1951 that Stockhausen visited Herbert Eimert, who was a critic for the *Kölnischer Rundschau*, and asked him to review a third performance of *Burleska* at the student hostel in Kerpener Strasse. Eimert did not suspect that the tall student was a musician, and asked if he was studying medicine. They soon found themselves engaged in expert conversation on New Music. When Stockhausen started talking about his thesis on Bartók's sonata for two pianos and percussion, Eimert, who produced the late-night music programmes at WDR (West German Radio) in Cologne, immediately thought about a broadcast on Bartók. A little later Stockhausen showed him a twelve-note sonatine for violin and piano – his last 'free piece' for the final exam – and Eimert proposed a radio production. With Stockhausen at the piano and Wolfgang Marschner (concert-master of the WDR Symphony Orchestra till 1950) playing the violin, the work was recorded and broadcast for the first time on 24 August 1951.

Eimert was a gently patriarchal figure whom many people found rather unapproachable. In the following years he was to become Stockhausen's paternalist sponsor, paving the way for his first performances and employment at the radio station. Eimert himself had dabbled in composition. The bases of his musical thinking were measure and number; he was deeply impressed when he later found these features in the construction of the Moorish Alhambra Palace in southern Spain, describing it as 'serial music in terms of architecture'.

In 1946 Darmstadt had begun hosting the International Summer Courses in New Music – a sort of summertime university – at the instigation of Wolfgang Steinecke, a musician, critic and, at that time, cultural adviser to the city of Darmstadt. The teachers in the early years included Heiss, René Leibowitz (from Paris), Wolfgang Fortner and Edgard Varèse (from New York); it was Steinecke's hope that this institution would give rise to a 'musical Bauhaus'. Since 1949 a series of concerts had been set aside for the younger generation. Stockhausen submitted his *Drei Lieder* to Darmstadt for the 1951 summer series, but they were rejected. (It is quite possible that in the summer of 1950 five songs were composed, two of which were subsequently destroyed. In a postcard to Detmar Seuthe, dated 7 January 1951, Stockhausen wrote that he had selected only three of the five songs for Darmstadt.) Eimert, who was a member of the jury, told him later that the texts were felt to be too gruesome and the music too old-fashioned. This led Stockhausen to replace the text of the first song with a German translation of Baudelaire's poem 'Le Rebelle'. In June 1951 he interrupted work on his Bartók thesis and, on Herbert Eimert's advice, made his first trip to the International Summer Courses in Darmstadt.

3 Awakening after a Musical 'Zero Hour' 1951–3

> So one can say that by the middle
> of the twentieth century the great
> 'Romantic' arch that had displayed
> so many extreme offshoots actually
> seemed to have reached its end...
> and an orientation away from mankind
> began. Once again one looked up to
> the stars, and started an intensive
> measuring and counting.
>
> Stockhausen

The Middle of the Century: A Musical 'Zero Hour'

With the deaths of Bartók and Webern in September 1945, a musical epoch came to an end. Webern had reduced thematic composition to the ultimate in motivic cells of just two or three notes. Bartók and Stravinsky had completed a striking revolution in the field of elemental rhythm, and in 1951 Stravinsky was to begin a circumspect reorientation towards the twelve-note music of Schoenberg and Webern. In the middle of the century music underwent a radical change whose effects were felt at various points in Europe and in New York. While Stockhausen was still a student in Cologne, evolving his first ideas about musical processes, a few young composers had already made a fundamental break with the past and taken the first steps along a new path for music.

The central figure in this new beginning was the Frenchman Olivier Messiaen. Both a mystic and a rationalist, Messiaen had an enormously broad knowledge of music, and his outlook greatly influenced a group of young composers after the Second World War. His courses at the Paris Conservatoire later acquired legendary status. During his stay at the Darmstadt Summer Courses in 1949 Messiaen composed the piano study *Mode de valeurs et d'intensités*. He had been working with scales of his own invention, which he called 'modes', and with rhythmic series or cells, inspired in a variety of ways by the music of other cultures and styles of the past. For him it was natural to shape pitch and rhythm independently of one another. In this piano piece Messiaen took a decisive step further: apart from the pitch modes and a series of time-values, he set up series for loudness and tone-colour (on the piano, mode of attack). Throughout the study each pitch of the mode is coupled with a particular duration, volume level and mode of attack, so that each note acquires a uniquely defined quality as a single sound. The phenomenon of the single sound was in the air.[1] At the same time the composer's relationship to these sounds had reached a critical point. The four properties of a note – pitch, duration, loudness and timbre, soon referred to as parameters – became equally privileged structural constituents in the music, and the musical note was thus reduced to its naked material, and physically measurable, existence. The character of a note or a key, and the connection of rhythm with the pulse, or breathing, seemed to be things of the past. Perhaps this is related to Messiaen's compositional crisis after 1951, which he overcame by spending seven years writing works based exclusively on birdsong. For young composers this situation demanded a complete re-orientation of their musical consciousness – a transit through a point zero – if they were not to fall back on traditional musical elements.

At the start of 1951 Pierre Boulez, a pupil of Messiaen, was at just such a point zero in Paris. Having concerned himself both with Stravinsky's approach to rhythm and with the twelve-note music of Schoenberg and Webern, he was now engaged in Cartesian doubt. It was around the time of Stockhausen's piano sonata, or perhaps a little later, that Boulez composed the first part of his *Structures I* for two pianos – a completely rationally ordered piece of music.

I wanted to make an experiment that set out from the 'degree zero of writing'. Originally, this first *Structure* in particular was going to be named after a picture by Paul Klee, *An der Grenze des Fruchtlandes* ... I borrowed the material from Messiaen's *Mode de valeurs et d'intensités* ... For me this was an essay in doubt, in Cartesian doubt: I wanted to question everything, to make a *tabula rasa* of the whole musical inheritance and begin again at degree zero, so as to see how one could arrive at a new way of writing, starting from a phenomenon that lay outside one's own experience.[2]

György Ligeti gives an equally striking description of his experience of this musical degree zero while he was living in Budapest. Around 1950 he was in a compositional predicament, since the post-Bartókian style he had been using no longer seemed to be 'the right path' for him. Ligeti had begun to imagine a music in which melodic and rhythmic characteristics as such were completely erased in favour of a static yet luminous web of sound, whose timbre was constantly changing.

It was then that I first began to conceive of a static, motionless music, with no development and no conventional rhythmic figures. These ideas were vague at first, and at the time I lacked the courage and the compositional and technical abilities to put them into practice ... In 1951 I began to experiment with very simple sonorous and rhythmic structures, building up a new kind of music from degree zero, so to speak; I did this in a frankly Cartesian way, in that I regarded all the music I knew and loved as being, for my purposes, irrelevant and even invalid. I set myself problems such as, what can I do with a single note? or with its octave displacements? with an interval? with two intervals? What can I do with specific rhythmic relationships that could serve as the basic elements of a rhythmic and intervallic aggregate? The result was several little pieces, mainly for piano . . . At any rate, the isolation in which I was working more or less condemned my would-be self-liberation to failure, since the familiar Bartókian idiom still came through, even if it was not as dominant as in my earlier music. So my pieces from that period strike me as being pretty heterogeneous in style, naïvely lacking in orientation, not even half-way decent as solutions.[3]

At the end of 1956 Ligeti left Hungary, and it was only when he arrived in Cologne in 1957 that he could realize his musical ideas of 1950–1.

Darmstadt 1951

The tense atmosphere of this upheaval in music also cast its shadow on the Darmstadt Summer Courses, and that year many events coincided to make it a notable event. In conjunction with the second international twelve-note congress, and as a climax, the 'Dance around the Golden Calf' from Schoenberg's opera *Moses und Aron* was to be premièred in the presence of the composer. In addition there was a music and technology conference on the acoustic world of electronic music, at which the Bonn physicist and phoneticist Werner Meyer-Eppler would present synthetic sounds produced on a melochord for the first time. Pierre Schaeffer was invited from Paris to present examples of his *musique concrète*. About one hundred young people came to these courses; among them, besides Stockhausen, were Hans Werner Henze and Bernd Alois Zimmermann, Bengt Hambraeus, Gottfried Michael Koenig, Bruno Maderna, Luigi Nono and Heinz-Klaus Metzger (later a well-known critic).

The young composers also included Messiaen's former pupil Karel Goeyvaerts, from Antwerp. In Paris he had made an intense study of some of Webern's scores (the Piano Variations op. 27 in particular, but also the Symphony op.21) and had discovered, so he felt, an extensive conscious structuring of the 'musical material'. Only the rhythm was not yet integrated into the structure. Since the end of 1950 Goeyvaerts had been composing a sonata for two pianos that was to incorporate the organization of all four parameters of a note within an overall structural idea. To this end he had evolved what he called his 'synthetic number' principle. A specific rule allocated a number to each value within the series for each parameter, and the sum of the four parameters was always

34

seven. Behind it lay a transcendental, perhaps almost religious attitude: the structural idea should be the image of an ulterior, absolutely serene spiritual one that is present at every instant, in all parameters of the piece, both temporally and spatially. The composer was to be the 'sound-crafter' of this 'static music'.

The connection of the religious and the rational was close to Stockhausen's heart, and the meeting with Goeyvaerts was an inspiration, coming as it did after his first efforts at composition in the isolation of his Cologne studies. Stockhausen and Goeyvaerts had both enrolled in Schoenberg's composition course and were disappointed when Schoenberg was forced to cancel because of illness. Theodor Wiesengrund Adorno had been chosen as his replacement. In his autobiography (published in 1983) Goeyvaerts described the atmosphere in Darmstadt that year and his meeting with Stockhausen:

There were many conversations at the Marienhöhe. We had a great need for contact at that time, because in that post-war period we were working on our own, more or less isolated. There was great sympathy for what other people were doing. From the first day on we were showing our scores to one another. And immediately you could tell that 'serialism' was in the air. But my ideas abut 'static music' did not get much of a hearing . . . My principle of the 'synthetic number', linking the parameters, still amounted to 'brain-games'. Just one young man saw something in it, and asked me more about it afterwards: Karlheinz Stockhausen. I still remember how he tried to explain the 'spiritual bases' of my new technique to other people over lunch. I had told him everything in a mish-mash of German and English, but despite my stammerings he quickly grasped it all.[4]

After we had talked about it for a long time, Karlheinz thought he had discovered a resemblance to Hesse's *Glass Bead Game*. I did not agree at all, since Hesse is dealing with an image of human knowledge and not with something as intangible as the trace of a mode of existence – without time and space.'[5] 'Even before my sonata for two pianos got its turn [in Adorno's class], Karlheinz knew about its construction from top to bottom.[6]

Stockhausen and Goeyvaerts had practised the second movement of the sonata, a sparse sequence of notes, and Adorno's first response was the provocative question, 'Why did you compose that for *two* pianos?' There was laughter in the room. Goeyvaerts, with his shaky grasp of German, felt insecure. Then Stockhausen stood up, quiet and confident, and gave a lucid analysis of the second movement, which was coolly received by Adorno. He was reminded of Hauer's music; he asked about motives, antecedents and consequents. This representative of twelve-note music, which he was putting forward in Darmstadt as the latest musical development, was faced with an unknown young student from Cologne whose polite but firm reply to all his objections was, 'Professor, you are looking for a chicken in an abstract painting.' Adorno dubbed Goeyvaerts and Stockhausen 'Adrian Leverkühn and his famulus', an allusion to Thomas Mann's novel *Doktor Faustus*. Three years later he spoke of this scene in a radio lecture and justified himself: 'The critic cannot be reproached for not understanding these recent products of rampant rationalism, since according to their own programme they are not to be understood but only to be demonstrated. Ask what is the function of some phenomenon within a work's total context of meaning, and the answer is a further exposition of the system.'[7]

Twelve-note music was the main theme in Darmstadt that year, and statements that already sought to extrapolate the consequences of Schoenberg and Webern attracted little attention, even from contemporaries. One of the few exceptions was the young Venetian Luigi Nono, whose *Variazioni canoniche sulla serie dell'op. 41 di Arnold Schoenberg* had made a lasting impression the previous year. The subject of one of those conversations at the Marienhöhe was the relationship of words and notes. Stockhausen and Goeyvaerts firmly espoused the thesis that 'a word is only musically usable if its acoustic substance can be integrated into the musical structure of the notes. Nono, on the other hand, was concerned only with the emotional content of the text as a stimulus to composition.'[8] Even then the opposing points of departure that would distinguish Stockhausen's and Nono's paths in the fifties were clearly evident.

The music critic Antoine Goléa had come to Darmstadt from France, and in the course of his lecture on new developments in French music he played the recently issued recording of Messiaen's *Quatre études de rythme* for piano, the fourth of which (now the second), *Mode de valeurs et d'intensités*, assumed great importance for Stockhausen. It must have been in the following days, in some corner of the Marienhöhe, that Goléa let Stockhausen and Goeyvaerts hear the recording again. Stockhausen was fascinated. He listened to this piano music three or four times and sensed its relationship to Goeyvaerts's sonata. Goeyvaerts had often talked about his teachers, Milhaud and, especially, Messiaen, and his courses in rhythmic technique and analysis at the Conservatoire. Stockhausen began to see Messiaen as one of the crucial figures in a new beginning, and for the first time he thought of continuing his studies with him in Paris.

The première of Schoenberg's 'Dance around the Golden Calf', conducted by Hermann Scherchen, was a success; Schoenberg died only a few days later. Stockhausen and Goeyvaerts had been to the rehearsals too, but they were disappointed, and in a letter to the pianist Yvette Grimaud, Goeyvaerts wrote: 'C'est du Verdi sériel' (It is serial Verdi). To them, Schoenberg was part of a bygone world.

Examinations

Back in Cologne, Stockhausen's relationship to Bartók had changed. Bartók's sonata lay further from his heart than formerly, and studying it from his new point of view he discovered many contradictions and crudities within the wonderful organization. The weeks in Darmstadt had set many things in motion, and Stockhausen appended to the stylistic summary of his examination thesis a more general section on rhythm and metre in which, for the first time, he made a distinction between 'duration' and 'interval of entry' (though he calls duration 'length' and the interval of entry 'time-length').

After finishing this, he hitch-hiked to Hamburg to see Doris Andreae. On the journey all the compositional considerations and musical experiences of the last weeks, which had been plaguing him while working on Bartók, suddenly intensified and came together as the idea for a composition. He had an intuition that the composer does not construct the idea for a work but is merely the witness of its emergence from within.

The couple who had picked me up went for coffee. I waited outside, sitting on a stone, took out some paper and made the first sketches for the whole form of *Kreuzspiel*. Then we drove on to Hamburg, where I began *Kreuzspiel*, essentially just as I had sketched it . . . and as I had seen and heard it inside my head, while these people were talking about something quite different. In a dream or a daydream a really strong pressure swells up inside like a bubble. It is both hearing and seeing at once: you see a written score and hear the overall sound without being able to say what comes next or how it will look in detail. But you hear it as a whole, as a landscape or mountain is seen from a great distance, and that is what is most important.[9]

'Mosaik', the original title of *Kreuzspiel*, marks a completely fresh start in Stockhausen's composing. There are no twelve-note rows with melodic motives – though Stockhausen is writing with all twelve chromatic semitones – nor any rhythmic motives. When Stockhausen sketched the formal plan of the piece, he drew up the process by which the individual parameters run their course.

These weeks at the end of summer 1951 were not just a new musical beginning, for there were changes in all directions. Stockhausen had

9 August 1956 in the garden at 6 Meister-Johann-Strasse: Stockhausen, Doris Stockhausen and Karel Goeyvaerts

decided on a firm relationship with Doris Andreae and had become engaged to her in Hamburg. His course was completed and he took steps towards studying with Messiaen and Milhaud in Paris from January 1952. He saw his life in terms of the radical events occurring mid-century, and in a letter to Goeyvaerts at this time he described Schoenberg's 'Dance around the Golden Calf', Hesse's *Glass Bead Game* and Thomas Mann's *Doktor Faustus* as the last paving-stones of a long development. Messiaen's *Mode de valeurs et d'intensités* and Heidegger's *Holzwege*, which Stockhausen had been reading in the previous months, were a new departure. Heidegger had prefaced his collection of essays (published in 1950) with a commentary in which Stockhausen recognized much of his own personal situation. Heidegger noted that 'Holz' is an old word for woodland, and that the woods are full of paths – 'Holzwege' ('blind alleys') – that suddenly come to an end in front of untrodden ground. Within the wood each one runs separately. Often it seems as though one is like another, but this is not so. The woodcutters and foresters know these 'paths to nowhere' and understand their meaning.[10]

In the middle of October the oral exams took place, and Stockhausen passed with distinction. For his principal study (piano) he played the Bagatelles op. 24 by Kurt Hessenberg, a rondo by Prince Louis Ferdinand of Prussia and pieces by Bartók and one by Schubert. For the composition option he had submitted the *Drei Lieder*, which Hermann Schroeder marked 'very good'. As he declaimed Gottfried Benn's 'Chopin' in the elocution exam, the dichotomy between author and musician may have surfaced once more. But the choice had already been made.

18 October 1951: Preparations for the Founding of the Cologne Electronic Studio

As the state exams were taking place, a decision was reached at Cologne Radio that would soon have a direct impact on Stockhausen's life and composition. On 18 October Herbert Eimert, Werner Meyer-Eppler and Robert Beyer had a meeting there with a number of senior colleagues and engineers from the radio. They agreed to recommend to the director that 'the process of creating music directly on tape proposed by Dr Werner Meyer-Eppler'[11] be initiated in Cologne. This was as a preliminary to the installation of the electronic studio at Cologne Radio, its goal being the production and investigation of synthetic sounds: a step with enormous consequences. Meyer-Eppler was at the head of the Cologne initiative, but Herbert Eimert was the propelling force. As a senior producer of the late-night programmes he had the necessary influence at the radio station, and was able to persuade the director that the first sound experiments should begin in 1952 and that an electronic music studio should be made available within the foreseeable future. That evening WDR Cologne broadcast a late-night music programme in which Werner Meyer-Eppler, Herbert Eimert, Robert Beyer and Friedrich Trautwein discussed 'The Sound World of Electronic Music', and Meyer-Eppler presented examples of melochord sounds.

Once the first usable tape equipment appeared at the end of the forties, music without musical instruments became possible. Pierre Schaeffer, who had begun his experiments in *musique concrète* in Paris in 1948, was interested in the sensual side of sound; everything that could be captured by microphone, from everyday noise to instrumental sounds, became for him the basic material of a new world of sound. The first tape compositions were created through the technical manipulation and alienation of such *concrète* sounds in his experimental Club d'Essai studio at Paris Radio.

At the end of 1951, a few weeks after the founding of the Cologne project, the first New York 'Music for Tape' experiments took place. In January 1952 came the première of John Cage's *Imaginary Landscape no. 5*, a four-minute tape piece whose material consisted of any sections from forty-two randomly selected gramophone records. In May of the same year, at Columbia University, Otto Luening and Vladimir Ussachevsky presented their first attempts to expand the timbral possibilities of classical instruments through reverberation, echo and distortion effects.

In the context of the beginnings of tape music in Paris, Cologne and New York, the definition of a musical tone may come into question. The standard answer is audible vibrations, acoustically and physically measurable sound. This area has been the subject of intense research. The work of Hermann Pfrogner and Heiner Ruland, for example, has led to greater understanding of sound that goes beyond the one-sided kind of answer.[12]

Kreuzspiel and a Composition Commission for Donaueschingen

Once his exams were over Stockhausen returned immediately to the composition of *Kreuzspiel*, finishing it early in November. It provides a good example of the way Stockhausen's works ofen come into being. At the start the idea for the piece is like a vision, its processes grasped only in an intuitive way. Then it is sketched out, often undergoing minor transformations of detail. Stockhausen's initial plan for *Kreuzspiel* was to write it for high soprano and piano. The phonemes of the name Doris, transformed in various ways, were to be incorporated into the construction. Then he thought of piano, high female voice and male voice, before finally deciding on oboe, bass clarinet, piano and three percussionists. The sketching is followed by 'hard work': the idea is worked out in terms of the individual parameters – the chains of numbers, combinations and permutations – and eventually the whole thing is notated. After it has been heard a few times, minor corrections are made to achieve the greatest possible clarity. (In the 1959 revision of the work, for example, Stockhausen reduced four percussion parts to the final three.)

In *Kreuzspiel*

the idea of a crossing of temporal and spatial procedures is presented in three stages. In the first the piano begins in the extreme outer registers and progressively – through crossing of registers – brings into play six notes 'from above' and six notes 'from below'; the middle four octaves (the joint range of oboe and bass clarinet) are increasingly exploited and, at the moment when an even distribution of pitches throughout the entire range has been achieved, the series governing durations and dynamics have been crossed in such a way that the initially aperiodic series are converted into a durations series whose values are progressively shortened and a dynamics series whose values grow progressively louder ... The whole process then runs backwards in mirror form, so that at the end of the first stage all the notes are again in the extreme registers of the piano; as a result of the crossing process, however, the six notes from 'up top' are now 'down below', and vice versa. In the second stage the whole formal process described above is carried out from the centre outwards: everything begins in the middle octave with oboe and bass clarinet, extending to the extreme registers (piano) and back ... The third stage combines the two processes.[13]

Each note was exactly defined in all parameters, as a unique, self-sufficient point of sound.

For Stockhausen as a composer, music even then was not the expression of human feelings and passions, but rather an attempt at a re-creation, a reconstitution of cosmic order and natural laws in sounds. His view of the middle of the century has thus been very different from that of Boulez and Ligeti, for example. He believed it inaugurated a new epoch in which the 'great "Romantic" arch that had displayed so many extreme offshoots actually seemed to have reached its end, in music ... and an orientation away from mankind began. Once again one looked up to the stars, and started an intensive measuring and counting.'[14] Stockhausen liked to compare the points of sound in *Kreuzspiel* to 'stars in the night sky, each one of them an individual'.[15]

Even if it was influenced by Goeyvaerts's and Messiaen's piano pieces, *Kreuzspiel* is an extraordinarily masterful achievement for a 23–year-old, and it already bears Stockhausen's unmistakable mark: the composing of a process, the genesis of a form; processes in music that are like those of life itself – construction, destruction and transformation; procreation, life and death in terms of music. Stockhausen had already experimented with this in his piano sonata, and – at a literary level – it was the main motive of the story 'Geburt im Tod'.

Stockhausen showed the completed score of *Kreuzspiel* to Eimert, whose response was distinctly reticent. He did not find the same spontaneous access to this work as he had had to the sonatine, and said, 'If

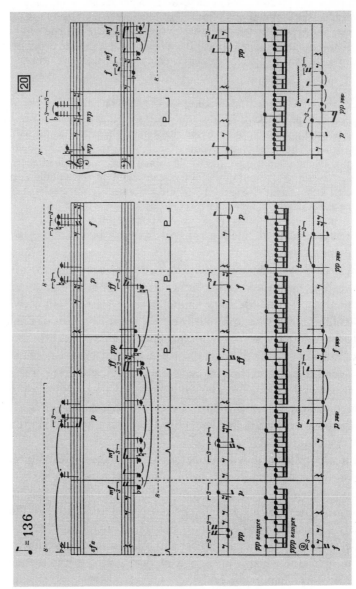

10 *Kreuzspiel* for oboe, bass clarinet, piano and three percussionists, bars 14–20 ('six notes "from above" and six notes "from below"')

you make music like this, you will have to be patient for twenty years until you get a performance.'

Many letters passed between Cologne and Antwerp at this time. Acquaintance with Goeyvaerts in Darmstadt had turned into close friendship, and they discussed everything, from the newest musical project to the most personal matters. In a letter of 23 November Stockhausen reported that he had just started working on his first orchestral composition. Of the first movement, whose original title, 'Studie für Orchester', he later changed to *Formel*, Stockhausen wrote:

The new piece will give rise to vigorous discussions between us; its general outlook is very different from that of *Kreuzspiel*. Just one indication: instead of the very precisely formed single notes there are little complexes, almost electrically evolved, and actually harmonic as well as melodic (please take harmonic and melodic in the right way: in the sense of an individual characterization of each complex); so instead of single notes, it is these little crystalline blooms that pass through a register form (first movement = eighteen phases).[16]

From the 'sound points' of *Kreuzspiel*, Stockhausen had now turned to 'sound complexes' or 'sound chains'. At the opening of the work the twelve chromatic notes are successively brought into play in twelve brief sections whose pitch chains gradually accumulate: Stockhausen was to call these sections 'limbs'. Each limb is marked by different features in respect of dynamics, tempo, rhythmic structure and instrumentation, etc. This twelve-limbed formation unfolds spirally through the different octave registers in twelve major sections.

A little later Stockhausen was summoned to Eimert's house, where Heinrich Strobel, director of the Donaueschingen Festival, was staying. Was he able to compose an orchestral piece, a commission for Donaueschingen? Stockhausen talked about his 'orchestral study', and said yes without too much hesitation. It was agreed that he would send a two-piano version of a major part of the work to Hans Rosbaud, the conductor. His daily schedule was already crammed: there were unexpected formalities for the forthcoming stay in Paris, a late-night broadcast on Bartók's sonata for two pianos and percussion, and a radio recording of *Kreuzspiel* (Eimert had, after all, risked a radio production), as well as the final appearances with the conjuror Adrion. Stockhausen had toured Germany with Adrion for well over a year; small but noteworthy events, sometimes poetic, sometimes dramatic, were constantly occurring.

Improvising at the Piano for the Conjuror Adrion

Stockhausen and Adrion had got to know one another at the end of the summer of 1950. Adrion was looking for a student pianist who could improvise accompaniments to his 'magic chamber art'. Stockhausen confessed to the conjuror much later that at that first meeting in the student hostel, as he was improvising on the grand piano to some samples of Adrion's art, he had 'stage fright from head to toe'.

Their joint performances took them from Oldenburg, in the north of Germany, right down to Franconia. The sponsors included colleges, theatrical societies and cultural clubs as well as some vicars and booksellers. When they arrived at a new venue they would go straight to the hall to check the stage, the lighting and the acoustics – and the grand piano, which usually caused a mini-drama of the kind that Adrion, a sensitive observer, recalls:

Karlheinz Stockhausen would seat himself at the piano, utterly composed, his eyes narrowing to a tiny slit, his head imperceptibly straining upwards. He played one note, then another, then a third, struck a few chords, and on his face you could see more and more clearly his displeasure at the instrument's unsatisfactory condition – and then there would be this look of unspeakable suffering, of reproach mixed with despair, from my distressed partner, and the exclamation (sometimes more of a scream), 'How am I supposed to make your magic music for you on this heap of shit!?' And with equal regularity he would slam the lid shut.[17]

Stockhausen has lasting memories of an appearance at Miltenberg; the vicar smoked fat cigars and had connections at a textile factory where Stockhausen purchased his first suit. He needed one urgently, since he was soon going to travel to Hamburg to be introduced to Doris Andreae's relatives. Adrion remembers Delmenhorst in particular; the power suddenly went off during the performance and the local priest had all twenty-five huge church candles brought in so that the performers could continue their show in a mysterious semi-darkness. (Something similar happened over twenty years later in London, where half-way through one of Stockhausen's lectures the power went off again. The composer calmly kept talking, with the twilight from the streets outside providing scant lighting in the lecture hall.)

Stockhausen used the many unfilled hours in hotel rooms and railway stations to concentrate on his work, and throughout the last months of 1951, according to Adrion's reminiscences, he only got to see Stockhausen when he was on stage. At a performance in Krefeld Adrion was standing in front of his assembled audience, waiting for his pianist; but he did not come. Finally he went off to look for him, and found him in his hotel room, immersed in the new work for Donaueschingen.

During these months there must have been strong conflicts within Stockhausen's music-making: when improvising for Adrion he could let his intuition run free, achieving certain things he could never have written. A newspaper review of one of his performances with Adrion commended Stockhausen as 'a pianist gifted with extraordinary intuition, whose imaginative playing contributed greatly to creating the right atmosphere, and thus to forging a link between public and performer'.[18] While he was composing, however, when single notes derived from numbers had to be 'formed into music', into points or formulas on paper, Stockhausen often felt 'insanely frustrated', as he once told Rudolf Frisius. The last performance Stockhausen and Adrion gave together took place in Cologne in the chamber hall of the Belgisches Haus at the Neumarkt on 10 December 1951. At the time Adrion noted: 'Last evening with Stockhausen – and the best.' The end of Stockhausen's tours with Adrion meant the end of his improvising for a living, though later he would sometimes improvise at the piano. Something comparable to the 'intuitive music' of the late sixties thus existed even then.

Shortly before Christmas Stockhausen went to Hamburg. He and Doris Andreae wanted to get married on 29 December, just before his departure for Paris. The imminent separation was not easy for either of them. Adrion and Goeyvaerts came to Hamburg as witnesses. The four of them celebrated the eve of the wedding. They had received a stack of plates from a restaurant and smashed them one by one on the doorstep of the house. Stockhausen was fascinated by some particularly beautiful-sounding fragments, and he happily went on striking them for some time. In the marriage register Goeyvaerts gave his occupation as 'Toonkundige', which Stockhausen translated as 'sound-crafter'. The wedding took place before a small circle of guests and there was a splendid feast. Goeyvaerts made an after-dinner speech, people danced, and until late at night Adrion was conjuring little surprises from the suits and blouses of the bride's distinguished Hanseatic relatives.

It was around this time that Stockhausen received a telegram confirming the commission for Donaueschingen. In the first week of 1952 he travelled via Antwerp to Paris, arriving there on 8 January.

Paris: Studies with Messiaen and Milhaud

During his first weeks in Paris Stockhausen lived in almost monastic isolation. He was devoted only to his work; he went to Messiaen's courses and Milhaud's classes, seizing any opportunity to learn French. He had found lodgings to the south of the city, in the student quarter of the boulevard Jourdin, among people of every conceivable colour and nationality. For the first months he shared a room with a Turkish mathematics student who often had female visitors; he 'mostly needed the room to himself . . . and I learned there and then to compose with full concentration in any corner, with any level of noise around me'.[19]

As well as working on the commission for Donaueschingen, Stockhausen composed two piano pieces, designated A and B, as a present for his wife's birthday on 28 February. A year later, slightly revised, they were retitled *Klavierstücke III* and *II* and put together with *Klavierstück I* (originally 'Klavierstück C', written shortly after the first two) and *Klavierstück IV* (written soon after 'Klavierstück C') to form a cycle. The conception of *Klavierstücke I-IV* is extremely radical and the cycle makes no concessions to the player; for the first time adjacent single notes are formed into higher-level groups of notes by specific common properties, foreshadowing a transition in Stockhausen's composing from 'points' to 'groups'.

At the end of January Heinrich Strobel came to Paris. He cheerfully complained to Stockhausen about the younger generation, which no longer cared for Schoenberg, Stravinsky and Hindemith. The previous year he had had Boulez's *Polyphonie X* performed at Donaueschingen. 'Write music, not mathematics,' he told Stockhausen. 'Last year it was Boulez, this year it is you. I am like the manager of a department store: I have to seek out exceptional, new, interesting things, even if they do not mean much to me.'

Gradually Stockhausen began to feel at ease in Paris. Every Sunday he went to mass in a different church and then wandered through the streets and parks, along the Seine and through the museums. He had set great hopes on the composition classes, but the ones with Milhaud, held in the composer's flat, were a great disappointment. Stockhausen had played the recordings of the choral and sonatine. Milhaud found the last movement of the sonatine 'amusing, just like 1920', and the choral good. He seemed to find everything good and nice, and after each piece he said, 'Merci, mon ami.' To finish, Milhaud played a recording of his Quartets nos. 14 or 15, 'then we were dismissed with his blessing'. After

11 Messiaen's analysis class at the Paris Conservatoire, March 1952. *At the piano:* Olivier Messiaen; *back row, third from the right:* Stockhausen

a few weeks Stockhausen abandoned these classes, which made the effect of Messiaen's teaching all the stronger. For a whole year he went twice a week to Messiaen's course in aesthetics and analysis.

Many things I knew already from my studies in Cologne. But most of it I knew without it mattering to me: it was dead. Messiaen awakened the dead. He interpreted the neumes of Gregorian notation in such a way as to be able to make a piano piece, *Neumes rythmiques*, out of them. He turned the *podatus, clivis, porrectus* and *torculus* into elements of a new composition. He transformed Indian rhythms into elements of his own music. In the Tierra del Fuego he had noted down rhythms and a few melodic formulas, from which he made two piano pieces. Modes from all periods and peoples, birdsong: wherever he goes, Messiaen takes along his little notebook and notates what he hears. Then he goes home, and orders, transforms and composes his 'objects'. Messiaen is a glowing crucible.

47

He absorbs sounding forms and mirrors them in terms of his own musical intellect.

That was very clear to me: he showed it quite openly. And thus from the start I was able to guard against it in my own work. I got to know much old and new music, studied scores, listened with insatiable curiosity . . .

But I got to know it in order to separate myself from it; to hear what had already been done, what had already had its life, so that I would not repeat or revive anything. My realm became that of invention. More and more I listened to what was inside me, rather than outside . . .

Invention and amazement at the as yet unheard: from the single sound to the form.

Marvelling.

Communicating.

In many respects Messiaen did the opposite of what I wanted. He never tried to convince me. That made him a good teacher. He did not give instruction in composition, but showed how he understood the music of others and how he worked himself.[20]

The months in Paris proved to be an exceptionally fertile period; in the course of 1952, Stockhausen's most productive year to date in terms of opus numbers, he wrote six new works. Yet this fruitful time began in February with a debilitating crisis that almost led to his giving up work on his piece for Donaueschingen. He struggled with the lifelong task he saw before him: to compose *new* music, to hearken to what came to him as 'visage' (in a letter to his wife dated 4 February 1952 Stockhausen described such an intuitive process at length, calling it a 'visage'),[21] and to carry it through as purely as possible, without the intervention of personal touches. His proximity to Messiaen – 'What can stand next to his work?' – intensified the dilemma. He wrote about his predicament in his letters to Goeyvaerts; 'May God show me the true way – I shall seek to do nothing but make myself ready. There are times now when I have a singular longing to welcome the End, to relinquish everything human and to enter into the One and Absolute. But I also feel I have still been given much to fulfil before it can all be left behind.'[22] By the beginning of March the crisis was past.

'His passion for innovation was so all-consuming that I was unhesitatingly reminded of Champollion'

In January 1984 Messiaen was asked to set down his memories of Stockhausen as a participant in his courses. Although some of what Messiaen says is already familiar and some has to do with himself, much light is shed on teacher and pupil.

I came to know Karlheinz Stockhausen in 1952; he was still rather young: barely twenty-five! It was at the time when I, as professor of harmony at the Paris Conservatoire, had been transferred to an analysis class, which was specially created for me by Claude Delvincourt. In it there were two categories of pupils: students who came because they felt like it, and composers from the composition class, for whom it was compulsory. I had been particularly asked to analyse sonata form, above all in relation to the sonatas and symphonies of Beethoven . . . From 1956 I was king in my little academic universe, and there, from 1956 to 1979, I could do whatever I wanted. What I wanted to cover was Stockhausen, Boulez and Xenakis themselves and the whole of ultra-modern music (including *musique concrète* and electronic music); but also Monteverdi, Gesualdo and Claude le Jeune; Mozart, Wagner, Debussy and Stravinsky as well as Schoenberg, Berg and Webern; the Middle Ages with its plainchant, Adam de la Halle and Guillaume de Machaut; ancient and exotic things, Greek metre, the Indian decî-tâlas, Balinese music and Japanese gagaku.

Alas! Stockhausen never knew these happy times! When he came to me, not only was I immersed in fugue and sonata form, but I had made a firm decision never to have disciples, and had absolutely forbidden myself to talk about my own personal researches. So Stockhausen was very unhappy in my class. [This was not the case, though once or twice in the correspondence with Goeyvaerts Stockhausen says he was sometimes bored by Messiaen's classes.] I treated him kindly and with the greatest possible respect, since I knew for certain that I was dealing with a real genius who had to be guided towards his true path. After a year he left me and went to Herbert Eimert, with whom he was initiated into electronic music. Then he left Eimert, to soar up with his own wings. In fact, Stockhausen did not need a teacher. The few musical encounters he has had in his life were merely springboards for his future works. His passion for innovation was so all-consuming that I was unhesitatingly reminded of Champollion, who passionately applied himself to learning Coptic in the hope that one day he would be able to read Egyptian hieroglyphics. Just as Champollion realized the dream of a lifetime and suddenly discovered the sound of the hieroglyphs when he had the idea that the names of the kings and queens within a cartouche on the Rosetta Stone were not to be pronounced in Greek but in Coptic, so Stockhausen fervently sought out everything that could aid the development of his genius and, luckily, everything served its purpose. Ultimately, remote from every teacher and every influence, he wrote the great works that the whole world knows today: *Gesang der Jünglinge* for a child's voice multiplied electro-acoustically; *Gruppen* for three orchestras; *Carré* for four orchestras and four choruses; and *Momente* for soprano solo, a chorus of sixty-four, and thirteen instrumentalists, which present many 'moments' at once and a great 'moment' in the explosion of primordial life. Since these splendid successes Stockhausen has made many about-turns, always spectacular, always unexpected and always yielding new masterpieces.

I had the great joy of meeting him again just recently, when he sat next to me in the Paris Opéra at a performance of my *St Francis of Assisi*. I shall never forget a word of the intimacies we exchanged that evening.

49

Acquaintance with Boulez and New Works

At the beginning of March 1952 Stockhausen was invited to visit Pierre Boulez, who had heard about him through Heinrich Strobel. Both rapidly became engaged in a conversation about their own works – the following year Boulez told Heinz-Klaus Metzger that he had been very impressed by the 'radicality' of *Klavierstücke I-IV* – as well as by new French music and John Cage. (Boulez had corresponded with Cage since 1949, but in October 1952 was to distance himself from the latest developments in Cage's music.) So began a friendship that, in spite of all the differences between the two personalities and their work, was based on mutual understanding and respect. For years Boulez was the only person whose musical judgements interested Stockhausen. Boulez was then at work on a *concrète* study in Schaeffer's studio; in the evening he took Stockhausen along to the Club d'Essai and made him known there.

Eight weeks later the orchestral work for Donaueschingen was completed, but there had been a change of plan. Stockhausen had set aside the 'Studie für Orchester', since it seemed to him too melodic and motivic; what he sent to the conductor Hans Rosbaud instead were the second and third movements of the work he had sketched in November 1951, now entitled *Spiel*, which were written more in the spirit of *Kreuzspiel*. Stockhausen later said, 'I have never again composed a work that is divided into movements.'[23]

Directly after *Spiel* Stockhausen composed a new piece, the *Schlagquartett* for piano and 3 × 2 timpani (reworked at N'Gor in 1974 as a *Schlagtrio* for piano and 2 × 3 timpani). Again, its musical process is clearly reminiscent of organic and reproductive processes. Herbert Hübner of North German Radio in Hamburg wanted to record it for radio broadcast, and also secured a performance within his concert series 'das neue werk'. In a letter to Hübner written from Paris on 11 November, Stockhausen described the compositional idea behind the quartet:

Two entities, starting from a state beyond what can be physically represented or perceived, arrive at a temporally and spatially limited field. Their relation is that of opposite poles. Each of the two principles appears in a multiplicity of guises, corresponding to the multiplicity of possible realizations in the time–space field they have both entered.[24] . . .

The two entities (twelve-note melodies) now move towards one another from the extreme high and low registers and assimilate one another. At the moment of their complete concordance (when all the sound spaces are equally filled by each), a new entity (a new melody) emerges from the middle. It unites in itself the twofold polarity of the preceding pair. The two generating entities (principles)

12 ?Baden-Baden, summer 1952. *Left to right:* Gerth-Wolfgang Baruch, then music producer at South-west Radio, Stockhausen and Heinrich Strobel

vacate the time spaces in the same way as they had steadily occupied them before. In so doing they distance themselves from one another once more, and return again to the state that lies beyond physical representability. The third entity remains on its own, accomplishing the same passage through the time spaces and the same return.[25]

Darmstadt and Donaueschingen 1952: First Performances

At the end of June Stockhausen went back to Hamburg via Cologne, where he met Werner Meyer-Eppler and listened to the first experiments with electronic sounds by Robert Beyer and Herbert Eimert at the radio station. A little later, on 21 July, one of his works was premièred for the first time. *Kreuzspiel* had been accepted for the younger generation concerts at the Darmstadt Summer Courses and put on a programme with works by Boulez, Maderna, Nono, Camillo Togni and Bernd Alois Zimmermann. Maderna himself played one of the percussion parts and Stockhausen conducted. For most listeners the piece came as a shock: no motives, no rhythm, just seemingly disconnected single notes. There was restlessness in the hall and tension rose. When the bass clarinettist, with cheeks bulging, unexpectedly played a low note fortissimo, a few people burst out laughing. Stockhausen went on conducting with the utmost concentration. But the spell was broken; the unrest increased and the piece ended amid hoots and shrill whistling. Herbert Fleischer, one of the lecturers, roundly accused Friedrich Wildgans of having deliberately played the clarinet so loud because he disliked the piece. It made no difference, though: *Kreuzspiel* became the scandal of the evening.

During August Stockhausen and his wife went on an extended hitch-hiking trip through France. On returning to Hamburg he began a new orchestral composition, 'Kontrapunkte', the first version of the work that was renamed *Punkte* early in 1953.[26] Once the piece was finished, on 30 September, Stockhausen travelled to Baden-Baden for the rehearsals of *Spiel*.

I played the piano part in the orchestra conducted by Hans Rosbaud. During the final rehearsals before the première Rosbaud's comments gave me the impression that he would be glad if I were to shorten the piece considerably. I decided to tell him 'on my own initiative' that I would like the second movement to end in the middle, where the mirroring begins. He was visibly relieved. So at Donaueschingen the première consisted of the first movement and the first half of the second.

The percussion involved every possible new timbre, and therefore included instruments never used before in the orchestral literature. For instance, I used a large drinking-glass, which is struck with a metal rod and is meant to ring through many pauses as an important 'marker'. Altgraf Salm, at that time the curator of the Prince of Fürstenberg's museum of valuable beer and wine goblets, did me the honour of letting me select a particularly beautiful-sounding goblet from the collection.

At the première, just before the ending we had decided on, there was a big build-up leading to a pause, and the glass was supposed to be struck at the beginning of it, ringing on through it as a bright, brilliant sound. Rosbaud gave one of his incomparable big cues for fragile sound sources and the percussionist, in the heat of the moment, struck so hard with his metal rod that the goblet smashed into a thousand pieces – all over the seats, the music stands and the floor – and the whole pause was filled with these splintering sounds. Then there was a loud final sound and the piece was over. The audience reacted in the now legendary scandalized fashion that all my early compositions seemed to provoke. By that time I had progressed much further and did not want the piece ever to be played again.[27]

After the performance a slim little man, radiating energy and amiability, came up to Stockhausen. He introduced himself as his prospective publisher and congratulated him on his piece. It was Alfred Schlee from Universal Edition in Vienna. Stockhausen was extremely pleased; he had no difficulty in accepting Schlee's offer and promised to send scores. *Spiel* had made an immediate, powerful impression on Schlee; after so many works by Schoenberg imitators during those years, it stood out as a 'creative explosion'. It was the start of a long friendship and collaboration.

Schaeffer's Club d'Essai and *Kontra-Punkte*

Stockhausen was back in Paris at the end of October. Boulez's departure that autumn had left a vacancy that Schaeffer had allocated to Stockhausen, but Schaeffer's budget and studio time had been cut back and Stockhausen had to wait. Then the chance arose of working in a little-used experimental studio at the Technical College of the PTT (French Post Office, of which the radio station was then an affiliated sub-branch). The task of this studio, which was under the control of the physicist and information theory expert Abraham Moles, was to conduct systematic research into sound. The equipment and other facilities struck Stockhausen as being even more limited than in the sparsely equipped main studio. He soon became familiar with the technology, and spent the next six weeks working very intensively in the rue Barrault.

Stockhausen started with systematic timbre analyses of glass, wood and metal sounds; later he analysed the sound spectra of various exotic instruments that he was able to record in the Musée de l'Homme. He was allowed to undertake his own experiments and, after some initial

53

13 Donaueschingen 1952: Luigi Nono and Stockhausen. This photo was taken by Alfred Schlee, who had been struck by both faces even before the première of *Spiel*

attempts, he began work at the start of December on a *concrète* étude based on six different prepared piano sounds, a tape composition whose underlying structural idea was to be manifest in each single sound. In a letter to Goeyvaerts of 3 December he wrote: 'I now wanted a structure, to be realized in an *Etude*, that was already worked into the micro-dimension of a single sound, so that in every moment, however small, the overall principle of my idea would be present.'[28] Yet the further Stockhausen penetrated into the acoustic conditions, the greater the difficulties became; 'The very thing we want to control gets ever more imperfect, the closer we look at it.'[29] Two days later Stockhausen very clearly stated what he wanted: 'We shall use electronic sound production in the future . . . and we shall govern the material – it shall not govern us.'[30]

It was around this time that Stockhausen made experiments with the studio's own frequency generator. He had learned from Goeyvaerts that these test generators used in studio technology produced sine tones, the individual partials of a sound spectrum. By superimposing sine tones, he attempted for the first time to produce synthetic sound spectra: 'The work was extremely arduous; as there was no tape recorder in the studio, I had to copy each sine tone on to disc and then copy it from one disc to another!'[31] Some doubt has been expressed over these attempts, but Abraham Moles confirms them: 'It is absolutely true that Stockhausen . . . while working on sound production in the rue Barrault made many experiments with a sine-wave generator. Some of these experiments were done with great precision, and with all the care for which he is renowned.'[32] But on account of the technical arrangements in the studio, his efforts were completely inadequate and unsatisfying.

On 15 December the *concrète* étude was finished – it lasts two minutes and twenty seconds – and Stockhausen played it to Schaeffer. Schaeffer clearly felt slight disappointment in this young German composer who was not interested in his advice:

It was really strange; when Messiaen came into the studio he said, 'I would like next to no sounds' – those were his words. When Stockhausen came, he said, 'I shall work with a single sound.' And Boulez came and wanted to make a study on a single sound . . . And they had to come to *me* with this desire, in a situation where I had discovered exactly the opposite approach . . . OK, Stockhausen came, he took a tiny bit of sound, about 10 centimetres of tape, and he said; 'I am going to cut this sound into millimetre pieces, and make a permutation out of it.' I said, 'You poor thing, don't do that, you'll only get a load of background noise, and that's just not interesting!' . . . He absolutely refused to follow my advice; he did not want any advice at all, and since what he had in mind could be done on his own, I sent him off to the rue Barrault to cut his tape into millimetre fragments. So he got down to the splicing and came back very happy, and we said, 'Well, fine, let's have a listen to it.' So we played the tape – it was only 10 centimetres long, perhaps 50 centimetres with the permutations – and all you heard was 'Shuuutt'. That was Stockhausen's sound study: a sort of little 'Shuuutt'. He was terribly pleased with it – me, not at all! I really do not know how he would view this episode in retrospect – what I remember is a charming young man who certainly would have been in a position to give and receive, someone who could have been involved in a mutually interesting exchange of ideas, but just did not want to listen to any rational view of things and clung on to his 'Study on One Sound' with a perfectly natural sense of ambition.[33]

The study, long thought lost, was rediscovered by Rudolf Frisius.

Two days after finishing his étude Stockhausen travelled to Hamburg, but the projected performance of the *Schlagquartett* had fallen through. Hübner had accepted the work for radio broadcast, but it seemed to him too risky for his concert series 'das neue werk'. Then Karl Amadeus Hartmann, who knew Stockhausen from Donaueschingen, intervened and programmed the work in the Munich Musica Viva concerts he was organizing; the première took place on 23 March 1953.

The last composition of the Paris period was a new piece of chamber music, *Kontra-Punkte*, which Stockhausen had already sketched before going to Hamburg in December. His first mature composition, it is a masterpiece of consistently composed serial music. The structure is based on sixes: six timbres, six tempos, six temporal series and six dynamic levels. A 'pointillist ensemble style' for ten soloists is transformed

irregularly but steadily into a soloistic style, articulated in terms of 'groups', which gradually focuses on the piano part . . . The six different dynamic levels (ppp-sfz) successively become pp. The big differences between very long and very short time-values are abolished; what remains is medium, very similar time-values. From the contrast between vertical and horizontal pitch connections, a two-part, monochrome counterpoint emerges.[34]

But in the wake of his work in the rue Barrault, Stockhausen found instrumental music a compromise, at least in one respect. Half-way through January 1953 he wrote to Goeyvaerts, lamenting the 'imperfection' and 'inadequacy' of instruments. 'If only a clarinet could stay exactly the same over three octaves for eight minutes!'[35]

It was only after completing *Kontra-Punkte* that Stockhausen returned to Paris, in mid-January. He had been planning further tasks in the studio, but Schaeffer declared that his personal experiments were at an end and gave him the task of classifying particular sounds and noises. The studio for electronic music at Cologne Radio was due to be opened in May, and Eimert had held out the prospect of employing Stockhausen as an assistant. On 27 March Stockhausen left Paris, determined, after his initial studio experience with Schaeffer, to carry out sound synthesis consistently in Cologne.

4 Electronic Music: A Musical Homunculus 1953–5

> Today, musical imagination calls
> for sounds that no one has ever
> heard. Many people find that disconcerting.
> Stockhausen

May 1953: A New Music Festival at Cologne Radio

When the first four electronic pieces by Beyer and Eimert were presented in conjunction with the opening of the electronic studio on 26 May 1953, the spectators sat – for the first time in a German concert hall – with no musicians in front of them: the stage was empty and the music came from huge loudspeakers. No subsequent performance of electronic music was to elicit quite the same reactions as those that morning: they ranged from dismayed hostility to naïve, progressivist fascination. Hans Heinz Stuckenschmidt described this first encounter with the world of synthetic sounds in words that have often been cited since: 'It was as if sonic projectiles from the mineral realm were surging up into the human world. Metals seemed to sing; technological forms such as the spiral became sound. A whole chain reaction of interweaving sensory impression was unleashed; a menacing upper- or underworld of associations flashed by in panoramic vistas.'[1]

Stockhausen's *Kontra-Punkte* was premièred that evening, conducted by Hermann Scherchen. WDR had accepted the work for the New Music Festival, and since returning from Paris to Hamburg Stockhausen had reworked the score and written out the parts. Originally *Punkte* was to have been played, but Stockhausen, who took a very critical view of his own works, had decided after considerable reflection to withdraw it temporarily; he had proposed that *Kontra-Punkte* should be performed instead.

At that time the complicated rhythms and rapidly changing dynamic levels of serial music caught most interpreters unprepared, and the rehearsals for *Kontra-Punkte* were quite a saga. They show the adverse performance conditions that serial music had to contend with in its early days. The difficulties began as soon as Stockhausen arrived in Cologne,

58

14 Herbert Eimert and Stockhausen in the electronic studio of WDR Cologne, 1953–4

where he was welcomed with the news that the pianist had sent her part back. She had overestimated her abilities and had not had enough time to practise. With only six days to go, former fellow student Gerhard Weidemann agreed to take her place. Another fellow student, Klaus Weiler, who was acting as page-turner, played the bottom notes as 'second pianist' in complex passages that Weidemann could not master and, when that was not enough, Stockhausen himself acted as 'third pianist'. At the first rehearsal the harpist developed a heart condition and bile complaint, so she withdrew. The harpist from the radio dance orchestra was talked into playing, but he could barely read music and Stockhausen had to have extended rehearsals with him.

When Scherchen arrived four days before the performance, he seemed hardly to know the score. Stockhausen told Klaus Weiler, that Scherchen had invited him to his residence in Gravesano, on Lake Lugano, to receive an explanation of the score – but it had no effect. During the rehearsals Scherchen was able to conceal his insecurity. At one of the breaks the head of New Music, Eigel Kruttge, came in to reassure the musicians, since the schedule seemed likely to be insufficient: 'Keep going! No one's going to blame you.'

Stockhausen was very angry because in four sessions Scherchen had rehearsed nothing new. More importantly, Scherchen's eruptive, jerky cues were making the musicians nervous again, and all the rhythms were turning into accents and syncopations. Although Stockhausen had accomplished so much in his own rehearsals that the playing was not too bad, on the last day, when the pianist was having difficulties with the ending, he settled for a truncated performance: better to have 350 good bars than 500 bad ones. The piece provoked strong views for and against. Some listeners would surely have found it hard to believe that Stockhausen talked to Eimert about beauty being the ideal of his music in a late-night music programme shortly after. The pretext for the conversation was the première of *Kontra-Punkte*. 'I want to invent *new* music, for I believe I have something new to say ... I am not looking for the new at *any* price. The price I pay is the old style – in order to find a new beauty, with the necessary luck ... Today and in the future, as in the past, it will always be a matter of discovering what is beautiful, of drawing close to beauty, of writing beautiful music.' When Eimert asked what traditional heritage he was continuing, Stockhausen named Anton Webern.

In Darmstadt in 1951 Webern had been an important topic in his conversations with Goeyvaerts. On his return from Paris Stockhausen had once more advocated Webern's music to Eimert and Kruttge at the

WDR. The two pieces he had heard in Darmstadt – the Five Canons op. 16 (in 1951) and the Four Songs op. 12 (in 1952) – had 'deeply moved' him. After the New Music Festival he had written to Goeyvaerts that there might be some sounds in Beyer's and Eimert's tape pieces that indicated possible paths forward, but all in all they had nothing musically sensible to offer. Only one piece at the New Music Festival had been significant: Webern's Quartet op. 22, which had been particularly beautiful. When Schlee sent him all the printed Webern scores from Vienna in mid-June, Stockhausen was able to study Webern's music more closely.

Darmstadt 1953

The 1953 Darmstadt Summer Courses brought a new development: for the first time the focus was on Webern as well as Schoenberg, and seven of his works were performed. Eimert had used the seventieth anniversary of Webern's birth as an opportunity to arrange an evening with Stockhausen and Nono entitled 'Webern and the New Generation' (on 23 July). He also read texts by Boulez and Goeyvaerts, who had been unable to come to Darmstadt that year. The evening, and Stockhausen's lecture in particular, made history in Darmstadt. Stockhausen analysed the first movement of Webern's op. 24, the concerto for nine instruments, portraying the structural proportions as antecedents of timbre composition, that is, of electronic music. No one had expected Stockhausen to give a conventional analysis, and he indeed provoked much indignation. The very same night the Swiss composer Armin Schibler drew up a broadsheet that talked of inhumanity and the degradation of music to mathematics, and distributed it to all. The whole affair, crowned by the defamatory accusation that all the composers who spoke at the Webern evening were also communists, went to ministerial level. Stockhausen learned of this later; since his wife was shortly expecting their first child, he was in Darmstadt for only one day.

Thirty-two years later Stockhausen commented on his Webern interpretation:

When people have something specific in mind, something they want to put into practice, they look for justifications. And that is why my analysis of the Webern Concerto was so savagely attacked at the time. They said that was not what Webern meant, he was up to something quite different, he was thinking in terms of motives. So all these Webern pupils became just incredibly angry about this analysis . . . They did not understand that of course it was a one-sided interpretation, because I too had something specific in mind, and said that that was already implicit in some works bequeathed by tradition. Perhaps we see in these

61

works only the things that we find personally important, and that is why we can constantly reinterpret traditional music: we always have new ideas of how to do things, and so we find ourselves modernizing a composition that is not widely regarded as important, or a composer, or the whole style of an epoch.[2]

Studie I: A Musical Homunculus

There was another reason for the brevity of Stockhausen's stay in Darmstadt besides the personal one: since June he had been experimenting and working every day in the electronic studio at the Cologne Radio building in Wallrafplatz. Eimert, who was artistic director of the studio, had engaged him as an assistant, thus sparing him the worry of how to make enough money. At this stage there could be no thought of earning a living solely from composing and concerts.

The electronic studio was in a recording room next to 'The 2' – the control room for the Small Broadcasting Hall. Apart from the recording equipment and a few technical accessories there were two electronic instruments: a two-manual melochord, sounding rather like an organ, and an electric monochord, also with two manuals, on which any pitch could be produced, with no breaks, by sliding a finger along a ribbon. They could not be used for sound synthesis since their timbres could not be changed. After becoming familiar with these instruments, Stockhausen appropriated a piece of test equipment, a sine-wave generator, and experimented with a ring modulator into which he fed melochord tones and sine tones. (The effect of a ring modulator is to suppress both the frequencies fed into it, letting their sum and difference be heard instead.) But these efforts too involved difficulties. 'You would not believe,' Stockhausen wrote to Goeyvaerts in Antwerp,

how awful these scratchy, braying, irritating sounds are (to say nothing of the sinusoidal form of the measuring waves, whose whistling causes physical pain through sheer pressure on the eardrum and gets on my nerves like almost nothing else I know!!). Lots and lots of patience is needed to tame such little brutes, to calm them down and clean them up nicely. And there is no rule of thumb, because as soon as you make the slightest change to the basic frequency or volume level, each sound becomes wild, crude and awful again if you try to make it audible in more than one function.[3]

By the end of July Stockhausen was already immersed in a first electronic composition, *Studie I*: 'I am building up sounds from sine tones for a new piece. It is going very well, and I already have a fair amount of experience with it . . . It is unbelievably beautiful to hear such sounds,

62

which are completely balanced, "calm", static and "illuminated" only by structural proportions. Raindrops in the sun.'[4]

For studio technician Heinz Schütz, Stockhausen's inventive assistant during the early days, the laboratory experiments with Beyer and Eimert were conducted in the same atmosphere as may have surrounded Gutenberg's first attempts at printing.

> The real trail-blazing period of the studio began with Stockhausen. He was working at a scientific level, and with him everything was conducted in terms of exact calculations. He rapidly got to grips with the materials, and knew exactly what he wanted. He always brought along mathematical sheets and drawings, which were applied directly to the work of composing. As for the realization, he was precise to the point of pedantry, and was never satisfied with the technical quality.[5]

It seems as though, in the euphoria of his work, Stockhausen was convinced at that time that the future of music lay in electronic sounds. He once said to Schütz, 'In twenty years no one will talk about Bach and the classics any more.' In the radio building there were surreptitious mutterings about the musicians in the electronic studio. They were regarded as 'slightly crazy', and the director expressed the fear that the music being produced there was in danger of losing the human element.

Work in the studio was endless and painstaking. The pitch of every note was notated in hertz and its loudness in decibels. Each one had to be produced individually on the generator, recorded and cut to the right length: one second corresponded to 76.2 centimetres of tape. A sound spectrum in *Studie I* consisted of up to six superimposed sine tones. The work generated a prospective score notation that had to embrace three distinct areas: time, pitch and dynamic processes (so-called envelopes). Stockhausen was repeatedly impeded by technical problems: excessive tape noise and defects in the four-track equipment that made it necessary to synchronize the individual sine tones manually. All his investigations – the assemblage of all kinds of sound spectra, with overtone-related partials, or noiselike spectra with inharmonic proportions – were tied up with his composing. Scientific research *per se* never interested him. From any viewpoint, Stockhausen's *Studie I* was a bold and courageous piece of pioneering, arising from the goals he had set himself as a composer. With it he had engendered a musical homunculus, which thrust open the door to all conceivable synthetic sounds and noises and made it possible to look at the acoustic anatomy of any sound.

Stockhausen and his wife had moved into a little flat in Köln-Lindenthal at 4 Klosterstrasse. The main event of that September was a private one: the birth of his daughter Suja. On the 24th, just before midnight, he had taken his wife to the hospital, and at seven o'clock he was back at work in the studio. Numerous calls were exchanged.

At the moment when the hospital rang to say that my wife had given birth to a daughter (who I then named Suja), I told the technicians, 'Now we must do something really special!' Then I took a sound (an unused one, which was one of many pieces of tape lying around on the studio floor) that was very noisy, and really sounded like the cannon ringing out during carnival on the Rhine, and I inserted it into my sacrosanct study; and there it sits to this day, making a fearful noise, and no one but me knows what it is doing there: that it is a clap of thunder to greet the birth of my daughter Suja.[6]

This 'reverberated sound of 108 hertz' was also a sort of breakthrough in Stockhausen's way of composing:

a first insert, a little bit of devilment that did not actually belong in the construction of the whole thing; but perhaps it shows a certain spirit in me, in my whole nature – that I can always allow myself to escape from my own house, from my own system, from my own world, whenever I have the feeling I really should be able to do that, I ought to permit myself that. And then that sort of thing happens.[7]

Ever since then Stockhausen has constantly broken into the strict formal plans of his works, adding new sounds that fascinated him or formal modifications that he found necessary, as 'inserts' or 'windows' in the work.

One day that autumn the young Swiss architect Paul Gredinger, who had read about the Cologne studio in a newspaper, arrived at the door, to offer them his services. 'Everything was already set up, polished and sparkling', but since Stockhausen found him an extremely stimulating person to talk to, Eimert let him stay, and helped him to get a commission in the following year. Gredinger was ready to abandon his profession and start all over again in music. He had done voluntary work for a while with Max Bill and had been occupied with Le Corbusier's Modulor idea. The Modulor was to become important to Stockhausen, for he was able to recognize in it the same kind of thinking about organization and mediation as existed in serial music. Evolved in the late forties, the Modulor was a brilliant but abstract procedure for reducing the dimensions of buildings and all their individual constructional details to a basic scheme of measurement derived from the human body. Le Corbusier

was always stressing that for almost a thousand years musicians had been able to use well-organized scales for their constructions ... and that as an architect he wanted quite modestly to propose the blue and red series of proportions ... One série was related to north European man, with an average height of 180 centimetres, and the other to Mediterranean man, with an average height of 170 centimetres; both *séries* are based on a Golden Section division, from which whole systems of further proportions may be derived.[8]

For Stockhausen serial thinking grew increasingly to be an all-embracing attitude to life, so much so that its traces were even visible in the layout of his own flat. Koenig remembers that in the one in Köln-Braunsfeld there was a big window with curtains sewn together from strips of various widths, using a whole scale of shades of green, all arranged according to Stockhausen's serial principle. Later Stockhausen was to say, 'Serial thinking is something that's come into our consciousness and will be there forever; it's relativity and nothing else . . . It's a spiritual and democratic attitude toward the world.'[9]

Studie I was completed in November 1953. Stockhausen's financial problems were solved for a few months when WDR commissioned two electronic works, with *Studie I* counting as the first. In the meantime Goeyvaerts had been in the studio, and Stockhausen realized Goeyvaerts's *Nummer 5 mit reinen Tönen.*

At the beginning of December Boulez arrived in Cologne with Henri Pousseur and Michel Fano, whom Stockhausen already knew from Paris, to hear *Studie I.* Both the piece and Stockhausen's theoretical concepts aroused the spirit of contradiction in Boulez. There were heated debates, and for a while no further discussion on this topic was possible between them. Unruffled, Stockhausen continued as though driven by an invisible force, and conceived a second electronic work.

January to May 1954: *Studie II* and New Piano Pieces

At the end of January Stockhausen astonished his friends by commencing a composition for piano. In the previous months he had been making sketches for a cycle of six piano pieces. He was experimenting with new possibilities in instrumental music, a step that signalled the beginnings of a move away from Goeyvaerts. (Around the same time he started what was to become a very extensive correspondence with Pousseur.) Goeyvaerts wanted to admit only sine tones as 'pure' material, but Stockhausen told him that qualitatively one should not regard a sine tone more highly than a note on a piano or the realization of music via a machine operated by humans more highly than music made by pianists. Writing for sine tones or for piano was simply a matter of the composer's conception.

In the next fourteen months Stockhausen produced *Klavierstücke V–VIII*, which he revised several times and in some cases completely rewrote.

Work in the studio was now showing its first influences on his instrumental music: using effects with harmonics, echoes and various degrees of pedalling, he invented new shadings of piano timbre.

Pousseur had also composed an electronic piece, *Seismogramme*, which needed to be realized. Once Eimert started composing again and Gredinger was working on his *Formanten*, studio time had to be shared, and Stockhausen made only slow progress with his new piece, *Studie II*. Its structure has been described as

a triumph of serial unity. Everything is based on fives, from the five main sections (each with five subsections) to the five-note sine-tone chords based on a $^{25}5$ scale.

In a $^{25}5$ scale the interval from one note to the next is slightly larger than a semitone.] One doesn't hear the individual pitches, since they have been reverberated; instead, one hears sound-mixtures of varying width. The narrower they are, the more nearly one can hear a central pitch . . . in fact, one could call *Studie II* a 'consonants' study, in comparison with the 'vowel sounds' of *Studie I*.[10]

In the following years a whole series of eminent people, including composers and conductors, visited Cologne Radio to find out about electronic music. Paul Hindemith, Stockhausen's erstwhile model, came to a performance of one of the electronic studies and was absolutely incensed at the piece; as Stockhausen was later to recall, he

did not utter a single printable word, and off he went. I was deeply shocked, because I respected him as a master craftsman, had played his works and knew and greatly admired the *Marienleben* and *Mathis der Maler*. I was thus disappointed that this man simply denied my musicality. Since then I have understood why. He really was a pure *Gebrauchsmusiker* [utilitarian musician]. What I had done was something he could not recognize.[11]

Darmstadt 1954

When Wolfgang Steinecke asked Stockhausen in November 1953 for a new piece to be performed in Darmstadt, he proposed *Klavierstücke I-IV*. Stockhausen did not receive final consent until the following May, and with so little time left it was not easy to find someone who would be prepared to perform these rhythmically complicated works. Probably acting on a suggestion from Pousseur, Stockhausen turned to the Belgian pianist Marcelle Mercenier and soon secured her agreement.

Stockhausen spent the period from mid-June to mid-July with his wife at Schlee's summer house, near the little village of Mantersdorf in the Hohe Tauern region. After the exhausting studio work of the past twelve months, this was an absolutely essential break. Stockhausen went strolling

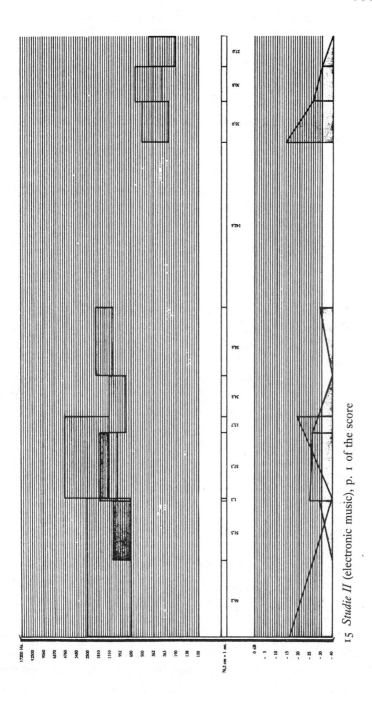

15 *Studie II* (electronic music), p. 1 of the score

in the mountains and enjoyed the calm offered by the secluded house. He did not want to spend even a moment thinking about music; he just wanted to eat, sleep and recover, as he wrote to Pousseur. All the same he began composing a song – a gift for Pousseur's imminent wedding – but could not get to the end of it and threw it aside.

As the performance drew closer, Marcelle Mercenier was getting nervous, for the pieces were harder than she had expected. She wrote to Stockhausen about her problems, and was invited to Cologne for a run-through. At first she replied that it was still too soon, but then she came. The journey to Cologne and the subsequent strict examination must have been a baptism of fire for Marcelle Mercenier. In Darmstadt a week later, on 21 August, she played *Klavierstücke I-IV* as well as *Klavierstück V*, which had been composed that year. As might have been expected, the performance ended in uproar. Whistles and boos overwhelmed the applause of friends. The pianist repeated *Klavierstück V* as an encore and the audience reacted with the same vehemence. *Klavierstücke I-IV* are dedicated to her by way of thanks for her courageous advocacy.

After the performance a seventeen-year-old student, fascinated by this new kind of piano music came up to Stockhausen and asked, 'How do you compose like that?' He was Hans Günther Tillmann, later a participant in Stockhausen's first Darmstadt composition course. In 1954 Tillmann became Stockhausen's first composition student and went regularly to Köln-Lindenthal for lessons. He has said that Stockhausen attached particular value to carrying out every single step in composing absolutely consciously. Tillmann wanted to become a composer and, after matriculating, sought Stockhausen's advice. 'There are only two possibilities,' came the answer; 'either you study the scientific and acoustic fundamentals with Meyer-Eppler, or compositional craftsmanship with me.' Tillmann settled for Meyer-Eppler.

Meyer-Eppler and Studies in Bonn

Something new emerged for Stockhausen's totally organized music in 1954: aleatory and statistical processes. That spring he had informed Pousseur that for some while he had been studying acoustics with Meyer-Eppler, experimenting and learning a great deal. In the autumn Stockhausen told Hermann Braun, a fellow student at Cologne, 'Totally organized music leads to sterility. The big thing now is aleatory processes!' When WDR awarded Stockhausen a grant, he enrolled officially at Bonn University, aiming to graduate in a subject related to electronic music.

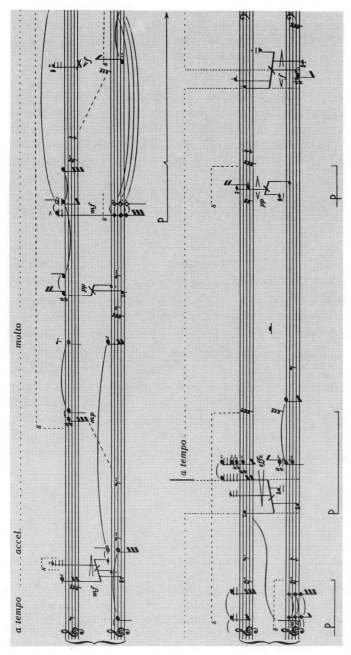

16 *Klavierstück V*, p. 4 of the notation (diamond-shaped notes = depress keys silently)

He studied phonetics, communications theory, philosophy and musicology. The main attraction, though, was undoubtedly Werner Meyer-Eppler, a lecturer at the Institute of Phonetics and Communications Research, which at that time was still small. Stockhausen later referred to him as the best teacher he had ever had.

Meyer-Eppler, a brilliant and imaginative mind, yet also a modest man who was happy to remain in the background, had mastered several languages and often played the piano for relaxation. Originally professor of theoretical physics, after the de-Nazification process he had stayed out of the squabbles over the reallocation of chairs and had transferred to the arts faculty, specializing in phonetics. There he gained a second professorship. He became familiar with the vocoder, an artificial speech apparatus, when the American Homer Dudley visited Bonn in 1948. In 1949 he was involved in the diffusion of information theory, which had just been developed in the USA, and began to apply it to the investigation of language and acoustics. For the purposes of this type of schematic thinking, which had grown in response to questions posed by electronic communication of information, the world consisted only of measurable 'parameters' and everything was reduced to mathematical formulas. That year Meyer-Eppler wrote his book *Elektrische Klangerzeugung* and started his experiments and research at the institute in Bonn. Since then he had constantly drawn attention to the possibilities of electronic music. In his investigations he applied mathematical and physical methods: speech, musical notes and indeed, everything audible became 'sound signals'. Sonic processes without an orderly acoustic structure were investigated by Meyer-Eppler using statistical methods derived from information theory. He described such phenomena, whose outcome is only measurable in broad terms and whose detail depends on chance, as 'aleatory'.

Meyer-Eppler 'always said: *alea* means dice, and "aleatory" means to have chance operations. And in the seminars we actually threw dice.'[12] Many experiments were made in these classes:

trying to compose artifical texts and using cards, lottery, roulette or telephone directory numbers in order to determine their structure ... we would take a newspaper and cut the text up into smaller and smaller units – three syllables, two syllables, one syllable, sometimes right down to individual letters. Then we would shuffle the pieces like cards, arrange the new text and study the degree of redundancy that would decrease the more you cut up the original newspaper text ... It is from such experiments that I derived the inspiration to compose my first sounds with statistical characteristics, staying within a given field of certain limitations. Of course, I still used deterministic notation in order to record these indeterministic textures. So it was a chance operation leading to a deterministic

17 At the Institute of Phonetics and Communications Research of Bonn University, 1959: Werner Meyer-Eppler is giving a lecture on 'drum- and pipe-languages'

18 In Bilthoven (Holland), at concert-organizer Walter Maas's home, 1957. *Left to right:* composer Ton de Leeuw, Stockhausen, Edgard Varèse and Maas

picture – somewhat like a [Jackson] Pollock painting by comparison with an [Alexander] Calder mobile. Once a Pollock canvas is dry it looks as if it were a final painting – despite the aleatory elements that went into its making, while the Calder mobile shows the changes in the wind.[13]

Stockhausen's fellow student Georg Heike (himself a composer and violinist) remembers him as being more of an observer than an active participant in the seminars.

Stockhausen always pricked up his ears when he believed there was something he could use in his music: he followed the proceedings from a composer's point of view. Meyer-Eppler was proud of Stockhausen, and mentioned him to others as his pupil.

We both studied musicology with Schmidt-Görg. Stockhausen gave a paper on the connection between harmony and temporal structure in Mozart's works. [This is Stockhausen's first demonstrable concern as a composer with Mozart; he wrote a major article on cadential rhythm in Mozart's work in 1961.] At the time Schmidt-Görg regarded his explanations, which were put across with great conviction, as a somewhat eccentric and hypothetical, but none the less noteworthy piece of research.[14]

His numerous commitments meant that Stockhausen could not regularly get to Bonn. In March 1956 he broke off his studies; they no longer offered him anything new, and his compositional projects absorbed all his interest and time. The meeting with Meyer-Eppler was an important pointer to Stockhausen: it made an impact on his scientific conceptions and led him to introduce scientific terms, such as aleatory, and micro- and macrostructure, into music.

19 October 1954: The Première of *Studie I* and *II* and Acquaintance with Cage

On 19 October 1954 *Studie I* and *II* were premièred in the Large Broadcasting Hall of Cologne Radio, along with other works composed in the past twelve months by Eimert, Gredinger, Goeyvaerts and Pousseur. In his autobiography Goeyvaerts described the atmosphere at this concert:

The very name 'electronic music' had an electrifying effect, and everyone who wanted to be a part of the snobbish avant-garde of those years (and there was a whole crowd of them in Cologne) was there. It was a remarkable performance: the audience, opulently dressed, sat quiet as mice through Eimert's verbose elucidations. The music came out of two enormous loudspeakers on the stage, which made the situation even crazier . . . That's not on! That's impossible! They had to think immediately in terms of a new kind of listening, a new objective for music . . . But up to this very day, that is how people listen to electronic music, apart from the crazy hats and purple-dyed hair.[15]

19 Stockhausen and John Cage in the summer of 1972 in Munich. Stockhausen's *Sternklang* was performed as part of the artistic programme for the Olympic Games

Another important event took place that day: Stockhausen and John Cage got to know one another. Cage and the American pianist David Tudor had come to Cologne as part of their first tour in Germany, and had performed new American piano music in the first part of the concert. Four years younger than Messiaen, Cage had the same kind of key position in New York as Messiaen held in Paris, though he did not teach at an institution. Since the beginning of the fifties a group of young composers and artists had gathered round Cage and been much influenced by him: Earle Brown, Morton Feldman, Christian Wolff and also David Tudor. Tudor has confirmed that at the mid-point of the century New York too underwent a radical change in music, in painting, in the whole of society. The musicians around John Cage saw time in a new perspective – as a field, like an artist looking at a canvas. All at once everything could be seen as a whole: space and time became one. In New

73

York there were many points of contact between the various arts, and Cage and his circle were engaged in a stimulating exchange of ideas with visual artists such as Robert Rauschenberg, Alexander Calder and Jackson Pollock.

Cage came from Los Angeles and had studied with Henry Cowell and Schoenberg during the latter's exile in California. At the time Schoenberg said of his pupil that he was 'not a composer, but an inventor – of genius'. Since the early forties Cage had shocked American concert-goers with his percussion compositions and pieces for prepared piano (screws, bolts, pieces of rubber and similar objects were fastened between the strings of the piano to mute its sound). In 1951, the year of upheaval in Europe, Cage had made a decisive change that had been anticipated some years earlier.

It was around the middle of the forties, when I was deeply disturbed for two reasons: one of them was personal, and the other was that I could not see a useful function for music any more, not for the way I was composing at the time. I was in such a mess that I thought about psychoanalysis. But the psychiatrist I went to said he could fix me up so that I composed more than I had done before, and I was writing far too much already. By chance I read a book by Aldous Huxley entitled *The Eternal Philosophy*. It was a collection of short maxims, not just by oriental teachers but by western ones too, including Meister Eckhart . . . Gradually I began to get the feeling that the direction that had most to say to me was that of Zen, as cultivated in Japan after it had come from India and been evolved in China. As I reached this view, by chance Dr Suzuki [the Zen philosopher Daisetsu T. Suzuki] came from Japan to teach in New York, and for three years I attended his lectures. After that I no longer needed psychoanalysis.[16]

In 1951 Cage composed his *Music of Changes* for piano. The combination of elements, which had already been drawn up on a chart, was determined not by the composer but by a threefold tossing of coins based on the I Ching, the ancient Chinese book of oracles. Music as composition, and the personality of the composer, had become minor matters for Cage – the present moment and the arbitrary here and now came to the fore, and would mark his music in future. Only a year later he produced the 'silent piece' 4'33" for an instrumentalist, inspired by Rauschenberg's monochrome white canvases, whose colour was altered by changes of the daylight or by the shadows of observers standing in front of the pictures. Throughout the four minutes and thirty-three seconds not a single note is sounded – it is a piece of silence in which only the noises of the listeners and the environment are heard. This American's nonchalant lack of tradition and his innovations, which were so surprising to a European, made a great impression on Stockhausen:

Cage is the craziest spirit of combination I have ever come across; he is not so much an inventor – which is how he is usually described – as a finder; in addition, he has that indifference towards everything known and experienced that is necessary for an explorer; on the other hand, he lacks the imperative power to imagine sound, the visionary element that haunts one.[17]

Although Stockhausen and Cage were worlds apart, they must have sparked off something in one another during those days. A little later Cage wrote to Stockhausen:

I should have liked to be longer with you. I doubt whether our differences of thought would have changed, or indeed our differences of useful means, ways of working except in the way in which, of their nature, they change. But what I respond to is your own relation to your work (what I sense of it) which rises up in the most affirmative and life-communicating way.[18]

David Tudor was a pianist such as Stockhausen had never previously encountered. Before the concert he spent a few days with Stockhausen and played him works for piano by Cage's circle: parts of *Music of Changes*, a piece by Christian Wolff for prepared piano and Morton Feldman's *Intersection III*, in the score of which, instead of notes, there were three horizontal systems of boxes for the high, medium and low registers of the piano and figures in the boxes gave the number of notes to be played. The dynamics and rhythmic placement were completely free. 'Stockhausen was fascinated by two things,' remembers Tudor:

the kinds of attack I had developed for *Music of Changes*, and the clusters in Feldman's piece. At the time I was the only pianist performing this music. Of course, I was also interested in finding new things in Europe and taking them back home. I was like a messenger between the States and Europe. The meeting with Stockhausen was the start of a creative exchange that lasted for about ten years.[19]

Tudor was used to having a co-creative role in the performance of such works, which was a novelty for Stockhausen. When working further on the *Klavierstücke* Stockhausen was doubtless inspired by Tudor's capabilities; *Klavierstücke V-VIII* were later dedicated to him.

December 1954: The Start of Stereophony and a Meeting with Varèse

At the beginning of December Stockhausen went to Hamburg for a performance of *Kontra-Punkte* conducted by Bruno Maderna. In the same concert Maderna gave the German première of a work in which orchestral and tape sounds were combined for the first time: *Déserts* by Edgard Varèse. A group made up of wind instruments, percussion and piano alternates with the mutated sounds of factory noises and ship sirens and motors, coming from two loudspeakers. Varèse, who was born in France in 1883 and emigrated to the USA in 1915, had already created a revolution in the early thirties with his work *Ionisation*, written for forty percussion instruments. He had come to Hamburg from Paris, where the première of *Déserts* under Scherchen had created a scandal and had been the first stereo transmission on French Radio. At the concert Stockhausen operated the volume controls regulating the tape for Varèse. Stockhausen had said in a letter to Pousseur in the autumn that stereophony was now the great task lying ahead of him. It is conceivable that it was this December performance that gave him the first ideas for the kind of stereophonic combination of electronic music and orchestra that he planned for the original version of *Gruppen*.

In later years Stockhausen met Varèse a few more times. On his first trip to America in 1958 he visited him in his New York apartment and found him 'unbelievably friendly, like a loving father'. Seven years after Varèse's death, he said to Jonathan Cott, 'I liked him very much . . . Varèse had great ideas . . . During his last ten years or so he was apparently more interested in astronomy than in music. He went to see a scientist friend of his in an observatory in order to watch the stars. Varèse's concepts went really far beyond his technical means.'[20]

Darmstadt 1955

When the city of Darmstadt handed out its commissions for the tenth Summer Courses, Stockhausen was asked to write for piano. Once again it was Marcelle Mercenier who performed these new pieces, *Klavierstücke VI-VIII*, for the first time, and once again she became very nervous as the performance drew near. She had been able to prepare just the first pages of *Klavierstück VI* and would play only if Stockhausen agreed to turn the pages. She travelled to Darmstadt in a state of unease, and was greeted there on 1 June by a tense and unruly audience.

At the performance I sat next to her to turn the pages. A few minutes after the start there was already noise in the hall: listeners were laughing, talking louder and louder and scraping their chairs. Suddenly Boulez yelled a few spicy French pejoratives at some female listeners who were sitting in front of him and could not help giggling. There was peace for a moment; then the noise began again, even louder. The pianist got nervous. In addition, in the pauses in the piece, a cricket could regularly be heard chirping somewhere up in the rafters, and each of his accompaniment figures earned him a roar of laughter. Finally people began whistling wildly and applauding. I was probably far too annoyed to laugh at the whole situation; I snatched the music from the piano (to this day, I can still see the pianist's shocked expression) and rushed out of the hall with the music under my arm. I do not know what I wanted to happen. (I learned later that my flight produced total mayhem. Mademoiselle Mercenier was so embarrassed that she went looking for my wife, finally found her and asked her to take a bow in my place.) I ran outside, where it was pitch-black, then to my room on the first floor of the building, and locked myself in. After a little while I heard steps, there was thunderous knocking and Nono shouted that I absolutely must come back. I told him there would be no more playing till there was calm in the hall. He ran off again, and must have made some kind of address to the public. Then he came back, and we went into the hall together. It was now quiet there. So Marcelle began again from the top. After a few minutes, however, the noise was just as bad as before. She broke off, because she could no longer hear what she was playing.[21]

Two days later, in the same hall where the cricket had accompanied Stockhausen's *Klavierstücke*, there was a Music Critics' Discussion among Luigi Rognoni (Milan), Claude Rostand (Paris) and H. H. Stuckenschmidt. Its theme was music since 1945, and in particular the newly commissioned works to be heard in Darmstadt. A few representatives of the younger generation were also on the stage, including the composer of the scandalous piano pieces. As so often in the last few years, the main question was, 'Is that still music, or is it just maths and calculations in sound?' When the flautist Kurt Redel had his chance to speak, he asked about the composition technique of the *Klavierstücke*: 'We're all professionals here, surely we can understand one another.' But Stockhausen answered proudly and provocatively, 'Who here has my professionalism?' and thereby elicited the same response as his music had had: boos and applause.

Stockhausen felt that these *Klavierstücke* marked an important turning-point in instrumental music. On the whole electronic music made possible the exact quantitative realization of a composer's ideas, and he had now discovered the 'Empfindungsmass' (instinctive measurements), of the instrumentalist. Little groups of notes to be played 'as fast as possible', for example, or staccato attacks after which the pedal was depressed immediately, so that the note sounded on softly, could only ever be executed by the pianist as 'statistical' approximations to the values in the score; at each performance the approximate values would be different, always arising on the spur of the moment. 'Above all,' wrote Stockhausen in the programme note for the première,

it is a matter of communicating a new feeling of time in music, in which the infinitely subtle 'irrational' shadings, movements and displacements of a good interpreter are sometimes more helpful in achieving the goal than a centimetre ruler. Such statistical formal criteria will give us a completely new, previously unknown relationship to the question of instruments and their construction. It will no longer be a matter of instrumental music *or* electronic music, but of instrumental music *and* electronic music. Each of these worlds of sound has its own conditions, and its own limits.[22]

5 Spatial and Aleatory Music 1955–60

> In electronic music, generators, tape recorder and
> loudspeakers should yield what no instrumentalist has
> ever been capable of. In instrumental music, on the
> other hand, the player, aided by the instrument and
> the notation, should produce what no electronic music
> could ever yield, imitate or reproduce.
> Stockhausen

Paspels, Summer 1955: A New Conception of Musical Time

Early in August Stockhausen retreated from the confines of his tiny flat
in Cologne to a little village in the Swiss Alps to compose a work for
electronic music and large orchestra commissioned by the WDR – it was
later to become *Gruppen* for three orchestras. A change of home was
planned; his wife was expecting a second child and wanted to go on
holiday '(something wives quite reasonably expect of their partners in
summer), but I never wanted to take a "holiday", so I went south . . .
while my wife travelled north and spent a few weeks by the sea'.[1] In
Paspels, a tiny village in Graubünden, he took a small, inexpensive attic
room, with a window looking out on the mountain panorama, in the house
of the pastor, who was a friend of Gredinger.

It always seems to be unusual circumstances – periods of solitude or
personal crises – that set new ideas in motion; during the isolation of
these weeks, while working on the orchestral part of *Gruppen*, Stockhausen
found a new way of shaping musical time, one in which his experience
in the electronic studio played an important role. In the course of his
experiments he was confronted with the following phenomenon: if a taped
sequence of rhythmic pulses was speeded up to about eight pulses a
second, the individual sounds could still be clearly heard. At a higher
speed, from about sixteen pulses upwards, there began a continuous
'rumbling', which turned into a clear pitch at around thirty pulses per
second. (The intermediate range between eight and sixteen sounds per
second was largely indefinable). Stockhausen seized upon this, regarding
pitch too as a temporal process, but transposed into an area where it was
no longer perceived as such. After profound reflection he was able to set
up a scale of durations corresponding to the twelve-note row, thereby
solving an old problem of serial music: the forming of pitch and duration
from a single principle. 'It was the time when the concept of the "time

spectrum" was discovered. Temporal layers were subdivided, just like the overtones of a fundamental pitch: 1:2:3:4:5:6 up to 1:27, or with even more periodic subdivisions over a "fundamental time-value", as I called it.'[2]

Stockhausen very rapidly came up against another difficulty: how was a conductor to direct several overlapping time layers for just one orchestra? There seemed to be no solution, but the one he finally found led unexpectedly to new musical possibilities. He divided the orchestra into three groups of equal size, to be placed at different points in the hall, each with its own conductor. Now there could be movement of the sound in space, alternation between two orchestras, rotations of the sound round all three orchestras; only a few passages were conceived in terms of a single common metronomic tempo.

His daily view of the mountain chain had a direct effect on the work, for Stockhausen converted it into musical structures.

In *Gruppen*, whole envelopes of rhythmic blocks are exact lines of mountains that I saw right in front of my little window. Many of the time spectra, which are represented by superimpositions of different rhythmic layers – of different speeds in each layer – their envelope which describes the increase and decrease of the number of layers, their shape, so to speak, the shape of the time field, are curves of the mountains' contours which I saw when I looked out of the window.[3]

Stockhausen's first sketches were couched in terms of a combination of orchestra – with metrically indeterminate tempo markings for the orchestral musicians – and multi-channel electronic music, with further orchestras on tape. Soon after having the idea of the three conductors, Stockhausen gave up the electronic sounds completely, and what had been thought of as electronic music was notated in the orchestral parts. When a few pages of the score had been written out, the aleatory tempo indications proved impractical, so they had to be dropped. About a year later Stockhausen summarized his ideas on the unified temporal structure of pitch and duration in the essay '. . . how time passes . . .', probably the most influential text on music theory of the fifties.[4]

By the time Stockhausen returned to Cologne at the end of September, the temporal, timbre and spatial structure of *Gruppen* had been composed. His wife had acquired a large flat in a villa-like two-family house in the peaceful Köln-Braunsfeld district (6 Meister-Johann-Strasse). *Gruppen* was put aside till the beginning of 1957 since Stockhausen had to write two important new pieces.

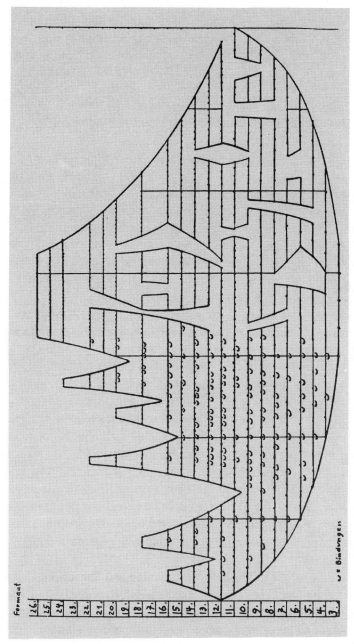

20 Fundamental spectra over seven basic durations (mountain panorama at Paspels)

Gesang der Jünglinge

After the concert on 19 October 1954 work in the electronic studio
had entered a new phase. The era of elementary studies was over, and
Stockhausen was planning to write a mass for electronic sounds and
voices. The young composer Gottfried Michael Koenig, from Brunswick,
had become the studio's second permanent assistant in the summer. On
being shown the 'critical letter' Koenig had written to Eimert outlining
his ideas about electronic music, Stockhausen had commented, 'He is as
good as here.'

In the summer of 1955 the brilliant theoretician Heinz-Klaus Metzger,
a pupil of Max Deutsch and Theodor W. Adorno, came to Cologne.
Along with Koenig, he formed the spearhead of a minor invasion of
composers, writers and painters who were drawn to Cologne by Stockhausen's work in the electronic studio. Thirty years later Metzger's characterization of Stockhausen at this period was pointed: 'When I came to
Cologne, Stockhausen's outlook on things stood on two legs: one was the
Catholic faith, the other was positivist science.'[5] Metzger and Koenig
adopted a critical stance towards religion.

Stockhausen felt it was not just the artistic aspect of the mass – the
combination of electronic sounds and the human voice – that was important; the mass was to be a sacred work, written from personal conviction,
and he hoped that it could be performed in Cologne Cathedral. Eimert
applied to the archbishop's diocesan office, but was refused: loudspeakers
had no place in church. It was a bitter disappointment for Stockhausen,
for whom a day without prayer or a Sunday without mass was unthinkable.
But he did not drop his plan for a sacred work. At the close of the
Catholic mass, just before the last prayer, the priest may on certain
occasions recite the *Benedicite*. The text – at that time still read in Latin
– is the Song of the Youths in the Fiery Furnace from the Apocrypha to
the Book of Daniel. One Sunday around the end of 1954 or the beginning
of 1955, as the *Benedicite* was being recited in the Braunsfeld church, the
electronic mass became *Gesang der Jünglinge*, later the most famous of all
electronic works.

By the time he left for Paspels, Stockhausen had already finished a few
seconds of the tape. He had immersed himself in phonetic and acoustic
studies, making many experiments in the studio. Electronic sounds and
the human voice were to combine within a timbre continuum extending
from the sine tone to 'white noise', the extreme electronic form of sound.
To this end, a twelve-year-old boy had sung various passages from the

Song of the Youths, and specific pitch sequences, which were recorded on tape. The incorporation of the human voice posed new problems, and called for a number of extremely diversified electronic sounds; Stockhausen found that there was probably no more complex timbre structure than that of sung speech. The discovery of multi-layered time spectra also had an impact on *Gesang der Jünglinge*, and the realization of the tape became harder and more protracted than that of *Studie I* and *II*. For a long time Stockhausen had to work at night, completely on his own. By the beginning of 1956 about three minutes of this work, conceived for five groups of loudspeakers distributed around the hall, had been completed.

At that time I was building up complex sounds whose individual time layers contained an unbelievable diversity of fragments: specific noise components mixed with vowel components, and single notes with chords. There was one sound lasting only four and a half seconds that we literally worked on for six weeks. So I said, 'Look, we can't go on like this! Otherwise ten years will go by, and I still won't have finished this piece that only lasts a few minutes', and then I invented completely different processes in which the three of us – myself and two musical and technical collaborators – each used a different piece of equipment. One of us had a pulse generator, the second a feedback filter whose width could be continuously changed and the third a volume control (potentiometer). I drew graphic representations of processual forms. In one such form, lasting twenty seconds, for example, the first of us would alter the pulse speed, say from three to fourteen pulses per second, following a zigzag curve; the second would change the pitch curve of the feedback filter, in accordance with another graphic pattern; and the third – using yet another graphic – would change the dynamic curve. This kind of process resulted from graphic curves that simply represented in lines what I was later to describe in words in the text compositions *Aus den sieben Tagen*. So we sat down to realize one of these processual forms, one of us would count 3, 2, 1, 0, then off we went. The stopwatch was running, and at twenty seconds each of us had to be finished. 'Should we do it again?' 'Yes, I made a couple of mistakes here. I went up twice here instead of down.' So the whole thing was done again, until the best possible realization had been achieved. Each processual form consisted of several different layers. These were copied over one another, and thus there came about a form that resulted from the interaction of three 'realizers'. The agreement that we would meet at a certain point after a certain length of time but that in between everyone would go his own way (because what happened during the intervening period could only be statistically notated) permits a formal layer to come about *processually* – by 'aleatory' means, as my teacher Meyer-Eppler used to call it in the context of information theory.[6]

The performance of all the electronic works composed in the previous eighteen months – once again various guests had been working in the studio – had been set for 30 May 1956. This put Stockhausen in an awkward situation, since by the end of March only seven of the piece's planned twenty minutes had been completed. So Stockhausen had to decide to shorten it, and it was announced in the printed programme as *Gesang der Jünglinge* (Part I), duration: thirteen minutes. (For the second part, still unrealized, Gottfried Michael Koenig remembers that Stockhausen considered working the names of his friends into the textual permutations of the list of affirmations.)

The electronic music was to be heard between an orchestral concert earlier in the evening and a concluding discussion, 'Unheard-of Music: Composers without Audiences?'. The main item of the orchestral concert was the première of Schoenberg's last work, the incomplete setting of one of his own 'modern psalms': 'O Du mein Gott, alle Völker preisen Dich'. And so it came about that Schoenberg's testament and Stockhausen's first sacred work – worlds apart, though only five years separated them – were premièred together.

Gesang der Jünglinge was the first example of electronic spatial music. The audience was seated 'within the sound', surrounded by four loudspeakers on the walls and a fifth to the front, in the middle of the concert platform (the plan had been to hang it from the ceiling, above the listeners' heads, but this was not permitted). They heard sounds that rotated and wandered to and fro between the loudspeakers: Stockhausen had incorporated the spatial dimension into the work's serial composition process. It seems quite plausible to view this spatial music, in which the ideas of music as a temporal art and space as a dimension of the plastic arts join in a 'musical plasticity', as expressing the desire for a new realm of musical experience in which the 'inner' and 'outer' interpenetrate in accord with Novalis's lines, 'Time is inner space – space, external time. Temporal figures and space and time arise conjointly.'[7] The performance provoked turbulent demonstrations in the hall as well as frenetic applause. Doors were slammed, one appalled listener yelled, 'That's blasphemy!' and the like, so that Heinz-Klaus Metzger found himself reminded of 'some celebrated events in Viennese provincial history, or the première of *Le Sacre du printemps*, where the proceedings may well have been even more unruly'.[8]

Zeitmasse

While Stockhausen was in Paspels composing *Gruppen*, he was asked to write a little piece in celebration of Heinrich Strobel's tenth anniversary of service at South-west Radio.

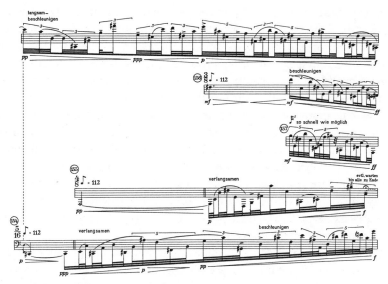

21 *Zeitmasse* for five woodwinds, p. 37 of the score

There I was, working like the devil, calculating the overall time structure, and I get this letter saying . . . that everyone had to write a little piece. So what did I do? I sat back, and I had to write something really quickly, by that evening. I did not allow myself to take any time over it. And then, suddenly, I hear this whole little four-minute piece. I really chuckled to myself about it . . . All four minutes really came in a dream. And that confirmed for me that this kind of intuitive composing still worked.[9]

The piece, an occasional composition for contralto and wind trio (flute, clarinet and bassoon) in 4/4, was soon sent off to Strobel. For his text Stockhausen had chosen a brief statement by Strobel himself, translated into French by Antoine Goléa: 'On cherche pour trouver quelque chose. Mais au fond, on ne sait pas ce qu'on cherche au juste. Et cela est vrai non seulement pour l'Allemagne musicale' (We are seeking to find something. But we really do not know quite what we are looking for. And that is not only true of musical life in Germany).

After returning to Cologne Stockhausen substituted a cor anglais for the contralto, added an oboe and expanded the two pages of notation to a work lasting about ten minutes: a wind quintet entitled *Zeitmasse*, in which, as in *Gruppen*, Stockhausen composed with various simultaneous time layers. It was recorded in December by the WDR Wind Quintet, directed by its oboist Wilhelm Meyer, and broadcast in January with an introduction by Heinz-Klaus Metzger.

85

The year after (1956) the piece was expanded, and its temporal aspects were revised. Stockhausen now latched on to those things that had seemed unrealizable in the orchestral parts of *Gruppen*: alongside exactly prescribed metronomic tempo markings, the players were, for the first time, simultaneously given aleatory tempos, that is, play as fast as possible, as slow as possible (within one breath), play quickly and then slow down, etc. A polyphony of 'time measures' is unfolded in the alternation and interpenetration of these two extremes. The première of this definitive version of the work was scheduled in the brochure for the 1956 Darmstadt Summer Courses, but since the parts could not be completed in time, the performance had to be called off at the very last minute. When Stockhausen showed Boulez the score in Darmstadt – for all the friendship that existed between the two composers, there was also lively competition – he made the rather cutting remark that Stockhausen would do better to stay in the electronic studio. Stockhausen completed a fair copy of the score, and sent it to Boulez in Paris. Suddenly, even Boulez showed interest in *Zeitmasse*, and conducted the first performance himself on 15 December 1956 in the course of his Paris concert series Domaine Musical; Messiaen came with some of his pupils, and greeted Stockhausen warmly. Later Boulez was to cite *Zeitmasse* as one of Stockhausen's best works.

In the summer of 1956 Stockhausen composed a new piano piece – his celebrated *Klavierstück XI* – in which, for the first time, aleatory principles were applied radically to the shaping of the overall form. The period from summer 1955 to summer 1956, when Stockhausen was in his twenty-eighth year, was full of new developments and gave rise to important works: in *Gruppen* and *Gesang der Jünglinge* Stockhausen embarked on spatial music; with the wind quintet *Zeitmasse* and *Klavierstück XI* came two exemplary pieces of aleatory music. These four are generally regarded as masterpieces. A first decisive peak in his output had been reached.

Darmstadt 1956, *Klavierstück XI* and Darmstadt 1957

At the 1956 Summer Courses the disagreements of succeeding years over aleatory techniques and John Cage were already being foreshadowed. Even before *Klavierstück XI* was performed it provoked controversy. Nineteen groups of notes – all derived from the same basic principles, whereby the pitches and the rhythmic structures are interrelated – are distributed irregularly over a sheet of paper measuring 53 by 93 centimetres. The pianist is to look 'without prior intent' at the sheet of paper, and begin with whatever group his or her eye happens to light on first. Tempo, dynamics and mode of attack are free. At the end of each group is a tempo indication, a dynamic level and a mode of attack, all determining the way the next group (again, selected by a random glance) is to be played. That year David Tudor had come to Darmstadt for the first time. After the performance of *Music of Changes* and a seminar in which Tudor had analysed it, Stockhausen and Boulez had engaged in a long and heated verbal duel.

I told Boulez about *Klavierstück XI*, which I had written shortly before. At first he was astonished then became angry and abusive: he could not understand such nonsense. I was afraid of fixing everything exactly in the notation, and wanted to brush off responsibility. All this time, Tudor was laughing slyly. Then more than a year passed before Boulez sent me the first sketches of the five formants of his Third Sonata.[10]

Boulez's Third Sonata also turned out to be a piece with aleatory formal principles.

Three years earlier Morton Feldman and Earle Brown had composed scores with interchangeable formal elements. When Stockhausen heard of this from Tudor in Cologne, he initially lost interest in further work on *Klavierstück XI*. In 1972 Tudor reported that he had 'told him he must not consider any other composer but should go ahead and do it anyway, and that led to *Klavierstück XI*. Stockhausen was our man in Europe, the most friendly to Cage's music and that of the other Americans.'[11] It was Tudor who gave the première of *Klavierstück XI* on 22 April 1957 at the Carl Fischer Hall in New York, playing two versions that were very different in length. It was intended that he would perform the piece in Darmstadt, but he was ill and therefore unable to go.

In 1957 a changing of the guard was signalled in Darmstadt: Wolfgang Fortner, Hermann Heiss, René Leibowitz and Ernst Krenek gradually withdrew, and the generation in its thirties, Boulez, Nono, Pousseur and Stockhausen, took over the composition teaching. Each year aroused greater expectations, and Steinecke, who had very skilfully steered the Summer Courses through all their difficult moments, was constantly asking, 'What comes next?' or 'What are you going to do next year?' That year Stockhausen spoke about the relationship of speech and music, with reference to Boulez's *Le Marteau sans maître*, Nono's *Il canto sospeso* and his own *Gesang der Jünglinge*: a relationship seen from the varying standpoints of 'the atheist, the idealistic communist and the metaphysician', as he described Boulez, Nono and himself in a radio version of

87

David Tudor, Piano Recital   **Carl Fischer Concert Hall, New York City. Monday, April 22, 1957 at 8:45 P. M. Program:**

VIII. Schlagfiguren[v] . . . . Bo Nilsson
Nr. 2 Klavierstuck VI . . . . . Karlheinz Stockhausen
Variations I" . . . . Henri Pousseur
Nr. 4 Klavierstuck XI*** . . . . Karlheinz Stockhausen

Cercles (I: Spirales. II: Rondes)" . . . Bengt Hambraeus
Bewegungen*** . . . . Bo Nilsson
Impromptu et Variations II[v] . . . . . Henri Pousseur
Nr. 4 Klavierstuck XI . . . . . Karlheinz Stockhausen

[v]1st NY Performance   "1st US Performance   ***1st Performance

22 David Tudor gave the première of *Klavierstück XI* at an evening recital of contemporary German, Belgian and Swedish music. John Cage, who designed the poster, had to search for a printer with 'European' typefaces – a rarity in New York

the lecture. The conversation with Nono at the Marienhöhe was thus continued six years later at the lectern.

The central theme that led to sharp disagreements between the young composers that year was aleatory factors in instrumental music. Taking *Zeitmasse* and *Klavierstück XI* (given its German première by Paul Jacobs) as examples, Stockhausen spoke about the irreplaceable significance of the interpreter, set next to music in which 'only measurement, the ruler and the clock hold sway'. In his article 'Alea: On Chance in Music' Boulez polemicized extremely sharply against Cage, and Stockhausen could tell that his words were also intended as covert side-swipes at *Klavierstück XI*. The next year Cage himself came to Darmstadt.

Cologne, Metropolis of New Music, and the Première of *Gruppen*

For Stockhausen 1957 was the year when he wrote out the score of *Gruppen* for three orchestras, a task that spread over many weeks. At this time Cologne was invaded by composers, a number of whom stayed for a few years; some became adopted citizens. Mauricio Kagel came fron Buenos Aires, Franco Evangelisti from Rome, Cornelius Cardew from London and Herbert Brün via Jerusalem, Paris and Munich. Cologne was becoming a metropolis of New Music. Ligeti was one of the first, arriving in February 1957 after a dramatic flight from Hungary. After political tensions there relaxed in the summer of 1956 and Ligeti could hear the German late-night music programmes on his radio without jamming, he wrote to Eimert and Stockhausen. In the first days of November, as the Red Army's shells exploded all around and his housemates took refuge in the cellar, Ligeti heard a piece of Stockhausen on the radio for the first time: *Gesang der Jünglinge*. He asked Stockhausen for tape copies of several works and these were sent to him. In December, after the failure of the uprising, he fled to Vienna and from there to Cologne a few weeks later. When he collapsed shortly after his arrival, he was taken to Stockhausen's flat since the address was found on a bit of paper in his coat.

In the following six weeks conversations about *Gruppen* and other scores extended far into the night. Ligeti revived and moved into a flat of his own, and for a while he worked in the electronic studio. In the wake of his experiences there he was able to realize musical ideas dating back to 1951 in orchestral works such as *Apparitions* and *Atmosphères*. When viewing those years, it should not be forgotten that the composer Konrad Boehmer, a seventeen-year-old genius studying at the Apostel-Gymnasium in Cologne, was loudly proclaiming that the history of music began with Stockhausen.

Among the others who came to Cologne were the poet Hans G. Helms, who wanted to realize his experimental sound poem 'Fa:m' Ahniesgwow' in the electronic studio, and the unpredictable Korean action artist Nam June Paik, whose performances often caused real alarm; the painter Mary Bauermeister returned after studying in Ulm and Saarbrücken. It was a fluctuating, intellectually invigorating environment – part bohemian, part experimental – in which every innovation in the art galleries or in literature was the subject of daily conversation. Soon Hans G. Helms was playing host to

a literary circle which, though the personnel constantly changed, met every

89

Sunday for many hours of the afternoon and evening in my bower on the Hohenzollernring, studying Joyce's *Finnegans Wake* on the basis of the direct experience or acquired knowledge of thirty different languages. Metzger, Koenig, Kagel, Evangelisti, Ligeti and Brün, and sometimes Jean-Pierre Wilhelm and Manfred de la Motte, all made their own personal contributions to our collective exegesis.[12]

Stockhausen had his own circle, and was later to nominate the publisher Ernst Brücher, director of the DuMont art publications, as his closest friend at this time. Brücher had got to know John Cage in the USA in the early fifties; he was involved in all the activities in Cologne and enthusiastically encouraged the avant-garde's ventures. From 1963 he had Stockhausen's *Texte zur Musik* (Texts on music) published by DuMont Verlag. Stockhausen's friends included the composers Pierre Boulez, Henri Pousseur, Luigi Nono and Bruno Maderna, and the painters Jean Tinguely, Harry Kramer and Horst Egon Kalinowski (both became famous through the 1964 Documenta in Kassel), who often went with him to galleries. Paul Klee's *Bildnerisches Denken* (published in 1957) was a revelation to Stockhausen, since much of this book seemed to him to be applicable to music. A thorough investigation of the parallel development (and reciprocal effects) of music and painting in the post-war era has yet to be undertaken.

The house in Meister-Johann-Strasse welcomed everyone. If a visiting musician were short of money, a phone-call to Doris Stockhausen ensured an invitation to dinner. She knew how to create an atmosphere that made every visitor feel at ease. It was she who made it possible for Ligeti to stay for some time. as well as Earle Brown, Cardew, Heinz-Klaus Metzger and Pousseur, and later Stockhausen's assistants Hugh Davies, Rolf Gehlhaar and Joachim Krist. Stockhausen once said that for a creative person, the significance of such a wife simply could not be put into words. It was thanks to Doris that for years he was able to compose without day-to-day worries. The education of their four children – after Suja came Christel (1956), Markus (1957) and Majella (1961) – was left entirely in her hands. Stockhausen had time for nothing but his work.

Composers and critics from all over Europe travelled to the première of *Gruppen* on 24 March 1958. Otto Tomek, Kruttge's successor as director of New Music at WDR, had arranged a two-day festival within the Musik der Zeit series: thirteen works in three concerts, including six premières. Since the main Broadcasting Hall was unsuitable, the performance of *Gruppen* was moved out to the site of Cologne's industrial

23 The three conductors of *Gruppen* for three orchestras during a break in
rehearsals. Left to right: Pierre Boulez, Bruno Maderna and Stockhausen

fair. At the morning dress rehearsal the Rheinsaal looked like an army
camp, and that evening everything was sold out.

To meet the requirements of the score, which calls for a total of
109 musicians, 10 percussionists were hired from the surrounding civic
orchestras. The rehearsals often strained the patience of the conductors
(Boulez, Maderna and Stockhausen) to the limit, the main problems being

the players' lack of experience with New Music and their sometimes open hostility to it. The three had met earlier for a series of 'dry' conductors' rehearsals, since a single mistake could have had catastrophic consequences; the result was a fruitful, inspiring collaboration. The première of *Gruppen* was one of the main musical events of the fifties: the movement of sounds in space, the extremely sophisticated and varied sound of the orchestra and the whole compositional conception of the work brought Stockhausen an outstanding success.

Among the listeners to *Gruppen* at Donaueschingen in the autumn of 1958 was Igor Stravinsky, who congratulated Stockhausen after the concert. When he saw the metronome marking 63.5 in the score he laughed and said, 'Of course, "point five" – the German professor.' He discussed details of the piece in his published conversations with Robert Craft. At the end of the sixties he was to make disparaging comments about Stockhausen and other members of the avant-garde.

Darmstadt 1958

In the summer of 1958 Stockhausen gave a lecture in Darmstadt on music in space in conjunction with a tape recording of *Gruppen*. He spoke for the first time about his idea of a spherical auditorium for music, in which there are rings of loudspeakers at many levels and the listeners sit in the middle on a sound-permeable platform. The sound can move around the sphere and resound simultaneously from every part of it, whereas in the traditional arrangement the sound of the instruments, in simple terms, radiates out to the periphery from a single point of origin. Furthermore, it can be controlled in many ways by loudspeakers. The inner experience of sound is projected outwards. It is the ideal image of a spatial music whose listeners must be open to a completely new dimension of sound. It is no longer merely a matter of sounds being mono- or polyphonic, but also of their location and movement in space.

That same year Cage came to Darmstadt for the first time, and his three studio presentations caused considerable uproar, providing fresh fuel for the arguments about aleatory music. In his second lecture, 'Indeterminacy', he discussed *Klavierstück XI*, among other pieces.

The indeterminate aspects of the composition of the *Klavierstück XI* do not remove the work in its performance from the body of European musical conventions. And yet the purpose of the indeterminacy would seem to be to bring about an unforeseen situation. In the case of *Klavierstück XI*, the use of indeterminacy in this sense is unnecessary since it is ineffective. The work might as well have been written in all of its aspects determinately. It would lose, in this case, its single unconventional aspect: that of being printed on an unusually large sheet of paper which, together with an attachment that may be snapped on at several points enabling one to stretch it out flat and place it on the music rack of a piano, is put in a cardboard tube suitable for safekeeping or distribution through the mails.[13]

Cage provoked controversy in all directions. When one of the participants asked him what his composition technique amounted to, he answered, 'I have several composition techniques: I work with lead pencils, sometimes with ink, and sometimes with crayons.'

1958: New Experiments and First Tours

If 1957 was a year of composing for Stockhausen, 1958 was a year of experimentation. *Klavierstück XI* was only a beginning, and it led, once *Gruppen* had been completed, to a variety of new ideas that Stockhausen wanted to try out in another cycle of piano pieces. 'Stencils (cardboard cut-outs) were to be placed over an (exactly notated?) text,' wrote the pianist Herbert Henck,

so that, depending on their position, different sections of the text would be seen and played. Another permits several possible continuations, in that the notation branches off into three separate staves; these paths diverge yet again, and come back together again, etc. (admittedly, this form is only shown in terms of empty staves). Yet another piece seeks (as in *Refrain?*) to achieve formal multiplicity through the use of transparent plastic.[14]

But ultimately none of these was composed. It is not possible to say for certain what held Stockhausen back, but Richard Toop has suggested two reasons: the lack of an overall formal idea matching up to Stockhausen's requirements; and the fact that shortly after some other composers produced pieces using the same ideas, so that Stockhausen may have lost interest in pursuing them further. ' "Musical graphics" was in the air,' it was said about 1959,[15] the period of Cage's *Variations II* and Kagel's *Transicion II*; and Evangelisti and Pousseur wrote similar scores. Everyone who met Stockhausen at that time took a look at what he was doing. And Stockhausen made no secret of his ideas; he was always talking about whatever preoccupied him.

Experiments were also taking place that year in the electronic studio. His experiences with *Zeitmasse* and *Klavierstück XI* suggested that the combination of electronic sounds and instrumental music was within reach. For his new work, *Kontakte*, Stockhausen had set himself a task that required extensive trials: the entire pitched and unpitched world of percussion instruments – metal, wood and skin – was to be brought 'in contact' with electronic sounds. The two realms would sometimes simply coexist, sometimes have points of contact and sometimes – the ideal – fuse together. New kinds of spatial projection of sounds would be created by the loudspeakers distributed on the four walls of the auditorium. Three percussionists and a pianist would play, following aleatory prescriptions, one player for each channel. It was necessary to try to produce sounds in intermediate areas so that a constant transition between metal, wood and skin would be possible. The main sources were the short noisy clicks, or 'pulses', of a pulse generator that Stockhausen had already used for a few sounds in *Gesang der Jünglinge*. Driven on by his tireless pioneer spirit, he and Koenig worked on these experiments well into the autumn of the following year.

Stockhausen was now sufficiently well known abroad to be invited to give more concerts and lectures. In the spring he went to Denmark, Sweden, Finland and Italy, and in October to the Warsaw Autumn (an annual festival of New Music founded in 1956) and the Journées de la Musique Expérimentale at the World Fair in Brussels, always for performances of the *Klavierstücke, Zeitmasse* and his electronic works. In the course of that year's World Fair, Stockhausen recollected over thirty years later, there was a major forum 'Towards the Fraternity of Mankind',

and Cocteau made a speech on behalf of the west, while Shostakovich as president of the Union of Soviet Composers spoke on behalf of the east. The only name that Shostakovich singled out for condemnation – as the arch-representative of 'decadent capitalist culture' – was Stockhausen. I was thirty years old at the time.

A little while later this same Shostakovich wrote me a private letter, saying he was very impressed by my music, and would welcome it if I made a tour of the Soviet Union with my interpreters. He recommended writing to a particular Soviet concert agency's address. Maria Judina, a fabulous Russian pianist who was friendly with Pasternak, Shostakovich and other famous Russian artists, described for me the conflicts between the official and private behaviour of her composer friend, and other Soviet artists.[16]

At that stage, though, the tour of the Soviet Union failed to materialize.

In November Stockhausen and his wife, who accompanied him on most of his travels, flew to the New World for the first time. In Los Angeles Leonard Stein, Schoenberg's former assistant, and Lawrence Morton, who directed the Monday Evening Concerts there, had invited him to lecture and conduct *Kontra-Punkte* and *Zeitmasse*. Thirty lectures throughout the United States and in Canada then ensued.

Each day followed a similar pattern: in the morning they flew in the customary rumbling turbo-prop machine to the next destination, and that evening he gave the lecture (mainly in big auditoriums with about five hundred listeners). Before or after came the inevitable cocktail party on campus, where he met the big figures in local music. In between there were visits to institutes and meetings with innumerable American artists and scientists. In New York he got to know Robert Rauschenberg, who had been friendly with Cage since 1951 and is often regarded as the first representative of pop art. Rauschenberg worked everyday, used-up items into his own pictures or 'objects' ('combine-paintings'); for Stockhausen this was an important lesson in how old, broken, ugly things have a beauty of their own. He made Rauschenberg a present of the original manuscript of *Klavierstück IV*. They often met again in the early sixties. In spite of their ephemeral aspects, the cocktail parties had their attractions:

We got to know the most interesting people . . . Right at the outset, we met most of the composers living in New York. A month later we were back in New York. And then we met most of them again, several times over, as well as the ones who could not come the first time: Varèse, Virgil Thomson, Aaron Copland, [Harry] Partch, [Teo] Macero, Gunther Schuller, Christian Wolff, Earle Brown, [Michiko] Toyama, Morton Feldman, Milton Babbitt and many others. Dreadful as such parties are – seldom is there a real conversation and everyone just gossips away over their whisky – I really cannot recollect ever having seen all the German composers getting together so peaceably.[17]

In all the lectures Stockhausen mentioned Cage, whose name had scarcely been heard before. New Music did not fare well in the USA.

For all the fantastic technical possibilities, the sheer prosperity of the country and the wonderful quality of the musicians, present-day music is virtually dead: and this in America, the much vaunted land of progress. An unspeakable amount of music is reproduced and listened to: but only superficial stuff, ephemera – or else old music, written fifty to two hundred years ago in Europe.[18]

Darmstadt 1959, *Zyklus* and *Refrain*

During the rehearsal period of *Gruppen* Stockhausen had been all too aware of the difficulties most of the twelve percussionists were having with their parts; afterwards he talked to Steinecke, suggesting that he set up an instrumentalists' course and a percussion competition in Darmstadt. Since there were no viable solo percussion pieces, Steinecke responded,

'If you write a piece for percussion, I'll have a competition.' The reason for writing *Zyklus* for one percussionist was thus pedagogic.

In the score Stockhausen had notated various gradations from explicitly fixed to open, 'variable' passages, and organized them into a cyclic, 'curved' form: the sixteen spirally bound pages may be read both normally and upside down. The percussionist begins with any page and then plays forwards or backwards through the whole cycle, ending with the first stroke of the initial page; all the instruments are arranged in a circle round the performer. One critic wrote of *Zyklus*, Stockhausen's first graphic score: 'The initial impression is that one is looking not at a score, but at a drawing by Paul Klee.'[19] The young Cologne percussionist Christoph Caskel, whom Stockhausen had got to know at the *Gruppen* rehearsals and with whom he had discussed the working-out of the score of *Zyklus*, proved to be a most suitable interpreter; on 25 August 1959 he gave the première in Darmstadt. *Zyklus*, the test piece for the competition, later became the most frequently played solo percussion work in New Music and inspired a wave of writing for percussion.

After finishing *Zyklus* Stockhausen held his first composition course in Darmstadt. Sixteen composers from seven countries were accepted, some of whom were the same age as or even older than Stockhausen: Gilbert Amy, David Behrman, Konrad Boehmer, Sylvano Bussotti, Friedrich Cerha, Giuseppe Englert, Friedrich Goldmann, Dennis Lee Johnson, Milko Kelemen, Hermann-Josef Kaiser, Joachim Limmer, Kurt Schwertsik, Emile Spira, Ernst-Albrecht Stiebler, Hans Günther Tillmann and La Monte Young. Instead of following the standard procedure and discussing works the participants had brought with them, Stockhausen demanded that each student composed a work during the barely three-week course. The meetings were in seclusion, and neither guests nor the press were admitted. An important innovation introduced by Stockhausen was the combination of theory and practice: throughout the entire course Tudor, Caskel and the Italian flautist Severino Gazzelloni were available to give advice. On the first day Stockhausen encouraged the composers to formulate in words the idea, formal concept and general plan of a piece, and the next day he gave a critique of the individual projects.

Alongside his composition course, which some people felt to be very exclusive, Stockhausen gave a public seminar on music and graphics in which he presented works by Cage, Kagel, Bussotti and Cornelius Cardew and analysed *Zyklus*. Resentment against Cage and what some regarded as the dissolute tendencies of his 'compositional anarchy' was still smould-

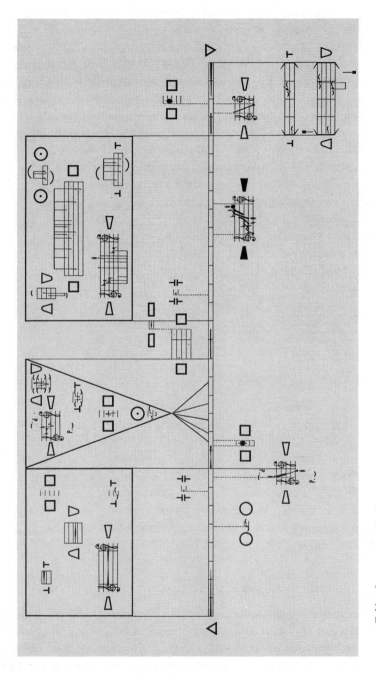

24 *Zyklus* for a percussionist

ering. In his seminar Stockhausen described himself, not unjustly, as 'perhaps the extreme antipode to Cage'.

A few days later Nono launched a sharp attack on Cage in his lecture 'Past and Present in the Music of Today'. Although Stockhausen's name was not mentioned, it was clear enough to whom he referred as 'those who set chance and its acoustic by-products as *perception* in place of their own decisions, and are afraid of personal decisions, and the freedom these involve'.[20] At the evening concert devoted to his own composition seminar Stockhausen spoke of 'statistical structures' and Nono, a Marxist, saw this in terms of 'fascist mass structures'. The conflict between the two friends erupted into violent argument, and it was years before they spoke to one another again.

Some weeks after Darmstadt, *Refrain*, a piece commissioned for the Berliner Festwochen, was performed by David Tudor (piano), Cornelius Cardew (celesta and antique cymbals) and Siegfried Rockstroh (vibraphone, cowbells and glockenspiel), percussionist in the Cologne Radio Symphony Orchestra. Written in June and July immediately after *Zyklus*, it is a fine example of 'polyvalent' composition. The score consists of two large-format pages of notation; on the first, which has a rotatable plastic strip fastened to the middle, the staves form a semicircle above and below the centre, whereas on the second page they are laid out in the usual horizontal way. Each new position of the plastic strip, on which the 'refrain' (little melodic fragments, glissandos, clusters, etc.) is notated, produces a new version of the work. Furthermore, Stockhausen no longer indicates the length of notes in terms of metric values but with six symbols; they range from small notes (as first used in the *Klavierstücke*) for 'as fast as possible', to a little flat rectangle (rather like a longa in mensural notation) meaning 'allow to die away completely'. Six different degrees of 'loudness' are represented by six different sizes of black dot (like circular note-heads). The concert on 2 October was the first 'composition evening' to be devoted to Stockhausen's work; *Kreuzspiel*, *Zeitmasse*, *Zyklus* and *Klavierstücke I, IV, V, VII, VIII* and *XI* were also played.

1959: Moment Form, *Kontakte* and *Carré*

After his return from America Stockhausen again began thinking about musical time, though not in terms of compositional requirements. The cause was the almost daily flights during his six-week tour. What had been sensed as a sort of dream when he was a child lying on his back in the meadows – the timelessness of the drifting clouds, the simply endless

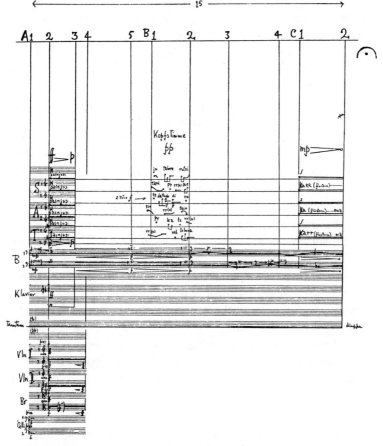

25 *Carré* for four orchestras and four choruses, p. 3 of the score for
Orchestra I and Chorus I (Orchestras II-IV and Choruses II-IV tacet)

dome of blue sky – he now experienced consciously inside the aeroplane.
Here time and space assumed wholly changed perspectives: he was aware
of the slowest rates of change and the broadest spaces.

My whole time feeling was reversed after about two weeks . . . I had the feeling
I was visiting the earth and living in the plane. There were just very tiny changes
of bluish colour and always this harmonic spectrum of the engine noise . . . And
I really discovered the innerness of the engine sounds and watched the slight
changes of the blue outside and then the formation of the clouds, this white
blanket always below me.[21]

In certain situations the sense of physical lightness and the excitement of
rapid movement during a train or car journey set Stockhausen's creative
process in motion – as in *Kreuzspiel*, and later in *Prozession* or *Mantra*.

99

This time the experience of flying had him making sketches on the plane for a new work – *Carré*, spatial music for four orchestras and four choruses – that would emanate the calm and spaciousness of these flights. The orchestras and choruses were to be positioned at the side of a square-shaped hall, the choruses singing phonemes and pitches woven into the fabric of the orchestral sound; words would emerge at a few points, with the name Doris becoming audible at the end. I 'thought I was already very brave in going far beyond the time of memory, which is the crucial time between eight- and sixteen-second-long events. When you go beyond them you lose orientation. You don't recall exactly if it was fourteen or eighteen seconds, whereas you'd never make that mistake below that realm of memory.'[22] This led to the development in Cologne of a new way of shaping time: 'moment form'. Employed first in *Kontakte* and *Carré*, it determined the formal structure of most of the works from the sixties. The experience of the instant becomes the defining dimension of time. A moment: an experiential unit, a formal unit that can exist on its own account, in which 'concentration on the Now – on each Now – simultaneously makes vertical cuts that break through the horizontal conception of time into a timelessness that I call eternity'.[23] Many such moments, one after another. Metronomic duration recedes into the background; indeed, it should be 'transcended, blown apart'. It is the search for a temporal structure with the tendency 'to transcend the ultimate time, death'.

At that time, for example, I wrote articles about what would happen to a man who sat in a dark prison cell for a long time hearing just one sound, a door slamming, then nothing again for a year, then another door slamming. What I meant by that was that there would have been one sound which lasted a year, because the prisoner wouldn't have thought of any other sound, *that* was the sound for a year. And like this, we can imagine eternity, an eternal duration. And that led me then to the concept of *moment form*, where I said that a moment lasts not just an instant – according to our time system a fraction of a second or a few seconds – but it can last an eternity if it isn't changing.[24]

In the autumn of 1959 Stockhausen began the realization of *Kontakte* in his 'alchemist's kitchen'. Rhythms were spliced together from pulses, and loops from the rhythms. These were allowed to run for hours and the entire result was recorded. In a neighbouring room a new loop was prepared, and also in a third.

So there were loops running everywhere, and you could see it through the glass windows between the studios. Finally I used the fast-forward on the tape recorder to accelerate the tapes so they were already four or five octaves up, then the

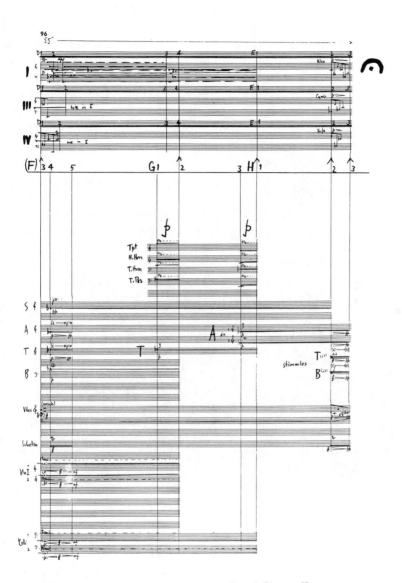

26 *Carré*, p. 96 of the score for Orchestra II and Chorus II
(Orchestras I, III and IV are at the top)

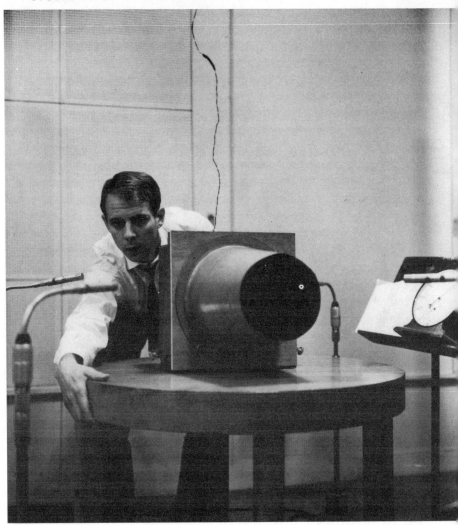

27 Stockhausen experimenting with new 'spatial projections' for *Kontakte* in the WDR electronic studio, 1959

result went up another four octaves – so then I was up eight octaves – until finally I got into an area where the rhythms were heard as pitches and timbres.[25]

Strange sounds, never heard before, occurred in the 'no man's land between skin and metal'; the nature of the percussion sounds made it impossible to tell whether they were coming from the loudspeakers or being played by a percussionist; the 'decomposition' of a sound, whereby a complex one gradually breaks up into its component parts; extremely long sounds, and others so short they could barely be perceived – it was a highly differentiated microworld of synthetic sounds.

As the performance date drew near, Stockhausen was confronted with the same problem as in *Gesang der Jünglinge*, and he again had to bring an electronic work to a close before the planned end. The realization of the last six or seven minutes had taken several weeks.

I spliced the result on to what was already finished, and listened to it in context. Then I turned white as a sheet and went out of the room and just cried my eyes out, because I knew it was all going too fast. I had to remake the whole thing! When I said that to my colleagues, they thought I was crazy. Then we remade all the last part, with every duration lengthened in the ratio 2:3, so that it had a more organic effect; otherwise everything stayed the same.[26]

The rehearsals with the four instrumentalists then began. Stockhausen had imagined that from performance to performance the musicians would react 'variably' to the electronic music, within the limitations of an open score. The playback of the electronic music was to be altered by the musicians in relation to what they were playing – by starting and stopping the tape, changing the dynamics, closing and opening various channels. But Stockhausen was not satisfied with the results of the first rehearsals. Caskel recalled: 'The realization of the aleatory indications in the score initially made the musicians feel insecure. It was only after exact discussions with Stockhausen about how these sections should sound that they could actually be played, so by the end of the second rehearsal Stockhausen had already decided on a score that would be fixed in every detail.'[27] He reduced the three percussionists to one and had the pianist playing a few percussion instruments, leaving Tudor as the pianist and Caskel as the percussionist. On 11 June 1960 they gave the première at the thirty-fourth World Music Festival of the ISCM (International Society for Contemporary Music) in Cologne.

The performance proved a disappointment for Stockhausen. Whether it was the audience's irritation at often being unable to categorize the sounds, or the unusual length of the piece (more than half an hour) or the poor ventilation of the hall, the listeners accorded *Kontakte* friendly but restrained applause. That evening, when Brücher invited people to a celebration with fireworks at his house in the Hahnwald, talk centred on Kagel and his effective piece *Anagrama*, which had been the second première of the afternoon. *Kontakte* was electronic music of the highest possible artistic level, yet, with the exception of Kagel and Koenig, Stockhausen's friends kept quiet about it. When Stockhausen played it to Boulez in the studio, the latter's 'only comments were that he was disturbed by an octave up to middle E, a few "realisms" (motor-like noises) and a diatonic melody'.[28] Later, along with *Gesang der Jünglinge*, *Kontakte* became the most highly esteemed of all electronic works.

'The Resistance to New Music'

On 24 April 1960, a few weeks before the première of *Kontakte*, Hessian Radio in Frankfurt broadcast a conversation between Stockhausen and Theodor W. Adorno in which the philosopher and music-sociologist discussed with the composer the difficult position of contemporary music – the 'Resistance to New Music', as Adorno entitled their talk. Whereas performances of Stravinsky and Schoenberg before the First World War had given rise to obvious controversies and stormy protests, the resistance to New Music was now characterized by indifference. For many traditional concert-goers contemporary music had simply become the concern of a small specialist circle. The gulf that opened up between audiences and New Music with the beginnings of Modernism seems, even now, to have stayed unbridged and essentially unexplained.

Towards the end of the fifties various people noisily accused contemporary art of having been artificially produced by enterprising managers, and the continuing attacks from various camps did not help composers. For Stockhausen, as for Adorno, there was no doubt that composing was a creative process that arose from inner necessity. 'What I do,' said Stockhausen to Adorno,

is also ultimately my music, in some kind of way, even if sometimes I do not understand it myself, because it suddenly comes to me, because it occurs to me ... people greatly underestimate the necessity of what one senses within oneself: I have to do *this* today and I have to do *that*. People underestimate this force; they seem to think, if we confront this composer often enough with a few trenchant critics, and if we do that publicly every now and then, and have a discussion, as is getting more common these days, then it will all change, or at least we shall put a spoke in his wheel. Do they really imagine that we are that gutless, that we have so little confidence in what we have to do? It has nothing to do with demands made on others; it is a demand we make on ourselves; and I know this too from my friends, whom people are always trying to tear to shreds.[29]

Stockhausen was seriously considering leaving Germany. Foreign centres of music had often made approaches to him.

A year and a half before this radio conversation, a considerable sensation had been caused by a lecture entitled 'What is Music?' given by Friedrich Blume, the eminent Kiel musicologist, editor of the encyclopaedia *Die Musik in Geschichte und Gegenwart*, and president of the German Society for Music Research. In an opening address at the Kassel Musiktage on 3 October 1958 Blume (for whom music was inseparable from a 'pitch material founded upon natural sound') asked,

Is it permissible that we should take an axe to one of God's most perfect creations, and then, from the ruins, erect a caricature that apes the Creator? Is this not impudent arrogance? Does it not verge on blasphemy? It may well be that this way of generating sounds, which can be produced and reproduced only through mechanical equipment, is a mirror of our era of atom-splitting and total automation. But – and my electronic colleagues must forgive me for affirming this openly – this utterly denaturalized product of the montage of noises derived from physics no longer has anything to do with music. Here the limits have definitely been exceeded.[30]

What was conceived as a contribution to musicological discussion was regarded by composers as an all-out attack. Boulez, Wolfgang Fortner, Bernd Alois Zimmermann and others, along with Eimert and numerous critics, responded, often in very impassioned terms, in the March edition of the music journal *Melos* (edited at that time by Strobel). Stockhausen joined in with a collage of quotations and his own succinct *aperçus*, including a parody of a nineteenth-century nursery rhyme that is his own personal, sharply ironic reply to Blume's oration in Kassel:

> The flowerlets were sound asleep,
> Products of Nature's love.
> Their little heads did upward peep,
> To Man, who lives above.
> The axe rings out against the tree,
> Sound-gen'rated in phantasy,
> Sleep on, sleep on,
> Sleep on, as long as good for ye!
>
> The Devil rises from the Pit,
> His blasphemies are serial.
> Sparks of electrons start to spit,
> Shaded flecks from darkest Hell.
> This must be outright levity,
> Music it only *seems* to be,
> Sleep on, sleep on,
> Sleep blessedly but rapidly![31]

Alongside confrontations with audiences, music critics and musicologists, there were those with composer friends. In a letter of 14 May 1960 to Adorno, with whom Stockhausen corresponded regularly in a distinctly intimate vein, he wrote:

Your great strength is evident in the number of your opponents; your great weakness is that your opponents are no real opponents. It is the same for me with my numerous pseudo-opponents. In reality I have two opponents: Boulez and Cage – or Cage and Boulez. Boulez counters with the technique of getting through my guard and lopping off limbs, Cage with the technique of silence and cutting loose. My technique is one of surprise attacks, and taking a stand. When I read your books or your articles, I know that I am truly an opponent of yours, though we may not even suspect this when we meet. Now and then I discover a sentence of yours that sends shudders through my spine. And I strike back, if I have not already done so, with weapons that are sinister and sharp. In my music, things have happened lately that are so much at odds with your thinking that you will surely be astonished if you discover them one day. You will be struck just as I know I was struck; but this time, secretly and dangerously.[32]

After the inception of aleatory music and Cage's visit to Darmstadt, serial music was no longer regarded by all its former protagonists in Darmstadt as a generally valid musical principle. Towards eleven o'clock at night on 16 June Heinz-Klaus Metzger read out his 'Cologne Manifesto' in the painter Mary Bauermeister's studio, sitting face to face with Stockhausen. Every day around then, always late in the evening, the studio housed a counter-festival to the ISCM World Music Festival, which was taking place at the time and where Stockhausen's *Kontakte* had just been premièred. In front of a densely packed international audience, Metzger stated his commitment to a 'negative aesthetic' – to the ending of any kind of generally applicable musical language – and to John Cage and his compositional anarchy. The phalanx of Cologne combatants was gradually breaking apart and drifing in all directions: Metzger was already living in Florence, Ligeti was in Vienna and Cornelius Cardew had gone back to London; a few years later Koenig went to Holland.

Paspels, Summer 1960: *Monophonie*

That summer Stockhausen retreated once again to the pastor's house in the alpine hamlet of Paspels as he wanted to compose undisturbed. Two premières were scheduled for the autumn: Heinrich Strobel had ordered a new orchestral work for Donaueschingen, and Herbert Hübner was planning the first performance of *Carré* at Hamburg Radio.

The programme booklet for that year's Darmstadt Summer Courses announced a lecture by Stockhausen, but from Paspels Stockhausen sent a manuscript entitled 'Polyvalent Form' to Heinz-Klaus Metzger, with the request to read it for him in Darmstadt. It consisted of ideas, episodes and personal data relating to the development of music in recent years – Boulez, Cage, Stockhausen – as well as a response to Metzger's 'Cologne Manifesto'. Metzger was given the opportunity to add his own commentary at specified points in the lecture. As Stockhausen began work on the composition of the 'one-note-music' of *Monophonie* in Paspels, Metzger was reading in Darmstadt:

I am composing a piece with just one note . . . All is to become one, and yet remain itself (individuality of timbre). Transformations within the note, instead of transformations *of* the notes . . . Yesterday, read Beckett: 'What prevents the miracle is the spirit of method to which I have perhaps been a little too addicted.' And later: 'For it is all very fine to keep silence, but one also has to consider the kind of silence one keeps. I listened.' [Stockhausen had been reading Beckett's novel *The Unnamable*.] The piece will be a monotone, and endless. That it must be endless, I have known since the performance of *Kontakte*. One note from eternity to eternity – and everyone can listen for as long as they wish. I no longer have any reasons to make an end – or indeed a start: *every* end will be a start. If that happens very often and many times in succession, each instant is simultaneously an end and a start . . . Perhaps people will now stop asking me whether I have used a twelve-note row, and if so, which . . . Even if there is not a single series that can be measured by numbers or the clock, the piece is still a serial composition . . . The work is without end. I have composed it in such a way that it can be played for any length of time and that, because of the way it is set out and by virtue of the collaboration of conductor and players, it can be constantly renewed. An infinite form, from which we shall take as much as we need.[33]

Without score or sketches, neither of which has yet been published, it is hard to imagine either the sound or the form of the work. *Monophonie* imposed many difficult performance conditions and, when Strobel fell out with Rosbaud, who was to conduct the piece, it remained unfinished. The winds, percussionists, guitar and two pianists were to be at many different levels (an idea later taken up in 'Luzifers Tanz'). The strings were to play out of sight behind the curtains to the side and at the back, with a second conductor (a similar effect to that of *Trans*, but the other way round).

28 October 1960: The Première of *Carré*

Since 1958 Stockhausen's commitments had grown considerably, and for several months on end he had to work simultaneously on *Kontakte* and *Carré*. This was only possible because he had involved Cornelius Cardew, the young Englishman who became his assistant, in the realization of

Carré. The piece was sketched in such a way that, with certain limits, Cardew could invent the textures himself; the result was a fruitful collaboration like those of an architect's office or the ancient schools of painting. The realization of *Carré* was begun around the same time as Stockhausen was composing *Zyklus* and *Refrain.* In it too the durations are not metrically notated, but drawn on the staves as horizontal strokes, proportionally. From April 1959 Cardew worked for several hours each day in Stockhausen's house,

aided, irritated, confused, encouraged and sometimes even guided by [Stockhausen's] eagle eye, or his voluminous notes, or his random narrations as he worked on his experiments for what later became *Kontakte* (for piano, percussion and four-track tape).

At the end of three months or so . . . a rough score had come into existence; I had an obscure idea of what the piece would be like, and Karlheinz's more whimsical notions about the piece had been abandoned, and all seemed set when, on the eve of my return to England, Karlheinz sprang the idea of the 'insertions' (episodes outside the general run of the piece – at this stage they had very little in common with what they eventually became) which were to delay the completion of even the rough score until March 1960, when I completed the last page (containing 3,000-odd notes) of the last insertion (comprising ten or so such pages) in a sun-filled library in Amsterdam.[34]

The première of *Carré* was similar to that of *Gruppen*: a move from the hall of Hamburg Radio to the Planten un Blomen festival hall, difficult rehearsals calling for a great deal of patience and a swarm of young composers from all over Europe who had travelled to Hamburg to hear it. Among them were Krzysztof Penderecki from Poland, who had come to Germany for the first time, and the gifted Swede Pär Ahlbom, who later withdrew from public musical life and dedicated himself to the development of improvisation. The conductors were Andrzej Markowski, Michael Gielen, Kagel and Stockhausen. Ahlbom remembers how, during the final rehearsal (which was to be issued as the gramophone recording) the roar of an aeroplane slowly approached the hall, growing ever louder. The performance once again provoked the audience into passionate demonstrations for and against.

In July of that year Meyer-Eppler had died, quite unexpectedly, and Stockhausen finally abandoned the doctorate he kept postponing because he had too much other work. He had reached the pinnacle of compositional quality and perfection of sound in both instrumental music (in *Gruppen*) and electronic music (*Kontakte*). Whether aleatory methods could be further developed in instrumental music and, if so, how, were now open questions, so there was some doubt as to which direction Stockhausen would take in the years following *Carré*.

6 From Moment Form to Live Electronics 1961–5

> In the first works I withdrew into
> extremely monistic thinking. Then
> I slowly expanded this to tri- and
> polyvalent thinking.
> Stockhausen

Mary Bauermeister and the Lintgasse Studio

Towards the end of 1959 the painter Mary Bauermeister rented a big studio in the attic of an old gabled house at 28 Lintgasse, in the old part of the city not far from the Rhine. The daughter of a professor of anthropology and genetics, she was gifted in both mathematics and the arts, yet ran away from school three months before matriculating 'so as not to have to study mathematics'. She spent a year with Max Bill at the Hochschule für Gestaltung in Ulm, and then went on to the State School of Art and Craft in Saarbrücken. Together with the painter and photographer Haro Lauhus, and Cornelius Cardew, she began to organize concerts and exhibitions in her studio in 1960, and it rapidly became a meeting-point for all those involved in the arts in Cologne.

Stockhausen, who was already the driving force behind the electronic studio at WDR, arranged for John Cage (and thus the whole American Cage school) to come to Europe, and to Cologne in particular . . . This studio automatically became the place where everyone stayed; there were mattresses everywhere. Heinz-Klaus Metzger, for example, lived in our bath-tub. There was always some artist or other making the daily pilgrimage to WDR to get their commission, or not . . . Cardew, our programme organizer, had access to everyone, Lauhus had good ideas and I [by selling pictures] provided the money . . . We tried to add those things that were not going on here. We performed Cage [what was probably the première of the live electronic work *Cartridge Music* took place on 6 October 1960] because he was not understood and because the pianist David Tudor had brought along lots of scores. He brought us George Brecht, La Monte Young and all the Japanese. We had performances with Bussotti, Merce Cunningham and many others.[1]

The climax of these events was the counter-festival where Metzger read out his 'Cologne Manifesto'. A constantly changing crowd native or elective Cologne inhabitants came along; Bernd Alois Zimmermann visited, as did Boulez and Cage if they were staying in Cologne. And from time to time Stockhausen turned up.

In January 1961 a relationship developed between Stockhausen and Mary Bauermeister that was to have fruitful effects on their artistic work for many years. But Stockhausen, now thirty-three, was faced with a deep personal conflict, since he still felt tied in every respect to his wife and children and did not want to split the family up. It is easy to imagine how the environment of Catholic Cologne in the early sixties, friends and enemies alike, reacted to this new relationship: reproaches and attacks were not slow in coming. There was also a physical threat from Mary Bauermeister's former partner, who was devastated by his loss; his pursuit of Mary Bauermeister, Stockhausen and his family went on for months, culminating in a brawl in the summer of 1962. From January 1961 Stockhausen welcomed every opportunity to move around; later he said he found himself 'on the run for years' and 'forced into a very complicated kind of life'.

A few months later, at the end of May, there was another, albeit less momentous conflict. Herbert Eimert, the artistic director of the electronic studio, a prolix propagandist for serial music and especially electronic music, had come back from the Schwetzingen Festival full of enthusiasm for the première of Hans Werner Henze's chamber opera *Elegy for Young Lovers*; in his review in the *Kölnischer Rundschau* on 24 May he called the opera a 'masterpiece'. 'With a sure hand,' he wrote, 'Henze's music makes use of the latest achievements in sound. It breathes, lives and floats within a transparent, unusually colourful world of sound and texture, it has a magic atmosphere, it is rhythmically captivating right down to its virtuoso jazz effects, it is dramatically thrilling.' For Stockhausen, as for most serial composers, Henze's totally different world had always been an old one; this enthusiasm was like a betrayal of serial music, and it was this that he accused Eimert of with great vehemence and broke with him because of it.[2]

A disagreement between Eimert and Stockhausen seemed to have been on its way for some while. Eimert had ambitions as a composer, and liked to see himself described in the press as the father of the 'Cologne School' – which indeed he was, but as an influential promoter and publicist rather than as a composer. Stockhausen had been his draught-horse, but the horse had now become the coachman.

Darmstadt 1961

In 1961 Stockhausen held his second special course at Darmstadt on the composition of instrumental music, with David Tudor taking part once again. Its theme was the new temporal structure of moment form, which

Stockhausen dealt with exhaustively on the first evening. 'Most of the participants came from far away, and were fatigued from the journey,' related the Viennese composer and horn player Kurt Schwertsik. 'Stockhausen had begun at 6.30 p.m. and, with one break, he went on teaching until 3 a.m., at full intensity and concentration. Many people could not follow what he was saying, and some Americans kept falling asleep due to jet-lag. The next day everyone had to start composing, and Stockhausen was sometimes amazed at how helpless a few of them were.'[3] Among the other students were Michael von Biel (Germany), Jack Brimberg (USA), Aldo Clementi (Italy), Makoto Shinohara (Japan) and Mary Bauermeister. 'To the astonishment of the composers,' said Stockhausen, she 'showed that in her painting the same compositional problems that are decisive for current musical writing have led to new optical inventions and discoveries.'[4] The shared principles of their work led the director of the Stedelijk Museum in Amsterdam to invite Mary Bauermeister and Stockhausen to hold a joint exhibition of 'Pictures and Electronic Music' two months later. Mary Bauermeister's pictures were accompanied by a continuous taped programme of electronic music. From June 1962 to April 1963 the exhibition was shown at the five most important modern art museums in Holland: Amsterdam then Schiedam, Groningen, Den Haag and Eindhoven.

As well as the composition seminar Stockhausen gave a second course on electronic music, in which he analysed *Kontakte* in great detail. In his public lecture 'Invention and Discovery', which made history and which has been much quoted ever since, he looked back at the musical developments of the past ten years, taking examples from his own work:[5] a development from points of sound via groups to statistical sound complexes, which can be composed determinately, variably and polyvalently. All forms may recur as developmental forms, seriate forms and moment forms – that is, dramatic, epic and lyrical forms (as Stockhausen later called them) – in all possible combinations. No one suspected at the time that this lecture would mark the end of the era of Wolfgang Steinecke, who died unexpectedly on 23 December as the result of an accident. The following words from Stockhausen's obituary of Steinecke reveal how much those eleven years in Darmstadt had meant to him: 'That great round face from the "Land of Smiles" now exists as part of my "Memories of Youth". Since 1951 I have been unable to get away from the feeling that every year I was having to take an exam in Darmstadt – fronting up to this man with his broad shoulders who wore "baggy trousers

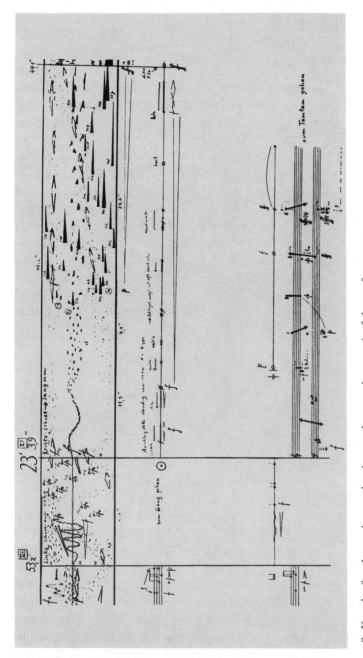

28 *Kontakte* for electronic sounds, piano and percussion, p. 26 of the performance score (*top*: graphic representation of the electronic music; *middle*: percussion; *below*: piano; composer's autograph

like a Russian".'6 Steinecke's death raised the question of whether the Summer Courses could go on at all.

Originale: 'I = Music Theatre'

Shortly before Darmstadt, early in July 1961, Stockhausen and Mary Bauermeister spent four weeks in Finland, where Stockhausen gave lectures on the Jyväsklä summer university courses. He took with him a commission from the Cologne theatre producer Arthur Caspari, who had had the idea of 'making theatrical use of the cultural situation in Cologne, and particularly the circle around Stockhausen'. The music-theatre work *Originale* grew out of animated conversations with Mary Bauermeister in barely two weeks of seclusion in the summer house of the famous Finnish biographer of Sibelius, Erik Tawaststjerna, on Lake Saimaa. This piece, often regarded as Stockhausen's 'happening', stood at the opening of the Fluxus and happening movements of the sixties, at a time when the last vestiges of tradition had been thrown overboard and the last taboos had been broken. At last everything was possible, even the topless cello playing of the American Charlotte Moorman in Nam June Paik's *Opéra sextronique* in New York in 1967, which led to both being arrested for indecent exposure.

Paik, Helms and some painters had already staged exciting 'actions' at the studio in Lintgasse and also in Jean Pierre Wilhelm's Gallery 22 in Düsseldorf, and Paik was to become a central figure in the Cologne performance of *Originale*. Stockhausen knew all the Cologne artists, so it was natural for him to combine the city's artistic activities with some of the city's best-known 'originals'. Stockhausen constructed the work's overall form – eighteen scenes, organized into seven structures; the passage of time is determined by a performance of *Kontakte*. Within this, he let the 'originals' portray themselves, as kinds of inserts: Helms was a poet, Mary Bauermeister a painter, Caspari a producer, Stockhausen himself a conductor of five actors, and a child (from the Stockhausen family) played with toy bricks. Caskel and Tudor appeared in a variety of exotic costumes. Among the many other participants were a sound engineer, a cameraman, a wardrobe mistress, a female attendant from Cologne Zoo's monkey house and a newspaper vendor known throughout the city for her witty comments on the headlines. With a large enough stage, up to three structures could be performed simultaneously on different planes, the structures being mutually interchangeable. To the right of the stage was a concert grand, to the left, Caskel and the tape recorders.

29 Mary Bauermeister's *Sand-Stein-Kugelgruppe* (1962)

30 Mary Bauermeister in the Lintgasse studio, around 1960

Birdcages with doves and budgerigars hung from the ceiling; there was an aquarium of goldfish, and various domestic plants were placed all around. On the walls were two huge stopwatches, a cuckoo clock and an hourglass.

The city had made the Theater am Dom available free of charge for this undertaking, but after only two of the twelve performances it had become a civic scandal: the little boy with the earthworm on his tongue and the frog in his apron pocket had given his first music-theatre performance, and everyone had yelled out, 'Ugh!!!' Stockhausen and Caspari were given an alternative: either the performances had to end or the city's subsidy would. The main cause of offence was the actions by Paik. Moving like lightning, he threw peas up at the roof over the audience, or straight at them. Clad in a dark suit, he smeared himself all over with shaving cream, emptied a bowl of flour or rice over his head and jumped into a bath-tub full of water. He submerged, then ran to the piano, began playing a sentimental salon piece, tripped over and banged his head several times on the keys. Paik's absurd actions changed every day and made immediate use of any special situation. Once, when he knew that the 'informal' painter Karl Otto Götz was in the audience, he poured inky water over his head, ran out to the toilet, flushed it and came back wiping his hair with a toilet roll. For those in the know, this created structures similar to those in Götz's paintings.

Faced with these official demands, the ensemble at once decided to continue under its own financial auspices. It hired the theatre – Mary Bauermeister raised the money from various patrons within twenty-four hours – and gave ten further performances, most of which were sold out. The reaction of the critics, who had doubtless expected something else from music theatre, ranged from bewilderment to cynicism. Twenty-five years later Caspari's impression was

that Stockhausen would gladly have performed the score exactly the same way each time, achieving an increasingly perfect realization. I, on the other hand, preferred flexibility and improvisation to convention and perfection. Within such a balance, Paik and Alfred Feussner were a splendid, almost unquestionable match for one another [Feussner, who was one of the actors, changed his texts every day, constantly confusing his colleages and Stockhausen too with the completely unexpected reactions that arose] and of course even Stockhausen did not have much trouble recalling the actual principle underlying the 'originals'.[7]

For some time Stockhausen had been planning to build a peaceful weekend retreat where he could compose undisturbed. His acquaintance with various Cologne artists, and in particular the rehearsals and performances of *Originale*, had already given him the idea of a small artists' colony, when a piece of land in Kürten, in the Bergisch region, became available. Stockhausen's congenial architect was Erich Schneider-Wessling, a former student of Frank Lloyd Wright and Richard Neutra, and also a visitor to the Lintgasse studio, who later became part of the Fluxus movement. The artists' colony, Schneider-Wessling remembers, soon turned out to be unrealistic for financial reasons, but the plans for a single house were drawn up in December 1961. Three principal ideas had a marked effect on the concept of the building: integration of the house into the surrounding natural landscape; the house as a communications centre – living together, working together; and an interpenetration of interior and exterior, of house and nature. After a tedious preparatory period, building started in May 1964.

Sicily 1962: *Momente*

From January to the end of March in 1962 Stockhausen and Mary Bauermeister lived in Sicily. Baron Francesco Agnello (director of the Palermo New Music Week, in which Stockhausen's *Punkte* was to be premièred that autumn) had put at their disposal his once magnificent but now rather dilapidated *palazzo* in the little village of Siculiana on the south coast. It was winter and, despite its southerly position, the building was cold as ice. Stockhausen and Mary Bauermeister retreated into a single room, with a piano and two tables, which had to be heated by gas. While Mary Bauermeister worked on pictures for her exhibition in Amsterdam, Stockhausen started on a composition that would preoccupy him intermittently for the next eleven years, *Momente* for soprano solo, four chorus groups and thirteen instrumentalists. The starting-points for this work are three characteristic kinds of moment: K-moments (sound or timbre), M-moments (melody) and D-moments (duration), to which are added i-moments (informal or indeterminate elements) that 'neutralize the three groups of moments'. It is no coincidence that the generative moments K, M and D bear the initial letters of the names Karlheinz, Mary and Doris. A conflict that was proving hard to overcome in his private life is established here on a musical level, and resolved. The individual, innately closed moments are opened up, and further moments arise from the interplay of the three basic moments: a K-moment combines with a D-moment, resulting in a KD-moment; an M-moment is heard within a D-moment, and from this comes a D(M)-moment, etc. All encounters were possible, everything could interpenetrate, appearing in inserts as an 'announcement' or a 'memory'. The polyvalently conceived score was to be reassembled and regrouped by the conductor for each performance.

Stockhausen found a new method of composing for this work. He had learned the structural properties set up for each individual moment by heart – the relative amounts of silence, sounds, female voices, male voices, etc. – lain down on his bed and then tried to imagine something arising from these possibilities. 'All the conceivable aural images flew to and fro inside me. In my imagination I constantly shuffled them around, interchanged them . . . until I found whatever pleased me most. Then I would hastily try to get it down in notation. Often it would slip my memory. So I simply lay down once more, until I found it again, and finally wrote it down.'[8] 'What I had discovered was really a completely new method. And the sediment of this is to be seen in the overall form: in this symbiosis of proportions, the assemblage of materials and the unified musical conception.'[9]

It may be helpful to consider a little further the influence of both artists on one another. Mary Bauermeister explained:

For my painting, Stockhausen meant structure and form . . . Something like the *Sand-Stein-Kugelgruppe* would be inconceivable without Stockhausen's *Momente* . . . Conversely, what he saw in my work was the possibility of loosening rigid structures. He was really drilled in strict composition. So I brought a certain freedom by saying: if you have made a schematic form, you can unmake it too.[10]

For the *Sand-Stein-Kugelgruppe*, one of many picture-objects created in Siculiana, Mary Bauermeister had made the central part simply by rolling a few largish round stones over the base of the picture and fastening them wherever they had come to rest. She wanted to arrive at the arrangement of the stones freely, not through logical consideration, not through laws. 'With Stockhausen the overall form was always built up, constructed, and the details rather more free; with me it was always the other way round. He started from law, I started from anarchy.'[11]

Another way in which they stimulated each other, particularly during these first years, was by reading and discussing various books together; in physics, for example, Albert Einstein and Werner Heisenberg, and in biology, Konrad Lorenz and Adolf Portmann. Stockhausen introduced Meister Eckhart, and Mary Bauermeister brought *Western Way, Eastern Way* by the Japanese Zen philosopher Daisetsu T. Suzuki. After the disappointingly empty experience of a Protestant confirmation, she had ostensibly rejected the church and become an atheist. Yet she took the rebirth of humans for granted, which Stockhausen described as her 'Goethean pantheism'. Probably the most important book for Stockhausen at that time was Gotthard Günther's *Idee und Grundriss einer nicht-Aristotel-ischen Logik*, published in 1957. Günther, who had emigrated during the Third Reich, was concerned with the 'transcendental aspect' of logic and later, during his exile in America, with cybernetics. In his book he introduces into logic the distinction between I-subject and you-subject, so that the classical dualistic subject-object logic gives way to a 'logical trinity' of I-subject, you-subject and object. A decade later Stockhausen had this to say about Günther:

He shows the possibility of a post-Hegelian, and, by that, a post-Aristotelian way of thinking in at least a three-dimensional and n-dimensional logical system . . . There's no perception without the perceived and no perceived without the perception. People always think they're in the world, but they never realize they are the world. They are identical with what they see and hear, whether they like it or not.[12]

Stockhausen broke off his ties with the Catholic church at this time. Günther's book became an intellectual act of emancipation, and its effect was still evident in the programme notes for the 1965 performance of *Momente* in Donaueschingen:

Up to the end of my student days my thinking was stuffed so full of dualistic pairs of concepts such as object / subject, reason / emotion, being / meaning, material / ideal, thematic / athematic, tonal / atonal, periodic / aperiodic, homo-phonic / polyphonic, pitch / noise, sound / silence, etc., that a latent doubt in all dual values began to overcome me. In my first works I retreated into extremely monistic thinking. Then I slowly expanded this to tri- and polyvalent thinking.

Vertical and horizontal and vertical and diagonal and vertical and spatial and curved.

Homo and poly and homo and hetero and homo and mono and. And and either and or and and.

AND.[13]

The text climaxes in a quotation from Günther's book: 'Reflection is repetition.'[14]

As Stockhausen came on stage in front of the soprano Martina Arroyo, the chorus and instrumentalists, to conduct the première of the as yet incomplete *Momente* in Cologne on 21 May 1962, he was greeted with lively applause, mixed with hisses and vigorous rattling of tin cans. The audience was not responsible for this reception, however: the clapping and box-rattling were part of the score. Aroused by this unorthodox opening, some listeners grew rowdy, so Stockhausen broke off the per-

31 Stockhausen on a concert tour in Rome, summer 1962. *Left:* Kurt Schwertsik; *right:* David Tudor

32 Darmstadt 1961. *Left to right:* Pierre Boulez, Stockhausen and Theodor W. Adorno. The blackboard on its side contains Stockhausen's illustrations to his seminar on *Kontakte*

formance, went out and came back shortly afterwards, greeted once more by the chorus applause, to begin a second time. *Momente*, various moments of which are a portrait of Mary Bauermeister, always cheerfully humming, singing and laughing, is a continuation of 'what was begun in *Gesang der Jünglinge* and in *Carré* for four orchestras and choruses: an "abolition" of the dualism between vocal and instrumental music, between sound and silence, between pitch and noise – combined with the attempt to integrate and mediate between the most varied articulatory possibilities'.[15] The raw material ranges from the most banal noises to sounds of impressive beauty, from simple vocal sounds and exclamations to elevated texts: parts of the Song of Solomon, a passage from William Blake, as well as lines from one of Mary Bauermeister's letters from New York (in the 1965 Donaueschingen version) and his own texts, names, exclamations and phoneme sequences. He found a use for everything. The performance in Donaueschingen in 1965, expanded by new moments, was a great success. The complete *Momente*, in a new 'Europe Version', was performed with the soprano Gloria Davy in Bonn on 8 December 1972. Now lasting almost two hours, it had developed from an audience-provoking experimental work to one of the full-length classics of New Music.

Darmstadt 1962 and 1963

Once it had been decided that the Summer Courses would continue, the music critic Ernst Thomas was appointed as Steinecke's successor. Steinecke's death brought to an end the important Darmstadt years, the years of post-Webernism, of strictly organized serial music and the open forms of aleatory music. After these developments, the whole question of what to do next hung more heavily over the Summer Courses than it had in previous years.

It was at the beginning of the sixties that composers from eastern Europe began to make a name for themselves: Ligeti, who had lectured at Darmstadt since 1959, Penderecki and Witold Lutosławski were just three of the best known. Ligeti's 'micro-polyphony' and Penderecki's string and percussion effects gave an important stimulus to instrumental music. Composers living in eastern Europe were often forbidden to travel abroad. Since 1957 a small group of Polish composers, including Włodzimierz Kotoński and Kazimierz Serocki, had come regularly to Darmstadt, but Leonid Grabovsky and Valentin Silvestrov from Kiev, both of whom had enrolled in Stockhausen's electronic music seminar in 1961, had to cancel at the last moment; the same thing happened the following year to György Kurtág, who had wanted to participate in Stockhausen's composition seminar.

At Darmstadt in 1962 Stockhausen gave ten seminars on composition and instrumentation, in which a new tone, the expansion of 'monistic thinking' to 'polyvalent thinking', was clearly perceptible. Kurt Schwertsik wrote the following text in November 1987:

darmstadt/stockhausen/liebesträume:

in 1961 stockhausen had revealed to us the significance of the moment: of 'not yet', 'not any more' etc. i had written a piece for piano & percussion (later called 'marche funèbre', as one movement of my liebesträume)

the percussion instruments were mainly piled up in the piano & thus prepared the notes played on the keyboard.

the following winter I cut up liszts liebesträume with a razor blade held behind my back & patched the resulting fragments into a nice collage; with the intention of putting familiar sounds in unfamiliar contexts. a similar intention gave rise to a piece based on a series of major and minor triads. at the time i felt very lonely and isolated.

in 1962 i went to darmstadt with this piece. at that time stockhausen was interested in the possibility of organizing the various parameters using quite different methods, instead of the usual effort to find one *unified* form of organization for all parameters. according to stockhausens new point of view, a note was the result of various preformed components. each participant could give a talk, and I used mine to criticize this procedure. stockhausens amiable & understanding reaction was to recommend to me his method of dealing with things from which he wanted to separate himself: to embrace them!

in general it seemed to me that his tolerance of intelligently uttered criticism was frankly unlimited. however much certain ideas fascinated him, he was free from any kind of dogmatism. during these summer courses I wrote another movement based on the previous winters triad series & the four above-mentioned pieces were then played in the shed near the beer-tent. the triads provoked ironic 'oho's', people screwed up paper and threw it, and sometimes people banged a drum that was standing around. to my astonishment there was general rejoicing after the piece. i was overwhelmed by the applause of this phalanx of good-humoured people. stockhausen was sitting right up front and smiled as he threw a wrapped sugar cube of the kind you always find in coffee houses. i bowed in thanks, but he called to me: 'read what's on it', and i read 'please give us the honour again soon'.

The next year Stockhausen held a series of seminars on the topic of complex forms. He gave the participants the task of encapsulating the 'complexity of the world' in music, and hinted how this might be achieved. Otto Tomek explained: 'Stockhausen investigated this complexity in terms of five different areas: those means we come across today that are more or less preformed, both historically and technically; the formal types extending from collective masses to individual shapes; the relationships between time and space; the positive–negative relationship between sound and silence; and finally the actual types of style.'[16] In his second course Stockhausen presented a thorough and brilliant analysis of his orchestral composition *Gruppen*, the score of which had recently been published.

Locust Valley, Long Island: *Punkte*

At the beginning of October 1962 Stockhausen travelled with his family and Mary Bauermeister to the USA; he had been asked to spend six months there by the composer and pianist Jack˙Brimberg, one of his Darmstadt pupils, on condition that he give his host regular composition lessons. Brimberg had bought a villa belonging to a member of the Rothschild family in a little place called Locust Valley on Long Island for just this purpose. He invited many guests from New York high society so that he could display the famous German composer. Cage, Feldman and Tudor also came. Stockhausen visited Rauschenberg in New York, and through Tudor he got to know the painter Jasper Johns; he saw the first pop-art exhibitions of Andy Warhol, Roy Lichtenstein, Claes Oldenburg and Robert Indiana. In a letter of congratulation to Schwertsik, who had just married, he wrote:

In the shock-tactic New York exhibitions of painting and optical objects a distinctly analogous Neo-realism (that is the official title) is going on at the moment; every imaginable kind of functional object and lots of advertising posters are montaged, multiplied, 'naturalistically' copied, etc., without modification. Authentic bathroom walls, chamber-pots, freezers (with built-in sirens), lots of noise-producing objects (Tinguely with built-in radios, Wesselmann with radios and TV sets). Would certainly interest you. As stimulus. And de-stimulus.[17]

Brimberg's house lay in absolute stillness, surrounded by parkland and woods. New York was too far away for anyone to be side-tracked, even 'just once'. The children went to primary school. Out of reach of all the Cologne tittle-tattle, Stockhausen worked on the new version of the orchestral piece *Punkte*, composed in Hamburg in 1952 but withheld at that time. He had already begun this version early in the summer of 1962, during another four-week stay in Finland when he had again lectured at the Jyväskylä summer university. But the score had not been finished, and Stockhausen had to cancel the performance in Palermo. The première was then set for autumn 1963 in Donaueschingen. Stockhausen had promised Strobel the score by 'the first day of the Fishmoon' (Pisces) –

21 February. On 27 February a worried Strobel telegraphed: 'Today ninth [*sic*] day of Fishmoon. News urgently requested, otherwise Donaueschingen performance seriously endangered.' At that time Stockhausen and Strobel enjoyed corresponding in a rather Dadaistic style. Stockhausen's telegraphed response a day later ran: '*Punkte* [Points] sent off. Superfish malade. Adieu', to which Strobel replied on 1 March: 'Subfish delighted by airmail-points. Wish meilleure santé for Mister Superfish. Good luck.'[18]

During these months in America Stockhausen and Mary Bauermeister jointly studied a little book published in 1959 by the biologist and cyberneticist Wolfgang Wieser: *Organismen, Strukturen, Maschinen*. They were astonished to learn how the shapes of certain creatures result from those of others, if individual growth processes are imagined as being speeded up under particular conditions. If the rear part of the Diodon fish, for example, is spread the result is the generically related Orthagoriscus. 'You can observe how nature creates divergent species by expanding certain parameters – blowing them up or shrinking them,' said Stockhausen later in relation to Wieser's book. 'Parametric transformations – that's what serial music is all about.'[19] The 'optical' idea of spreading, remembers Mary Bauermeister, raised the question of what corresponded to spreading and shrinking in the acoustic realm. Stockhausen had composed register-spreadings as early as 1951, in *Kreuzspiel*. The traces of Wieser's book may be found only a little later in Stockhausen's *Plus-Minus*, in which 'musical organisms' are expanded and contracted, as in many other works. Stockhausen responds as a composer to whatever he experiences.

When Stockhausen and his family flew back to Germany at the end of March, Mary Bauermeister stayed on in America. With five hundred dollars lent to her by Doris Stockhausen, she decided to build up a career as a painter in New York.

On 20 October *Punkte* was premièred in Donaueschingen, conducted by Pierre Boulez. A later introductory programme note reads:

In the new version 'points' are only seldom simple tone points: they become the *centres* of groups, formations, swarms, vibrating masses, the *nuclei* of *micro*musical *organisms* . . . As I was composing, sometimes so many sound layers piled up on top of one another that the result was more sound volumes than empty space. (Why do we always think of music as sound structures in empty space, as black notes on white paper? Is it not equally possible to start out from a homogeneously filled sound space, and leave out music, by erasing the musical figures and forms?) . . . So I composed *negative forms* too: holes, 'rests', pits of various shapes

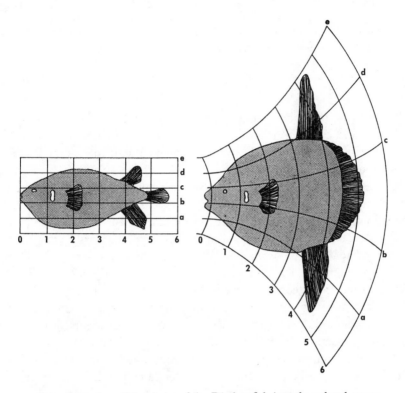

33 Transformation of the shape of the Diodon fish into the related genus Orthagoriscus by means of transformed coordinates (after Thompson)

whose edges were more or less sharply defined... After the performance I revised the score twice more.[20]

The Cologne New Music Courses

When Herbert Eimert retired in 1963, Stockhausen assumed artistic directorship of the electronic studio. The thirty-fifth year of Stockhausen's life was, broadly speaking, the beginning of his activities as a composition teacher outside Darmstadt. In the summer term that year he directed the composition master class at the Basle Conservatoire. He lived in the house of Paul Sacher, at that time one of the conservatoire two directors and conductor of the Basle Chamber Orchestra, which was renowned for its many premières. 'Stockhausen was not in Basle all the time,' reported Hans Ulrich Lehmann, one of the students:

But every three to four weeks he was there for several days, teaching six hours a day. He analysed *Momente* very thoroughly, then *Zyklus*, and other compositions of his ... he also presented the theories we knew of from his published writings. And then he analysed and discussed the compositions put forward by course participants. This was most refreshing after Boulez's classes the previous year, where discussion was very sharply focused on details of the pieces, on changing individual notes and chords, etc. Stockhausen dealt far more with the overall layout, the broad formal basis, instead of going into details.[21]

Basle was followed by visiting professorships in the USA in 1964 and 1966–7, and above all by Stockhausen's work as artistic director of the Cologne New Music Courses, which began in autumn 1963 at the Rheinische Musikschule in Cologne.

At the end of the fifties Stockhausen had talked to Kurt Hackenberg, the senior cultural adviser to the city of Cologne, about the idea of a permanent music university based on the Darmstadt model. The plans went into details of the organization and building management, but nothing had been followed up. When the active and energetic Hugo Wolfram Schmidt took over the directorship of the Rheinische Musikschule – the oldest conservatoire in West Germany – in 1962, he had in mind 'a completely new conception of a high-level music school for the rising generation of young musicians'.[22] As early as October 1961 he had invited Stockhausen to lecture at the Rudesheim Music Weeks that he held at the beginning of each term for music-education students from the Frankfurt Musikhochschule. Soon after came the first conversations.

In July 1962 Stockhausen presented a plan for a New Music institute. There was no model; the colleges and conservatoires were largely stultifying in academic tradition. For this new school, every step had to be posited on the existence of New Music. Only artistic work, allied to public musical life, could determine the form and content of artistic training.

Considerations of this kind formed the basis of the structural plan for a Cologne New Music school. It divided into ... two sections: (a) composition courses; (b) courses for instrumentalists ... The lessons of the composition courses were to be followed through in practice as well as in theory ... No deskwork without practical realization. To this end, final concerts with larger or smaller ensembles, or even an orchestra, were arranged in advance ... Daylong tuition, planned beforehand, was provided in each of the main subjects on a cyclic basis – as opposed to the switching every hour from one subject to another that had hitherto been typical of all music schools. So instead of an hourly timetable, there was one for days, weeks and months ... This new principle of dividing time has been constantly maintained. It was not just the teaching material that was revolutionary, but also the method, namely working on a given task in a collective of lecturers and course participants ... Stockhausen was not out to hide any compositional secrets: he clarified how a piece came into being, he

34 At rehearsals for the Donaueschingen performance of *Momente* in the great hall of WDR Cologne, 1965

ensured that he and his work were understood. Certainly he could be challenging, and he himself was challenged. But throughout the years of collaboration with me, Stockhausen's yes always meant yes, and no meant no. We could rely on his word, and we had to try to understand his opinions. And yet neither he nor any of the other lecturers had an authoritarian teacher–pupil relationship. Open conversation determined the situation. And with these young composers it could not have been otherwise.[23]

The Cologne Courses – first tested on a three-month basis and then implemented for six – made an immediate international impact, and the number of students increased rapidly. The teachers included Luciano Berio, Earle Brown, Luc Ferrari, Włodzimierz Kotoński, Koenig and Pousseur. Caskel, Aloys Kontarsky (piano) and Siegfried Palm (cello) formed the core of the instrumental course. Among other visitors were Martina Arroyo and Cathy Berberian (singing), Michael Gielen (conducting), Johannes Fritsch (viola) and Vinko Globokar (trombone). Ernst Thomas came to regard Stockhausen's teaching in Cologne as being in competition with his composition courses in Darmstadt, and presented Stockhausen with the alternative: Cologne or Darmstadt. Stockhausen did not hesitate to turn his back on Darmstadt.

In the summer of 1963 he made a lightning trip to New York to see Mary Bauermeister. After a few lean months she was giving painting courses for housewives, schoolchildren and amateurs within the summer programme of Fairleigh Dickinson University (Rutherford, New Jersey), and he too lectured there. Following this they rented a little flat in Mehlemer Strasse in Cologne, and then went to Sicily, where an expanded version of *Momente*, which had evolved in the previous few weeks, was to be performed at the beginning of October as part of the Palermo New Music Week. Palermo became a '*Momente*-shock', for it emerged in the rehearsals that the Italian chorus could not cope with the score, and Stockhausen was forced to cancel the concert.

Plus–Minus, an extreme example of Stockhausen's new, open method, developed from a number of conversations with Mary Bauermeister in Siculiana and Palermo. A 'process composition', it was written by way of preparation for the first of the Cologne New Music Courses.

I wanted to write a composition that would summarize as many as possible of the formative laws that I have become aware of in my work of recent years and would be so formulaic that it would permit many interpretations, and so could serve as a basis for realizations by other composers or performers. While working on *Plus–Minus* I was constantly thinking about creating the necessary conditions for living organisms, for 'musical living entities' that are always absorbing and

128

expelling material and are subject to an irreversible development process; that can undergo mutations, but can die too.[24]

The score consists of seven pages with events represented in terms of graphic symbols and seven pages of pitch materials. The two must be combined with one another in layers, following specific rules. When Stockhausen handed out the 2 × 7 pages and a commentary in the first hour of the course, everyone was astonished. The realization of this work demanded study of both the traditional and the very latest ways of writing; as Pierre Mariétan, one of the participants, wrote in an essay, it stimulated 'the composer's imagination to the highest degree'.[25]

New York and Philadelphia, January to June 1964

In January Stockhausen flew to the USA for another six months. During his earlier trip, while the Cologne Courses were still in the balance, he had accepted a visiting professorship at the University of Pennsylvania in Philadelphia. He immediately began a concert tour of North America – initially with Caskel, Tudor and Max Neuhaus, and then on his own – featuring *Kontakte, Zyklus, Refrain* and several *Klavierstücke*. The tour was organized by the concert manager Judith Blinken, whom Stockhausen had got to know the previous year; he later dedicated *Mikrophonie II* to her. The tour was to open with a Stockhausen Evening in New York. Its announcement caused a rush on the concert hall of Hunter College, and three hundred people had to be turned away. The audience included Leonard Bernstein, Lukas Foss, Edgard Varèse, numerous Greenwich Village beatniks and curious industrialists from the electronics industry. But many of those who had come expecting a lecture on the development of musical form since 1951 were to be disappointed. Stockhausen gave just one brief introduction after the interval: 'Our time is a time of beginning, not of conclusion.' It was more important to listen than to hear him giving a commentary on his music. The music was greeted with genuine and loud applause, and had a friendly reception in the much feared New York press.

The tour took an adventurous turn at Boulder, Colorado, where the concert had been organized by Alvin King, a composition teacher at the university. He was an enthusiastic amateur pilot, and over a meal he revealed he had just traded in his street-hopper for a four-seater propeller machine. They suddenly had the idea of continuing the tour in his sports plane. Caskel said he was quite happy to stick with the scheduled flight, so the next morning King, Stockhausen, Mary Bauermeister and Tudor set out in the direction of Los Angeles, the next stop on the tour. 'From Colorado,' related Mary Bauermeister,

we flew over the Rocky Mountains in the direction of the Grand Canyon. When the fuel started running out over North Arizona, King made radio contact with the next ground station, and had to put down on the tiny landing-strip of a huge Indian reservation. The next settlement, Tuba City, was an hour's walk away and turned out to be populated only by drunken Indians; the hotel was a wretched dive, with staff who did not exactly arouse much confidence. Naturally there was no aeroplane fuel, but using some sort of mixture of lawn-mower fuel and petrol, or something like that, we managed to get to Flagstaff, the next largish place, just before dark, and spent the night there. The flight next morning over the deep sandstone gorges of the Grand Canyon, with their many shades of red, was impressively beautiful, and the further west we flew, the more the gorges were gradually transformed into their 'negative images': into single rocks and rock formations reaching up into the sky.

From Los Angeles we went on to San Francisco. That day the weather did not look too promising, and King flew across the desert in a northerly direction. Soon a storm loomed up; we said nothing, but just looked outside uneasily. To get to a calmer zone, King took the machine high up above the clouds ... To make things worse, we lost radio contact. In a strangely composed mood, we awaited our end until finally, just before our destination, the weather relented, and the sea appeared below us. As King landed the machine safely in San Francisco, we lay overjoyed in each other's arms.[26]

Afterwards the three men visited Harry Partch, who lived on an old chicken farm in Petaluma, not far from the city. He demonstrated his self-built instruments, tuned to his own scales, and late that night, full of enthusiasm, the three men went back to their hotel.

In February, after the tour was over, Stockhausen and Mary Bauermeister (who had had a term contract with the New York Galerie Bonino since autumn 1963) rented a sixteenth-floor apartment in Manhattan at 116 Riverside Drive. From here Stockhausen drove regularly to Philadelphia. His composition course took the same form as the one in Cologne a few months earlier: a realization of *Plus–Minus*.

New York, the melting-pot of nations and races, made a profound impact on Stockhausen; he saw it as an image for the future of how currently fragmented humanity could live together. A little later, in a radio text on Varèse for WDR, he wrote: 'Anyone living in New York today is confronted daily with the collision of all races, religions, philosophies and customs, and with the frictions between the conventions regarding the civilization and culture of all nations ... New York, the first model for a global society, is unquestionably an indispensable experience for a contemporary artist.'[27]

35 Cologne New Music Courses 1966–7. *Left to right:* Gérard Masson (*above*), Mesias Maiguashca (*below*), Guido Baggiani, Stockhausen, Victor Saucedo, Marcel Goldmann (*below*) and Jean Yves Bosseur (*above*)

During these months Stockhausen visited several electronic studios in the USA and Canada, conducted the successful American première of *Momente* in Buffalo and composed further moments of this work in New York. He got to know the happenings artist Allan Kaprow and the experimental poet Jackson MacLow, and guests at Riverside Drive included the Beat poet Allen Ginsberg and his poet friend Peter Orlovsky.

After Stockhausen's return to Cologne Kaprow and Charlotte Moorman, with help from Mary Bauermeister, prepared a New York staging of *Originale*, and at the beginning of September Stockhausen's 'music theatre' had five new performances in Judson Hall, a little concert hall opposite Carnegie Hall. According to the participating Fluxus artist Dick Higgins,

Kaprow had talked with Stockhausen about his performance and had got his agreement. Stockhausen wanted to avoid a repetition of the style and effects of the première in Cologne. So Kaprow got together a big ensemble, about forty-five people, consisting of the best and most experienced artists, happenings authors and musicians. The result was a big colourful circus: Kaprow at his very best.[28]

Paik was carried over as a key figure from the Cologne performance, but Mary Bauermeister had given her place to a New York painter, Brown, the consequences of which left a 'bad odour'. A small group of American Fluxus artists had staged a revolt against Stockhausen as a representative of the 'serious music' that rejected jazz. Under the leadership of George Maciunas, the rather eccentric Fluxus ideologist, they had demonstrated against a Stockhausen concert in front of the New York Town Hall that April, much to the amusement of the public and press. They had handed out leaflets and carried around sandwich-boards with various slogans, of which 'Stockhausen go home!' was the least offensive. This time, as soon as people left the subway train, they were greeted by placards culminating in the demand, 'Stockhausen – Patrician "Theorist" of white supremacy: to go hell!'; the New York press suspected this was a publicity ploy by Stockhausen.

In Judson Hall the percussionist Max Neuhaus stripped down to his red stockings, to roars of laughter, and pianist James Tenney had his hair piled up like a Mephisto; Paik once again daubed himself with shaving cream, clambered into a tub of water and drank from his shoe. The whole thing was played out at several stage-levels, a monkey danced and sheep-dogs barked (this had been planned for Cologne, but could not be realized because of the opposition).

While Allen Ginsberg sang mantras – he and Jackson MacLow took part as poets – Brown, who was dressed in an 'obscene' spacesuit, lit a fire in a red pail. The fire emitted evil-smelling fumes and most of the audience fled from the hall. Brown had been sneaked into the perform-ance by Maciunas to sabotage it. He was replaced by the Japanese painter Ay-O, and, luckily, further sabotage acts were spotted in advance and prevented. Among the guests at the turbulent première were Varèse and Stefan Wolpe; the piece caused a considerable stir, as well as much amusement.

Allen Ginsberg provided the following anecdotal note as a brief memoir of the performance:

Taking part (invited by Charlotte Moorman) in Stockhausen's originale perform-ance was a blessing. I chanted *om gri maitreya* in avant-garde context rather than high school, street or academic conference; encountering Nam June Paik I drank water from his shoe – so we became friends. Since then Nam June Paik has engaged me in many video projects from chanting to rocknroll to conversation with my dead father the poet Louis Ginsberg. Thanks Karlheinz Stockhausen.

Beginnings of Live Electronics: *Mixtur* and *Mikrophonie I* and *II*

One consequence of these unsettled years of constant travel was that, up to the summer of 1964, Stockhausen had completed only one piece, the polyvalent process composition *Plus–Minus*. *Klavierstücke IX* and *X* had been realized in 1961, and since 1962 he had been writing a huge 'work in progress', *Momente*. An unsolved compositional problem that had preoccupied him since the end of the fifties was the synthesis of electronic and instrumental music. The machines in the electronic studio allowed him to shape a sound right down to its microstructure and to treat dynamics and tempo without regard for the limitations of an interpreter. Pure tape composition, however, lacked the tense, electric atmosphere created by an interpreter. The use of aleatory factors in instrumental music had added the dimension of the co-creative interpreter; on the other hand, the traditional instruments and their timbres had long been known and were more or less unalterable. By the time Stockhausen came back from the USA at the end of June, the solution to this problem was within his reach. After his arrival he began the orchestral composition *Mixtur*, a commission from the American Koussevitzky Foundation, and after a few weeks' uninterrupted work it was done. Stockhausen was aware of a few tricks used in pop music, whereby instruments were connected to microphones, but these sound effects struck him as too superficial; writing the score was an adventurous experiment, since there was no experience in this field to draw on. *Mixtur* inaugurated a new cycle of pieces in which the equipment of the electronic studio was combined with instruments: Stockhausen's 'live electronic' music. A symphony orchestra is divided into five groups – brass, woodwind, strings, pizzicato strings and percussion – placed as far as possible at different points in the hall. What each group plays is recorded by microphones; the sound is transformed by other musicians at mixing desks, to which ring modulators and sine-wave generators are connected, and played back simultaneously over the loudspeakers, producing a quite remarkable 'mixture timbre'. The work consists of twenty moments with names such as 'Mixture', 'Mirror', 'Brass', 'Tuning Pitch' and 'Silence'; the order of the moments may be reversed and a few of them may be interchanged.

As ever when Stockhausen discovers something new, he worked straight

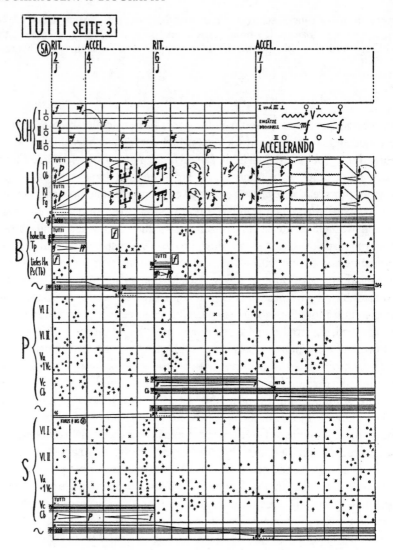

36 *Mixtur* for orchestra, sine-wave generators and ring modulators:
p. 3 of the *Tutti* moment

on, with feverish activity. Directly after *Mixtur* he began a second live electronic composition using only one instrument: a tamtam 1.55 metres in diameter, which he had bought a few years earlier for *Momente*. In August 1964 he experimented with it in the garden. He set the tamtam vibrating using various objects found around the house – glass, cardboard, metal, wood, rubber and plastic; a strongly directional microphone was attached to an electronic filter and the output of the filter was connected to a loudspeaker through which the outcome could be heard. 'My collaborator Jaap Spek was inside the house and improvised changes of the filter settings and volume level. We simultaneously recorded the result on tape. For me, the tape recording of this first experiment in microphony was a discovery of capital importance.'[29]

In New York Mary Bauermeister was occupied with similar phenomena in the realm of optics around this time, and the two exchanged letters about their work. At the exhibition in Amsterdam the artist had placed magnifying lenses on her pictures so that small structures could be seen more clearly. The visitors were always walking off with the lenses, however, so in the summer she began to fasten them securely on her pictures, the result being effects of magnification as well as light and colour.

For Stockhausen two things stood at the forefront of his new work: just as a doctor uses a stethoscope to listen to a body, so the microphone was to make audible the 'inaudible vibrations' of the tamtam, with its rich store of sounds and noises; at the same time movements of the microphone elevated the whole process of microphone recording to an artistic level. Stockhausen had discovered a realm of noise that fascinated him, but now he had to find an appropriate notation. He divided his new piece, *Mikrophonie*, into thirty-three moments, whose names all describe a particular realm of 'noise': 'clashing-creaking-thundering', 'crinkling-cackling', 'chirping-snorting-grunting' or 'rebounding-grating'. Following a specific combination scheme, the moments are divided between two groups of three players apiece – the groups play mainly in alternation. The first player strikes the tamtam with a great variety of instruments, the second picks up the result with a hand-held microphone, and the third alters the sound by means of filters and potentiometers.

At the beginning of October, the notation of the first two moments having been finished, the players met for a first practice. In the period before the première in Brussels on 9 December over fifty rehearsals took place – probably the most that have been necessary for a work by Stockhausen. The young English composer Hugh Davies, who had just finished his studies at Oxford and became Stockhausen's new personal

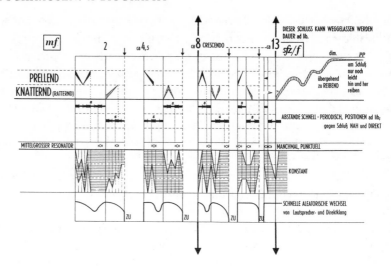

37 *Mikrophonie I* for tamtam, two microphones, two filters and two potentiometers. Moment: 'prellend, knatternd' (*top:* tamtam; *middle:* microphone; *bottom:* filter/potentiometer

assistant in November, reported on the last weeks of preparation in his 'Mikrophonie Diary':

27 November: Rehearsal of group I 7–10 p.m. I arrived in Cologne this morning to start work as Stockhausen's personal assistant. By the time of the rehearsal I was tired, and hardly began to understand what the piece is all about.

29 November: Sunday. In the morning I go up the tower of [Cologne Cathedral] with Stockhausen and his family. Probably the last proper relaxation we will get before the performance on 9th December. Rehearsal 2–6 p.m. group II.

2 December: Rehearsal 10 a.m.-1 p.m. I come a bit later, as I have to order a complete score . . . to be photocopied for me. 2–5 p.m. rehearsal, with Stockhausen's students from the [Cologne courses]. In the morning we have problems with both of the microphones, one appears to have been *kaputt* when they started, the other shortly after I arrived. Spek puts them right when he comes later on, and then has difficulty with his loudspeaker and filter . . . today is the first time the two groups have rehearsed together, exactly a week before the concert.

4 December: Rehearsal 10 a.m.-2.15; 2.30–4.15; 4.30–5.30 p.m. Group II in the morning, without the filters, as Spek had taken them to the customs . . . In the lunch break Stockhausen improvises on the piano, first in a fairly modern style, then something more nineteenth-century . . . Spek comes back with all the electrical equipment, including two much handier potentiometers . . . We three stay

136

until 6.30 p.m. while Spek sets up all the equipment again. Stockhausen plays some jazz on the piano: *Lil' Darlin'*, *Summertime*, a song from the *Dreigroschenoper*, *Tea for Two* etc., in a fairly racy style, at times a bit reminiscent of George Shearing, quite interesting rhythmically.

5 December: Rehearsal 10 a.m.-1, 2–4 p.m. Schlee (director of UE) comes. The electrical equipment is working very well now.

6 December: Our last day rehearsing in Cologne, 10 a.m.-2.45 p.m. Schlee comes again for a few minutes, and Stockhausen's family for longer. Stockhausen's wife finds a few things being used as instruments that have been missing from her kitchen recently!

7 December: Spek drives Stockhausen and myself in a van, with all our equipment and Caskel's percussion instruments for *Kontakte*, to Brussels.[30]

The players at the première were Christoph Caskel and Aloys Kontarsky (tamtam), Johannes Fritsch and Bernhard Kontarsky (microphones) and Stockhausen, Hugh Davies and Jaap Spek (filters and potentiometers). This first performance of *Mikrophonie I*, the unleashing of an elemental world of noises under the constraint of electronic equipment, also marked the forming of the Stockhausen Group, which, with many membership changes, was to go on playing Stockhausen's live electronic works all over the world until well into the seventies.

From autumn to the beginning of winter in 1964 Stockhausen was living on his plot of ground in Kürten, where a sauna had already been built. When Mary Bauermeister came to Germany for a few months, the sauna was where they lived and worked; parts of *Mixtur* were written here. The house, which was not finished until the autumn of the following year, has many original features: painted white, it has a dark-stained wooden roof that runs parallel to the incline of the hills; above this is a smaller top floor whose roof slopes in the opposite direction. The windows are big, and each room has a different hexagonal shape and its own door to the outside. The small stairway leading up to the house goes back to one of his earlier drafts, in which a stairway was to lead from the bottom of the valley right up to and through the house, finishing on the hill-top, where the *Momente* tamtam was to stand. In the course of many years the composer has planted this ample plot of land, which stretches to the edge of the forest, with all kinds of trees and shrubs.

Stockhausen's next field of experimentation in live electronics was the combination of song and electronic equipment. From the middle of March to the middle of April in 1965, during another stay in America with Mary

38 In front of his self-designed house at Kürten, 1965

Bauermeister at Glen Ridge, New Jersey (not far from New York), he wrote *Mikrophonie II* for twelve singers, Hammond organ and four ring modulators, a WDR commission. As Hugh Davies recollected, the work was originally conceived for chorus and tamtam, but the two types of forces turned out to be too contrary and Stockhausen replaced the tamtam with a Hammond organ. Like *Mikrophonie I* the work consists of thirty-three moments, but this time in a fixed order. Three first sopranos, three second sopranos, three first basses and three second basses are each ring-modulated by the Hammond organ. As a text Stockhausen used Helmut Heissenbüttel's *Einfache grammatische Meditationen* of 1955, the only occasion to date on which Stockhausen has set contemporary literature (apart from his own texts). The following is the first of the five sections of text:

a [tautologies]
the shadow I am casting is the shadow I am casting
the position I find myself in is the position I find myself in
the position I find myself in is yes and no
situation my own situation my own specific situation
groupings of groupings are moving over empty surfaces
groupings of groupings are moving over pure colours
groupings of groupings are moving over the shadow I am casting
the shadow I am casting is the shadow I am casting
groupings of groupings are moving over the shadow I am casting and
disappearing

Mikrophonie II is a piece of many facets, of many different sounds. To continually find new nuances of sound, Stockhausen has the chorus members singing in all kinds of ways: mellifluous 'bel canto', 'Don Cossack style', 'cool à la jazz', 'seductively' or 'sleepily'; in 'witch-like' and 'demonic' passages the song of the ring-modulated voices becomes grotesquely distorted. Adapting a phrase from Robin Maconie's book on Stockhausen, Orpheus's descent into the electro-acoustic underworld has begun.[31]

The première of the work took place along with the first German performance of *Mikrophonie I* on 11 June 1965 in the Great Hall of Cologne Radio, and marked Stockhausen's début as director of the electronic studio. Two electronic pieces by a second, younger generation of composers working in the studio (Michael von Biel and Johannes Fritsch) were premièred in the same concert. That afternoon Stockhausen had given a prefatory lecture in which he outlined what the term 'New Music' meant to him. It was impossible not to notice that he was also talking about his experiences with live electronic music:

New Music is not so much the outcome or audible result of the way modern composers think and feel (though it is that too) as a music that is uncanny, new, unknown, even to those who happen upon it or let it come about. Such New Music is found rather than invented – no one even suspects it in advance, so it does not express anything that was known or felt *previously*. Rather, once we have heard it, it *creates* a new way of thinking and feeling. Such thinking and feeling as is created by New Music can then be built on as part of our experience and our learning processes. But the process of innovation always runs on ahead.[32]

In an interview in 1982 Stockhausen added a further nuance to this idea; that of something mysterious and hidden that the composer 'listens in' to, something, moreover, that is perceived with amazement, that immediately provokes a very alert, inquisitive state and is profoundly impressive.

The performance of the expanded version of *Momente* and the première of *Mixtur* that autumn were followed by Stockhausen's first lecture tour in England, where the attitude to the latest development in music had for a long time been very reserved. After giving evening lectures at the universities of Oxford, Cambridge and Glasgow, in London Stockhausen found a particularly interested and open-minded audience that was quickly won over by his relaxed and drily humorous manner.

Three days before the première of *Mixtur* Edgard Varèse died in New York. As chance would have it, Varèse's *Poème électronique* was also in the concert programme, and at the beginning of his introduction to *Mixtur*, Stockhausen made mention of his 'fatherly friend' in terms that led Karl H. Wörner, who had written the first book on Stockhausen in 1963, to comment,

His words on that occasion, spoken freely and without preparation, deserve to have been published, for I must confess that I have never heard or read any declaration made by a younger composer about an older colleague that was more grateful, more appreciative and more sympathetic towards such creative greatness, human warmth and artistic significance as passed on with Varèse.[33]

7 'A Music of All Countries and Races' 1966–8

> I wanted to come closer to the
> realization of an old dream: to
> take a step further in the direction
> of composing not 'my' music, but
> a music of the whole world, of
> all countries and races.
>   Stockhausen

Japan, January to April 1966: *Telemusik*

Through the good offices of his composition student Makoto Shinohara, Stockhausen was invited by Japanese Radio (NHK) to Tokyo for a few months to carry out two commissions in the electronic studios in celebration of the station's fiftieth anniversary in 1965. Stockhausen had kept putting off his journey because of other commitments, but finally, under pressure from Tokyo, the date of departure was set for 19 January 1966. Mary Bauermeister had decided to await the arrival of her first child, which was due in February, in Germany and come over to Tokyo later. So Stockhausen flew to Tokyo on his own; three days later, on 22 January, his daughter Julika was born.

'My arrival in Japan,' said Stockhausen later, 'made such an enormous change to my life that I felt like someone coming out of the provinces into the big wide world.'[1] It was similar, albeit on a different scale, to the change experienced at the age of eighteen and a half when he left the village seclusion of Altenberg to study in Cologne, and it came about eighteen and a half years later. (A third such key year, of even greater import, was Stockhausen's fifty-sixth, when he addressed the question of death in his opera *Samstag* from *Licht*.) He lived in a sort of dream world, and was so fascinated by all things Japanese that he transformed himself and soon became 'more Japanese than the Japanese'.

The time difference of eight hours meant that for the first week Stockhausen could not get to sleep.

I was glad of this, because sound-visions, ideas and movements went ceaselessly through my head whenever I was lying awake. After four sleepless nights and four days of working in the studio for eight or nine hours without any viable result – I had to cope not only with a foreign language, food, water, air and the yes/no confusion, but also with a completely different technical set-up in the studio – one vision came again and again. It was just what I wanted: a vision of sounds, new technical processes, formal relationships, pictures of notation, human relationships, etc. – all at once and in a network too tangled up to be unravelled in *one* process. It was to preoccupy me for a long time.

In all this I wanted to come closer to the realization of an old dream: to take a step further in the direction of composing not 'my' music, but a music of the whole world, of all countries and races.[2]

First Stockhausen had to face an inner conflict. Could he compose exactly the same kind of piece in Tokyo as in Cologne? If so, why travel to Tokyo? But what if he were to imitate gagaku or noh, Japanese music? That implied a contradiction between how one lived and what one did. Up to now Stockhausen had always avoided musical quotations, regarding them as showing a lack of orginality. But in the Cologne studio the previous year he had begun work on a tape composition, *Hymnen*, whose material was national anthems from all over the world. Stockhausen had not been able to complete the piece in time for a première before the trip to Japan. 'I was already more or less prepared to come to terms with material that I would previously have regarded as unusuable. Then, in Japan, there was this breakthrough, where I used the Japanese elements literally like photos, acoustic photos, which I transformed, allowing them mutually to modulate one another.'[3]

It was more than just a matter of Japanese music, however. The new work became a 'tele-music', in which Stockhausen sought to combine tape recordings of music from China, the mountains of Vietnam, Bali, the Shipibo Indians of the Amazon, a sevillana from a Spanish village celebration and music from Hungary and the southern Sahara, with his own electronic music. His intention was to create not the arbitrary juxtaposition typical of collage but a 'meta-collage' whose elements influenced and penetrated one another at a higher level. The rhythm of one event would intermodulate with the dynamic curve of another, his own electronic chords with the dynamic curves of a Japanese priest's chant, the priest's chant with the one-note song of a Shipibo Indian, and so on – the modulation of one musical event into another, of one musical style into another.

Telemusik had taken a few days to get under way, but then the project rushed ahead. The atmosphere and even the whole attitude to life in the Tokyo studio were fundamentally different from that in Cologne. Almost every hour a bowl of tea was passed round and they ate bitter little cakes. Stockhausen's technical assistants were introduced to him as 'Buddha of the tape recorder', 'Buddha of the filter' and 'Buddha of the generators', only partly in jest. They had to converse in broken English, but the

39 Japan, 1966: outside the Buddhist Todai-ji temple in Nara

technicians adapted to Stockhausen so easily that by 2 March the seven-
teen-and-a-half-minute work was already completed.

Stockhausen grasped every available opportunity to absorb the ancient
court culture of Japan. 'Whenever I could, I would sit still somewhere,
in Kamakura, in Kyoto, in Nara – leaning against a tree, gazing into the
valley, listening in the evening to the bells, these great temple bells that
summoned and answered one another . . . I sat for hours in temples . . .
every tiny detail fascinated me.'[4] He was often accompanied by Aiko
Miyawaki (a painter and sculptress from an old Japanese family), and
Wataru Uenami (the director of the electronic studios), who were both
friendly and helpful.

On one of the first Sundays they went to a noh-theatre performance;
then came gagaku music, kabuki, sumo wrestling, innumerable tea cere-

monies and much else. The climax of the Festival of Dedicating the Water (Omizutori), a six-week Buddhist ceremony at the Todai-ji temple in Nara, lasted three days and three nights: Stockhausen was able to witness it from a side-room next to the altar room, peering through cracks in the thin wooden wall. All the music and the religious ceremonies showed that the Japanese experience of time is completely different. The European feels at home with the middle range of tempos, 'whereas the extremely rapid actions and reactions of the Japanese, and their very slow movements and long waiting times . . . allow far fewer changes to take place in the middle range'.[5]

Whereas people in Europe always lay stress on transitions, on musical bridge-passages, for a Japanese the typical temporal sequence is a sudden leap from one time layer to the other, and indeed to extreme opposites . . . I became aware that such processes are the most profound things underlying all music, irrespective of whether it is traditional or modern. For me as a European, the Japanese and their music were utterly modern. For me it was new music, a new life.[6]

Having been joined by Mary Bauermeister, they went together to visit Daisetsu T. Suzuki, then over ninety years old, whose work they had studied, five years earlier. Perhaps Stockhausen faced a dilemma within himself in respect of the sounds he produced 'in the laboratory'. As he was telling Suzuki about his work, he said,

You know, I make sounds in a very artificial way . . . That's a new method, as opposed to the natural way of producing a sound with your voice. [The Zen philosopher's response to this is fascinating: he addresses not the external facts but the attitude that lies behind them.] 'I cannot understand your language. I cannot understand why you say this is artificial and this is natural.' I said, 'What do you mean? By using this apparatus and equipment, that's artificial.' And he said, 'That is quite natural.' 'Well, OK,' I said, 'what is not natural?' He said, 'It would only be artificial if it went against your inner conviction. You're being completely natural in the way you do it.' And then I said, 'Wonderful, I'll forget about my western education, and the way we call things artificial and natural. When we speak about a homunculus we think it's an artificial man that they tried to make in medieval times.' He said, 'That is quite natural. I don't see anything wrong with it.'[7]

The première of *Telemusik*, which Stockhausen had dedicated in grati-tude to the people of Japan, was given at Japanese Radio in Tokyo on 25 April. The concert included the first performance of *Solo* (for a melody instrument and feedback), in versions for flute and trombone. The second commission, it was written in Tokyo during March and April, though the earliest sketches date back to the time of *Plus–Minus* and *Mikrophonie I*. The piece is brilliantly conceived but hard to realize. What the soloist plays is recorded on tape, played back over loudspeakers after a short time-delay and then commented on in all kinds of ways. The soloist improvises chords, blocks or a polyphonic counter-voice to his or her own playing.

At the end of April, after extremely cordial farewells, Stockhausen left Japan. He returned to Germany via Hong Kong, Cambodia (Angkor), Bangkok, New Delhi, Tehran, Beirut and Istanbul. He spent a few days in each place, visiting temples and ancient cultural sites and giving talks on his works at the radio stations. A brief but memorable encounter with an Indian village musician during this journey was described two years later in his 'Freibrief au die Jugend' (Open letter to the young):

In India, on a country road between Agra and Jaipur, I met a musician who played for me (and sang too) on a little string instrument he had made himself. He was one of the few really wonderful musicians I have met during my lifetime. He owned literally nothing, and when I asked him whether he would sell me his instrument for twenty dollars – a sum it would have taken him years to earn (he got, so the Indian driver who was translating for me said, at best something like ten cents a day, from villagers or passers-by) – he just looked at me blankly. Tears ran down his cheeks, and he shook his head. I was so ashamed, I could have died.[8]

On 16 May Stockhausen arrived back in Germany.

A Mondrian Exhibition in Den Haag, and *Adieu*

Just before leaving for Tokyo Stockhausen had met the highly promising organist Wolfgang Sebastian Meyer to talk about a work for organ. Shortly afterwards the organist, who was only twenty-seven, was killed in a car accident in Italy. In June his father, Wilhelm Meyer, who was the leader of the WDR Wind Quintet and who had played *Zeitmasse* on many European tours, asked Stockhausen for a new piece for a forthcoming tour of Asia. But it was impossible for Stockhausen to interrupt his work for an extended period – he was fully occupied with *Hymnen* – so he declined.

A few days later Stockhausen drove to Den Haag to see an exhibition of works by Piet Mondrian. In the wake of his discovery of Paul Klee, Mondrian too became important to Stockhausen at the end of the fifties. Rather like Webern in music, Mondrian had reduced the elements of painting to their ultimate, simplest phenomena: vertical and horizontal lines, and the three primary colours, red, blue and yellow, along with black and white. The exhibition at Den Haag, one of the most comprehensive so far, gave Stockhausen an uneasy feeling:

Once Mondrian had chosen the elements for a painting and had immersed himself in the contemplation of their relationship and once he had shifted around the 'strips' that he worked with instead of painted lines, which were done afterwards, until he was entirely happy with the relationship of the criss-crosses, and of the white and coloured planes, he must sometimes have been able to finish a picture in a single afternoon. Why have I never been able to do that sort of thing? Why do I always work for months or even years on a composition? Why do I always feel that a work ought to call for a long period of highly concentrated work???[9]

It was with these thoughts that Stockhausen returned. He remembered the request for a wind quintet, and the death of the young organist. In the autumn of the previous year Stockhausen had once composed a piece within a few hours. When a student at the Cologne Courses had asked him about the process that brought a composition into being, he had spontaneously drafted *Stop* (for orchestra) on the blackboard and had planned the details during a single seminar session, explaining each individual decision to the students. Back in Kürten Stockhausen retired to his workroom, and the wind quintet *Adieu*, dedicated to the memory of Wolfgang Sebastian Meyer, was created in one weekend. Soft sounds that seem to come from far away, a static music, consisting of few notes. On 30 January 1967 *Adieu* was played for the first time, in Calcutta; the official première took place in Tokyo on 10 February.

The composition of the new wind quintet was a touchstone for Stockhausen. He was now certain that he too could complete compositions in a short space of time. In the following years there would be a new cycle of works, each written in a few days: *Prozession, Kurzwellen, Spiral, Pole* and *Expo*.

Darmstadt 1966

After the dissension caused by Stockhausen's teaching at the Cologne Courses, Ernst Thomas once again invited the much sought after composition teacher to Darmstadt in 1966, and Stockhausen accepted. In previous years Thomas had tried to focus work in Darmstadt by congresses on a principal theme, and this year it was to do with music theatre: 'New Music – New Stage'. Stockhausen's reappearance was welcomed by the participants. In his seminar he dealt with the things that were of immediate concern to him: syntheses of electronic, instrumental and vocal music. His accounts of *Telemusik* and Japan and of *Momente* and *Mikrophonie* enthralled many listeners, and the first performance of the complete *Klavierstücke*, given by Aloys Kontarsky, was greatly admired. But Darmstadt had changed: 'The highly charged atmosphere, the constant excitement or provocation of Kranichstein's intellectual cauldron has turned into a prosaic works convention . . . The discussions that followed the numerous papers were devoid of all heat and pungency. But the sobriety has none the less achieved an intense approach to work,' reported Wolf-Eberhard von Lewinski.[10] It seemed as though everything had become very pallid and mediocre. This was also the subject of a conversation after Adorno's lecture on the function of colour in music, his last at Darmstadt before his death three years later. Singer Carla Henius wrote about it in a memoir of Adorno:

As we were sitting relaxing over a beer, we all grumbled rather peevishly at the alarmingly modest quality of the course participants, about inadequate compositional contributions and about the eternal and inevitable lack of rehearsal time. But since none of those present – Adorno, Stockhausen, Ernst Thomas, Karl O. Koch, Joachim Klaiber and myself – was able to say where the root of the general malaise lay, our joyless commentaries were little more than 'objections not sustained'.

Silence had alread begun to settle . . . when suddenly Stockhausen turned to Adorno and in a cutting tone, albeit extremely politely, scornfully enquired why he was doing nothing to redress the situation. He was still the idol of countless student groups, people listened to him, and consequently he could not get out of saying what people really wanted to hear from him, namely how things could be done better.

Everyone was naturally rather shocked at the mercilessness of this unexpected frontal attack. Yet Adorno seemed to feel neither provoked nor driven into a corner. He did not even sit up in his uncomfortable tavern chair, but after a brief pause for reflection, without raising his voice, said very calmly, 'I cannot do that – I have not learned how to do it.' His profession was to ponder things, and to write books, not to become a dilettante organizer, possibly causing unforeseeable damage . . . Stockhausen was the first to concede that Adorno was right.[11]

The 'negative dialectician' and the 'metaphysician' had a high regard for one another, but had never managed a deeper level of mutual understanding. Twenty years later Stockhausen viewed Adorno as a man whose facial expression, with his glasses, had something owlish about it, and who, when asked about the deeper meaning of the whole, grew nervous, grasped for his glass of wine and shut up.

California, November 1966 to April 1967

Stockhausen had been invited to spend six months at the University of California in Davis as visiting professor in composition. After his arrival at the start of November 1966 he began work on a commission from

Leonard Bernstein for the 125th anniversary of the New York Philharmonic Orchestra in 1967: *Projektion* for orchestra. Stockhausen had found
lodgings in the artists' quarter of Sausalito, facing San Francisco from
the opposite end of the Golden Gate Bridge; the house had a direct view
of San Francisco Bay. California, equidistant from Europe and Asia, had
always been a focal point for eastern philosophy and religion within
the USA. At that time San Francisco was the goal of American hippie
pilgrimages, and psychedelic pop music was in its heyday. Stockhausen
got to know this side of California too. Some pop musicians, including
members of The Grateful Dead, came to his public lectures, and at San
Francisco's famous Fillmore West auditorium Stockhausen saw the group
Jefferson Airplane, along with the psychedelic light shows that were
becoming popular. He also had friendly contact with members of a hippie
commune in the neighbourhood. It seems to have been during these
months that the idea of repeated lives on earth first became a serious
preoccupation of Stockhausen. On meeting the anthropologist Nancy
Wyle he felt he had already known her for a long time, and later he told
Mary Bauermeister 'To love is to recognize.' In an interview twenty years
afterwards he expanded on the idea of 'recognition':

Autobiography is merely the conscious expression of a much more far-reaching
memory, I am sure of that. I have found myself back in places where I had
already been in an earlier life: in Japan, India and central America I have
recognized particular houses and streets as *déjà vu*. How often I have met people
with the secret certainty that I know them well. I really do not know where my
autobiography begins, but I know that it is already very old.[12]

Stockhausen had so many things to occupy him that *Projektion* progressed only slowly. A joint music and dance project was conceived
with the American choreographer Jay Marks, who was preparing dance
compositions based on *Kontakte*, *Refrain* and *Klavierstück X* with the San
Francisco Modern Dancers. Stockhausen and Marks spent many hours
in discussions and planning sessions. Project X (the working title) 'is
every choreographer's dream,' said Marks. 'It is a theatre piece in which
the dancers' movements produce sounds that are picked up by contact
microphones. At each performance the sounds are filtered and transformed electronically, so that the music for the dance is created by the
dancers themselves.'[13] It was intended to be premièred as Stockhausen's
commission for the Bremen Pro–Musica Nova festival in May 1968.

Stockhausen had set aside the months of March and April for work
on *Projektion*. He intended that the playing of the orchestra on the stage
would be matched by two films of the same orchestra, projected on to

screens; the conductor on the stage and the two on film would give signs to one another, and the playing of the three orchestras would be completely synchronized. Whereas *Gruppen* for three orchestras had been practically 'stillborn' – it was almost never done with the right layout of the orchestral groups as usually there was some emergency compromise on the problem of space – *Projektion* was meant to obviate this by means of the two 'film orchestras' and their playback on separately mounted loudspeakers. Stockhausen had sketched out the whole work and begun the orchestration, but when he left, *Projektion* was incomplete.

After a short trip to the Yosemite National Park, Stockhausen and Mary Bauermeister were married in San Francisco on 3 April 1967; their son Simon was born later in the year. By way of a California farewell, Stockhausen's friends and students organized a fancy-dress party on a houseboat. Dressed in a grey kimono, Stockhausen was sitting amid thunderous rock music when Jay Marks went over to him. 'Stockhausen smiled at me as I said goodbye. "What do you think of that music?" I asked. "It really blows my mind!", he called out in his almost too perfect English.'[14] At the end of April Stockhausen went back to Germany. Rolf Gehlhaar, a member of his composition class at Davis and a Yale graduate, followed him back to Kürten a little later as his new assistant.

Prozession: A New Beginning in Ensemble Playing

A Scandinavian tour was scheduled for the end of May, and Stockhausen was looking for another piece for the programme. At first he had thought of a version of *Solo* for Harald Bojé and his new electronium, a rebuilt electric Hohner accordion played on a table. But Stockhausen was not satisfied with the potential of the realization. On a railway journey from Cologne to Basle (where the oboist Heinz Holliger was to give the European première of *Solo* on 2 May at the ISCM Festival), an animated conversation with Rolf Gehlhaar gave rise to the idea for a piece for ensemble: a musical process in which – even more radically than in *Plus–Minus* – the indications for the players would consist essentially of only three symbols, plus, minus and equals signs. Plus would mean higher, faster, louder or more segmented, minus would mean the corresponding opposites and the equals sign would mean the same or similar. The musical material was to be 'events' from earlier pieces by Stockhausen. Each performer was to react and establish a relation to such an event, or to the playing of one of the other participants. This was a little reckless, since at the time the ensemble consisted of only two pianists, Bojé and

Kontarsky, and the other musicians from *Mikrophonie I*: Johannes Fritsch, who played viola, and the percussionist Alfred Alings. Back in Cologne the composer summoned the ensemble to Doris Stockhausen's house in Marienburger Strasse. He presented the new work and got the musicians to react to the simplest possible elements – a rhythm or a pitch sequence – using the plus, minus and equals signs.

A little later, on 21 May, the première of *Prozession* took place at the first stop on the tour, Helsinki. Kontarsky was at the piano, Alings at the tamtam with Gehlhaar as microphonist, Fritsch played viola with contact microphone and Bojé played his electronium. Stockhausen controlled the four loudspeakers at the sides of the hall, as well as a filter for viola and tamtam. In the rehearsals the musicians had still been reacting mainly to their own playing, but were gradually beginning to respond to each other, and the combination of the ensemble's various characters and capacities proved successful. In 1985, almost twenty years later, Rolf Gehlhaar summed up the players:

> Kontarsky was the perpetual wag, sometimes a bit coarse and forceful, but controlled and refined. Bojé, a true man of the Ruhrgebiet, liked to creep off into a corner, yet everything that he didn't show outwardly was churning away inside him – a fabulous pianist. Fritsch, always full of ideas, versatile, had a good ear and a lively imagination, but was sometimes rather careless. And Alings, slow and calm, was very dependable. He didn't do much that was new, though he could surprise you now and then. I was taking my first steps as a composer, had lots of ideas and liked experimenting – I was always hanging on to sounds for a very long time, introducing regular durations and periodicity into the playing.[15]

Prozession brought a new beginning to the ensemble playing of the Stockhausen Group. In the course of the performance they had to invent new things, to be instantly creative, and from the concentration of working together and reacting to one another a music emerged whose whole was more than the sum of its individual parts.

Darmstadt 1967: *Ensemble*

After the previous year's reconciliation with Darmstadt, the 1967 Summer Courses operated essentially under the Stockhausen banner, so that people talked jokingly but appropriately about a Rhineland Music Festival, or a Stockhausen Festival. Along with performances of *Mikrophonie I*, *Mixtur* (première of the version for chamber orchestra) and *Prozession* (first German performance), the main event was the evening concert comprising *Ensemble*, the result of Stockhausen's composition course that

40 Darmstadt, 29 August 1967: *Ensemble*, a studio concert of Stockhausen's composition course, given in the Ludwig-Georgs-Gymnasium

year: a four-hour simultaneous concert of works by the participants, each of whom sat with an instrumentalist on a rostrum in a gymnasium as the audience wandered from one to another.

Some months before the twelve young composers had been informed that they should bring a tape with twenty-five sound events (and a tape recorder) or a short-wave radio. During the two-week course each one was to compose as sharply profiled a piece as possible, with a complete individuality of gesture that distinguished it from the others, alternating between duos for instrument and tape, and solos for instrument or tape alone. Eleven instrumentalists from Hudba Dneska, a Czech ensemble from Bratislava conducted by Ladislav Kupković (flute, oboe, clarinet, bassoon, horn, trumpet, trombone, violin, cello, double bass and percussion), and Aloys Kontarsky (piano) also attended. The *Ensemble* evening was created during the course, with Stockhausen composing the overall plan and eight inserts. As he wrote in the programme, it was 'an attempt to introduce a new form into the traditional "concert". We are accustomed to comparing various compositions played one after another. In *Ensemble* the "pieces" of twelve composers are performed simultaneously.'[16] Gehlhaar, who was one of the twelve, described the course and the performance that took place on 29 August:

The concentrated effort and cooperation with which the participants worked on this project were amazing. The atmosphere was electric. Not that Stockhausen tyrannized us, but he made it rather clear that he expected two things from us: work . . . [it] was not over once the parts had been written and assembled. That was only the beginning. The rehearsals and the performance were to test us perhaps more than we had expected. The decisions we had postponed until the performance were important ones and often had to be made with little time for thought. The relationship between composer and instrumentalist sometimes resembled that between coach and player, or between player and fan, or between God and man. Peixinho often, as if possessed, beseechingly got on his knees in front of the double-bass player so that he could give him instructions and influence him more effectively. Beurle swarmed around the violinist with his little information slips, rose on to the tips of his toes at important crescendos, sank to his knees for particularly delicate decrescendos.

Farmer liked the idea of playing from the balcony. Several times during the performance Stockhausen would point his finger into the air, trying to tell Farmer to play a very high pitch. Farmer, of course, thought it was time to go upstairs, and would immediately make his way there.

The efforts of the musicians must be considered no less than heroic – four hours of concentrated playing, *thinking*, producing sounds that some of them politely referred to as barbaric, others as injurious to their technique. Nevertheless they survived. Both.[17]

Hymnen

When Stockhausen's *Hymnen*, electronic music and *musique concrète* with soloists, was given its first performance on 30 November at a WDR concert in the main hall of Cologne's Apostel-Gymnasium, it sparked controversy. Stockhausen was regarded by many as the front-runner of the musical avant-garde; yet the material of this almost two-hour work, divided into four parts (regions), consisted of about forty national anthems from the most diverse countries all over the globe. It was not intended as parody or as the unmasking of antiquated nationalistic thinking, which is why the left-wing critics attacked him so sharply. Instead he wanted to continue what he had begun with *Telemusik*: to write not his own personal music, but a music that incorporated the people of all races and nations. Stockhausen had been collecting national anthems from every country

(137 in all) since 1964 and, in the wake of his experience with *Telemusik* in Japan, he completed the work in a few months after his return.

During a press conference preceding the performance Stockhausen referred to national anthems, the 'what' of his composition, as musically 'the most banal and obvious things imaginable'; they served him as placard-like identification signs for the nations, as a pop-art gesture in his music, comparable to the banal, everyday pictorial motifs of the American pop-artists, whose work Stockhausen knew well. In his conversations with Jonathan Cott, Stockhausen compared Jasper Johns's 'maps' and his hand-painted bronze cast of a beer can with what he was doing in *Hymnen*:[18] something old and familiar is alienated, placed in new contexts, and thus revitalized and made interesting again. But the 'how', the compositional shaping of the materials and the intention behind his work, are of a very different order.

Just as *Telemusik* is bound up with the experience of Japan, so the background for *Hymnen* may be seen – though not so directly – as the USA, and in particular the city of New York (an important centre for American pop art). Stockhausen's aim is to transcend the incoherent juxtaposition of differences, the way nations bounce off one another; *Hymnen* gives shape to a lofty future vision of how humanity can live together, which he had sensed ever more clearly in the preceding years: the divisive factors in races, nations and religions come to form a richly interactive coexistence, in which an individual person is important as one segment of a multi-faceted whole. 'America, I have written you this music from the heart,' said Stockhausen three years later in the programme for the American première of the orchestral version of *Hymnen*. 'You could be a model for the whole world, if only you lived as this music proclaims possible.'[19]

Johannes Fritsch regarded *Hymnen* as Stockhausen's greatest composition, a successor to Beethoven's *Missa Solemnis*, Mahler's Eighth Symphony and Schoenberg's *Moses und Aron*. The most important aspect of this multi-level work is the confrontation of the Composer-Ego with the world.

The piece begins with a chaos of short-wave radios, and collective utterances (the '*Internationale*'). The subject awakens: the play begins, as the composer with his Promethean powers goes out into the world. He then becomes a doubter (in the confrontation with '*Deutschland, Deutschland*') and lastly an observer of the processes he has set in motion. In the scherzo the innate forces of the musical development overwhelm the Ego. [Fritsch had previously drawn parallels with the four movements of a symphony.] Finally, through a sort of pull to the centre

153

in the Fourth Region, the subject regains strength, until it divides: one part disappears in sound, and the remaining part becomes its own observer. Memories sweep past . . . The Ego has conquered the world.[20]

In all this, Stockhausen himself is the great crucible he once described Messiaen as being. Impressions of childhood, the experience of nature and personal factors become sound within his pieces and are integrated into their formal plan. In *Hymnen* one hears the buzzing circlings of a little sports plane, a young child's experience as a cowherd in the Bärbro-ich meadows (at the start of the Second Region), the plunging masses of water at the Yosemite Falls in California, which re-emerge in the Fourth Region as several minute-long, powerful glissando sounds that move downwards but never become lower as new ones begin imperceptibly at the top – and the name of a Finnish girlfriend, Iri, which Stockhausen shouts into the enormous blocks of sound in the Fourth Region since he 'felt somewhat strange toward Mary because she was the only person I really loved . . . so that she'd listen to me and forgive me'.[21]

The work ends with the anthem of Stockhausen's own 'Pluramon', 'a symbiotic being combining aspects of both a pluralist and a monist . . . he lives in the Harmondie, which is a combination of harmony and mundus – the world'.[22]

Mexico, January to March 1968, and Madison: Composition of *Stimmung*

Stockhausen was to give a series of lectures and concerts in Mexico City at the end of January. Beforehand he went to Hawaii with Nancy Wyle and then visited the ancient temples and cultural sites of the Mayas and Aztecs. On all his travels Stockhausen has studied buildings and temples.

Even as a student I counted the windows every time I went along a street in Cologne: how many to the left, to the right, how many on top, how many below, whether there was the same number of windows, whether they were the same size and how they were arranged.

It is like a sixth sense of mine and it always makes me measure architecture because of course I know that a temple, in all its dimensions, reflects the profound secret of a harmony that is mathematically sound, and that good music is the same. That is why it fascinates me.

In Mexico I would sit for hours in the ruins of temples, absorbing what the Mayan religion is and the particular character innate in a Mayan temple. Each temple awakens its own religious feelings as part of its atmosphere. The atmosphere is simply there, it just has to arouse a religious feeling, to reanimate that feeling within people. That is something I have experienced, and always in a new way, in Cambodia, India, Thailand, Turkey, Greece, Syria, Lebanon, in Tunisia

41 The Stockhausen Group in Amsterdam for the 'Holland Festival', 1968. *Left to right:* Alfred Alings, Rolf Gehlhaar, Stockhausen, Johannes Fritsch, Harald Bojé and Aloys Kontarsky

and Morocco, in Persia and Israel. And each time I ask myself why the temple was placed in those particular surroundings, where the sun would rise, in what ways it would shape the daily life of the community. I gain enormous enjoyment from making sketches each time I can explore a temple.[23]

But it was not just the Mexican buildings that left a deep impression; the whole aura of the historical past gave rise to an almost obsessive fascination that allowed Stockhausen to transpose himself back into those times:

becoming a Maya, a Toltec, a Zatopec, an Aztec, or a Spaniard – I became the people ... I relived ceremonies, which were sometimes very cruel ... Perhaps I'm still a child concerning this: I imagined a priest standing on top of the 108th step of a pyramid, shouting for the sacrificial victims to be brought up. In the end it was terrible how many people they offered. You get the impression that such ceremonies were constantly taking place.[24]

From Mexico Stockhausen travelled to Madison in Connecticut to join Mary Bauermeister, who had been staying with the children on Long Island Sound in a house belonging to her brother. Still influenced by his impressions of the previous weeks, he immediately began a commission for the Cologne vocal sextet Collegium Vocale. It was wintertime in Madison and Long Island Sound was frozen. There were unbelievably strong winds, and I just watched the white snow on the water in front of my two windows. That was the only landscape I really saw during the composition of the piece.'[25] It was Stockhausen's first purely vocal work since the choruses of his student period. He tried out a few things, rejecting them all until he started intoning various sequences of phonemes, listening carefully to their spectrum – perhaps this was inspired by the singsong of his nine-month-old son – and settled on a compositional idea: *Stimmung*. Over a single static chord, that is sustained for over an hour (a six-note 'timbre spectrum' comprising the second, third, fourth, fifth, seventh and ninth partials of a low B flat), the singers freely bring into play different 'sound models'. Stockhausen assembled phoneme sequences, each with two or more vowels, into sound models that are to be sung in such a way that various overtones predominate. 'One hearkens to the inner sound, to the inner harmonic spectrum, to the inner vowel, to that within',[26] though in this case what Stockhausen means by 'inner' is not a spiritual or mental 'innerness' but the acoustic microworld of sounds themselves.

The pitches and timbres in *Stimmung* are serially ordered while the tempos are organized according to the proportions of the overtones. To reach beyond the almost purely phonetic aspect of the sound models,

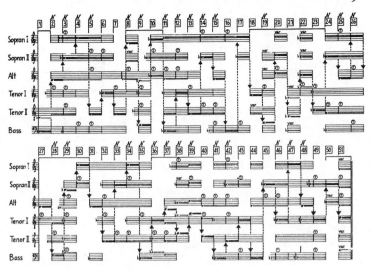

42 *Stimmung* for six vocalists: form scheme

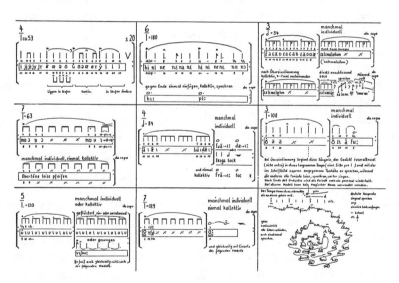

43 *Stimmung*: eight sound models for female voice

44 *Kurzwellen* for six players and short-wave receivers, first quarter of the score

each singer is also given a series of names of gods, compiled by Nancy Wyle from all the earth's cultures – Stockhausen's affirmation of a common thread underlying all religions. These 'magic names' are called out at freely chosen points and integrated by the other musicians into whatever sound model they are singing. A series of erotic poems written for Mary Bauermeister in California a year earlier is also drawn into the work. In *Stimmung*, as in certain parts of *Licht*, religious and erotic elements intermingle in a way that some listeners have found disconcerting.

Stockhausen returned to Europe in March to fulfil concert obligations. He and Mary Bauermeister were to spend two months apart before deciding once again whether or not it would be desirable to go on living together.

Kurzwellen

Stockhausen had been invited to give lectures and concerts in Prague and Bratislava in early April 1968. Czechoslovakia was the third east European country following Poland and Yugoslavia to permit access to New Music. Stockhausen and his ensemble played *Prozession, Hymnen, Kontakte, Zyklus* and *Klavierstück X*. Alfred Schlee, who travelled with them to the Czech capital, was to describe the Prague of that brief spring as an overly happy city. People were in such a state of euphoria that it was difficult to see how they would re-establish contact with everyday life. Everywhere, not just in Prague, there was a sense of imminent revolution, leading to worldwide political unrest, and demanding free forms and improvisation within the arts.

Back in Cologne, a new process composition with plus, minus and equals signs, *Kurzwellen*, was created for Bremen within a few days, as Project X with Jay Marks had failed to materialize. The starting-point for the players' improvisation was no longer earlier compositions but completely unforeseeable 'events' from short-wave receivers: mixtures of Morse-code signals, fragments of speech and intrusions of music. Stockhausen was attracted to short-wave sounds by more than the search for different acoustic material for a new piece. For years he had felt that short-wave receivers transmitted not only the music and sounds of mankind, but also something else: the murmurs of the atmosphere, or even distant spheres, spheric pulses and sounds, as Stockhausen once said – a twentieth-century quest for the harmony of the spheres through the guise of technology and electricity.

The première of this 'quodlibet from a universe of sound, extracted from the musico-technological universe', to use the pertinent words of one critic, took place on 5 May 1968 as part of the Bremen Pro Musica Nova festival.[27] As was to be expected, it provoked many conflicting opinions in the press.

8 *Aus den sieben Tagen* 1968–70

> But it would be bad if you did not at
> least suspect that in your best moments you
> are inspired by intuition, and moreover
> by the presentiment that you have within
> yourselves the possibility of a higher
> existence, which is what sustains your life.
> Stockhausen

May 1968: *Aus den sieben Tagen*

The year 1968 and particularly the days from 6 to 13 May are a focal point in Stockhausen's biography, leading to a radical change in his work that was to have more extreme consequences than any of the previous ones. As student unrest reached a climax after the attempted assassination of Rudi Dutschke, and the May uprising fermented in France, Stockhausen returned to his house in Kürten after the première of *Kurzwellen*. He was expecting the arrival of his wife and children from America, but instead he found a letter: Mary Bauermeister was not coming and had decided to end their relationship. At that moment the emotional tensions of the year-long alternation between being separated and being together unleashed depression, and Stockhausen 'just could not go on'. He sent Rolf Gehlhaar to Cologne so as to be alone, and telegraphed to Madison, begging Mary Bauermeister to come. Stockhausen waited in vain for an answer, and

on the second day of waiting – I had absolutely resolved not to go on living – she became unimportant to me. Even by the second day I noticed that things were happening inside me that no longer had anything to do with this personal situation. During that period I mostly did nothing . . . just sat and found myself asking: who am I, what do I want, what is my goal? I still remember how – it was at the end of the second or third day – I was wandering around in my room. In my bookcase I discovered an old, out-of-print book. It was Satprem's book about Sri Aurobindo. A girl had given it to me one day during a seminar in California. I had never read it but I brought it back home with me. I found that what I was reading was in extraordinary accord with the feelings about life and the spiritual mood that was in me at that moment. I felt that this spirit was entirely kindred to mine, and I identified completely with these ideas.[1]

It was not the first time that an apparently random external stimulus had set something in motion within Stockhausen, something that was already at work below the surface, demanding to be developed. But the experience of this book was more profound. Coming at a crisis point, it was the impulse for a catharsis that immediately generated new music.

On 6 May Stockhausen had begun a hunger strike to induce Mary Bauermeister to return, and for seven days he ate no food. On the evening of the second day, in an extremely intense, highly alert and sensitive frame of mind because of the circumstances, he wrote a text composition for the first time: 'Richtige Dauern' (see below). The player is given a brief, concentrated text, which generally outlines the formal course of the piece and whose content corresponds to a musical process. There are thus no more 'events' or motifs: for the first time the performer is left utterly alone with his or her musical inspirations of the moment.

play a sound
play it for so long
until you feel
that you should stop

again play a sound
play it for so long
until you feel
that you should stop

and so on

stop
when you feel
that you should stop

but whether you play or stop
keep listening to the others

at best play
when people are listening

do not rehearse

In the following days he wrote fourteen more text compositions, later assembled under the title *Aus den sieben Tagen,* as well as a number of philosophical and poetic aphorisms in which he described his relationship to his wife and some of the extreme experiences of those days.

'Goldstaub', the last of these text compositions, written late in the evening of 10 May, runs:

> live completely alone for four days
> without food
> in complete silence, without much movement
> sleep as little as necessary
> think as little as possible
>
> after four days, late at night,
> without conversation beforehand
> play single sounds
>
> WITHOUT THINKING which you are playing
>
> close your eyes
> just listen

This was exactly the situation Stockhausen found himself in that evening:

I had eaten nothing, I was living just as the text says . . . and then on the fourth evening I opened the lid of the piano and played just one note . . . today, I still think that was like the first note of my whole life, of my whole existence, as if I had never heard a note before – how this note shocked me: everything within me was so still, so empty . . . for days on end I had heard nothing but birdsong, and this note hit me like a bombshell – I was super-electric, super-sensitive – and after a long gap, after the first note had completely died away, I played another one . . . and so I heard notes of a length, a beauty, an inner life such as I had never heard before.[2]

Of the fifteen texts in *Aus den sieben tagen*, only twelve are text compositions in the narrow sense. 'Oben und Unten' is set out as an improvised theatre piece. Two others, 'Litanei' and 'Ankunft', are rather generally formulated affirmations of the new beginning marked by *Aus den sieben Tagen*. Stockhausen's concern here is to permanently open up the creative process, the composer's realm of musical ideas, and to make it accessible to ensemble playing. This reveals Stockhausen's affinity with Sri Aurobindo, probably one of this century's most significant representatives of Indian intellectual life, who implanted revolutionary thinking in the ancient spiritual tradition of his country. Above all, Stockhausen found confirmation of his musical path from *Prozession* via *Kurzwellen* to *Aus den sieben Tagen*.

Satprem represented Aurobindo's first essential thoughts in terms of yoga: to restrain all the thoughts and stimuli that normally fill our consciousness, to think nothing, and through this empty state to produce the prime conditions for receiving intuitions from a level of consciousness higher than that of daily life. Satprem wrote: 'It is obvious that we must first leave the old land, if we want to discover a new one within us – everything depends on the decisiveness with which we take this step.'[3] That affected Stockhausen directly. It was fundamental to both the pieces preceding *Aus den sieben Tagen* that the score prescribed the minimum and the composer took the risk of completely trusting the players' intuition during the performance. Furthermore, Stockhausen found that Aurobindo's image of the world and mankind came very close to his own experiences and ideas of the last few years.

Four weeks later, on 16 June, he wrote his celebrated 'Freibrief an die Jugend' in response to a request from the French *Journal Musical*, and in it he summed up everything that had strongly influenced him at this time. The younger generation was in revolt from Berkeley to Berlin and from Prague to Peking. And perhaps those months were an awakening not just to a political sensitivity, but something broader: a symptom of the younger generation's search for a new, creative awareness. 'Permanent revolution, constantly start everything afresh, let nothing stultify' – these were the watchwords. Stockhausen felt himself caught up in the upheavals: 'Once again we are making a revolution. But this time across the whole globe. Let us now set ourselves the highest possible goal: a gaining of consciousness that puts the whole of humanity at stake.'[4] He always came back to what was, for him, the central issue of a new, higher consciousness, and at the end he posed the question that might already have occurred to many of the readers: 'What has all this to do with music? Today we must address the Whole. If we grasp that, we shall also produce the right music to make people aware of this Whole.'[5]

It is a question that has constantly been posed in this century, the question of the limits of human awareness, or even the existence of another world. Stockhausen could see that his music required a different type of musician: one who knows that there is something higher than the self and is prepared to develop this higher consciousness gradually. To Stockhausen it had become clear that this realm could be revealed either by spiritual exercise or by an extreme situation in one's life.

Darmstadt 1968: *Musik für ein Haus*

That summer Stockhausen lectured once again at the International New Music Summer Courses in Darmstadt. It is significant that he immediately sought to make the new world of *Aus den sieben Tagen*, with all its consequences and intensity, bear fruit in his composition course. He had undertaken to lead the fourteen students to the limits of their own consciousness. They were to write text compositions that would be performed simultaneously at the end, in a concert lasting many hours, in all the rooms of the Georg-Moller-Haus, the Darmstadt masonic lodge.

After a series of concerts in the musically tradition-bound city of Vienna, where a row arose when the festival director, Michael Gamsjäger, tried to prohibit Stockhausen from chalking the word 'Vietnam' on his tamtam, the composer went to Darmstadt at the beginning of August. He began his course with a presentation of *Prozession* and then placed his *Aus den sieben Tagen* texts in front of the class: 'Now I have nothing more than these little texts. I do not know which way things are heading with me.'[6]

Each participant was given a text to meditate on later. But as soon as Stockhausen had read out a text, he asked everyone what kind of musical process, what duration, dynamic and tempo and what kind and number of instruments they associated with this text. Then he explained: 'I do not want a spiritualist seance – I want music! I do not mean anything mystical, but everything absolutely direct, from concrete experience. What I have in mind is not indeterminacy, but intuitive determinacy!'[7] At first they were startled and confused, and it took all Stockhausen's pedagogic skill to guide them towards what he wanted. He recommended that they become familiar with Aurobindo. Some text compositions were produced, but Stockhausen was not satisfied with the results and kept putting the participants in surprising situations to make them open to new experiences. On one occasion he quite unexpectedly brought the 10 a.m. start of the seminar forward to 5.30 in the morning, and as the students came into the room, still half asleep, a tape of Japanese gagaku and temple music was playing. The next few classes began at 4.30 a.m. and then, after a few days, started late in the afternoon. Stockhausen played works of his own several times over. He took the class in a rented bus to a service at a Jewish synagogue in Frankfurt and another morning they went to a Russian Orthodox church; he arranged to have a Catholic mass read in a Capuchin monastery, specially for them. What he wanted to get across was how higher consciousness may be experienced in religious

45 Darmstadt 1968: Stockhausen's composition course *Musik für ein Haus*. *Left:* Stockhausen; *right:* Rolf Gehlhaar

ceremonies and what kind of effect the architecture and atmosphere of a sacred building contributes to this.

Towards the end of the course Stockhausen assembled the text compositions into an overall plan as *Musik für ein Haus* and, once the instrumental soloists from the Stockhausen Group and a few other players had arrived, the rehearsals commenced. The novelty and difficulty of the tasks for all concerned often created tensions, and Stockhausen was subjected to sharp attacks. But the result was a successful performance on 1 September that soon set a trend.

The search for new, mobile forms of concert-giving begun in *Ensemble* and *Musik für ein Haus* was to go on preoccupying Stockhausen and was resumed whenever the opportunity arose. He was no longer concerned with performing single pieces of music on a stage, but with a total event in which the auditorium was permeated by sounds in motion. In the following years the audience too would have to get used to some unconventional situations: the music having already started when they arrived; the fixed seating having been changed, or not being there at all, so that they had to improvise a place to sit; wandering round during the performance and selecting their own programme (an exciting but testing process for both sides). It was to be some months, however, before Stockhausen was to give the first performance of one of his *Aus den sieben Tagen* text compositions with his ensemble.

Madison, September 1968: *Spiral*

Mary Bauermeister came unexpectedly to Darmstadt for Stockhausen's fortieth birthday. Directly after *Musik für ein Haus* he went back to Madison with her, to realize a commission from the American guitarist Michael Lorimer. In addition, a West German government representative had asked Stockhausen and the Düsseldorf painter and light-artist Otto Piene to make a joint artistic contribution to the German Pavilion at the 1970 World Fair in Osaka. After discussions with Piene, Stockhausen had already started work in Darmstadt. *Hinab-Hinauf* was to be a music–light–space project that united sound, sight and movement in one *Gesamtkunstwerk*. Stockhausen had managed to persuade Fritz Bornemann, the architect of the German Pavilion, to abandon his original concept and build a spherical auditorium. Stockhausen was elated by the prospect of composing music for the spherical auditorium he had conceived in the fifties. His main concern after May 1968 became the project's theme: the various levels of consciousness or existence of mankind and the cosmos. Fifty-five events lead in downward and upward motion, through experiences within eight different levels of consciousness, ranging from the highest level of pure, radiant light down to the microlevel of mere material. At first there is unity between music, the visual elements and spatial movement; then the realms diverge and are displaced, encountering each other in contrapuntal shifts, till at the end the highest level is reached once again, in a realm beyond space and time that Stockhausen depicted in a sketch from those Darmstadt days:

See all the light that the dead have seen.
Hear all the tones that the dead have heard.

See all the light that the unborn shall see.
Hear all the tones that the unborn shall hear.

Time stands still.
Space stands still.

In this time it does not matter –
when you were born.

In this space it does not matter
in what country you were born.

In this time and space it does not matter
whether you are a child, man or woman.

The animal became human.
The human will become a spirit.[8]

In contrast to *Hinab-Hinauf*, the piece for Michael Lorimer was progressing slowly. The young American guitarist wanted to show Stockhausen

all the possibilities of playing the guitar, and of the compositions for guitar written so far. In September I began a work for guitar, but did not get far with it, since I lacked the necessary enthusiasm to check the finger positions for each chord and each passage. Finally I put the work to one side and began the composition of *Spiral*. Lorimer came to Madison, was very surprised by the result and probably somewhat disappointed, since after practising intensely for several days he found the piece 'much too difficult', and would have 'preferred something easier'.[9]

Spiral, written for a soloist with short-wave receiver, became the key solo piece of the following years. In the score Stockhausen again employs the plus, minus and equals signs from *Prozession* and *Kurzwellen*, but extends them further by means of new symbols for ornamentation, polyphonic articulation, periodic divisions, echoes and so on. It places very high demands on the improvisatory capacity of the player or singer, who must rise above his or her acquired skills at each performance whenever one of the score's several 'spiral processes' is reached. Stockhausen described the spiral process thus:

Repeat the previous event several times,
each time transposing it in all parameters,
and transcend it beyond the limits
of the playing/singing technique that
you have used up to this point
and then also beyond the limitations

167

of your instrument/voice.
For this all visual and theatrical possibilities
are also brought into play.
From this point on, retain
what you have experienced in the extension
of your limits, and use it in this
and all future performances of *Spiral*.[10]

Eight months later, on 15 May 1969, the oboist Heinz Holliger gave the première in Yugoslavia, at the Zagreb Biennale, using theatrical elements to create a very humorous effect. At the 1970 World Fair in Osaka *Spiral* was played over 1,300 times in many different versions.

The Premières of *Stimmung* and 'Es'

In October 1968 Stockhausen returned to Germany to teach once again at the Cologne New Music Courses. After a series of concerts at home and abroad, the much awaited première of *Stimmung* took place in Paris on 9 December at French Radio. The performance planned by Alfred Deller for the Stour Music Festival in England in July had had to be cancelled because an unexpectedly large number of rehearsals were necessary to learn the new vocal technique.

The six members of the Collegium Vocale Köln sat with legs crossed on cushions in the darkened foyer, intoning their sound models, bringing the 'magic names' into play and integrating them into a six-note sound spectrum lasting over an hour. Alfred Schlee, Stockhausen's Viennese publisher and friend of many years, who had attended nearly all Stockhausen's premières (including the series of scandals in the fifties), said the atmosphere that evening was 'uniquely beautiful'. Among the audience were Max Ernst and his wife, Dorothea Tanning, as well as Pierre Souvtchinsky, a friend of Stravinsky whom Stockhausen knew from his early years in Paris. It was on that evening that Stockhausen became personally acquainted with Max Ernst.

After *Zeitmasse*, this was the second of Stockhausen's works to be premièred in France. The press had difficulties with what seemed to them to be a completely new Stockhausen, and assumed that this unknown world of sound and the unusual length were the result of Stockhausen's trips to Asia. Directly afterwards, the first German performance of *Stimmung* took place at the Italian Institute as the final concert of the fifth Cologne New Music Course. Stockhausen made it known that this was

168

the last year he would teach at Cologne. He was not prepared to collaborate with Heinrich Lindlar, Hugo Wolfram Schmidt's replacement as director of the Rheinische Musikschule, since for years Lindlar had been writing negatively about Stockhausen's music.

Earlier, on 25 November, two pieces from *Aus den sieben Tagen* – 'Es' and 'Treffpunkt' – had been played in London as part of the Macnaghten Concerts by the Arts Laboratory Ensemble, with Hugh Davies and Stockhausen at the potentiometers. On 15 December the first official performance of 'Es' was given by the Stockhausen Group. Stockhausen had been invited to Brussels for the Rencontre de Musique Contemporaine and was asked for a première. The musicians chose the text with the title 'Es'. At first some persuasion was necessary to get the members of the ensemble to play at all on this basis. Harald Bojé wanted absolutely nothing to do with it – that kind of mental situation is not achieved in three weeks' rehearsal, he said later. Alfred Alings felt that Stockhausen was making life too easy for himself, just giving the players a text; and Kontarsky – according to Stockhausen – 'probably thinks the whole thing was humbug to this day'. Only Johannes Fritsch and Rolf Gehlhaar were immediately interested and fascinated by the musical aspects. Stockhausen convinced the others too and finally the rehearsals began. The text of 'Es' is Stockhausen's direct musical response to the starting-point for the kind of yoga that Aurobindo taught:

> think NOTHING
> wait until it is absolutely still within you
> when you have attained this
> begin to play
>
> as soon as you start to think, stop
> and try to reattain
> the state of NON-THINKING
> then continue playing

At the rehearsals the first versions of the piece were very short; just a few sounds would be played, followed by long pauses. Then gradually people started reacting to one another, and music took shape. The première, once again, was a typical risk on Stockhausen's part. A few critics took ideological exception to the formulation 'think NOTHING' (not surprisingly, given the politicized mood of the times) as well as to the background of this music, which was familiar from Stockhausen's 'Freibrief'. But the risk had a lasting effect.

Stockhausen was forty years old when he underwent the profound changes resulting from his experiences in May 1968 – changes that set free a new level of his personality. For some time he had been having dreams of exceptional intensity and clarity, going far beyond his everyday dreams. He constantly found himself flying, as an eagle or some other great bird. Often the dream was of a vivid reddish violet, which Stockhausen associates with the creative and intuitive sphere. This colour appeared mainly when performances of his works had been particularly successful. The transformation even had external symptoms. Stockhausen, who had never been much concerned with clothes, has had an unmistakable way of dressing ever since: white Mexican shirts ('at two dollars apiece') from a rural market in Oaxaca, light linen trousers from Hawaii and a grey-green, three-quarter length jacket that he found in a teenage shop in Cologne's Hohe Strasse.

'Intuitive music', as he baptized it, is still a very embryonic notion. Stockhausen was later to describe his *Aus den sieben Tagen* text compositions as a kind of 'music from utopia', meaning that it was only in the future that the playing of these pieces could be taken for granted. In the spring of 1969, giving an account of his path as a composer up to that time, he said,

Between 1950 and about 1965 we went through many stages of a primarily rational music, as the end-product of a long tradition, and gradually passed beyond the limits within which most music today is still being constructed. The task now is to steadily widen our experience beyond these limits, and let it feed back into the limited realm of rationality so that, for Heaven's sake, no new duality arises between what is intuitive and what is rational: a situation we know well from the lacerating crises of dialectical composing, which has led many exceptionally talented artists to the verge of silence and to a crippling of their creativity, even to the loss of the meaning of art itself.

The era of intellectual absolutism is coming to an end, and so too, therefore, is the era of artistic products that – in increasing measure – are primarily products portraying the human capacity to think.[11]

Madison, January to April 1969

Apart from new compositions 1969 brought further premières of pieces from *Aus den sieben Tagen*. Stockhausen spent the first three months back in Madison, finally completing the commission from Leonard Bernstein for the New York Philharmonic Orchestra. Since *Projektion* was lying unfinished, Stockhausen proposed expanding the tape of the Third, American Region of *Hymnen* with an orchestral part. Bernstein agreed, and in two and a half months an orchestral score lasting about forty-three minutes was composed.

While he was working on the orchestral parts, Stockhausen drove to see Lukas Foss; it was winter and a snow storm was raging over New York. Foss's apartment had been appointed as the meeting-place for discussions about a joint concert with Stockhausen and the Beatles. The other party (either one of the Beatles or a manager) was delayed for hours because of the weather, and finally Stockhausen returned home. A concert that would have united avant-garde and pop music for the first time never even reached the planning stage. In 1967 the Beatles had honoured Stockhausen by putting his photo on the cover of their *Sergeant Pepper* album. When John Lennon was murdered in December 1980, Stockhausen said in a telephone interview, 'Lennon often used to phone me. He was particularly fond of my *Hymnen* and *Gesang der Jünglinge*, and got many things from them, for example in "Strawberry Fields Forever". And his texts also made young people prick up their ears. In my eyes, John Lennon was the most important mediator between popular and serious music of this century.'[12] After John Lennon, Frank Zappa was probably the pop musician whom Stockhausen regarded most highly; during that stay in Madison he went to hear a concert by Zappa and the 'Mothers of Invention' in New York, and he later met Zappa.

In April Stockhausen returned to Germany, and from 28 May to 4 June he gave a series of seven concerts at the Théâtre National Populaire in Paris, in which the orchestral work *Stop* (in a Paris version conducted by Diego Masson) and 'Setz die Segel' from *Aus den sieben Tagen* were premièred. His family followed him back to Germany, since he and Mary Bauermeister had decided to attempt to live together in Kürten once again. The Madison studio was abandoned.

Further Performances of *Aus den sieben Tagen*

The ill-fated performance of 'Oben und Unten', the theatre piece from *Aus den sieben Tagen*, took place on 22 June at the Holland Festival in Amsterdam. The piece moves between the polarities of those things that are disgusting, ugly and reprehensible – expressed by an actor's words and gestures – and those that are pure, beautiful and spiritual – portrayed by an actress: between these two protagonists sits a child, who repeats what both of them say. The man's aura is reinforced by two 'noisy' instruments, the woman's by two instruments with clear pitches. During the rehearsals both actors asked Stockhausen, in writing, for set texts as a point of reference, since they felt incapable of inventing the texts freely, as Stockhausen demanded. He proposed quotations from the 'Words of Chairman Mao Tse-tung' for the man and passages from Aurobindo for the woman. The effect, however, was very forced and inartistic. The following performance of *Stimmung* (which was being broadcast live) was so disrupted by a few listeners' miaows, howls and imitations of the sound models that, after twice interrupting the playing and asking for quiet, Stockhausen finally had to stop. He and the singers had barely gone off when the stage was occupied, the microphones were grabbed and the airwaves used for musico-political propaganda. In the midst of the hullabaloo it was possible to make out the voice of the well-known Amsterdam composer Peter Schat: 'Whatever you think of this music, the composer has the right to have his music heard!'

In mid-July Stockhausen travelled with a few musicians to St Paul de Vence in southern France. Here, on 26 July, a quite different audience awaited him, for the obligatory critics were accompanied by the prosperous inhabitants of the Côte d'Azur. Every year the rich art dealer Aimé Maeght mounted a week of concerts, the Nuits de la Fondation Maeght, in the inner courtyard of his museum. On the programme was 'Unbegrenzt' from *Aus den sieben Tagen*, with three inserted versions of *Spiral*.

'Musicians were sitting on the roofs, in the courtyard and on the wooden ramps that were constructed for the audience,' Stockhausen told Jonathan Cott.

We started at 6.30 p.m., and when the people began arriving throughout the next hour they could already hear the music from far away. We played until about ten o'clock, integrating not only our instrumental and vocal sounds but also those of the frogs and cicadas and all the other animals which woke up to the rising of the late summer moon. And then, one after another, each musician started walking off, continuing to play, into the forest. (Every once in a while a musician would run back from the forest through the courtyard, only to disappear again, echoing in the night.)

We had built a special small wagon with an almost invisible string for Bojé and his Elektronium, and he was pulled away, while he was playing, through a little gate close to Miró's 'Cosmic Egg' into the Labyrinth of Miró. Michel Portal had two saxophones around his neck, Diego Masson walked around banging a tamtam, and I had a large sliding bird whistle and car horns. And then, one by one, all disappeared further into the pine forest – there was now a full moon, cicadas whirring, dogs barking. After a long time of not knowing what to do, the people tried to follow us, but when someone approached us we hid until he or she passed by. And then slowly they started dialogues of sound signals with us . . . When the people decided to go home they began walking to the parking lots. The last thing I remember occurred about 2.30 in the morning – a twenty-minute-long dialogue with car horns. I started it but then all the people who hadn't left began making horn music with each other, and as one after the other drove off, they exchanged sounds for miles down the road.[13]

At this time Stockhausen visited Marc Chagall, Max Ernst and André Masson, whose studios were not far away. Chagall received him extremely warmly and was visibly delighted to meet the composer whose music had often inspired him while he was painting. It was the start of a friendly relationship that lasted until Chagall's death in 1985; he was already eighty-two at the time. During the rehearsal for 'Unbegrenzt' Stockhausen also got to know Joan Miró, who was working on a series of lithographs; Stockhausen was asked to pick out the one he liked best and Miró signed it for him. He later offered Stockhausen the plot of ground next to his Majorca studio for a summer house, but Stockhausen amicably declined the offer. Miró and Ernst too listened to Stockhausen recordings when they were at work.

Darmstadt 1969

Having been invited once again to lecture at the Summer Courses in Darmstadt, Stockhausen decided to go with his ensemble and Vinko Globokar's Free Music Group and perform all the text compositions from *Aus den sieben Tagen* (with the exception of 'Goldstaub' and 'Oben und Unten') in six seminars, but not to give lectures on them. He was only willing to answer questions. The sheer concentration of 'intuitive playing' and the technical potential of the electro-acoustic equipment meant that the performances had a fascinating effect. To the listener, some pieces were like the tiniest structures of the human organism; others, with their long-sustained notes and ostinatos, evoked the breadth of space. At times the sound of the whole ensemble created music that was an orgy of noise; at others, especially in passages featuring the piano, there was a sense of tender empathy.

Stockhausen had sensed that *Aus den sieben Tagen* would have a baptism of fire in Darmstadt, where the student uprisings and the mood of criticism they had provoked had not failed to leave their mark. The politicization of the media in later years was already slowly getting under way. Many provocative questions were posed after the performances, and Stockhausen was not spared his share of criticism. He simply referred to his own experiences, and said, 'This is what I have learned; those who have ears to hear, let them hear.' He was conscious of Schoenberg's comment with regard to Eisler and his politically engaged music: it was better to make good music than hang a political cape round one's neck.

There was a disagreement between Stockhausen and Globokar (composer and trombone virtuoso) about who 'owned' the improvised *Aus den sieben Tagen* pieces. Globokar regarded himself as a co-composer, since he was creatively involved and thus assumed partial responsibility. Stockhausen asserted that the text, which defined the processual course of the piece, was his and that therefore he alone was the composer responsible for the music. This controversy later became a 'moral question' for Globokar, and on the record sleeves of *Aus den sieben Tagen* he had himself referred to as a trombonist who wished to remain anonymous. Stockhausen's riposte was, 'Of course you want to make your own reputation, and not be under Stockhausen's thumb.'[14]

'Music for the Beethovenhalle' and a Concert in the Jeita Grotto

After the première of 'Intensität' on 11 September at the Venice Biennale – the last for a while of a text from *Aus den sieben Tagen* – Stockhausen went to Corsica. He and Mary Bauermeister stayed as guests at the summer house of the French biographer of Mahler, Henri Louis de la Grange, and his friend Maurice Fleuret, who was later to organize numerous concerts for Stockhausen in Paris. Stockhausen admired de la Grange's meticulous research and wrote a preface for the first volume of his Mahler biography. In the Couvent d'Alziprato Stockhausen wrote his lengthiest text composition: 'Intervall', a duo for piano, to be played with eyes closed. He dedicated it to his two hosts.

In the following weeks Stockhausen composed *Fresco* and produced four tapes of sound events drawn from Beethoven's music in one of Deutsche Grammophon's studios in Hanover. He had been asked to make a contribution to the impending Beethoven Year. Then, in November, came two concerts that aroused considerable attention. The Bonn general music director, Volker Wangenheim, had heard about the *Ensemble* and *Musik für ein Haus* experiments, and offered Stockhausen all the rooms of the Beethovenhalle for an evening concert, a 'music for the Beethovenhalle'. Stockhausen proposed that simultaneously in all three halls and at four points in the foyer there would be a non-stop programme of many of his works lasting four and a half hours. Even a première was planned. Stockhausen had written *Fresco*, 'wall sounds for meditation', to be played by the Bonn orchestra (divided into four groups) in the foyer as the listeners arrived at the halls, and throughout the whole evening.

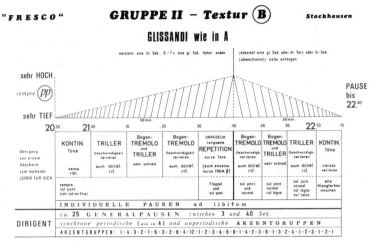

46 *Fresco* for four orchestral groups

A sympathetic orchestra could master the score of *Fresco* without difficulty: very slowly evolving bands and surfaces of sound enter upon and depart from a backdrop of silence. But the members of the orchestra, unaccustomed to contemporary music, rebelled during the rehearsals; at the performance on 15 November they were playing against their will and exuded ill-humour and incomprehension. Snatches of famous passages from the classics and local Rhineland songs, accompanied by the clatter of overturned ashtrays, music stands and beer bottles, could be heard in the foyer. All the standard seating had been removed from the halls, and a colourfully hybrid audience reclined on gym mattresses or wandered through the rooms where most of Stockhausen's pieces from the past fifteen years were being performed or played on tape. But some of the many young listeners, who had presumably expected simply an attractive and amusing evening, made such a noise as they walked around that Stockhausen and the musicians often had to ask for quiet. So the 'Music for the Beethovenhalle' turned out to be an impeccably conceived, ideal concert, but with an inexperienced audience and all those difficulties with German orchestral musicians that were all too familiar to Stockhausen.

Immediately afterwards Stockhausen travelled to the caves of Jeita, near Beirut. The success of the four concerts planned there for 22 to 25 November was even more in doubt than that of the Bonn project had been. Stockhausen and his ensemble were to perform his music in the vast upper stalactite cave of Jeita. In this brightly glistening subterranean

175

world the listeners sat on a gallery to one side, almost lost beneath the gigantic rocky dome. The musicians played on a platform constructed over the abyss. Down below, the rushing of an underground river could be heard. The entrance of the cave was approached by a little cable railway, and the visitors then had to walk for fifteen minutes through a tunnel and on through smaller caves until they reached the main grotto. Along the way they were accompanied by Stockhausen's music, coming softly from hidden loudspeakers. Max Ernst and André Masson had arrived from France. On the first evening Stockhausen shouted out their names and a dedication to these founders of surrealism, and the musicians answered and started transforming the sounds: Ma-ax. Ernst said later that at that moment it seemed as if he had died and was hearing his name on entering a new world.

The peculiar acoustics of the grotto had their own role to play: the sounds reverberated for a very long time and sometimes seemed to roll physically for hundreds of metres along the rock walls, accumulating in a manner never experienced in normal concert halls and stimulating the musicians to shape time and dynamics in a special way. A Catholic priest said of the performance of *Stimmung*, 'It was the longest prayer I have ever known, and the happiest.'[15] All four concerts were sold out, and the Lebanese press praised Stockhausen and his musicians in the most glowing terms.

On 17 December Stockhausen and his ensemble performed his contribution to the Beethoven Year in the Robert-Schumann-Saal in Düsseldorf: *Kurzwellen mit Beethoven Opus 1970*. He had confronted his musicians with the 'improbable special case' that

from all the short-wave receivers – however one tuned them – would come Beethoven's music, at one point interspersed with excerpts from the Heiligenstadt Testament. Instead of the short-wave receivers each of the four players has a tape recorder that can play back continuous recordings of fragments of Beethoven's music whenever the player turns up the loudspeaker. I have manipulated the tapes in such a way that they have the characteristic sound of short-wave transmissions. It is certainly in the spirit of Beethoven – who is a timeless, universal spirit – that the whole of his music (and not just a 'theme' from it) should be used as material for *immediate development*, in which not only segments, but *even the individual notes and timbres are spontaneously 'developed' at the moment they are heard.*[16]

47 The Stockhausen Group plays *Hymnen* in the great cave at Jeita, Lebanon, 25 November 1969

Osaka World Fair 1970: Concerts in the Spherical Auditorium at Osaka

A change was made to Stockhausen's Osaka project after he and Otto Piene had already made considerable progress on *Hinab-Hinauf*. The committee of the World Fair had rejected their concept, without giving reasons, and Stockhausen was asked to plan a daily five-hour programme of his works to last throughout the exhibition. In December 1969 and January 1970, with Osaka in mind, Stockhausen composed a new score for a 'duo', employing the same sort of symbols as in *Spiral*, in which both interpreters use short-wave receivers. It was later titled *Pole*.

In February Stockhausen spent three weeks in Bali, where he wrote another piece with short-wave receivers for Osaka – *Expo* for three soloists – and further text compositions. He visited temples and pagodas, and came across Ramayana performances, gamelan concerts and other examples of Balinese music and dance.

The following six months marked the peak of Stockhausen's concert-giving. Every day from 14 March to 14 September an afternoon and an evening programme of his works was performed in the German Pavilion at the World Fair. In addition to the musicians of his ensemble and the Collegium Vocale Köln, the players included Karlheinz Böttner (guitar), Christoph Caskel (percussion), Peter Eötvös (piano and 55–chord), Gerard Frémy (piano), David Johnson (flute), Mesias Maiguashca (sound projection), Michael Ranta (percussion), Edward Tarr (trumpet) and Michael Vetter (electrically amplified recorder).

The metallic blue spherical auditorium stood at the edge of a garden-like site, from which a broad spiral staircase led down into the underground exhibition halls of the German Pavilion. After walking through the cylindrical halls, visitors went up an escalator into roughly the middle of the spherical auditorium; they sat on ochre-coloured cushions on a sound-transparent platform opposite the entrance, just below the equator level. When conceiving *Hinab-Hinauf*, the idea had been that the audience would enter the auditorium at the base of the sphere and be moved up and down on the platform to Stockhausen's music and Piene's light projections. The sphere was roughly twenty-eight metres in diameter and held about six hundred people. Slightly elevated on the walls of the sphere were six little balconies – Stockhausen called them 'nests' – on which the soloists played. Stockhausen was seated at the mixing desk behind the escalator entrance, controlling the sound coming from fifty-five loudspeakers arranged in seven rings from the north pole to the south pole of the sphere.

48 World Fair in Osaka, 1970: Stockhausen at the mixing desk in the spherical auditorium of the German Pavilion. *Left:* Peter Eötvös

Stockhausen had taken into account the probable restlessness of the listeners, who would already have been exposed to many impressive events, and divided each afternoon programme into five or six different works. Every performance was briefly announced in English and Japanese as a new audience was admitted. In the evening the programmes were longer and went on to about 10.30. As soon as the musicians began playing with the lights lowered, there was an atmosphere of concentration. Many visitors felt the spherical auditorium to be an oasis of calm amidst the general hubbub, and after a while it became one of the main attractions of Expo 1970.

Here, for the first time, Stockhausen was able to work fully surrounded by the electro-acoustic movement of sounds. Using a technical set-up he had designed himself, he could project the sound in circular and spiral paths. A phenomenon that had preoccupied Stockhausen since 1958 had now become technically possible.

To sit inside the sound, to be surrounded by the sound, to be able to follow and experience the movement of the sounds, their speeds and forms in which they move: all this actually creates a completely new situation for musical experience. 'Musical space travel' has finally achieved a three-dimensional spatiality with this auditorium, in contrast to all my previous performances with their *one* horizontal ring of loudspeakers around the listeners.[17]

All the same, Stockhausen could not help noticing the variable quality of his *intuitive* pieces. They were very dependent on the physical and spiritual outlook of the musicians, some of whom had been taking drugs 'as a result of meeting American hippies who,' as Stockhausen put it, 'were contaminating the whole globe at that time with their psychedelic experiments'.

When the World Fair ended, attempts were made to preserve the spherical auditorium and rebuild it in a German city; Berlin, Munich and Cologne had shown interest. Stockhausen's preference was to have it on the roof of a much visited high-rise block, such as the Kaufhof in Cologne. But the costs of transport, reconstruction and maintenance were so high that the plan was rejected.

In mid-June Stockhausen left Japan and he and Mary Bauermeister visited the island of Ceylon, where the Kataragama Festival, a religious celebration by Hindhus, Buddhists and Muslims, was taking place. Sinhalese musical improvisations in a temple and memories of Japan stimulated the text compositions 'Ceylon', 'Japan' and six others.

On his return to Kürten Stockhausen received a letter from Fritsch and Gehlhaar in Japan. The composers among the interpreters in Japan were finding the same problem Globokar had had the year before in Darmstadt. Both of them informed Stockhausen that once their concert commitments in Japan were over, they wanted to leave his ensemble and form a group of their own, called Feedback, with David Johnson. Stockhausen was deeply hurt. Fritsch and Gehlhaar, whose assistantship had ended that year, had taken this decision in order to become independent from the man who had permanently influenced the way they thought about composing. Their departure was a great loss, since they had constantly been an important stimulus to the group's intuitive playing and had taken part in countless rehearsals and performances. A whole series of concerts in the coming months had to be cancelled, and Stockhausen reacted quickly. He replaced Alfred Alings, who had left the ensemble before Osaka, with Christoph Caskel. Peter Eötvös, the Hungarian composer, conductor and pianist who had played with the group since 1968, would now be a permanent member. In November 1970 the Munich composer and viola player Joachim Krist became Stockhausen's new assistant. Some months later he too joined the ensemble.

Darmstadt 1970

A few weeks after receiving the letter from Japan Stockhausen went to Darmstadt to teach at the International Summer Course. A new seminar project, 'Musik im Wald' (Music in the woods), an outdoor sequel to *Musik für ein Haus* to be rehearsed and performed in the woodlands around Schloss Kranichstein, had been abandoned by Stockhausen some months earlier. It seemed to be a time for looking back and, as in 1961, Stockhausen gave an account of the past ten years of New Music. His six seminars – 'Micro- and Macro-continuum', 'Meta-collage and Integration', 'Expansion of the Tempo Scale', 'Feedback', 'Spectral Harmonics and Expansion of Dynamics' and 'Spatial Music' – have become a cornerstone in the history of Darmstadt. Speaking with extreme concentration and dynamism, Stockhausen talked far into the night and stimulated the majority of students. That year in Darmstadt some things were being radically questioned. The younger generation was looking for new social structures; it demanded participation in the shaping of programmes, and there were 'delegations' and a 'plenary session'. But the contrast between these seminars and those of the previous year made it clear that Stockhausen's way of composing was about to take another turning. With the break-up of the Osaka ensemble and the retrospective of the past ten years of New Music, he had commenced – for the third time – a year of major changes.

9 Music as Gateway to the Spiritual 1970–74

> The essential aspect of my music is always
> religious and spiritual; the technical
> aspect is mere explanation.
> Stockhausen

Mantra: The Beginnings of Formula Composition

In the summer of 1968 Stockhausen had told the participants in his Darmstadt composition course, 'Those of you who know me know that I shall not be standing still in my current position, that is, using verbal notations like those of *Aus den sieben Tagen*.'[1]

In Osaka Stochausen began work on a commission for the 1970 Donaueschingen Festival: a sort of action-score for two pianists, relating back to an idea he had had the previous year during a flight from New York to Los Angeles: the pianists come on stage, miming various playing movements in the air, which, when they sit down are transferred to the keyboard, becoming single notes and chords. In the course of the music this process was to become a unity, a *Vision* for two pianists. As performers, Stockhausen thought of the Kontarsky brothers, the trusty piano duo. But after a two-week tour of Australia in which he presented his electronic works and gave lectures, Stockhausen lost all desire to go on with the piece. The main reasons may have been some unsatisfactory performances of the intuitive pieces and the question of the authorship of this music fermenting among the composers-cum-interpreters.

A year later, in his conversation with Jonathan Cott, Stockhausen explained: 'I felt that I wanted to develop further a kind of music that only I was responsible for and not only make music with our group or with other musicians where I proposed rather than "ordered".'[2] His mind made up, Stockhausen put *Vision* aside and took up another idea: a melody that had also occurred to him the previous year in the USA, during a car journey from Madison to Boston.

I was sitting next to the driver, and I just let my imagination completely loose . . . I was humming to myself . . . I heard this melody – it all came very quickly together: I had the idea of one single musical figure or formula that would be expanded over a very long period of time, and by that I meant fifty or sixty

49 Formula for *Mantra* for two pianists

minutes. And these notes were the centres around which I'd continually present the same formula in a smaller form . . . I wrote this melody down on an envelope.[3]

The idea of letting a melody, each note of which is characterized in a particular way (grace-notes, embellishments, trills, etc.), be a musical miniature that acts as a formula from which every detail of the composition is derived through permutations, expansions and compressions was the beginning of a change in Stockhausen's way of composing. The melody itself became the formula for *Mantra* for two pianists and ring-modulated pianos, his first exactly notated composition since *Carré*. The formal plan was created within seven weeks in Osaka, and on his return from Ceylon Stockhausen wrote out the music. Alfons and Aloys Kontarsky gave the first performance of *Mantra* in Donaueschingen on 18 October.

In the following years exactly notated works came into being alongside music composed in a more open way; *Ylem* (1972) is Stockhausen's last text composition to date, and in the mid-seventies he turned exclusively to formula composition. *Mantra* re-established links with the exactly notated works of the fifties, but the pendulum had swung from the single notes, the 'points' of the early days, to melody. For Stockhausen formula composition meant the end of an important achievement: his aleatory and intuitive music had probed the creative capacities of the instrumentalists, though in the works of the previous three years the emphasis had been

183

not so much on the work as a composition as on the common creative process of the whole ensemble. There is no question that Stockhausen was the most important, even irreplaceable part of it. His restless spirit, always looking for new things, and his tirelessly active imagination forced him onwards. In formula composition he had found a technique in which the formula – as a musical miniature – provides a compositional framework but leaves open the question of *how* it is to be worked out.

It is no coincidence that shortly after composing *Mantra*, Stockhausen rediscovered a work he had withdrawn in 1951 because it did not fit in with the 'point' style of that period. When Maurice Fleuret asked him for a new piece for the 1971 Journées de Musique Contemporaine in Paris, Stockhausen gave him the study for orchestra written just after *Kreuzspiel*. Viewed in retrospect, its melodious aspects and the way they were developed seemed like the germ of *Mantra;* Stockhausen now titled it *Formel*. He conducted the première himself on 22 October at the Théâtre de Ville. Compositions from his student period were also performed for the first time: Brigitte Fassbaender sang the *Drei Lieder* for contralto and chamber orchestra, Marcel Couraud's chamber chorus sang the *Chöre für Doris* and the chorale, and Saschko Gawriloff and Aloys Kontarsky played the sonatine for violin and piano.

A Year of Radical Change

The departure of Fritsch and Gehlhaar from the Stockhausen Group began another year of crises. In spring 1971 came the final separation of Stockhausen and Mary Bauermeister. When she and the children departed, it was the end of Stockhausen's life on the move between Germany and the USA – in future he would only leave his house in Kürten for concert tours, lectures and courses.

In the same year Stockhausen broke with Universal Edition, his Viennese publisher for many years, because a whole series of works had still not been printed. He had never made life easy for Alfred Schlee when it came to bringing out his often complicated and unconventionally notated scores: Schlee had to prevail on his printers to carry out instructions that were exact to the millimetre and increasingly demanding in terms of the artistic presentation of the scores. The publications fell further and further behind. Stockhausen found the situation intolerable, and looked for new ways of bringing out his works.

In the weeks surrounding the separation from Mary Bauermeister Stockhausen composed *Sternklang*, a 'park music', as a commission for the Berliner Festwochen of 1971. Five groups, each of four singers and instrumentalists with amplification (some of the instruments are combined with synthesizers), play in a park, as far apart as possible but within hearing range. *Sternklang* consists of sound models written on the same principle as those in *Stimmung*, derived from various constellations. Instead of the 'magic names' of gods, the musicians are given little drawings of constellations, which in good weather should be read directly from the night sky. They are integrated into the work as 'musical figures'.

Around four thousand people came to Berlin's English Garden on 5 June 1971 to hear the première of Stockhausen's park music. It had been raining for days, but just before the performance the last clouds drifted away and a clear starry sky formed a vault across the garden. Each group had a 'sound-runner' who carried its sound models to other groups, which musically integrated them. Torch-bearers ran ahead of the sound-runners, making a pathway for them through the audience. In a tutti passage during the last third of the work, everyone joined together in 'Aufwärts' from *Aus den sieben Tagen*. The groups involved were the Collegium Vocale, an expanded Stockhausen Group, Hugh Davies and Gentle Fire from London, and Roger Smalley and Tim Souster with Intermodulation from Cambridge. Just before midnight the last sound rang out – the park became silent, and the clouds drew together once more.

In the programme for *Mantra* Stockhausen had cited an extended passage from Satprem's book on Aurobindo concerning the magic and sacred effect of musical sound in ancient India. In the one for *Sternklang* he spelt out clearly what music meant to him: '*Sternklang* is sacred music . . . Music for concentrated listening in meditation, for the sinking of the individual in the cosmic whole. It is intended as a preparation for beings from the other stars and their arrival.'[4]

At the Height of His Fame

At the beginning of the seventies Stockhausen reached the peak of his popularity. His concerts in the spherical auditorium in Osaka were covered by the international press and television, and he was world-famous. The West German president Gustav Heinemann and his wife, who had got to know Stockhausen's music in Osaka, invited him to the Villa Hammerschmidt for a performance of *Stimmung*. Stockhausen also met Willy Brandt several times. When the city of Brühl decided to honour its long-ignored son Max Ernst with an eightieth-birthday exhibition, he requested Stockhausen's music for the opening. On 15 May Peter Eötvös and Harald Bojé played *Pole* on the steps of Brühl's Schloss Augustus-burg, with Stockhausen at the filters and potentiometers. The audience of diplomats in full dress and evening clothes was probably accustomed to softer sounds on such occasions, and presumably they gritted their teeth during the passages of drastic noise, much to the secret delight of the painter and his composer friend.

A large number of letters from all over the world arrived daily in Kettenberg, including many from young musicians. At the end of the sixties the post-war generation had discovered Stockhausen, and they streamed to his concerts, wherever he appeared. A few days before the New York première of *Hymnen* with orchestra Stockhausen told Jonathan Cott, 'I've had several letters during the last weeks from very young people in Germany . . . They make music in small groups at night in the forest, trying to make the music in harmony with the sound of the forest. And they are really trying to catch waves from distant stars . . . I think there's a new generation, a new consciousness.'[5]

The New York concert on 25 February 1971 turned out to be a breakthrough for Stockhausen in the USA. He was very popular there – his recordings could be found in shops among those of rock and pop musicians but he had not had many performances. *Hymnen* was to be the longest concert in the history of the New York Philharmonic, and the *New York Times* emphasized that 'most of the listeners were young, dressed youthfully à la mode: denims, long hair, hot pants, the works'. It was the first time the New York Philharmonic had played the 'German avant-garde post 1945', and Stockhausen himself conducted. The rehearsals had started in a frosty atmosphere because in an interview in the *New York Times* Stockhausen had likened working with the New York orchestra to 'scheduled factory labour' and complained about American orchestral musicians who just regarded music as a job. From the first session he had made great demands of the performers and had then been able to carry them along with him. Yet on the dot, the orchestral manager would put a hand on his shoulder and the rehearsal would be over.

The beginning of the concert was considerably delayed due to the unexpected demand for tickets. After intensive rehearsals with Stock-hausen the players' initial tension had relaxed, and the performance of the Third Region had something of a circus atmosphere. American musicians love contact with their audience, and during the Spanish anthem the cellist let his instrument whirl round on its spike. At the end of the concert Stockhausen was greeted with an ovation lasting for many minutes, and the evening was enthusiastically hailed as the opening of a

50 New York, 25 February 1971: première of *Hymnen* with orchestra in the
Philharmonic Hall of the Lincoln Center

new era in New York's musical life. The young people from the Green-wich Village arts scene, many of whom had pony-tails, applauded him frenetically; Stockhausen too had his hair, which had grown to shoulder length, tied back.

After the performance a remarkable figure came down the central aisle of the Philharmonic Hall towards Stockhausen – long hair, a beard, bare legs, galoshes on his feet, a staff in his right hand and a book in his left. Unembarrassed, and audible on all sides, he called out, 'Stockhausen, can I talk to you?' Back in the dressing room he played something on a flute he had made himself and sold Stockhausen the large volume beneath his arm. Called *The Urantia Book*, it was a cosmogony of the Urantia Brotherhood of Chicago, one of the innumerable religious groups in the USA.[6] The book was to prove important for Stockhausen in his great musico-dramatic cycle *Licht*.

The highlight of the year was the Festival of Arts Shiraz-Persepolis, a pomp-laden celebration of two and a half thousand years of ancient Persia. Empress Farah Diba loved the arts, and had the leading artists from all over the world invited: the performances were a rendezvous for the international jet set. That year the festival was dedicated mainly to Stockhausen's works: a night-time performance of *Hymnen* with soloists in the ruins of Persepolis and a series of concerts in Shiraz, including a day of 'Music in the City' when *Aus den sieben Tagen* could be heard at various places in the inner city from dawn to dusk. To end the festival *Sternklang* was played for the common people – a great attraction. As the gates of Delgosha Park were opened, early in the evening, a seething mass of about eight thousand poured up the star-shaped converging paths and the atmosphere was like a powder-keg. The mood of the musicians was very tense. The park had no broad grassy areas, so the spectators squashed together on the pathways, besieging the performers. Some of the many young people immediately clambered up the loudspeaker scaffolding and were hauled down again by the police, who were standing guard by the five groups of musicians. Stockhausen was convinced that his music would calm the listeners. And so it was. After half an hour of music the waves subsided. Over the whole scene was a starry Persian heaven – southerly constellations, a dark blue sky and stars that shone more brightly than in central Europe.

Whereas Stockhausen had become a symbolic figure in New Music abroad, in Germany, especially since his 1968 turn-about, he had become a target for criticism. Musical life had become politicized after the student revolt. Marx, Mao and Marcuse furnished fuel for arguments here too, and in the leftist camp the call for a music 'in the service of the class struggle' was growing louder. Even Cornelius Cardew in London had turned Maoist and thundered against his former teacher as a 'servant of capitalism'. Konrad Boehmer, who had been living in Amsterdam for some years, wrote about Stockhausen and 'Imperialism as the Highest Stage of Capitalist Avant-gardism', an allusion to Lenin's writings.[7] But in the hot-headed climate of those years music came to matter less than socio-political questions and ideology. For some Stockhausen was too élitist, for others too mystical; although malicious criticism did not make his life easy, he went his own way consistently and entered the arena of controversy when he had to.

Jill Purce, the Spiral and Musical Esotericism in Islam

In May 1971 Stockhausen got to know the English art historian Jill Purce in London. She had come along to a performance of *Spiral* because she was working on an extensive research project concerning the spiral as symbol and formal principle in nature, art and religion. An important basis for these investigations was her observations on the 'sensible chaos' of running water. She had also studied the researches of Theodor Schwenk.[8] All the formal contours of flowing water lead back essentially to spiral movements; the spiral seems to be the mobile trace, the expression of a cosmic life force – of what Rudolf Steiner in his anthroposophy dubbed etheric formative powers. Stockhausen was very interested in these phenomena, since at that moment he was planning a multi-media project commissioned by Kiel Opera House for the 1972 Aquatic Olympics – 'Aqua-Divina', on the holy power of water – and the music was to be played in the water. The work did not get beyond the planning stage. Stockhausen soon established a close friendship with Jill Purce, and part of her book *The Mystic Spiral*, as well as her essay 'The Spiral in the Music of Karlheinz Stockhausen' was written at Stockhausen's house in Kürten.[9]

Jill Purce had connections with the Sufi movement, a mystical current within Islam that had an important centre in London at that time. Through her Stockhausen discovered the writings of the Sufi musician Hazrat Inayat Khan, and in the following years he always gladly mentioned and quoted Khan, his favourite reading matter. In some respects Khan's ideas are reminiscent of the medieval theory of *musica mundana, musica humana* and *musica instrumentalis:*

189

What we call music in our everyday language is only a miniature, which our intelligence has grasped from that music or harmony of the whole universe which is working behind everything, and which is the source and origin of nature . . . Music is a miniature of the harmony of the whole universe, for the harmony of the universe is life itself, and man, being a miniature of the universe, shows harmonious and inharmonious chords in his pulsation, in the beat of his heart, in his vibration, rhythm and tone. His health or illness, his joy or discomfort, all show the music or lack of music in his life.[10]

Stockhausen had now become interested in esoteric writers of the most diverse kinds: for example, Jakob Böhme and Nostradamus, Robert James Lee (adviser to Queen Victoria), the theosophist Helena Blavatsky, and Jakob Lorber (1800–1864) described by his adherents as a modern prophet. At the age of forty-two this music teacher from Graz heard a voice saying 'Take up thy stylus and write', and he went on to produce twenty-five volumes of 'New Revelations'. Stockhausen later set one of Lorber's texts in *Sirius*.

Trans: A Composed Dream

Trans, the orchestral composition that followed immediately after *Sternklang*, has a special position among all the works written since 1968. Every detail of it relates back to a dream Stockhausen had in December 1970: an orchestra becomes visible with heads protruding from the clouds. Two rows of strings are bathed in a hazy purple light (the reddish violet from 1968); they play with stiff, puppet-like movements, producing a dense, static web of sound. Each time a Norn-like time-stroke rings out, with the whizzing noise of a weaving loom, the web alters. The string sounds are like a wall that sometimes opens, and behind them several groups of wind and percussion are heard playing parallel lines over a low-pitched melody line, like mixture stops on an organ. The whole effect is of a music from the beyond: there is something else, apart from this audible world, but it cannot be seen. Stockhausen had told Otto Tomek (who became festival director after the death of Heinrich Strobel in 1970) about his dream, and his plan to make a work out of it; a few weeks later *Trans* was commissioned for Donaueschingen 1971. Originally it was called 'Musik für den nächsten Toten' (Music for the next to die), and as he was working Stockhausen felt he was composing music that – like the *Tibetan Book of the Dead* – would help a dead person at the beginning of their journey to the beyond.

As the curtain rose at the première on 16 October, a general 'Ooohhh' rang out, part astonished, part ironic. The stage, illuminated in reddish

51 In the early seventies

violet, lay behind a gauze curtain; the strings were in black, like waxworks; the wind and brass were concealed behind a black wall, and their playing was heard amplified over loudspeakers. In an interview a little later Stockhausen used the effect of the concealed players to raise a question – a fundamental question, as he himself said – that had always occupied him: can a musician be replaced by a tape recording?

It *would* be possible to give a performance of *Trans* sometime in which there are absolutely no musicians behind the strings and the music is just played back on tape . . . And what then? Would people notice? . . . In perhaps ten or twenty years people will suddenly wake up and say . . . Can we have the orchestra playing back on tape too? *Or:* do the musicians really send out vibrations at the moment they play that are absolutely vital to music? I firmly believe so! . . . What we have called music up to now was just an excerpt from the music and never the whole music! It was just the acoustic waves. But we know very well that when we hear a musician play 'live', *if* he or she is inspired, then there is always something extra (usually not very much, unfortunately).[11]

The management of orchestras, lack of rehearsal time and tight deadlines, however, has meant that the wind parts in performances of *Trans* are generally taped.

The Beginnings of Scenic Music: *Alphabet für Liège*

Trans is the first piece in which all the visual elements – movements and colours – are incorporated into the composition. It is the start of what Stockhausen calls 'scenic music'. There were already isolated scenic elements in earlier works, for example at the start of *Kontakte*. When the audience is quiet, the pianist goes over to the tamtam standing in the middle of the stage and 'sets the global wheel in motion' by touching the upper edge of the instrument with a large metal knitting needle and moving the needle very slowly once round the full circle; the sound is continued in the loudspeakers and the piece begins. Since composing the music-theatre work *Originale* Stockhausen has jotted down many scenic notions or ideas for larger scenic projects in his sketch-books, but most of them have not yet been realized. There is an operatic project in which each protagonist uses a different style from music history, and the styles are then mixed and combined as if they were timbres. Another scenic project bears the title 'Das himmlische Parlament' (The celestial parliament). Almost all his works after *Trans* have been composed as scenic music, always in different ways. Two elements have come to the fore: the combination of movement and music, not as dance or ballet in the traditional sense but as gestures and movements that are conceived by Stockhausen himself so as to accord with the playing of an orchestra or a soloist; and the expansion of pieces of music into little scenes that are theatre too. Stockhausen's 'will to form' no longer leaves anything to chance: everything has to be shaped, integrated into the composition, 'musicalized'. It is the first step towards an all-embracing music theatre, which Stockhausen was to embark on in *Licht* six years after the première of *Trans*.

As Stockhausen once stressed, he almost always hears and sees something inwardly – often at night – and then seeks the place and time to realize it. When Belgian Radio commissioned a piece for the Nuits de Septembre 1972 in Liège, he responded in spring by producing the scenic music *Alphabet für Liège*. Stockhausen drafted thirteen 'musical pictures', all of them variants of one theme: sounds and their effects, from making acoustic wave-forms visible to an attempt at the magic mantra sounds of ancient Asia. Stockhausen had exchanged many ideas on this in conversations with Jill Purce. The effect of sound on matter was her second area of study, and she drew Stockhausen's attention to the research of Hans Jenny, who was making a phenomenological investigation of the vibratory effects of waves in tangible matter.[12] The whole event took its name from a musical alphabet that Stockhausen had drawn up. There were thirty little cards: *A*nrufen (invoking), *B*egleiten (accompanying), *C*haos, etc. All the players had to draw two cards and at any time they wished during the performance had to go over to one of the others and respond musically to what they heard in terms of whatever was on their card.

Stockhausen has imagined the work being performed in a labyrinth-like building. In the end they decided to use the underground level of a half-finished radio building in Liège: fourteen basement areas, all leading off from a central corridor. At the première on 23 September they presented a piece of scenic music lasting four hours. The walls had been whitewashed for the performance; the doors and studio windows had not yet been fitted. Hans-Alderig Billig, the bass in Collegium Vocale, with pianist Herbert Henck at the synthesizer made the vibratory form of sounds visible; Gaby Rodens from the Collegium Vocale sang into dough – 'Magnetizing food with sounds' – and Jill Purce let a pendulum swing above it. Wolfgang Fromme intoned mantras to 'harmonize the seven centres of the body'. Among the other scenes were 'Shattering glass with sounds', 'Massaging a human body with sounds' and 'Praying with sounds'. In Liège only eleven of the thirteen scenes were performed; Peter Eötvös was the 'musical director' and Stockhausen drew up a plan to regulate the whole thing. In this colourful display, ranging from the acoustic physics laboratory to esoteric practices – sometimes the hint of the fairground booth – Stockhausen hurled out the question, 'What are the effective domains of sounds, in inanimate matter, and mankind?'[13]

The key piece within *Alphabet* is the 'Indianerlieder' 'Am Himmel wandere ich . . .', twelve two-part songs based on texts by the American Indians concerning love, God and death. The first song uses just one note, the second two and so on until in the last all twelve semitones have been unfolded. The performers are given some freedom in the shaping of tempo, dynamics, fermata and pauses, but scenically the work is very exactly planned: 'The singers sit with legs crossed facing each other on a rug at the front edge of the stage at the eye-level of the audience. Every movement is exactly notated – from the rhythm of the eyelids to the ecstatic dance . . . The singers should only perform this music if they can completely identify with *what* they sing.'[14] In following years the songs were given many successful performances by the artists of that evening: Helga Hamm-Albrecht and Karl O. Barkey.

Professor of Composition in Cologne

In autumn 1971 Stockhausen took over as director of a composition class at the Hochschule für Musik in Cologne. The director Heinz Schröter had been asking him to do so for some years, but for various reasons he had not accepted the offer. Early in November, a few days after the premières of his student compositions in Paris, Stockhausen began his classes in Cologne, exactly twenty years after he had taken his own final exams there. At WDR, where fears seemed to have been expressed for some while that Stockhausen was becoming too overbearing as director of the electronic studio, the Cologne professorship was taken as an opportunity to relieve him of this post in 1973 on the grounds that it was not possible for someone to be employed at two different public institutions. Stockhausen has remained as 'adviser to the studio'.

Stockhausen's students over the next six years included his assistant Joachim Krist, Clarence Barlow, John McGuire, Robert H. P. Platz, Christian Petrescu, Wolfgang Rihm, Mark Tezak, Claude Vivier and Kevin Volans. Rihm's basic style was already established, and a few years later enjoyed a rapid rise to fame. In 1986, when Stockhausen was awarded the Ernst von Siemens Prize, Rihm gave the congratulatory address;

That was the first thing I sensed when, for a short period in 1972, I became a nominal Stockhausen pupil (and have been ever since 'under the surface'): your eyes were open, the air could be breathed and your head stayed free. We learn from the surroundings . . . Once during a class Stockhausen said, 'In every work there must be something that makes it utterly different!' That is my paraphrase, no doubt simplified by repeated use: but that was something that stayed with me – a blow struck at the right moment.[15]

The regular topic of Stockhausen's seminars, which generally took place in Kürten, was formula composition. Using the opening of *Mantra* as an example, he showed how a mantra is evolved (at that time he usually used the word 'mantra' rather than 'formula'), imbuing it with as much 'musical information' as possible, and then he would let his students create their own formula compositions. He analysed his own works – the 'Europe Version' of *Momente, Tierkreis, Harlekin, Amour* and many others – and constantly got the young composers involved in his own current projects. When the German Choral Association asked Stockhausen for a

52 Stockhausen and his children in the early seventies. *At the back, left to right:*
Markus, Christel and Suja: *in front:* Majella, Simon and Julika

composition that could be sung by an amateur chorus, he suggested to his students in the winter of 1973–4 that they should write simple choral pieces based on texts by Hazrat Inayat Khan (from a little volume of aphorisms, *The Bowl of the Cup-bearer*). Some of them reacted rather coolly. He began to compose one himself, the idea being they would be published together in a single volume. The project fell through, however, and Stockhausen's piece became the first part of *Atmen gibt das Leben . . .*, his choral opera.

In 1973 Stockhausen began the orchestral composition *Inori*, which called for a highly refined treatment of dynamics of sixty levels, extending from the first for one flute playing pianissimo to the sixtieth in which all instruments play fortissimo. The main topic of the 1974 summer term was the working-out of this scale of dynamics.

After the summer break in 1974, the dynamic scales for *Inori* having been completed, Stockhausen welcomed his students in a most unusual way. He came in, placed *The Urantia Book* on the table with a resounding crunch and said; 'If you want to go on being my pupils, you must read this!' He often spent his seminars talking about the book, which had made its full impact during work on *Inori*; he had a section dealing with the meaning of prayer translated for use in the programme for the forthcoming première in October 1974, though it was not printed since the Urantia Society of Chicago refused permission. *Inori* (a Japanese word meaning 'prayer' or 'invocation') became Stockhausen's great religious affirmation of the seventies.

Inori: A Musical Prayer

The background to *Inori* began in 1970 in Australia, where Stockhausen got to know the very young dancer Philippa Cullen. About three years later the Dai-Ichi Kangyo Bank commissioned a work for large orchestra 'to make a contribution to Japanese culture that will have a lasting value for posterity', and Stockhausen conceived *Inori*, a 'great musical prayer', as he later called it. It was Philippa Cullen's gifts as a dancer that gave Stockhausen the idea of having a dancer-mime portraying prayer gestures along with the orchestral music. Stockhausen studied the praying actions of various religions, and suggested to Nancy Wyle that she should make him a collection of illustrations from all kinds of cultures. He was concerned with creating a harmony of movement and music – one thinks of Rudolf Steiner's eurhythmy, especially the tone eurhythmy – and devised a 'chromatic scale of prayer gestures'.

Inori is evolved from a multi-dimensional formula in which rhythm, dynamics, melody, harmony and polyphony are developed successively in large sections. The formula consists of thirteen notes, each one associated with a particular dynamic, duration, tempo, timbre (that is, vowel timbre) and a prayer gesture. G is the central note, the 'heart' of the work. It is matched with the tempo of the human heartbeat, the syllable 'Hu' (according to Khan, 'the origin and end of all sounds, the holiest of all sounds') and a gesture close to the heart, with hands closed, which is related to a piannissimo dynamic and the longest duration.

When this gesture is performed in a forward direction, moving away from the body, this corresponds to a crescendo from pianissimo to fortissimo ... When the hands rise or sink, this corresponds to changes of pitch, ... when arms or hands drift apart stepwise, ... to a sequence of regularly shortening durations. The various prayer gestures are used as timbres and tempos. By means of these close connections between prayer gestures and musical degrees and intervals, even purely musical alterations are, as the length of the work increases, experienced as prayer.[16]

In 1973 the Brussels-based Ballet du XXième Siècle had opened a tour with *Stimmung*, using choreography by Maurice Béjart. At first there was talk of Béjart as the mime for *Inori*, but it came to nothing. When Stockhausen conducted the South-west Radio Orchestra in the première of *Inori* at the 1974 Donaueschingen Festival, on the podium between conductor and orchestra was the Moroccan dancer and mime Alain Louafi. Stockhausen had arranged a big photographic exhibition, with illustrations of prayer gestures. At that time it was clear that most music critics would find a religious work controversial. 'Of course I knew what a Red Hole Donaueschingen was then: so anti-religious that you can hardly imagine it. To set *Inori* in the midst of that – it was like being Gaudí.'[17] *Inori* was later performed in many European countries, sometimes with two dancers.

Darmstadt 1972 and 1974

While minimal music was the latest fashion in the USA, in Germany there was a new generation of composers whose music was known from the mid-seventies onwards as New Simplicity and New Tonality. They were in search of a new expressivity and were not interested in electronic music and experiments. In 1974 some of their works were performed for the first time in Darmstadt, and it was not long before they were giving lectures there: Hans-Jürgen von Bose, Hans-Christian von Dadelsen,

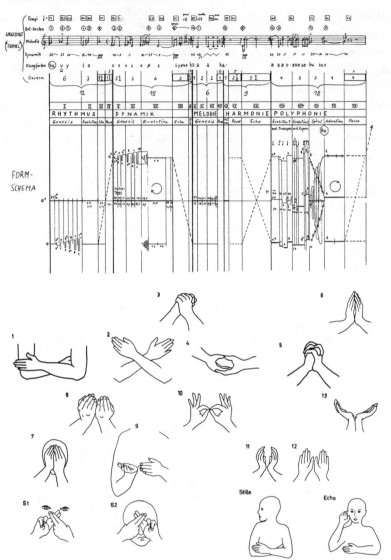

53 Formula and prayer gestures for *Inori*, adorations for one or two soloists and orchestra

Wolfgang von Schweinitz and the exceptional Wolfgang Rihm, to name but a few. Since 1970 some aspects of Darmstadt had changed; there were no courses in 1971 and from 1972 they took place every second year. Composition seminars by the 'big names' were gradually replaced by young composers' studios, and the emphasis was put on creating a forum for the presentation and exchange of all kinds of ideas and works. Another innovation was the instrumentalists' studio, in which tutors studied and performed works alongside students.

In 1972 Stockhausen had given seminars on *Stimmung* and *Mantra*. In 1974 he was in Darmstadt for the last time, having left a decisive mark on the development of New Music there over the previous twenty-three years. Since the score of *Mikrophonie I* had recently been published, he analysed the work, and discussed his 'Indianerlieder'. At the end of the *Stimmung* analysis he stated what was now important to him in his music:

The essential aspect of my music is always religious and spiritual; the technical aspect is mere explanation. I have often been accused of vague mysticism. These days, mysticism is easily misunderstood as something vague. But mysticism is something that cannot be expressed with words, that is: music! The purest musicality is also the purest mysticism in a modern sense. Mysticism is a very incisive capacity to see right through things. To this end, the intellect is a piece of equipment that serves intuition. Intuition, clearly, is not innately present in man, but constantly infiltrates him, like the rays of the sun. Thinking is a way of formulating things, of translating intuition in terms of our equipment, and our practical world – an application to the realms of perception.[18]

10 New Interpreters, New Instrumental Techniques 1974–7

> I do not believe in ensembles that step off a
> plane, work together for a few evenings
> and then split up again. At a theatrical
> performance or in concert, the
> performers must be *one* soul – like in the
> Indian and Balinese dance groups.
> Brotherhood on a 'supra-individual' level.
> Stockhausen

Herbstmusik, Acquaintance with Suzanne Stephens and New Works for Clarinet

At the beginning of 1971 Peter Eötvös, Stockhausen's assistant in the electronic studio at the time, moved from Hungary to Germany, and Stockhausen found him a farmhouse in Oeldorf, not far from Kürten. Soon some other musicians moved in: the Ecuadorian composer Mesias Maiguashca (Stockhausen's second studio assistant), the cellist Gaby Schumacher, David Johnson and Joachim Krist. The Oeldorf Group, as these musicians called themselves, organized a regular Summer Night Music series in the barn attached to their farmhouse, performing their own works and also inviting many guest artists: Philippa Cullen danced with a Theremin connected to a synthesizer; in 1973 the Yugoslav violinist Miha Pogačnik, who was to become famous for his Idri-Art Festivals, played Bach's partitas and in the same concert Stockhausen's 'Indianerlieder' were heard in Germany for the first time.

It was in this barn that Stockhausen began rehearsing a new work, *Herbstmusik*, in March 1974, six months before the première of *Inori*. *Herbstmusik* is a sort of staged outdoor music. Three people nail down a wooden roof, a quartet breaks twigs and branches, a trio threshes and a couple rustles and tussles in moist autumn foliage. Stockhausen was seeking to reveal the musical side of the rustic scenes he constantly witnessed as a child: the 'autumn music' of snapping and crackling wood, the rustling of straw and leaves, the many different rhythms of roof-building and threshing. 'I heard and saw the whole of *Herbstmusik* in my mind – and the names came at the same time.'[1] Stockhausen told Joachim

Krist that he would like to shape a whole series of traditional crafts into musical scenes; this plan has not yet been carried out.

The fourth player for *Herbstmusik*, in addition to Eötvös, Krist and Stockhausen, was found almost by accident. The American clarinettist Suzanne Stephens, who was due to perform in one of the Summer Night Music concerts, was staying in Oeldorf. Stockhausen immediately composed a little melody for the 'nailing the roof' trio, and for the last scene wrote a duo for viola and clarinet. After the tussles amid the leaves, a few tentative initial notes develop into a sophisticated duet, to which the couple slowly exits in spiralling movements. On 4 May 1974 the work was premièred at the Bremen Pro Musica Nova festival, but it seemed out of place on the stage of a concert hall; the atmosphere of the barn in Oeldorf was lacking, and perhaps the appropriate seasonal mood too. The 'breaking wood' quartet was greeted with ironic cries of 'heave-ho!' and at the end of the work, which had lasted about seventy minutes, there was only sparse applause.

Acquaintance with Suzanne Stephens soon blossomed into intense artistic collaboration and a personal friendship. The daughter of an American officer, brought up in the USA, Germany (Heidelberg) and France (Saumur on the Loire), she became Stockhausen's new partner. After completing her exams in the USA, she had come to Germany on a Fulbright grant; her many awards included the 1972 Kranichstein Chamber Music prize at Darmstadt for clarinet and ensemble playing.

In the early seventies Stockhausen began visiting Africa, Tunisia and the Canary Islands. He preferred to spend the dark, cold months of the year in warmer regions, especially by the sea; such surroundings were very conducive to work. In December 1974 he and Suzanne Stephens travelled to Cape Verde via N'Gor in Senegal. There, among other things, he wrote a first piece for clarinet, an ingenious melody with the title 'Sei wieder fröhlich'. At Easter 1975, in Morocco, Stockhausen began *Harlekin* which was completed at the turn of the year on Corn Island off the coast of Nicaragua. In this second composition for Suzanne Stephens the clarinettist (as 'Harlequin') dances to her own playing, Stockhausen having devised a choreography of mime, gesture and movement. Barely a decade later Stockhausen said,

I still go regularly to various spots on the planet, sometimes to Africa; I go every two years at least, and spend two or three months there. Whole sections of *Donnerstag* were composed there in a tiny, completely isolated house, looking every night at the most beautiful starry sky ... of a kind you just cannot see here. The same is true of the island on which I composed *Harlekin* ... There you see

54 'Sei wieder fröhlich', no. 1 from *Amour*, five pieces for clarinet

a starry sky ... so full of stars that you are profoundly moved, and you realize what a *quantité négligeable* our fate on this planet is, a tiny element, so to speak, in this massive cosmic clock, in this wondrous work.[2]

In the following years he produced further clarinet compositions, *Amour* and *In Freundschaft;* in 1977 Suzanne Stephens took on the role of the instrumental protagonist of Eve in *Licht*.

In the mid-seventies Stockhausen gathered a new ensemble of instrumentalists, singers and dancers, with whom he worked in close collaboration. He tried out and developed new instrumental techniques and timbres, especially for clarinet and trumpet, and further pursued the interlinking of music and movement. He has frequently given courses and numerous concerts with the group. Apart from Suzanne Stephens, its basic core includes three of his six children (four are trained musicians): Markus (trumpet), Majella (piano) and Simon (saxophone and synthesizer. 'I do not believe in ensembles that step off a plane, work together for a few evenings and then split up again ... the performers must be *one* soul – like in the Indian and Balinese dance groups. Brotherhood on a "supra-individual" level.'[3]

55 Kathinka Pasveer plays in a concert version of 'Kathinkas Gesang als Luzifers Requiem' in Odense, September 1987

56 Suzanne Stephens plays and dances *Der kleine Harlekin*, Odense, September 1987

In the summer of 1975, after four years without a publisher, the problem of bringing out Stockhausen's works was solved. Having negotiated with various well-known firms, none of whom could meet the conditions that he postulated for a collaboration, he founded his own publishing house. Jayne Stephens, Suzanne's sister, became the editor and the English composer James Ingram, who had been writing out scores for Stockhausen since *Inori*, became the copyist.

Musik im Bauch and *Tierkreis*

On Good Friday in 1975 a new piece of scenic music by Stockhausen was premièred at the Festival International d'Art Contemporain in Royan: *Musik im Bauch* for six percussionists and music boxes. Like *Trans*, it stems from a dream Stockhausen had had the previous year. The performance took place in the Haras stables in the little town of Saintes near Royan. A more than life-sized birdman, with an eagle's head and a tense and watchful expression, hung above the middle of the stage. The birdman, called Miron, was wearing a Mexican shirt and light linen trousers. To the left of the temporary stage, in front of a high, sky-blue wall, was a percussionist with sound-plates and tubular bell, to the right was a marimba with two more players and in the background three more players with antique cymbals and glockenspiel. The players came in one after another, and throughout the performance they moved like clockwork dolls. The sound-plates and the marimba (played with extremely slow movements) began together, and then the antique cymbals and glockenspiel came in: a brilliant, glittering sound. After a stroke on the tubular bell the three players at the back began to beat the air with their switches, making whirring, sizzling sounds: according to Stockhausen this was a ceremonial action to clear the air of evil spirits. The tubular bell sounded twice. The three moved towards the birdman with stiff movements, encircling him, prodding him with their switches; then they struck him, so that the Indian and other tiny bells sewn into his shirt produced a silvery sound, and trampled round him in a wild dance, with all the bells rattling and tinkling. When the tubular bell was heard for the third time, all three froze. Using a huge pair of scissors, the first player cut open the birdman's belly – a second cut, then a third. From its insides, to his astonishment, he extracted a little wooden music box and the melody for the zodiac sign of Leo was heard, disturbed by the playing of the sound-plates. The second and third players also found music boxes with zodiac melodies (Capricorn and Aquarius) in the belly of the birdman. They played along with their melodies on a tiny glockenspiel at Miron's feet. Then the six percussionists departed one after another; the music boxes were left behind, and their clockwork ran on till finally the sounds died out. After the performance there was applause but also puzzled booing.

In his book on Stockhausen Robin Maconie interprets *Musik im Bauch* as a fairy-tale for children, with reminiscences of Japanese noh theatre, but it is more like a ritual played out in Mexican Indian scenery. Birds have a particular significance in the myths of the Mexican Indians – for example, the 'plumed serpent' Quetzalcoatl – and among the Toltecs the eagle was regarded as a symbol of sacred mysteries. Some of these 'mysteries' were gruesome: the bellies of sacrificial victims were cut open and the entrails taken out. Reference has already been made to Stockhausen's striking affinity with Mexico. It was Nancy Wyle, with whom he had gone to Mexico in 1968, who built the birdman Miron for him.

In the autumn of 1974 Stockhausen had discovered the Jean Reuge music box factory in St Croix in Switzerland, and that winter, having composed the three melodies, he went there for a week to learn how music boxes were made. The whole of *Musik im Bauch* is based solely on three zodiac melodies – not necessarily those used at the première – and their extension to various lengths, including twenty-eight minutes on the marimba. In the spring and summer of 1975 Stockhausen wrote the melodies for the nine remaining signs of the zodiac and put them together as an independent work, *Tierkreis*. He steeped himself in astrological literature and began to study the twelve human characters associated with the zodiac.[4]

In inventing each melody I thought of the character of children, friends and acquaintances who were born under the various star signs ... Each melody has been composed with all its measures and proportions in keeping with the characteristics of its respective star sign, and listeners will discover many of the criteria when they hear a melody often and consider its construction exactly.[5]

Tierkreis was to become Stockhausen's most popular and probably most played work, performed by Gidon Kremer and amateurs alike. During the next two years further versions were made for solo instrument with or without harmony instrument, for voice – on a text by Stockhausen – in five different ranges and for various chamber ensembles.

57 *Tierkreis*, twelve melodies of the zodiac; Leo

Sirius: A Mystery Play as Science Fiction Story

In the spring of 1975 Stockhausen began preparations for a work commissioned by the West German government to celebrate the USA's bicentenary. *Sirius*, for electronic music and trumpet, soprano, bass clarinet and bass, is a visual and musical representation of the annual cycle. The four soloists represent the four seasons, times of day and points of the compass, the four elements, the four stages in the growth of plants (seed, bud, blossom and fruit) as well as man, youth, woman and beloved. The work was originally conceived for clarinet, soprano, trombone and bass, but after a concert in Paris at which his son Markus's playing in the orchestral part of *Hymnen* made Stockhausen fully aware of his abilities, the instrumentation was changed and he wrote a trumpet part for Markus.

Among the ancient Egyptians, whose mysteries were preoccupied with the four elements, Sirius was especially revered as the brightest star of the fixed-star heavens and its appearance there marked the beginning of the year. When it first became visible after the summer solstice, this was a sign that the flooding of the Nile, on which the fertility of the land depended, was imminent. Stockhausen considered Sirius the star for whose inhabitants 'Music is the highest form of all vibrations. For this reason, music there is the most highly developed of all things. Every musical composition of *Sirius* is linked to the rhythms of the star constellations, seasons of the year and times of the day, the elements and the existential differences of the living beings.'[6] It was following two dreams, which Stockhausen has never explained in detail, that Sirius became important to him.

This ninety-minute work should ideally be performed in a planetarium or in the open, under a night sky, with the stars moving above the listeners. It is divided into three parts: the 'Presentation' of the four soloists, a main section – the 'Wheel' of the passing year – and the final 'Annunciation', in which a message drawn from Jakob Lorber's teachings of Jesus in the *Great Gospel* is presented by the quartet:

Only this period of creation has the virtue – still indiscernible for you – that in the entire eternal infinite it is the only one in which I, creator of all worlds, have completely taken on the nature of the human flesh. I have chosen for myself within the entire, immense Universe, this particular capsule, and within this, the local universe whose central sun is Sirius, and among the 200 million suns rotating around Sirius, I have chosen just your earth to become incarnate as human being. Here I will raise, for all times and eternities to come, children completely similar to me, who, together with me, will some day reign over the entire infinite.[7]

Sirius is Stockhausen's attempt at a modern mystery play, clothed as a science fiction story. Lorber claims that the inhabitants of Sirius founded the human race thousands of years ago and have sometimes visited the earth since then. *Sirius* begins with the whining sound, rotating between the loudspeakers, of the brakes of the four spaceships in which the messengers from Sirius land on earth. After the Annunciation the spaceships rise up again with whining motors.

Stockhausen began the realization of the tape part in the middle of July; it was the first time he had worked in the electronic studio since *Hymnen*, and at the start there was little progress. 'I have never yet had such great difficulty in composing as I did with *Sirius*,' he said a year later.[8] In the initial stages, the sticky, impure air in the studio made him faint and he had to spend a week in hospital, where he fasted. During this time he evolved the entire musical conception of *Sirius* (as well as the concept of an ideal hospital in which painters and musicians too would live, as art therapists aiding the sick). The basis of the music lies exclusively in the twelve formula-melodies of *Tierkreis*, while the basis of the tape part is the melodies of the four seasons; Aries, Cancer, Libra and Capricorn. Using a voltage-controlled synthesizer, the four melodies are developed in many ways: transformed, combined with one another and fused together, sometimes with many melodies simultaneously. As he once remarked to Rudolf Frisius, Stockhausen regarded his compositional approach as a resumption and extension of the developmental techniques of Beethoven's middle period, techniques that had not been pursued further since that time.

On 15 July 1976 an incomplete version of *Sirius* (of the 'Wheel', only summer had been composed) was performed to celebrate the opening of the Albert Einstein Spacearium (planetarium) in Washington, DC. Markus Stockhausen (trumpet), Annette Meriweather (soprano), Suzanne Stephens (bass clarinet) and Boris Carmeli (bass) played and sang before an invited audience of 120 people, among them the then federal chancellor Helmut Schmidt and his wife, and the American vice-president Rockefeller. At the request of the West German government Stockhausen had dedicated his work to the American pioneers on earth and in space. In autumn of that year came further performances (including the autumn part of the 'Wheel') in Tokyo, Osaka, Paris, Berlin, Venice, Toulouse and Metz. The landing of the four inhabitants of Sirius and their message were not well received by many newspaper critics in Berlin. *Die Welt* cast doubt on 'the programmatic superstructure of the work' as being comprehensible only to initiates, 'to those fans of the occult, which has become so fashionable these days'.[9] In most other places *Sirius* had a more friendly reception, and in the Romance countries, especially Italy, Stockhausen was popular from then on.

Stockhausen was heard even in the USSR. At the end of the sixties, Alexander Rabinowitsch had played some of the *Klavierstücke*. Now the pianist Alexei Ljubimow and his ensemble performed text compositions from *Aus den sieben Tagen* in various cities, the highly esteemed Moscow percussionist Mark Pekarski played *Zyklus* and the chamber orchestra of the Bolshoi Theatre gave the octet version of *Tierkreis*. Stockhausen had had connections in Moscow since the early sixties, when recordings of his works were listened to behind closed doors and had a great influence.

At the end of 1976 Stockhausen interrupted work on *Sirius* to complete the choral opera *Atmen gibt das Leben . . .*, one movement of which had been written in 1974. The première took place on 22 May 1977 in Nizza at the Musée National Message Biblique Marc Chagall as a preliminary celebration of the ninetieth birthday of Stockhausen's friend. Stockhausen had given a concert there in the autumn of 1975, which included *Spiral*, the 'Indianerlieder' and *Inori*. For many years Chagall had wanted a Stockhausen première in his museum, and the commission from the French minister for religious affairs made it possible.

1977 began as a year of intense creativity. After *Atmen gibt das Leben . . .* came the festive, hymn-like orchestral work *Jubiläum*, commissioned to celebrate 125 years of the existence of the Hanover Opera House. In this formula composition, lasting about fifteen minutes, the orchestra is divided into four groups who play independently of one another. On 10 October 1977, while Stockhausen was in Japan, the Regional Orchestra of Lower Saxony, conducted by George Albrecht, gave the successful première. After *Jubiläum*, Stockhausen finished *Sirius*. The first complete performance took place on 8 August at the Festival of Aix-en-Provence as the closing event of the Sirius Centre courses; it was loudly applauded by the audience.

11 *Licht* 1977–91

> Various spiritual currents can come together in my
> work: it is a real dramatic arena. For me it is terribly
> important that this balance continues to exist –
> that the constructive forces of progress continue
> for the benefit of human creation and the human
> world, ever mindful of all the essential yet
> questionable aspects of this process.
> Stockhausen

Donnerstag from *Licht*: Michael's Day

Since beginning the composition of *Donnerstag* in the autumn of 1977, Stockhausen has worked exclusively on his *magnum opus, Licht*. He has set himself the goal of ending this seven-part work within twenty-five years, thus making an arc extending over the end of the millennium. A 'day' from *Licht* is to be completed approximately every three and a half years. In many languages and cultures light is an expression or image of the Divinity; *Licht* is Stockhausen's attempt to create a cosmic world theatre that summarizes and intensifies his lifelong concern: the unity of music and religion, allied to a vision of an essentially musical mankind. Stockhausen's world theatre is enacted not only on earth, for the plot also unfolds in the world beyond. It considers the destiny of mankind, the earth and the cosmos, in conjunction and confrontation with the spiritual essences Michael, Lucifer and Eve. Michael, the 'Creator-Angel of our universe', represents the progressive forces of development. Lucifer is his rebellious antagonist, and Eve works towards a renewal of the 'genetic quality' of humanity through the rebirth of a more musical mankind. Originally Adam was to appear alongside this primal mother, but Stockhausen restricted himself to a trinity of principal characters, seeing in Adam and Eve only different versions of one and the same essence. Michael, Lucifer and Eve each appear in three forms: as singers (tenor, bass, soprano) instruments (trumpet, trombone, basset-horn) and bodies (dancers). The significance of the seven days of the week and the divinities associated with each of them was derived by Stockhausen from various cultures and esoteric traditions; *The Urantia Book* was also an important source.[1] Stockhausen has organized everything into a huge seven-part cycle: Monday is Eve's day, Tuesday is the day of confrontation between Michael and Lucifer, Wednesday is the day of collaboration between all three, Thursday is Michael's day, Friday is the day of Eve's temptation by Lucifer, Saturday is Lucifer's day and Sunday is the day of the mystical union of Michael and Eve. The plot and the ideas for staging are essentially Stockhausen's own. Each day has its affiliated colours, symbols, plants and animals, etc.[2] *Licht* is Stockhausen's *Gesamtkunstwerk*; singing, instrumental music, tape sounds, movement, costumes and lighting – everything that happens musically or theatrically – is conceived as one unity. The compositional germ cell for the whole thing is a 'super-formula', conceived in terms of rhythms, dynamics and timbre, in which three individual formulas are combined (a thirteen-note Michael formula, a twelve-note Eve formula and an eleven-note Lucifer formula). The entire cycle is developed from this triple-formula polyphony, from the single note, via the musical and scenic details to the broader musico-dramatic context. Although the various sections of the operas are mainly fully composed, some give the interpreter greater freedom. Many passages in the music are melodious and readily singable; in particular, some parts of the Michael formula are very memorable and are reminiscent of leitmotifs.

For the trumpet, Michael's instrument, Stockhausen had an especially rich range of shades of timbre in mind. So he turned to the research centre IRCAM (Institut de Recherche et de Coordination Acoustique/Musique), opened in Paris in 1976 and directed by Boulez, and proposed that a 'sound transformer' be constructed there. A small fourteen-key manual producing fourteen different vowel colorations was to be attachable to the instrument or the player's chest, a little apparatus with filter and volume control that could be combined with any solo instrument. It 'must fit into a briefcase, as *hand luggage* to go under the seat in an aeroplane,' wrote Stockhausen to Boulez a little later.[3] Extended experiments in Cologne and Kürten showed that the sound quality of the transformer was not yet adequate for Stockhausen's purposes, and in March 1978 he decided on a purely instrumental solution using a highly varied mute-technique. In his role as an instrumentalist Michael was to produce richly varied trumpet timbres using six different mutes carried in a belt around his waist.

After almost exactly three and a half years the première of *Donnerstag* took place on 15 March 1981 at La Scala, Milan, directed by Luca Ronconi. Large parts of the work had been presented earlier in Donaueschingen, Jerusalem and Amsterdam, yet it had not been possible for Stockhausen to get a single opera house in Germany – which has more opera houses than anywhere else in the world – to show interest in his

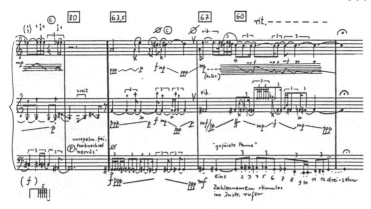

58 Super-formula for *Donnerstag* from *Licht* (*top:* Michael; *middle:* Eva; *below:* Luzifer)

work. Either his requests were left unanswered or he was asked – just as if he were some young composer – to send a few tapes, which then gathered dust in a cupboard somewhere. Some even kindly informed him that they 'were committed to other contemporary composers'.

In Milan there were unexpected obstacles and a scandal: owing to a strike by the opera chorus of La Scala, the work was premièred without the final act. In one brief part of this act the chorus is split up into solo parts. The singers had demanded a soloist's bonus and had been turned down, so they had fallen out with the theatre management. After five incomplete performances an agreement was reached and *Donnerstag* could be seen in its entirety.

The work begins in the theatre foyer with the 'Donnerstags-Gruss' for chamber ensemble, and then moves into the auditorium. Michael has made himself incarnate on earth to experience, for once, the fate of mankind. His father, a schoolmaster, shows him how to pray, act, hunt and shoot; his mother teaches him the names of the sun, moon and stars, and she laughs, sings and dances. Stockhausen said he reworked his own biography, including the smallest details (his mother's illness, his brother 'Hermännchen' and his father's death as a soldier), so as to depict simple life as realistically as possible without having to invent anything. After meeting Mondeva, a 'girl from the stars', and passing his music examination, Michael sets off, in Act 2, on a musical journey around the world: a trumpet concerto, with the orchestra as the world. A huge globe rotates slowly in front of a backdrop of the firmament, and Michael appears at various 'windows' in the globe. Along with the orchestra, he plays music tinged by the culture of each place: Japan, Bali, central Europe, New York, India and Africa. In central Africa he hears a basset-horn in the distance. Michael stops the globe and steps out, and Mondeva appears; the pair's melodic formulas twist round one another and interpenetrate until one of them plays the other's formula. After a musical 'mockery' by two clownish solo clarinet players and a 'crucifixion' by them, the orchestra's trombones, tuba and horns (the clarinet, second basset-horn and brass 'nail down what the trumpet and first basset-horn play'), Act 2 ends with a musical 'ascension'; the sounds of basset-horn and trumpet circle and glide over the loudspeakers, gradually rising up until they are artfully united in a trill.

In Act 3, 'Michael's Heimkehr', Michael has returned to his celestial residence, where he is welcomed by Eve with a choral hymn:

MIKAEL

Welcome Son of Love

MICHAEL Son of God

Protector of Mankind

LIGHT

Hermes-Christos

Thor-Donar

Sirius composed this hymn for you

Does it not please you?

Holy be your Work

MICHAEL

Musichel

'Invisible choruses' are heard on tape from all around. Eve now hands Michael three presents: plants, a light composition and, as a souvenir of his journey, a little globe. But a devil springs up who has been 'exiled to the very centre of the earth'. A musical Dragon Fight begins, from which Michael emerges the victor. The end of the act is a 'Vision', in which everything that Michael has experienced is mirrored above him.

It was shortly before midnight when the audience left La Scala. Five trumpeters on the rooftop terraces of the building and on three balconies around the opera square played single melodic 'limbs' from the Michael formula for at least half an hour: 'Donnerstags-Abschied'. The trumpet sounds mixed with the nocturnal noises of the still sleepless city.

The German newspapers responded to Stockhausen's first opera with headlines such as 'Strike Hinders World Redemption' (*Frankfurter Allgemeine Zeitung*, 18 March), 'Stockhausen's Cosmic Theatre Deficit' (*Süd-*

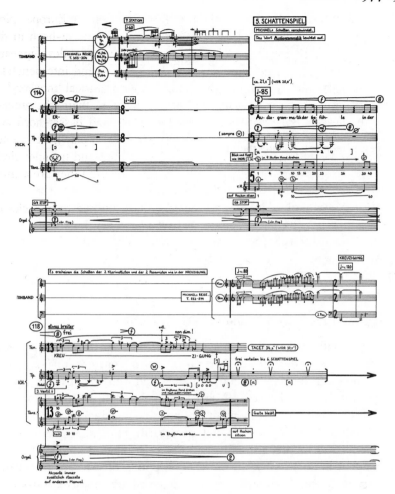

59 'Vision' for tenor, trumpet, dancer, Hammond organ, tape and shadow plays: Scene 2 of Act 3 of *Donnerstag* from *Licht*, p. 11 of the score

deutsche Zeitung, 17 March) or 'Global Theatre Fudged' (*Frankfurter Rund-schau,* 17 March). Stockhausen was used to being handled anything but gently in the German press. But after the composition of *Licht* the partly personal criticisms had piled up to such an extent that in September 1980 he decided to write an 'open letter', which he distributed widely:

NEVER since 1952 have I been *personally* attacked in the *German* press so unequivo-cally, and in so dirty and vile a manner as in 1978, the year of the first perform-ances of my work *Licht.* The . . . attack is directed 1. against the transcendental spirit in my works; 2. against the musical collaboration of my children . . . New formal principles, rhythm, melody, harmony, timbre composition, vocal technique, gesture, spatial composition, etc. – all these *musical* criteria are mentioned *nowhere*. No one has argued about the *artistic* quality of the named members of our family . . . The people of this country have a singular talent for denigrating its artists, and learning nothing from its history. Schoenberg, Thomas Mann, Hesse and many others emigrated – and not so long ago. Whether that was caused by National Socialism or God knows what other kinds of socialism, the effect is the same. I should just like to have this put on record: alone, even the strongest person can provide the necessary conditions for *free* creative work only up to a certain point.

In Italy *Donnerstag* was very popular, and in December 1981 it received the Italian Music Critics' first prize for the best new work of contemporary music. A new staging of *Donnerstag* at London's Covent Garden opera house, planned for 1983, was realized in September 1985 when for the first time Covent Garden opened its season with a work by a living composer.

Samstag from *Licht*: Lucifer and the Day of Death

Samstag, Lucifer's day, is the day of death, and work on his second evening of opera demanded that Stockhausen confront this age-old human question. Is death an end, to be awaited with fear or stoic equanimity? Not for Stockhausen. 'From childhood on, I quite often experienced death directly as the moment of a possible transition that can come at any time, something we do not necessarily have to spend twenty, thirty or forty years preparing for, and which is followed immediately by continuation in some other form. My conception of art and the whole of my work in composition have been stamped with this experience.'[4] Stockhausen's life-motto, 'Birth in death', now assumed its broadest dimensions: death on earth is seen as birth into a world beyond, as the possibility of a new existence in the 'light', in the *lux aeterna*, if the soul can maintain itself in clear consciousness. Many factors have left their mark on Stockhausen's image of death: the inner certainty of an ineradicable self and the constantly experienced presence of dead friends and relatives; but there are also the various conceptions of death in other cultures, his impressions as a traveller and the literature of the classic books of the dead. Stockhausen concluded his preparations for *Samstag* by studying the *Tibetan Book of the Dead*, and said at that time that he had inwardly come to terms with the question of death.

Whereas the realization of *Donnerstag* from *Licht* was fraught with many difficulties, the preparations for *Samstag* and the performance ran relatively smoothly. The four scenes of the work had been given concert performances in Metz, Assisi, Donaueschingen and Ann Arbor. On 25 May 1984 'Lucifer's Day' was given its stage première, once again in Milan with Ronconi directing, but at the Palazzo dello Sport instead of La Scala. This large oval hall on the fringe of the city was architecturally remarkable for its parabolic roof. Spectators entered by a wooden stairway, went over a platform that took them past the globe and other notable objects from the staging of *Donnerstag*, and then descended into the arena. There were no seats there, apart from a few rows on the outer tiers. Gae Aulenti, the stage designer, had draped the arena with a huge Lucifer face made of armrests and cushions, on which the spectators sat. The stage action took place within this face and to the four sides of it.

Once the lights are dimmed, four brass and percussion groups, posted up high on all sides, begin the evening with 'Luzifers Gruss'. Lucifer appears in the arena, dressed wholly in black. He soars up and down on a hydraulic chair, enveloped in swathes of fog and smoke. Lucifer dreams a piano piece, played for him by the pianist Majella. He wants to abolish time, and constantly counts up to thirteen, invoking the elements – air, water, earth, fire and light – in song. Finally, against his will, he enjoys the Eve-melody on the piano and dies, enchanted by this sensual human music.

At a cemetery with a legless grand piano as the grave, against which lean wreaths with bows and garlands, the cat Kathinka plays a requiem for Lucifer on the flute. She is the animal associated with Saturday. In *Licht* the flute, like the basset-horn, is linked with Eve. The requiem is not music of mourning, but music that helps the dead person to achieve rebirth, to find his way in the beyond. The cat slinks up the pyramidal steps to two big silver mandala discs standing to left and right above the grave. There she plays 'twenty-four musical exercises' for the dead man, which are illuminated on the mandalas. Six black percussionists accompany her with a clattering, howling, grating midnight music. 'Magic instruments' are attached to every part of their bodies. The six percussionists represent the 'six mortal senses': hearing, sight, smell, taste, touch and thinking. After the 'Release of the Senses' the cat disappears in the grave. But Lucifer's death was only pseudo-death – there is no death. With derisive laughter, he rises from his piano catacomb and strides through the hall – a gigantic black figure, portrayed by a dancer on stilts. Simultaneously, on the narrow side of the arena, a curtain with a drawing of Lucifer by Botticelli is hauled up. Behind it there appears a large wind

60 The première of *Samstag* from *Licht* on 25 May 1984 at the Palazzo dello Sport, Milan: the 'orchestral face' in Scene 3, 'Luzifers Tanz'; the orchestral musicians are 'going on strike'

band with percussion, arranged in six tiers in the form of a human face, with which Lucifer performs his dance. He lets the various parts of the face, the right eyebrow, the left eyebrow, the right eye and so on play out their dances, each on their own and against one another, rebelling for independence. Out of sight, Lucifer sings:

> If you, Man, have never learned from LUCIFER
> how the spirit of contradiction and independence
> distort the expression of the face . . .
> you cannot turn your countenance in harmony
> towards the LIGHT.

Then Michael enters in golden armour; his ideal is harmony, and playing together. In a brilliant cadenza for piccolo trumpet he protests against Lucifer's grimacing face. Lucifer drives him away with seven tamtam strokes, and the orchestra, touched, weeps a 'Tears Dance'. But then the cat appears again, on the tip of the face's tongue, and plays her 'Tip of the Tongue Dance', as if the face were impudently sticking out its tongue at Michael and the audience. She has brought a little demon with her, who dances as he unwraps fourteen letters of black ribbon from his body and forms them into the phrase 'Salve Satanelli' (Greetings, Satan's children). Lucifer's voice accompanies all this:

> If you have tested out your tenfold face
> in all the dissonances and rhythms of grimaces,
> it will fall apart, empty and hollowed out,
> before it can rise again, invisible to human eyes,
> on Sunday.

Suddenly the scene takes an unexpected turn. One brass player after another stops performing since the contractually agreed time has run out. The conductor is furious, and the theatre manager is called in. 'Luzifers Tanz' ends in staged chaos and disintegration. But what could easily be seen as a parody of the chorus strike of 1981 was actually sketched by Stockhausen before the trouble-laden première of *Donnerstag*.

The last scene, 'Luzifers Abschied', is reminiscent of a ritual procession. The sides of the arena turn into the aisles of the nave of a church, with hints of walls and columns. A 'wild, black bird' in a cage is borne in by twenty-six monks, thirteen of them in brown habits and thirteen in black; they enter at a brisk pace, singing, wearing wooden shoes and carrying Good Friday clappers and mass bells. Along with thirteen concealed tenors and accompanied by seven trombones and Hammond organ, they celebrate 'Luzifers Abschied'. Sometimes moving about, sometimes standing still they sing the text of St Francis of Assisi's 'Lodi delle virtù' in long, drawn-out notes divided by brief solos. When the church bells begin to ring, the monks set the bird free. A bulging sack has meanwhile 'fallen from heaven', and one by one the monks take a coconut out of it. Each monk throws his nut against an enclosed stone slab 'in front of the church' and is allowed to make a wish – a ceremony that Stockhausen had seen at the Kataragama Festival in Ceylon. The basses accompany the closing ceremony, singing and sounding their bells and clappers.

In the autumn of 1982, when Stockhausen and his ensemble spent several weeks giving courses and concerts at the Royal Conservatoire in Den Haag, he got to know the Dutch flautist Kathinka Pasveer. She took on the role of the cat in *Samstag* and joined the ensemble. Stockhausen

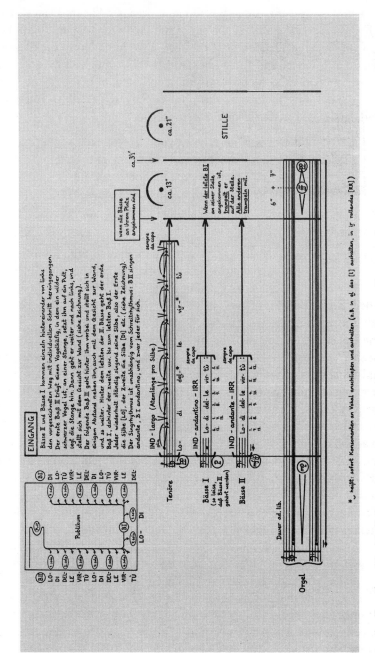

61 'Luzifers Abschied' for male chorus, organ and seven trombones: Scene 4 of
Samstag from *Licht*, upper half of p. 1 of the score

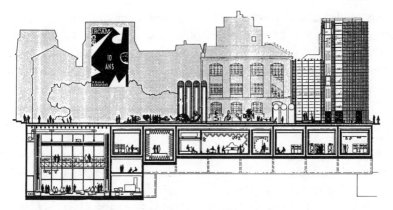

62 IRCAM, the spacious state-run research centre for electro-acoustics in Paris.
All the rooms lie underground, between the Georges-Pompidou Centre and the
St Merri Church. The outline of the Stravinsky Fountain, objects by Jean Tinguely
and Nicki de Saint-Phalle, may be seen at ground level

expanded 'Kathinkas Gesang als Luzifers Requiem' – originally conceived
for only six percussionists – to give the flute part the central role. Since
then he has constantly collaborated with Kathinka Pasveer.

Stockhausen has conceived *Licht* in such a way that all the scenes of
the individual days of the week may be performed as independent works.
In the spring of 1983 he made a concertante version of 'Kathinkas Gesang
als Luzifers Requiem' for flute and electronic music. Stockhausen realized
the electronic music in December 1983 and August 1984 in the electronic
studio at IRCAM in Paris, since the Cologne studio lacked the appropriate
facilities. What Stockhausen had first thought about in the early fifties –
the detailed, composed shaping of a sound's phase spectrum – was now
technically possible in Paris, thirty-three years later: the composition is
controlled right up to the 212th partial. The extremely varied realm of
electronic sounds, with its finely chiselled, astringent splendour, carries
echoes of the mosques and monuments of the Islamic world.

Montag from *Licht*: Eve's Day as Rebirth of Humanity

Stockhausen was frequently interrupting work on *Licht* for courses and
concerts in various European countries. In the autumn of 1984 he was
invited to Hungary for the first time to attend a performance of the
orchestral version of *Hymnen* and *Harlekin*. In mid-November he and his
ensemble flew to India for three weeks. The musicians gave concerts in

Delhi, Calcutta and Bombay, but it was also a cultural trip. Stockhausen saw buildings and ancient sites from Nepal to southern India, seeking contact with the music and choreographic arts of the subcontinent. He spent a few days at a Kathakali school in Cheruthuruthy (south India) and visited a dance school in Bombay. In Calcutta he met the sitar and subahar virtuoso Imrad Khan, but they could not collaborate because Khan and his students played without any scores, as is normal in Indian classical music.

While working on *Samstag* Stockhausen had decided that in *Montag* he would use synthesizers as a 'modern orchestra'. The main reason was his wish to have his sons Markus and Simon as interpreters (though ultimately Markus was not able to participate in the performances); but disgust and decades of disappointment with the whole orchestral system, its 'star conductors' and its musicians, must also have contributed. For a long time, Stockhausen had rejected working with synthesizers since, compared with the electronic studio, he found it lacking in creativity. But now that the use of the keyboard synthesizer was both technically and financially feasible, there began

a profound and unforeseeable change in the craft of composition. The direction in which this development leads is the one I spoke and wrote about from the very beginning: that every composer . . . creates his own world of sounds for every new work and . . . that while composing, he constantly checks what he is writing at the synthesizer, and in addition . . . listens day and night over headphones to his catalogued sound programmes.[5]

The electronic studio of 1953 had become portable.

As well as writing for synthesizer Stockhausen had tested out new instrumental techniques over several months with Suzanne Stephens and Kathinka Pasveer: 'new micro-scales, voiced and unvoiced (noise) consonant timbres, quarter-, sixth- and eighth-tone, all the way up to intervals undefinable is numerical terms, with as many as twenty-six steps within a major third'.[6]

On 7 May 1988 *Montag* from *Licht* had its stage première at La Scala, Milan, this time with an English team. As with the London production of *Donnerstag* from *Licht*, the director was Michael Bogdanov. Chris Dyer designed the stage settings and Marc Thompson the costumes. Including intervals, the performance lasts more than five hours.

Eve's day is devoted to the mythology of femininity: to fertility, creativity, giving birth, and eroticism. At the beginning of Act 1, 'Evas Erstgeburt', Eve sits beside the sea in the form of a huge female statue and is made ready for birth by twenty-one women (actresses). Tidal waves

63 Discussion after a dress rehearsal of 'Evas Zauber' in Metz, November 1986: children from the Chorus of Radio Budapest, Stockhausen and Kathinka Pasveer. *In the background:* Michael Obst (with score) and Andreas Boettger

are seen surging in the background. The music portrays the creation of a human body, which is simultaneously expressed in the sky in terms of various phases of the moon, and embryo development. From the statue's larynx, which is open and transparent, Eve sings as a triple voice (three sopranos); a mixed chorus is heard on tape, and three synthesizers and a percussionist play on either side of the stage. A musical formula evolves slowly, becoming 'increasingly lively'. (Originally singers in the chorus were to play the twenty-one women, while the men sang from the wings. But the women of the WDR chorus – the one heard on the tape – were not willing to appear as actresses.)

Montag from *Licht* is 'a musical celebration of the rebirth of mankind', and in the eighth of its nine stages the choir sings:

> Music for the festival of birth
> - rebirth -
> MONDAY from LIGHT
> EVE-day.
> ESA — JANA
> give us new life,
> shine into the night of death.
> Saturday Saturnlight
> Dahay of death LUCIFER-Day
> LUCIFER.
> Thy fire melts the ice
> changes the night of resurrection
> into light.

One by one fourteen extraordinary creatures are now brought into the world, seven boys with animal heads (lion, two swallows, horse, parrot, budgerigar and dog) and seven grey-haired boys ('little straw men'). The three Eve-sopranos give thanks in a 'birth aria'. Three sailors disembark from boats, bearing flowers, juices and fruits, and sing a second 'birth aria'. Various parts of the text (the forty-page libretto is, once again, Stockhausen's own) contain names and allusions from different mythologies: the three Greek Fates and the three German Norns, as in this passage from the sailors' aria:

> Urd uru
> urturu Geburt uru
> urukete tukete lachetu tukete lachetu
> Urd Werdandi ninini
>
> ruketu Urt Werdandi ruketu
> tukete tukete take teke tike toke tuke tu ketu
> Urrt jeketu urt Werdandi
>
> Skult Skult
> tubedube skuld tubedup
> Atropos Uksakka
> acqua acqua Samudra

Other long passages play with Dadaist texts and sound-painting, both reminiscent of children's verse – the text recedes as a bearer of meaning and becomes an acoustic element of the music. After extended choreo-

64 *Montag* from *Licht*, 'Fertilization with Piano Piece' from the beginning of Act 2.
At the piano: Pierre Laurent Aimard as 'budgerigar'; *in the background:* 'Eve's
children' as lily blossoms; *seated:* the 'women' (rehearsal photo)

graphic treatment of a stroll with the new arrivals in prams, the 'Baby-
Buggy-Boogie', Lucifer enters and everything freezes. He appears as the
double entity Luzipolyp, dressed in a spider-web of black: he is both
singer and croaking, rasping mime, the two drawn together by bands of
black gauze. In 'Lucifer's Fury' he mocks the birth and is finally buried
in sand by the women. At the end of Act 1, after the 'Great Wailings' of
the disappointed women, Lucifer emerges from the sea, comes to the
beach and yells out at breakneck speed: 'All back in!! The whole thing
back to the starrrt!!!'

At the beginning of Act 2, 'Evas Zweitgeburt', the sea is frozen over.
The women break up the ice with axes, singing as they work. Then
suddenly the auditorium becomes completely dark. Three rows of girls
with candles, dressed as lily blossom, come down through the audience
from the back. 'Eve's children' sing a song of praise and thanksgiving in
preparation for the second birth. As the lily children sing, Eve is fertilized
by a piano piece – the pianist is the budgerigar from the boy animals.
Eve's womb now glows red and green 'like a Christmas crib', and the

225

Partiturausschnitt aus AVE

65 'Ave' for alto flute and basset-horn; from 'Evas Zauber', Act 3 of
Montag from *Licht*

seven boys of the seven days come into the world. The heart of the female
sculpture opens up and Eve emerges as Coeur, as a basset-horn player.
She discovers the musicality of the boys and teaches them the 'Seven
Songs of the Days'. Eve multiplies herself into three further basset-horn
players – Busi, Busa and Muschi – and the boys are seduced and led
astray.

When the last act, 'Evas Zauber', opens, the ice has melted and the
Eve statue is seated on a verdant lawn. The boys have become men. Men
and women appear on stage and the women sing:

A musician,
a wonderful, tender, exciting musician
has come.
Everyone says
that he has magic powers.

226

66 January 1988: Stockhausen in the WDR electronic studio, now in Annostrasse

Ave, a mirror image of Eve (in German, Eva) dressed as a man, enters. Eve and Ave fall in love and play a duet together until a 'gracious entwining of the two, both musical and physical' is achieved. Several inquisitive children have come in and as Ave turns to them Eve draws back, disappointed. Her mirror image plays the piccolo, casting a spell on the children until they copy her like puppets. 'Sound scenes from all over the world' and 'childish humour celebrates a festival' are heard on the tape. Finally Ave exits as a 'child-catcher'; the children follow her, and as they ascend to 'higher worlds with green clouds', their singing carries on for a long time:

> Monday – born from LIGHT -
> Ceremony and Magic.

The piccolo and the children's voices are transformed into birdsong, and the Eve sculpture reverts to nature: a mountain with bushes, shrubs, animals, flowers and streams (this could not be done in Milan). The

227

creative act and the forces of nature have become one. Like the previous days, *Montag* begins and ends with a musical greeting and farewell.

Montag completes the three evenings dedicated to the three main protagonists of *Licht*, Michael, Lucifer and Eve. It is important to Stockhausen that before a performance the musicans tune themselves inwardly to what they are going to play, just as in the Kathakali theatre or the Ramayana dances the participants prepare for a performance through meditation; if they do not sense the 'presence of the gods', then they will not play, even if the audience has already gathered. Michael, Lucifer and Eve are, for Stockhausen, more than theatrical figures. They are the expression of a world beyond, to which terrestrial eyes are blind, but which is given concrete form by *The Urantia Book* and other sources. 'Not only most people from the world of music,' concedes Stockhausen, 'but the great majority of intellectuals ridicule me because I concern myself with such matters and because I compose such things.'[7] Many composers have described the act of creation as a kind of contact with supra-personal, divine forces. Here Stockhausen stands alongside Beethoven, Brahms and Wagner as well as Schoenberg and Messiaen. But when Stockhausen talks about the progressive and retarding forces in the evolutionary spiral, how can he tell which kind is inspiring him?

All my life I have been convinced that there is an angel constantly guiding me. Depending on the tasks I have set myself, and that have been set me . . . the angel changes . . . There are several of them. They specialize in particular subjects, stages of life, and also particular kinds of change of life and of creative activity. My angel is highly experienced in questions of music. It is certainly possible that if, for a moment, I do not invoke my angel, or if I get involved with the means, or with other spirits, then other influences may come into my work – I am not always pure, it is true. On the contrary, I am often exposed to lively mixtures of other people's tendencies – interpreters, technicians and many people I work with. So it is absolutely possible that I may receive satanic transmissions, and let them into my work . . . So to that extent, it is true, various spiritual currents may come together in my work: it is a real dramatic arena. For me it is terribly important that this balance continues to exist – that the constructive forces of progress continue for the benefit of human creation and the human world, ever mindful of all the essential yet questionable aspects of this process.[8]

Sixtieth Birthday Concert Series and a Première for the 600th Anniversary of Cologne University

At the time Stockhausen was working on *Montag* someone asked him how he felt about the conflicts arising from being world-famous, and the steadily mounting external pressures this caused. He answered, 'Even

für AVE habe ich drei Monate lang täglich mehrere Stunden mit den beiden Interpretinnen neue Mikro-skalen, stimmhafte und stimmlose (Rausch-)Konsonant-farben ausprobiert. Viertel-, Sechstel-, Achteltöne und in einfachen Zahlen nicht mehr definierbare Intervalle bis zu 26 Stufen innerhalb einer großen Terz (quasi '13-tel-Töne') mit all den unbeschreiblichen Klangfarbenchangierungen kommen in dieser neuen Komposition vor.
Dazu kommen noch die integrierten Bewegungen.

Auch bei der Komposition für diese traditionellen Instrumente habe ich ständig das Gefühl, ein Schüler an der Schwelle zu einer neuen Entwicklung der Instrumentalpraxis zu sein.

Seit 1970 hat sich in meinen Werken kontinuierlich eine neue Aufführungspraxis entwickelt:

Auswendigspielen;
ohne Dirigent singen und spielen und die Partien der anderen Musiker auswendig kennen;
alle Bewegungen stilisieren, oft gemäß detaillierter Notation;
ein 'Konzert' ist entweder ein einziges Werk ohne Unterbrechung, oder eine Komposition von 'Stücken', die miteinander in einem räumlichen und zeitlichen Prozeß verbunden werden;
möglichst besondere Kostüme für jede Komposition entwerfen;
pro Werk individuelle Beleuchtung gestalten;
alle unkünstlerischen Aktionen vermeiden.

Es wird deutlich, daß der Aufführungsstil für ein Konzert und für jedes Werk ganz eigen und unvergeßlich gestaltet ist, ähnlich wie die Klangfarben und die Form seit 1951 für jedes 'Stück' unverwechselbar von mir komponiert worden.
Das Schöpferische selbst ist Inhalt und Form jedes Werkes geworden.

Karlheinz Stockhausen
26. IV. 1987

67 Stockhausen's autograph instructions for 'Ave'

more than before, I have to learn to concentrate, and to say no. Increasingly, when I am offered a concert, I consider whether it is compatible with work on *Licht* . . . It often saddens me, because there are scarcely any conductors who want to perform my work. The works require too many rehearsals for normal concert managements, and conductors want to get from the first rehearsal to the concert as quickly as possible. Our most famous interpreters do not play my works because they do not want to spend time studying them . . . So I have to concentrate firmly on whatever project is next, and that, for the foreseeable future, means *Licht.*'[9]

Back in Kürten after the première of *Montag* in Milan, Stockhausen faced a year in which he would pay a high price for his fame: eleven concert series in nine countries, sometimes with only a couple of days between them. The cause of all this was the composer's sixtieth birthday, in August. The way was led by Cologne, a city that has not always done full justice to its great son, and has had a fair number of feuds with him. The Musikhochschule celebrated its former student and professor with a series of concerts and lectures in late May; the state premier of North Rhine-Westphalia, his old employer, gave the welcoming speech. In the second half of July Stockhausen set out on his first South American tour, which included seven ensemble concerts and three illustrated lectures in Rio de Janeiro. After these he journeyed across the country: 'four days of wonderful experiences – boat trips, folk music, mountain climbing, a Benedictine mass, and candomblé in a mulatto commune'.[10]

Returning to Europe in the second week of August, he went to Mozart's home town of Salzburg, better known for its cultivation of the traditional repertoire. At the Mozarteum's summer academy Stockhausen directed staged performances of seven of his works, and gave courses with his musicians. After this came concerts and other events at Swiss Radio (DRS) in Zurich, at the Frankfurt Festival, the Festival d'Automne in Paris, at Gütersloh in Germany and the Huddersfield Contemporary Music Festival.

While writing *Montag*, Stockhausen was asked to compose a piece for the 600th anniversary of Cologne University in November 1988. He was delighted to accept the invitation: 'While I was talking to the vice-chancellor . . . and his university colleagues, all kinds of feelings and memories came flooding back from the time when I went in and out of the main university buildings daily, forty years earlier, from the spring of 1947 to the autumn of 1951 . . . Since I am now working on *Dienstag* from *Licht* (the day of war), correspondence about the 600th anniversary made me think back to all those post-war discussions on the basic subject of "with God" or "without God" – discussions that animated the minds of the entire student body, bringing union and discord. There was Sartre's existentialism, appallingly atheistic and nihilistic, and in complete contrast there was also a fanatical new religiosity . . . and when I compare that situation with the one faced by my six children and their friends, most of whom studied or are still studying at the Musikhochschule and the university in Cologne, I see that the essential battle – the intellectual one – has not changed much.'[11]

Eleven years after *Der Jahreslauf,* another section of *Dienstag* was composed: the *Friedens-Gruss* for mixed chorus, solo soprano, nine trumpets, nine trombones and two synthesizers. This is the work that opens the fourth evening of *Licht.*

The festivities came at a time when the hopeless overcrowding of German colleges was being discussed in all the media, and many demonstrations were being staged. At the celebration of 4 November 1988 a number of students gathered in front of the Philharmonic Hall, waving banners and chanting slogans in protest at the critical situation in German universities. The police had created a narrow gangway, and checked every visitor going to the ceremony. During the official speeches – the speakers included the federal president Richard von Weizsäcker – further banners were unfurled in the back rows of the arena-like concert hall. Next came the *Friedens-Gruss:* down below, on the oval stage, were Annette Meriweather, and Michael Obst and Simon Stockhausen with their synthesizers, while the choir, trumpets and trombones were stationed in the top row of the rear gallery. Stockhausen had considered using a text by Albertus Magnus, a great schoolman who had taught in Cologne, but finally opted for a text of his own

which tries to resolve the feud between two ensembles through the provisional decree of the solo soprano:

> Let those with God
> and those who deny God
> love their neighbour -
> and their neighbour's neighbour!
> This brings peace and freedom.

This is followed by a synchronous, homophonic closing hymn which, however, naturally stresses the open disagreement between the two halves, one of which sings:

> We want peace, and freedom through God!

while the other half demands:

> We want peace, and freedom without God![12]

The work blended well with the controversial mood of the day.

1989 began with a two-week Telemusik Festival, during which Stockhausen's music was played at various places in the Netherlands. Following concerts at the conservatoire in Caen, a French town close to the English Channel, Stockhausen's birthday festivities took him back to Finland, after a gap of over twenty years. In March three concerts at the Helsinki Biennale were dedicated to Stockhausen and, as had usually been the case in the preceding months, the programmes consisted of staged performances from *Licht*. Finnish audiences had a high regard for Stockhausen's works from the fifties, Seppo Heikinheimo had written a book entitled *The Electronic Music of Karlheinz Stockhausen* and in 1967 the Stockhausen Group had premièred *Prozession* in Finland. Yet little was known about the *Licht* cycle. When the last sound died away at the end of the first concert in the Savoy Theatre, there was silence: not an empty silence, but silent astonishment that lasted a long time, allowing the music, and the sacral and humorous images, to reverberate in the listeners' minds. Such was the Finnish mentality. After a while Stockhausen broke the spell by applauding from behind his mixing desk, and this unleashed lengthy, warm applause. The audience included members of the younger generation of Finnish composers, notably Kaija Saariaho, who had met Stockhausen some years earlier at IRCAM.

Two performances of *Inori* at the Cologne Philharmonic Hall on 27 and 28 May, with Stockhausen conducting the highly committed Gürzenich Orchestra, ended the birthday celebrations in the same place as they had begun. These were the first performances of *Inori* in Cologne; a programme note pointed out that it had taken the work fifteen years to travel the thirty kilometres from Kürten.

Moscow: A First Concert Tour in the Soviet Union

One of the outstanding events in Stockhausen's many years as a concert artist was his first appearance in the Soviet capital in 1990. The circumstances leading to these concerts were complicated and, as so often with Stockhausen, fraught with obstacles. Stockhausen had constantly received letters and telegrams from Moscow, urging and imploring him to give concerts there. He had never been able to accept such invitations, since the details were always too vague and improvisatory, and there was often no mention of contractual agreements. In the USSR it is by no means unusual for major concert promotions to be organized much more hastily than in the west, and for programmes to be changed shortly before the concert. When the massive German festival Musikkultur heute was planned, involving about 150 concerts and music-theatre performances of post-war West German music in fourteen Soviet cities from September 1989 to June 1990, it naturally had to include Stockhausen. Eventually, though, negotiations between him and the German organizers broke down. He had the impression that they were inventing difficulties to put in the way of his proposed programmes (which included a concert performance of *Montag*), so he pulled out. His opponents claimed that his final proposal – a cycle of five concerts in at least three different cities – was impractical, however well disposed their Soviet partners might be; given two days of rehearsal, it meant that three concert halls would each be immobilized for a whole week. It was only through the tireless efforts of the Moscow-based musicologist Marina Tchaplygina, who had corresponded with Stockhausen for many years, that he finally got a direct invitation from the Union of Soviet Composers. Five concerts – back in harness with the Musikkultur heute festival – would be held in a hall at Lomonosov University, seating about five hundred people. Within hours they were sold out.

Late in the afternoon of 22 March 1990 Stockhausen and his ensemble landed at the Sheremetovo II Airport, and for a week they were embroiled in the Moscow atmosphere of glasnost and perestroika through which Mikhail Gorbachev was seeking to impose order on the social and economic chaos of his vast kingdom. A group of Moscow musicians who had performed various works of his were waiting for Stockhausen at the airport, along with friends in a semicircle of flutes, whistles, rattles and other percussion instruments. They gave him an unusual welcome, as pianist Ivan Sokolov recalls: 'As soon as we saw Stockhausen come through the glass doors, poised like an alert eagle, we cut loose. I played the opening of the Michael formula. For a few moments Stockhausen was taken aback; but then he gazed at us, abandoned his luggage trolley and started to conduct us.'[13] The rest of his ensemble turned up, the Russian musicians were introduced and Stockhausen invited them to spend the evening at his hotel.

When Stockhausen heard the concerts had sold out, he immediately offered to give each one twice, but the heavy-footed bureaucracy said no. After three days of concerts he was asked if extra performances were possible; this time it was he who declined. Rehearsals, interviews and conversations with the Union of Composers left him with little time. Stockhausen visited the Kremlin, and was deeply impressed by the walls of icons in the Orthodox churches. The concerts were a major event in the musical life of Moscow, and aroused great enthusiasm. The composer said later that he had never known an audience to understand his work so well, and have such discriminating artistic judgement. He was led to believe he would soon be invited back for more concerts in the USSR.

While he was in Lisbon for concerts mounted by the Gulbenkian Foundation early in May 1990, Stockhausen received a fax from the directorate of the Hamburg opera house, who since 1988 had been negotiating to be the first German house to stage one of his operas, in May 1991. Bogdanov and his team had been planning to give *Montag* a run of several days. Yet now the work could not be done: it seemed that the opera workshop was not able, after all, to construct the statue of Eve, and an outside firm had estimated the cost at 450,000 marks. In addition, the rebuilding of the pit area would have to be brought forward by three days, and to close the opera house for the eleven days needed to prepare *Montag* was just too expensive. Stockhausen wrote back that there must be some other solution for the statue, that people had known for ages about the rebuilding of the pit and that Bogdanov had only asked for the theatre to be closed for five or six days. But the first chance to see one of his operas in a German theatre was missed, and Stockhausen was extremely disappointed. Yet he continued to compose *Licht*.

Work on *Dienstag* and Skirmishes on Various Fronts

In the sixties Stockhausen had retreated to the country village of Kürten, hoping to work undisturbed in his house at the edge of the forest. Even in those days various animals belonging to his neighbour robbed him of peace and quiet. After a lecture at Cambridge University in 1973 he gave a good-humoured account of his troubles: 'It is the acoustic pollution of the environment that is worst of all. For almost six years now I have been tormented by my neighbour, who has several sheepdogs, five sheep and a parrot. The parrot starts squawking around six in the morning, and let me tell you, it brings out the devil in me! I am constantly dreaming up all kinds of unilateral action . . . it's an impossible situation.'[14] Even the sexagenarian Stockhausen got no peace. Further purchases of land and the removal of field boundaries greatly enlarged the property surrounding his house. Hunters entered his woods increasingly often, not only disturbing him but dismaying him by killing the few wild animals left in the area. Stockhausen wrote to the head of the local council and to the Ministry for the Environment in Bonn: 'At all times of the day I hear shots very close to my house: the wildlife is being killed – particularly on Sunday mornings and public holidays. Sometimes I find bloodstains on my lawn, or some dying animal the marksman failed to find. You can well imagine that every time I hear a shot, my peace of mind is shattered for some time, and that I lose all desire to compose for a 'humanity' that legalizes that sort of thing . . . There are very few animals left in my grounds; they disturb no one, and perhaps they are the last evidence of the wonders of the Divine imagination . . . On ethical grounds, I protest against this pointless, perverse killing on my lands, and seek information as to what judicial measures I should take to prevent it.'[15] Stockhausen was referred first to the Federal Office for the Environment in Berlin, and thence to the Ministry for the Environment of North Rhine-Westphalia – one of those Kafka-like situations where no one accepts responsibility.

In September 1988 Stockhausen learned that a high-tension cable was to run from the Rhine to the Dhünntalsperre in the north of the locality, passing right over Kürten. It was planned that the cable, along with pylons 45 metres high, would cut a swathe 50 metres broad through the fields and forests, and would go straight through Stockhausen's grounds. The composer became a prominent member of the local 'Citizens against Overhead Cables' group; again, he wrote numerous letters to corporate bodies, local authorities and ministries. He pointed out that research had shown that such cables were a threat to public health; exposure to the electromagnetic fields could cause cancer, even at a distance of 800 metres. Such cables had already been banned in the USA and the UK. As of May 1991 there was no sign of pylons in Kürten. Stockhausen said that 'the cable construction has obviously been delayed because of local response, but we are all worried . . . Well, we shall keep on fighting.'[16]

In comparison with this project, the authorities' sealing-off of Stockhausen's little music-house is a minor matter. Stockhausen had enlarged a three-room building erected on his land in 1965, modifying it so that he could store instruments and hold rehearsals there; in May 1986 it was closed off by the local building authorities, and their ban will only be lifted when the extensions have been torn down. Here, once again, an enervating battle against petty officialdom is under way.

Alongside these aggravating and time-consuming struggles on various fronts, Stockhausen was composing *Dienstag* from *Licht*. From August to

November 1990 he was back in the electronic studios at WDR Cologne, working daily on Act 2 (Invasion – Explosion) – which involves a twenty-four-track tape of electronic music produced on digital synthesizers. The new factor here is 'octophony': eight groups of loudspeakers arranged as a cube, permitting every conceivable vertical and diagonal movement of the sounds, at any speed. The opera was completed in the spring of 1991. Stockhausen has added tenor and bass solos to the 1977 version of Act 1 (*Der Jahreslauf*), in which Michael and Lucifer engage in intellectual combat; in Act 2 numerous trumpeters and trombonists will join battle on the stage. According to current plans, *Dienstag* will have its first performance in June 1992 at La Scala, Milan.

Notes

The following abbreviations are used in the notes:

Cott   Jonathan Cott, *Stockhausen: Conversations with the Composer* (New York, 1973).

Frisius   Rudolf Frisius, 'Wille zur Form und Wille zum Abenteuer, Interview mit Karlheinz Stockhausen vom 8. Januar 1978', in Stockhausen, *Texte zur Musik 1977–1984*, vol. vi: *Interpretation* (Cologne, 1989).

Kurtz I   Michael Kurtz, 'Ich halte dann den Finger vor die Lippen', interview with Karlheinz Stockhausen, 22 September 1980, in Stockhausen, *Texte zur Musik 1977–1984*, vol. vi: *Interpretation* (Cologne, 1989).

Kurtz II   Michael Kurtz, 'Lichtblicke', interview with Karlheinz Stockhausen, 24 January 1981, abridged in Stockhausen, *Texte zur Musik 1977–1984*, vol. vi: *Interpretation* (Cologne, 1989).

Sabbe   Hermann Sabbe, 'Die Einheit der Stockhausen-Zeit', *Karlheinz Stockhausen, . . . wie die Zeit verging . . .* (Munich, 1981) [= *Musik-Konzepte*, 19].

Texte I-VI   Karlheinz Stockhausen, *Texte zur elektronischen und instrumentalen Musik*, vol. i (Cologne, 1963); *Texte zu eigenen Werken – zur Kunst Anderer, Aktuelles*, vol. ii (Cologne, 1964); *Texte zur Musik 1963–1970*, vol. iii (Cologne, 1971); *Texte zur Musik 1970–1977*, vol. iv (Cologne, 1978); *Texte zur Musik 1977–1984*, vol. v: *Komposition* (Cologne, 1989); *Texte zur Musik 1977–1984*, vol. vi: *Interpretation* (Cologne, 1989).

Introduction: A Sirius Centre in France

1   Kurtz II.
2   Dietmar Polaczek, 'Unvereinbare Welten: Wie Karlheinz Stockhausen die Kölner Musikhochschule verliess', *Frankfurter Allgemeine Zeitung* (9 September 1977).
3   Kurtz II.
4   Ibid.
5   In ancient times significance was attached to seven-year periods in people's lives, for example by the Jews, Greeks and Romans. Cf. also Wilhelm Hoerner, *Zeit und Rhythmus: Die Ordnungsgesetze der Erde und des Menschen* (Stuttgart, 1978). In more recent times, Rudolf Steiner's anthroposophy indicated a seven-year rhythm in human development. See Rudolf Steiner, *Vom Lebenslauf des Menschen: Vorträge ausgewählt und herausgegeben von Erhard Fucke* (Stuttgart, 1980).
6   Johannes Fritsch, editorial, *Feedback Papers*, 16 (1978), p. 2.

1 Childhood and Youth 1928–47

1 Conversation with author (25 July 1981).
2 Kurtz II.
3 Ibid.
4 Heinz Josef Herbort, 'Von Luzifer lernen. Eine Reportage. Anmerkungen und Teile eines Gespräches', *Die Zeit* (1 June 1984).
5 Kurtz II.
6 Ibid.
7 Texte IV, p. 589.

2 Writer or Composer 1947–51

1 Kurtz II.
2 Hesse's reply to Stockhausen has not yet been found. Peter Lachmund told the author about the content of Hesse's written reply. The Hesse archives of Suhrkamp Verlag include three of Stockhausen's letters to Hesse, which Volker Michels kindly passed on to the author.
3 Wolfgang Pelzer (who studied in Freiburg from 1949), letter to author.
4 Texte II, pp. 235ff.
5 Klaus Weiler remembers hearing the sonata for two pianos and percussion with Stockhausen at the Robert Schumann Konservatorium in Düsseldorf at the beginning of December, but Stockhausen does not recall this. A second performance of the sonata that Stockhausen might have heard took place early in February 1951.
6 Texte IV, p. 376.
7 Ibid.
8 'Lachendes Musikleben: Musikalischer Humor in der Hochschule', *Kölnische Rundschau* (1 February 1951).

3 Awakening after a Musical 'Zero Hour' 1951–3

1 It may be noted that Rudolf Steiner, whose influence on the arts has been widespread, pointed to the experience of the single note as having significance for the future of music. On 21 February 1924, in the course of a cycle of lectures on tone eurhythmy, he said: 'Melody works through time. The chord is the corpse of the melody. And as far as understanding music is concerned, our time is in a quite hopeless situation. For all this reflection about the timbre within the overtones and that sort of thing involves a desire to extrapolate from each single note a kind of chord. So that today, in fact, sympathy for the harmonic within people is already embedded in the single tone. To questions about how music should develop, I have often given the answer: we must become aware of the melody within a note, within a single note. In each note there are a number of notes – three at least. But the one note that we hear as the note which is sounding, which is being produced with the instrument, that acts as present. And then there is another one, which is as though we were remembering it. And there is a third one there, which is as if we were expecting it. Each note actually evokes memory and expectation, as melodious neighbour notes.
'That is something that one day people will be able to demonstrate. We will find a way of making music a more profound experience, by making the single note into melody. These days people like to seek chords within the individual note, and ponder on how this chord lives in the overtones. So it goes beyond a purely materialistic grasp of music' (*Eurythmie als sichtbarer Gesang*, Complete Works, no. 278, Dornach, 1975, p. 48).
Steiner made his first comments on the experience of the single note on 29 September

238

1920, and answered a question related to these with the following: 'But I would like to know how we can understand musical personalities like Debussy if they are not regarded as being forerunners, perhaps very unfocused ones, of some future development lying in this direction. Once we can concede this, we realize that a very special possibility lies ahead of us, the possibility that people will compose in a completely different way from now, namely in such a way that the relationship between the composer and the reproducing artist will be a much freer one, that the player, the producing artist, has a much less determinate role, that he can be much more productive and will have much greater scope. But in the musical domain that will only be possible when the tonal system is expanded, if we really can have those variations that are necessary if things are to be decisively varied. And I can imagine, for example, that what the composer will produce in future will be more loosely formulated, but because it is more loosely formulated, the reproducing artist will need much more variation, far more notes, to express things properly. If we can find our way in to the deeper essence of the note, we can deploy it in a great variety of ways, by setting it out with its innate neighbour notes. In this way a very versatile musical life could result' (*Das Wesen des Musikalischen*, Complete Works, no. 283, Dornach, 1969).

2 Pierre Boulez, *Wille und Zufall* (Stuttgart, 1977), pp. 61f.
3 György Ligeti, 'Anlässlich *Lontano*', in the brochure for Donaueschingen 1967.
4 Karel Goeyvaerts, *Autobiografie* (Leuven, 1983), p. 54.
5 Karel Goeyvaerts, letter to author.
6 Goeyvaerts, *Autobiografie*, p. 54.
7 Theodor W. Adorno, 'Das Altern der Neuen Musik', *Dissonanzen: Musik in der verwalteten Welt* (Göttingen, 1956), p. 119.
8 Karel Goeyvaerts, 'Was aus Wörtern wird', *Melos*, 39 (1972), p. 159.
9 Conversation with author (11 December 1982).
10 Martin Heidegger, *Holzwege* (Frankfurt am Main, 1950), p. 5.
11 Werner Meyer-Eppler, 'Daten aus der Entwicklung der Elektronischen Musik in Deutschland', unpublished manuscript.
12 Hermann Pfrogner, *Lebendige Tonwelt* (Munich, 1981); Heiner Ruland, *Ein Weg zur Erweiterung des Tonerlebens* (Basle, 1981). Pfrogner and Ruland try to distinguish between *sonic resonance* (the physically measurable sound), *sound* and *tone*. Tone is the very essence of music, the product of the creative act of listener and musician. It is, in the sense used by Goethe, the 'moral', that is, spiritual, aspect of the tone experience, while *sonic resonance* represents its 'sensual', material side. In the experience of *sound* the listener and musician find themselves in an inner realm between the poles of spirit and sense. 'All these distinctions,' says Pfrogner, 'are to be understood according to Goethe, for whom Nature has "neither outside nor inside", but is rather "all of a piece" (J. W. Goethe, *Gedichte, Allerdings [Dem Physiker]*). In the same way the musical tone is a unity arising from the interpenetration of *tone, sound* and *sonic resonance*' (p. 195). This statement, of course, cannot be discussed further here; nevertheless it touches a central question of the music of our century.
13 Texte II, p. 11.
14 Hans Heinz Eggebrecht (ed.), *Karlheinz Stockhausen im Musikwissenschaftlichen Seminar der Universität Freiburg im Breisgau* (Murrhardt, 1986), pp. 34f.
15 Hermann Braun, conversation with author.
16 Sabbe, p. 22.
17 Alexander Adrion, 'Zaubern mit Stockhausen', *Frankfurter Allgemeine Zeitung* (20 August 1988).
18 'Bunte Märchen auf der Bühne: Alexander Adrion bezaubert das Publikum', *Westfälische Rundschau* (10 December 1951).
19 Texte IV, p. 52.

20 Texte II, p. 144.
21 'It has fallen to my lot to invent music. But it is not my intention to express what can be thought or felt, using notes as an image or similitude. There is just a growing familarity with the very simple material, with the limitations set on playing this or that, with the richness of the audible outcome. And at a certain moment there comes a visage – from all the known and unknown possibilities, I suddenly see some of them emerging and meshing together. And I just stay still and watch the things move round one another until suddenly there is stasis. Sometimes that takes a long time, and I have to call back the apparition and wait for it to stop moving. Then, when the visage is completely at rest, I seek my own way of finishing, of finding a reference point, of gaining insight. And I write it down. Some things are not achieved; that is exactly where I lack perfection. And I sense that clearly. Everything – I myself within everything I ever could be – is dependent on what we call the Idea' (Letter to Doris Stockhausen, 4 February 1952).
22 Sabbe, p. 57.
23 Texte IV, p. 53.
24 Texte II, p. 13.
25 Texte IV, p. 55.
26 In a letter of 14 January 1953 from Hamburg Stockhausen told Goeyvaerts he had started writing out a new chamber-music work, 'Nr. 5 für 10 Instrumente'. From his description it is clear that he was talking about the piece that is now called *Kontra-Punkte*. In the same letter Stockhausen said that in future he would be designating his works only by numbers (though the plan did not last long), and he mentioned *Spiel* and a work entitled 'Kontrapunkte' as nos. 2 and 4; at that time no. 1 was probably *Kreuzspiel* and no. 3 the *Schlagquartett*. If a letter of 4 November 1952 to Alfred Schlee from Paris is taken into account, it seems reasonable to surmise that 'Kontrapunkte' is identical with the orchestral work composed in September 1952 in Hamburg, which became *Punkte* in the spring of 1953. 'In the next few days my wife will be sending you two scores: "Schlagquartett" and "Kontrapunkte" . . . You might begin – if this seems good to you – with the publication of "Kontrapunkte" [the piece now known as *Kontra-Punkte* was not written out in Hamburg until at least two months later] . . . Moreover, this work departs widely from normal orchestral forces, that is, the usual instrumentation' (*75 Jahre Universal Edition*, exhibition catalogue for the Vienna Stadt- and Landesbibliothek in the Historisches Museum, December 1976–January 1977, Vienna, 1976, p. 67). In the letter Stockhausen also said that saxophones would need to be involved (the 1952 version of *Punkte* includes three saxophones), as well as nine percussionists, as in *Spiel*.
27 Texte IV, p. 53.
28 Sabbe, p. 42. In 'Stockhausen's Electronic Works: Sketches and Work-sheets 1952–1967', *Interface*, vol. 10 (1981), pp. 150f., Richard Toop reports on two tape compositions from Paris: 'Studie über einen Ton' (for two parts) and the 'Konkrete Etude'. He relates the passage from the letter to Goeyvaerts of 3 December 1952 to the 'Studie über einen Ton'. In the list of works in *The New Grove Dictionary of Music* the 'Studie über einen Ton' is listed (as 'Study on one sound') under 'unnumbered works and projects'. In a letter of 20 September 1984 to the editor of the dictionary Stockhausen wrote (in English): ' "Study on one sound" is the wrong title. It is in my work list as "Etude" (konkrete Musik). It is NOT discarded, but the *tape exists: my verbal radio explanation of 1952* exists on tape from that time; and the graphic notes with all details exist.' Toop's article describes sketches for two different *concrète* tape works with the same duration, so it may be that the 'Studie über einen Ton' never got beyond the planning stage.
29 Sabbe, pp. 42f.
30 Ibid., p. 43.
31 Texte III, p. 342.

32 Abraham Moles, letter to author (10 April 1987).
33 Michael Kurtz, 'Interview mit Pierre Schaeffer', *Zeitschrift für Musikpädagogik*, 33 (January 1986), pp. 16f.
34 Texte II, p. 20.
35 Sabbe, p. 47.

4 Electronic Music: A Musical Homunculus 1953–5

1   Quoted in Werner Kaegi, *Was ist elektronische Musik?* (Zurich, 1967), p. 132.
2   Eggebrecht, *Karlheinz Stockhausen*, p. 12.
3   Undated letter to Karel Goeyvaerts (*c.* June-July 1953), probably from Cologne.
4   Sabbe, p. 44.
5   Heinz Schütz, conversation with author.
6   Frisius, p. 147.
7   Ibid., pp. 147f.
8   Texte IV, pp. 402f.
9   Cott, p. 101.
10 Richard Toop, *Karlheinz Stockhausen: Music and Machines (1954–1970)*, booklet for the series of Stockhausen concerts given by the BBC at the London Barbican Centre, 8–16 January 1985, p. 25.
11 Karlheinz Stockhausen, 'Ein Gespräch über die Donaueschinger Musiktage (Erinnerungen und Ausblicke)', reprinted from *Almenach 1990*, Heimetbuch Schwarzwald-Bear-Kreis, series 14 (pp. 220–30).
12 Ekbert Faas, 'Interview with Karlheinz Stockhausen', *Feedback Papers*, 16 (1978), p. 27.
13 Ibid., pp. 27f.
14 Georg Heike, conversation with author.
15 Goeyvaerts, *Autobiografie*, p. 71.
16 Niksǎ Gligo, 'Ich traf John Cage in Bremen', *Melos*, 40 (1973), pp. 23f.
17 Texte II, p. 249.
18 John Cage, letter to Stockhausen (3 December 1954), quoted in Richard Toop's unpublished manuscript.
19 David Tudor, conversation with author.
20 Cott, p. 208.
21 Texte II, p. 45. What pieces were played on that day has not yet been established. Toop's manuscript (pp. 169f) suggests that Marcelle Mercenier had only mastered the first few pages of *Klavierstück VI*. Madame Mercenier informed the author that she had not played *Klavierstück VI* at all. The sound archive of the Internationales Musikinstitut Darmstadt contains three tape recordings of *Klavierstücke V-VIII*, made on 1 June 1955. The first has *Klavierstück V*, complete performance without disturbances, and *Klavierstück VI*, up to p. 12 of the Universal Edition score when the playing suddenly breaks off. The second is of *Klavierstück VII*, with 'obbligato' cricket from the start. The playing is undisturbed until the first line on p. 4 of the Universal Edition copy. After the fortissimo C sharp there is laughter and during the second line, sustained applause; the piece is broken off. On the third tape are *Klavierstück VIII*, uninterrupted performance, and *Klavierstück I* (as an encore?), both without the cricket.
22 Texte II, p. 43.

5 Spatial and Aleatory Music 1955–60

1   Frisius, p. 145.
2   Ibid., p. 155.
3   Cott, p. 141.

4 Texte I, pp. 99–139.
5 Heinz-Klaus Metzger, conversation with author.
6 Frisius, pp. 154f.
7 Novalis, 'Aus den Fragmenten', *Dichtungen* (Leipzig, 1939), p. 135.
8 Heinz-Klaus Metzger, 'Vokal, Instrumental, Elektronisch', *Melos*, 23 (1956), p. 222.
9 Texte IV, pp. 577f.
10 Texte II, p. 249.
11 David Tudor, 'From Piano to Electronics', *Music and Musicians* (1972), p. 25.
12 Hans G. Helms, 'Lauter Originale', in Wulf Herzogenrath and Gabriele Lueg (eds), *Die 6oer Jahre: Kölns Weg zur Kunstmetropole: Vom Happening zum Kunstmarkt*, exhibition catalogue for the Cologne Kunstverein, 31 August – 16 November 1986 (Cologne, 1986), p. 135.
13 John Cage, *Silence* (Cambridge, Mass., 1966), p. 36.
14 Herbert Henck, *Karlheinz Stockhausens Klavierstück X: Ein Beitrag zum Verständnis serieller Kompositionstechnik* (Cologne, 1980), pp. 75f.
15 Toop, unpublished manuscript, p. 251.
16 'Ich will weil es wird', in 'Ist der Sozialismus am Ende?', *Die Zeit*, 49 (1 December 1989).
17 Texte II, p. 220.
18 Ibid., p. 231.
19 Wolf-Eberhard von Lewinski, 'Klausur, Studio und Forum in Kranichstein', *Melos*, 28 (1959), p. 302.
20 Luigi Nono, 'Geschichte und Gegenwart in der Musik von heute', *Darmstädter Beiträge zur Neuen Musik*, iii (1960), p. 47.
21 Cott, p. 31.
22 Ibid.
23 Texte I, p. 199.
24 Cott, p. 31.
25 Texte IV, p. 365.
26 Rudolf Frisius, 'Prozesskomposition, Interview mit Karlheinz Stockhausen', in Texte VI, p. 405.
27 Christoph Caskel, conversation with author.
28 Texte II, pp. 206f.
29 'Der Widerstand gegen die Neue Musik', radio conversations between Theodor W. Adorno and Karlheinz Stockhausen, in Texte VI, p. 476.
30 Friedrich Blume, *Was ist Musik?* (Kassel, 1959), p. 17.
31 *Melos*, 26 (1959), p. 84.
32 Tibor Kneif, 'Adorno und Stockhausen', *Zeitschrift für Musiktheorie*, 4 (1973), no. 1, p. 34.
33 Texte II, pp. 251 and 253.
34 Cornelius Cardew, 'Report on Stockhausen's *Carré*', *Musical Times*, 102 (1961), pp. 619f.

6 From Moment Form to Live Electronics 1961–5

1 Gabriele Lueg, 'Gespräch mit Mary Bauermeister', in Herzogenrath and Lueg, *Die 6oer Jahre*, p. 142.
2 A minor event a few years later sheds new light on the Stockhausen–Henze relationship. When *Der Spiegel* published a very unflattering article on Henze late in autumn 1968, Stockhausen immediately sent a telegram, which was published in the magazine as a reader's letter on 9 December 1968: 'henze is as he is stop his music is as it was and is stop since the war the german press has tried to make henze into a musical model stop it is not so long since der spiegel chose him for its cover picture and rated his work

very highly stop why must a magazine as popular as der spiegel aggravate the general
fragmentation, enmity and hatred yet further and treat a musician so disgracefully?'
3 Kurt Schwertsik, conversation with author.
4 Texte II, p. 167.
5 Texte I, pp. 222–58.
6 Texte II, p. 243.
7 Arthur Caspari, 'Brief an Gabriele Lueg', in Herzogenrath and Lueg, *Die 60er Jahre*, p. 162.
8 Kurtz I.
9 Frisius, p. 146.
10 Mary Bauermeister, 'Fruhe Aktivitäten in Köln', in Ursula Peters and G. F. Schwarzbauer (eds), *Fluxus: Aspekte eines Phänomens*, exhibition catalogue for the Kunst- und Museumverein Wuppertal (1981–2), p. 202.
11 Mary Bauermeister, conversation with author.
12 Cott, p. 78.
13 Texte II, p. 32.
14 Gotthard Günther, *Idee und Grundriss einer nicht-Aristotelischen Logik* (Hamburg, 1957), p. 248. Günther is quoting his teacher Arnold Gehlen.
15 Texte II, p. 130.
16 Otto Tomek, in *Die Internationalen Ferienkurse für Neue Musik 1962–3* (based on broadcasts by Hessian Radio and WDR), p. 10.
17 Letter to Kurt Schwertsik (4 January 1963). The 'analogous Neo-realism' relates to Schwertsik's style of composition.
18 All from Heinrich Strobel, *Verehrter Meister, lieber Freund*, edited by Ingeborg Schatz (Stuttgart, 1977), p. 91.
19 Cott, p. 102.
20 Texte III, pp. 12f.
21 Hans Ulrich Lehmann, letter to author (20 July 1987).
22 From the introduction to a book about the Cologne New Music Courses that was compiled by Hugo Wolfram Schmidt for publication by Universal Edition but never issued.
23 Ibid.
24 Texte III, p. 40.
25 Pierre Mariétan, 'A nouvelle musique, pédagogie nouvelle, Kölner Kurse für Neue Musik 1963–1966', *Schweizerische Musikzeitung/Revue musicale suisse*, 106 (1966), pp. 283–92.
26 Mary Bauermeister, conversation with author.
27 Texte III, p. 227.
28 Dick Higgins, 'Postface', in Wolf Vostell (ed.), *Happenings* (Reinbek, 1970), p. 191.
29 Texte III, p. 61.
30 Hugh Davies, 'Working with Stockhausen', *Composer*, 27 (1968), pp. 8f.
31 Robin Maconie, *The Works of Karlheinz Stockhausen* (London, 1976), p. 198.
32 Texte II, p. 234.
33 Karl H. Wörner, *Stockhausen: Life and Work*, translated and enlarged by Bill Hopkins (London, 1973), p. 140.

7 'A Music of All Countries and Races' 1966–8

1 Texte IV, p. 442.
2 Texte III, p. 75.
3 Kurtz II.
4 Ibid.
5 Texte IV, p. 447.

6 Ibid., p. 454f.
7 Cott, p. 30.
8 Texte III, p. 294.
9 Ibid., p. 92.
10 Wolf-Eberhard von Lewinski, 'Alte und neue Experimente bei den Kranichsteinern', *Melos*, 33 (1966), p. 321.
11 Carla Henius, 'Adorno als musikalischer Lehrmeister', *Melos*, 37 (1970), p. 492.
12 Guido Canella and Luigi Ferrari, 'Musik und Tod, Interview mit Karlheinz Stockhausen', *Neue Zeitschrift für Musik*, 148 (1987), no. 5, p. 19.
13 Jay Marks, 'Conversation with Stockhausen', *Saturday Review* (30 September 1967).
14 Ibid.
15 Rolf Gehlhaar, conversation with author.
16 Texte III, p. 212.
17 Rolf Gehlhaar, 'Zur Komposition Ensemble', *Darmstädter Beiträge zur Neuen Musik*, xi (1968), pp. 37f.
18 Cott, p. 213.
19 Texte IV, p. 79.
20 Johannes Fritsch, 'Hauptwerk *Hymnen*', *Feedback Papers*, 16 (1978), p. 21.
21 Cott, p. 144.
22 Ibid.
23 Kurtz II.
24 Cott, p. 163.
25 Ibid.
26 Texte III, p. 109.
27 Erich Limmert, 'Bremer Musiktage mit 16 Uraufführungen', *Melos*, 35 (1968), p. 302.

8 *Aus den sieben Tagen* 1968–70

1 Kurtz I.
2 Ibid.
3 Satprem, *Sri Aurobindo oder das Abenteuer des Bewusstseins* (Berne, 1970), p. 29.
4 Texte III, p. 292.
5 Ibid., p. 295.
6 Fred Ritzel, 'Musik für ein Haus', *Darmstädter Beiträge zur Neuen Musik*, xii (1970), p. 12.
7 Ibid., p. 15.
8 Texte III, p. 164.
9 Ibid., p. 137.
10 Ibid., p. 136.
11 Ibid., pp. 124f.
12 Karlheinz Stockhausen, 'Modulationen wie bei Gustav Mahler oder den Minnesängern', *Die Welt* (14 December 1980). Shortly after John Lennon's death Stockhausen told the author that a reporter from *Die Welt* had interviewed him over the phone about Lennon's death. The author does not know whether Stockhausen authorized this text.
13 Cott, pp. 210f.
14 Texte IV, p. 530.
15 Harry Hamm, 'Andacht in der Grotte', *Frankfurter Allgemeine Zeitung* (5 January 1970).
16 Texte III, pp. 121f.
17 Ibid., pp. 154f.

9 Music as Gateway to the Spiritual 1970–74

1 Ritzel, 'Musik für ein Haus', p. 35.
2 Cott, p. 222.
3 Ibid.
4 Texte IV, p. 172.
5 Cott, p. 25.
6 *The Urantia Book* (7th edition, Chicago, 1981).
7 Cornelius Cardew, 'Stockhausen Serves Imperialism', *Listener*, vol. 87 (1972), pp. 809ff; Konrad Boehmer, 'Der Imperialismus als höchstes Stadium des kapitalistischen Avantgardismus', *Musik und Gesellschaft*, xxii (1972), pp. 137ff.
8 Theodor Schwenk, *Das sensible Chaos* (Stuttgart, 1976).
9 Jill Purce, 'The Spiral in the Music of Karlheinz Stockhausen', *Main Currents in Modern Thought*, xxx (1973), no. 1, pp. 18–27; Jill Purce, *The Mystic Spiral* (London, 1974).
10 *The Sufi Message of Hazrat Inayat Khan*, vol. ii (Geneva, 1973), pp. 78 and 149.
11 Texte IV, pp. 545f.
12 Hans Jenny, *Kymatik*, vols. i and ii (Basle, 1967 and 1972).
13 Some explanatory comments may be useful here. Is it not wrong to imagine that the essential factor in experiencing music lies with the physical and acoustic effects on the human body – the idea that the body is, so to speak, massaged with sound vibrations? Is it not more likely that the opposite is the case – namely that musical experience is an interior experience, a spiritual experience? In this context, we may remember Pfrogner's distinction between sonic resonance, sound and tone (see ch. 3, n. 12). Jacques Handschin has commented on this as follows: 'Music is not the sounds available on our instruments, but something that lives within us' (cited in Pfrogner, *Lebendige Tonwelt*, p. 7). Yet this music within us (it could also be called an inner aural capacity) has changed as music itself has developed, leading to a threshold at the middle of the century. On the one hand, music has been reduced to a physio-acoustic experience. We are confronted with the physical residues of what was once a spiritual world of sound, and we are probably making a great mistake if we assume that musical experience in the past was physio-acoustic as it is now. On the other hand, this legacy has severed a spiritual umbilical cord for mankind, whom the divine world has expelled from its creation, and we now face the question of musical freedom. This is the eye of the needle within the musical 'zero hour' considered at the beginning of Chapter 3. It has become possible to compose everything, even something absolutely arbitrary. In his essay 'Concerning the Spiritual in Art' Kandinsky sought a spiritual basis for painting. The question now is whether a comparable spirituality will be sought again in music, setting out from the assumption that the inner aural capacity can be regained. But no one knows how the world of music will look in the future. That is implicit in human freedom.
14 Texte IV, pp. 200 and 209.
15 *Ernst von Siemens-Musik-Preis 1986: Karlheinz Stockhausen* (1986), pp. 16ff.
16 Texte IV, p. 226.
17 Kurtz II.
18 Third seminar on *Stimmung*, 3 August 1972 (based on the author's notes, compared with the tape recording at the Internationales Musikinstitut Darmstadt).

10 New Interpreters, New Instrumental Techniques 1974–7

1 Texte IV, p. 246.
2 Herbort, 'Von Luzifer lernen'.
3 Roland de Beer and Paul de Neef, 'Interview mit Karlheinz Stockhausen', *Haagse Post* (4 December 1982).

4 Alfons Rosenberg, *Durchbruch zur Zukunft: Der Mensch im Wassermannzeitalter* (Bietigheim, Württemberg, n.d. [?1971]; V. M. von Winter, *Die Menschentypen: Die Psychologie der Tierkreiszeichen* (Frankfurt, 1982).
5 Texte IV, p. 275.
6 Ibid., p. 301.
7 Jakob Lorber, *Der Kosmos in geistiger Schau* (Bietigheim, Württemberg, 1977), p. 90.
8 Texte IV, p. 465.
9 Wolfgang Schultze, 'Getröpfel aus dem Kosmos: Im Berliner Planetarium wurde Stockhausens *Sirius* aufgeführt', *Die Welt* (30 September 1976).

11 *Licht* 1977–91

1 An extensive glossary of the names and concepts in *The Urantia Book* may be found in Clyde Bedell, *Concordex of 'The Urantia Book'* (Santa Barbara, Calif., 1986). *The Urantia Book* consists of mediumistic writing (like Jakob Lorber's publications), printed on 2,097 pages of India paper, and is not the result of scientific researches. The following may be noted: in the angelogy of the Christian Middle Ages the Archangel Michael is described as the 'visage of Christ'. In *The Urantia Book* Michael is a 'Creator Son', 'ruler of our local universe of Nebadon'. Over a billion years he has made seven 'bestowals', the seventh and last being his birth as a human, as Christ-Michael, in 7 BC at midday on 21 August in Bethlehem. Christ-Michael is not identical with the Son of God, as embodied in the Trinity of the Father, Son and Holy Ghost, which also finds a place in *The Urantia Book*.
  On the traditions concerning the Archangel Michael in pre-Christian and Christian times, see Nora von Stein-Baditz, *Aus Michaels Wirken* (Stuttgart, 1967), especially the essay of the same name by Ita Wegmann, pp. 11–30.
2 Rudolf Frisius writes: 'The seven days of the week and their melodies are nominated as symbols of the seven celestial bodies (Moon, Mars, Mercury, Jupiter, Venus, Saturn and Sun), of seven personal characteristics (courage, bravery, friendliness, industry, steadfastness, fearlessness and loyalty), of seven colours (green, red, yellow, blue, orange, black and gold), of seven mythological elements (water, earth, air, ether, flame, fire and light) and the seven senses (smell, taste, seeing, hearing, feel/touch, thinking and intuition)' ('Zeremonie und Magie: *Evas Lied*: Karlheinz Stockhausens neues Teilstück aus *Licht*', *Musik-Texte*, 17, December 1986).
3 Quoted in Markus Stockhausen, *'Michael's Reise um die Erde*: Eine Dokumentation über die Entstehung des Werkes bis zu seiner Uraufführung' (admission thesis to the Cologne Musikhochschule, 1979).
4 Canella and Ferrari, 'Musik und Tod', p. 19.
5 *Karlheinz Stockhausen*: 60. Geburtstag: 22 August 1988 (Kürten, n.d.), p. 39.
6 Ibid., p. 40.
7 Michael Kurtz, 'Wo Musik lebendig ist: Interview mit Karlheinz Stockhausen vom 17. Oktober 1986', *Zeitschrift für Musikpädagogik*, 38 (January 1987), p. 6.
8 Kurtz I.
9 Kurtz, 'Wo Musik lebendig ist', p. 3.
10 Letter to author (31 July 1988).
11 'Friedensgruss an alle planetarischen Studenten', in the brochure *600 Jahre Kölner Universität*, p. 10.
12 Ibid., p. 11.
13 Conversation with author.
14 Texte IV, p. 423.

15 Letter to the Federal Ministry for the Environment, Nature and Atomic Energy, Bonn (19 September 1989).
16 Letter to author (11 March 1991).

Select Bibliography

An extensive Stockhausen bibliography, compiled by Christoph von Blümroder and Herbert Henck, appeared in vols. 3 and 5 of the annual review *Neuland: Ansätze zur Musik der Gegenwart*, edited by Herbert Henck (Bergisch-Gladbach, 1983 and 1985); updated to 1986, it is reprinted in Stockhausen's *Texte zur Musik 1977–1984*, vol. vi: *Interpretation* (Cologne, 1989).

Writings of Stockhausen

Texte zur elektronischen und instrumentalen Musik, vol. i (Cologne, 1963).
Texte zu eigenen Werken, zur Kunst Anderer, Aktuelles, vol. ii, (Cologne, 1964).
Texte zur Musik 1963–1970, vol. iii (Cologne, 1971).
Texte zur Musik 1970–1977, vol. iv (Cologne, 1978).
Texte zur Musik 1977–1984, vol. v: *Komposition* (Cologne, 1989).
Texte zur Musik 1977–1984, vol. vi: *Interpretation* (Cologne, 1989).

Books and Articles

Burow, Winfried, 'Stockhausens Studie II', *Schriften zur Musikpädagogik* (1973).
Cott, Jonathan, *Stockhausen: Conversations with the Composer* (New York, 1973).
Eggebrecht, Hans Heinz (ed.), *Karlheinz Stockhausen im Musikwissenschaftlichen Seminar der Universität Freiburg im Breisgau*, publications of the Walcker-Stiftung, vol. 11 (Murrhardt, 1986).
Feedback Papers, 16 (1978), edited by Johannes Fritsch (issue dedicated to Stockhausen on his fiftieth birthday, including: Barlow, Klarenz, 'Hertzlichen Glückwunsch' and 'Colozentrische Weltkarte'; Bojé, Harald, '*Aus den 7 Tagen*, Textinterpretationen'; Eötvös, Peter, 'Wie ich Stockhausen kennenlernte'; Faas, Ekbert, 'Interview with Karlheinz Stockhausen'; Frisius, Rudolf, 'Von der Reihe zur Melodie'; Fritsch, Johannes, 'Hauptwerk *Hymnen*'; McGuire, John, 'Drei Träume'; Schiffer, Brigitte, 'Berichte aus Ägypten'; Volans, Kevin, 'Understanding Stockhausen').
Gehlhaar, Rolf, 'Zur Komposition Ensemble', *Darmstädter Beiträge zur Neuen Musik*, xi (1968).
Harvey, Jonathan, *The Music of Stockhausen: An Introduction* (London, 1975).
Heikinheimo, Seppo, 'The Electronic Music of Karlheinz Stockhausen: Studies in Its Esthetical and Formal Problems of Its First Phase', *Acta musicologica fennica*, vi (1972).
Henck, Herbert, *Karlheinz Stockhausens Klavierstück IX* (Bergisch-Gladbach, 1979).
Henck, Herbert, *Karlheinz Stockhausens Klavierstück X: Ein Beitrag zum Verständnis serieller Kompositionstechnik* (Cologne, 1980; English translation, *Karlheinz Stockhausen's Klavierstück X: A Contribution Toward Understanding Serial Technique*, Cologne, 1980).

Krüger, Walther, 'Karlheinz Stockhausen: Allmacht und Ohnmacht in der neuesten Musik', *Forschungsbeiträge zur Musikwissenschaft*, vol. xxiii (1971, enlarged 2nd edn, 1974).

Maconie, Robin, *The Works of Karlheinz Stockhausen* (London, 1976).

Manion, Michael, Sullivan, Barry, and Weiland, Andreas, *Stockhausen in Den Haag* (Zeist, 1983)[documentation of the Karlheinz Stockhausen Project at the Royal Conservatory in Den Haag, 27 October–1 December 1982].

Ritzel, Fred, 'Musik für ein Haus', *Darmstädter Beiträge zur Neuen Musik*, xii (1970).

Sabbe, Hermann, 'Die Einheit der Stockhausen-Zeit', *Karlheinz Stockhausen, . . . wie die Zeit verging . . .* (Munich, 1981) [= *Musik-Konzepte*, 19].

Tannenbaum, Mya, *Conversations with Stockhausen* (Oxford, 1987).

Wörner, Karl H., *Karlheinz Stockhausen: Werk und Wollen* (Cologne, 1963); translated and enlarged by Bill Hopkins as *Stockhausen: Life and Work*, London, 1973).

List of Works

(with dates of premières)

Sources: Stockhausen-Verlag Index of Works (1987); *The New Grove Dictionary of Music and Musicians* (London, 1980); Richard Toop's unpublished manuscript; the author's collection of concert programmes and scores. A few details have been added or corrected; a few premières could not be traced.

Published Works

The numbering is Stockhausen's. Nos.¹⁄₁₁ to 29 are published by Universal Edition, Vienna, no. 30 onwards by the Stockhausen-Verlag, Kürten.

¹⁄₁₁   *Chöre für Doris* (Choruses for Doris; on poems by Paul Verlaine) – 1950
1. *Die Nachtigall* (The nightingale); 2. *Armer junger Hirt* (Poor young shepherd); 3. *Agnus Dei* (Lamb of God)
P: Paris, 21 October 1971, ORTF (French Radio) Chamber Chorus, cond. Marcel Couraud

¹⁄₁₀   *Drei Lieder* (Three songs) for alto voice and chamber orchestra – 1950
1. *Der Rebell* (The rebel; text by Baudelaire); 2. *Frei* (Free; text by Stockhausen); 3. *Der Saitenmann* (The string man; text by Stockhausen)
P: Paris, 21 October 1971, Brigitte Fassbaender, Ensemble Musique Vivante, cond. Karlheinz Stockhausen

¹⁄₉   *Choral* (Chorale; text by Stockhausen) – 1950
P: Paris, 21 October 1971, ORTF Chamber Chorus, cond. Marcel Couraud

¹⁄₈   *Sonatine* for violin and piano – 1951
P: Paris, 22 October 1971, Saschko Gawriloff (violin), Aloys Kontarsky (piano)

¹⁄₇   *Kreuzspiel* (Crossplay) for oboe, bass clarinet, piano, 3 percussionists – 1951 (rev. 1959)
P: Darmstadt, 21 July 1952, Romolo Grano (oboe), Friedrich Wildgans (bass clarinet), Irmela Sandt (piano), Paul Geppert, Bruno Maderna, Hans Rossmann and Willy Trumpfheller (percussion; original version for 4 percussionists), cond. Karlheinz Stockhausen

⅙   *Formel* (Formula) for orchestra – 1951
P: Paris, 22 October 1971, Ensemble Musique Vivante, cond. Karlheinz Stockhausen

⅕   *Etude, musique concrète* – 1952

¼   *Spiel* (Play) for orchestra – 1952
P: Donaueschingen, 11 October 1952, SWF (South-west Radio) Orchestra, cond. Hans Rosbaud

⅓   *Schlagquartett* (Percussive quartet) for piano and 3 × 2 timpani – 1952 (rev. 1974 as *Schlagtrio* for piano and 2 × 3 timpani)
P: Munich, 23 March 1953, Hans Alexander Kaul (piano), Ludwig Porth, Karl Peinkofer and Hermann Gschwendner (timpani)

½   *Punkte* (Points) for orchestra – 1952 (rev. 1962, 1964 and 1966)
P: Donaueschingen, 20 October 1963, SWF Orchestra, cond. Pierre Boulez

1   *Kontra-Punkte* (Counter-points) for 10 instruments – 1952 revised 1953
P: Cologne, 26 March 1953, WDR (West German Radio) Symphony Orchestra, cond. Hermann Scherchen

2   *Klavierstücke I-IV* (Piano pieces I-IV) – 1952–3
P: Darmstadt, 21 August 1954, Marcelle Mercenier

3   *Studie I* and *II* (Studies I and II), electronic music – *I* 1953; *II* 1954
P: Cologne, 19 October 1954

4   *Klavierstücke V-X* – 1954–5 (*IX* and *X* were not realised until 1961)
P: *Klavierstück V*: Darmstadt, 21 August 1954, Marcelle Mercenier; *Klavierstücke V-VII*: Darmstadt, 1 June 1955, Marcelle Mercenier; *Klavierstück IX*: Cologne, 21 May 1962, Aloys Kontarsky; *Klavierstück X*: Palermo, 10 October 1962, Frederic Rzewski

5   *Zeitmasse* (Time-measures) for 5 woodwinds – 1955–6
P: Paris, 15 December 1956, Domaine Musical, cond. Pierre Boulez

6   *Gruppen* (Groups) for 3 orchestras – 1955–7
P: Cologne, 24 March 1958, WDR Symphony Orchestra, cond. Pierre Boulez, Bruno Maderna and Karlheinz Stockhausen

7   *Klavierstück XI* – 1956
P: New York, 22 April 1957, David Tudor

8   *Gesang der Jünglinge* (Song of the youths), electronic music – 1955–6
P: Cologne, 30 May 1956

9   *Zyklus* (Cycle) for a percussionist – 1959
P: Darmstadt, 25 August 1959, Christoph Caskel

10   *Carré* (Square) for 4 orchestras and 4 choruses – 1959–60
P: Hamburg, 28 October 1960, NDR (North German Radio) Orchestra and Chorus, cond. Michael Gielen, Mauricio Kagel, Andrzej Markowski and Karlheinz Stockhausen

11   *Refrain* for 3 players, piano and woodblocks, celesta and antique cymbals, vibraphone and cowbells – 1959
P: Berlin, 2 October 1959, David Tudor (piano), Cornelius Cardew (celesta), Siegfried Rockstroh (vibraphone)

12   *Kontakte* (Contacts) for electronic sounds – 1959–60

12½   *Kontakte* for electronic sounds, piano and percussion – 1959–60
P: Cologne, 11 June 1960, David Tudor (piano), Christoph Caskel (percussion)

12⅔   *Originale* (Originals), music theatre with *Kontakte* – 1961
P: Cologne, 26 October 1961, Arthur Caspari (director), David Tudor (piano), Christoph Caskel (percussion), Kenji Kobayashi (violin), Nam June Paik (actions), Belina (singer), Hans G. Helms (poet), Mary Bauermeister (painter), Edith Sommer (as herself), Wolfgang Ramsbott (cameraman), Walter Koch (lighting), Leopold von Knobelsdorff (sound engineer), Liselotte Lörsch (wardrobe), Mrs Hoffman (newspaper vendor), a child, Alfred Feussner, Harry J. Bong, Ruth Grahlmann, Eva-Maria Kox, Heiner Reddemann and Peter Hackenberger (actors)

13   *Momente* (Moments) for solo soprano, 4 chorus groups and 13 instrumentalists (text: Song of Solomon, Blake, Bauermeister, Stockhausen) – 1961–9
P: Cologne, 21 May 1962, Martina Arroyo (soprano), WDR Chorus, WDR Symphony Orchestra, Aloys Kontarksy (Hammond organ), Alfons Kontarsky (Lowrey organ), cond. Karlheinz Stockhausen; P of the expanded version: Donaueschingen, 16 October 1965, same forces; P of the definitive 'Europe Version': Bonn, 8 December 1972, Gloria Davy (soprano), WDR Chorus, Ensemble Musique Vivante, Harald Bojé and Roger Smalley (organ), cond. Karlheinz Stockhausen

14   *Plus–Minus*, 2 × 7 pages for realization – 1963
P: Rome, 14 June 1964, Cornelius Cardew (piano), Frederic Rzewski (piano)

15   *Mikrophonie I* (Microphony I) for tamtam, 2 microphones, 2 filters and potentiometers (6 players)- 1964
P: Brussels, 9 December 1964, Aloys Kontarsky and Christoph Caskel (tamtam), Johannes Fritsch and Bernhard Kontarsky (microphones), Hugh Davies, Jaap Spek and Karlheinz Stockhausen (filters and potentiometers)

16   *Mixtur* (Mixture) for orchestra, sine-wave generators and ring modulators – 1964
P: Hamburg, 9 November 1965, NDR Orchestra, Hugh Davies, Johannes Fritsch, Harald Bojé and Makoto Shinohara (ring modulators), Karlheinz Stockhausen and Jaap Spek (sound projection), cond. Michael Gielen

16½   *Mixtur* for small ensemble – 1967
P: Darmstadt, 23 August 1967, Hudba Dneska Ensemble, Harald Bojé, Johannes Fritsch, Rolf Gehlhaar and David Johnson (sine-wave generators), Karlheinz Stockhausen (sound projection), cond. Ladislav Kupković

17   *Mikrophonie II* (for 12 singers, Hammond organ and 4 ring modulators (text: Heissenbüttel, *Einfache grammatische Meditationen* – 1965
P: Cologne, 11 June 1965, WDR Chorus and the New Music Studio Chorus, Alfons Kontarsky (Hammond organ), Johannes Fritsch (timer), Karlheinz Stockhausen and Jaap Spek (sound projection)

18   *Stop* for orchestra – 1965

18½   *Stop*, Paris version – 1969
P: Paris, 2 June 1969, Ensemble Musique Vivante, cond. Diego Masson

19   *Solo* for melody instrument with feedback – 1965–6
P: Tokyo, 25 April 1966, Jasusuke Hirata (version for trombone), Noguchi (version for flute)

20   *Telemusik*, electronic music – 1966
        P: Tokyo, 25 April 1966

21   *Adieu* for wind quintet – 1966
        P: Calcutta, 30 January 1967, WDR Wind Quintet

22   *Hymnen* (Anthems), electronic music and *musique concrète* – 1965–7

22½   *Hymnen*, electronic music and *musique concrète* with soloists – 1966–7
        P: Cologne, 30 November 1967, Stockhausen Group, Karlheinz Stockhausen (sound projection)

22⅓   Third Region of *Hymnen* with orchestra – 1969
        P: New York, 25 February 1971, New York Philharmonic Orchestra, cond. Karlheinz Stockhausen

23   *Prozession* (Procession) for tamtam, viola, electronium, piano, microphones, filters and potentiometers – 1967
        P: Helsinki, 21 May 1967, Stockhausen Group, Karlheinz Stockhausen (sound projection)

24   *Stimmung* (Tuning in) for 6 vocalists – 1968
        P: Paris, 9 December 1968, Collegium Vocale Köln

25   *Kurzwellen* (Short-waves) for 6 players and short-wave receivers – 1968
        P: Bremen, 5 May 1968, Stockhausen Group, Karlheinz Stockhausen (sound projection)

26   *Aus den sieben Tagen* (From the seven days), 15 text compositions – May 1968
        1. *Richtige Dauern* (Right durations) for *c.* 4 players, P: Darmstadt, 1 September 1969, Stockhausen Group and Free Music Group (Vinko Globokar), Karlheinz Stockhausen (sound projection); 2. *Unbegrenzt* (Unlimited) for ensemble, P: St Paul de Vence, 26 July 1969, Roy Hart (voice), Michael Vetter (electrically amplified recorder), Free Music Group (Vinko Globokar) and Stockhausen Group, Karlheinz Stockhausen (sound projection); 3. *Verbindung* (Connection) for ensemble, P: Darmstadt, 2 September 1969, Stockhausen Group and the Free Music Group, Karlheinz Stockhausen (sound projection); 4. *Treffpunkt* for ensemble, P: London, 25 November 1968, Arts Laboratory Ensemble, Karlheinz Stockhausen and Hugh Davies (sound projection); 5. *Nachtmusik* (Night Music) for ensemble, P: Darmstadt, 1 September 1969, Free Music Group (Vinko Globokar), Stockhausen Group, Karlheinz Stockhausen (sound projection); 6. *Abwärts* for ensemble, P: Darmstadt, 2 September 1969, Roy Hart (voice), Free Music Group (Vinko Globokar), Stockhausen Group, Karlheinz Stockhausen (sound projection); 7. *Aufwärts* for ensemble, P: Darmstadt, 4 September 1969, Vinko Globokar (trombone), Stockhausen Group, Karlheinz Stockhausen (sound projection); 8. *Oben und Unten* (Over and Under) (theatre piece), man, woman, child, 4 instruments, P: Amsterdam, 22 June 1969, Sigrid Koetse (woman), Jan Retèl (man), Keesjan van Deelen (child), Stockhausen Group, Karlheinz Stockhausen (sound projection); 9. *Intensität* (Intensity) for ensemble, P: Darmstadt, 3 September 1969, Free Music Group (Vinko Globokar), Stockhausen Group, Karlheinz Stockhausen (sound projection); 10. *Setz die Segel zur Sonne* for ensemble, P: Paris, 30 May 1969, Stockhausen Group and Free Music Group (Vinko Globokar), Karlheinz Stockhausen (sound projection); 11. *Kommunion* (Communion) for ensemble, P: Darmstadt, 3 September 1969, Free Music Group (Vinko Globokar), Stockhausen Group, Karlheinz Stockhausen (sound projection); 12. *Litanei* (Litany) for speakers or choir; 13. *Es* (It) for ensemble, P: London, 25 November 1968, Arts Laboratory Ensemble, Karlheinz Stockhausen and Hugh Davies (sound projection); 14. *Goldstaub*

for ensemble, P: Kuerten, 20 August 1972, Peter Eötvös (electrochord, keisu, rin), Herbert Henck (voice, sitar, saucepan, 2 small bells and ship's bell), Michael Vetter (voice, hands, recorder), Karlheinz Stockhausen (voice, conch shell, cowbell, 14 rin, key and jar of water, Kandy-drum, ring of bells); 15. *Ankunft* for speakers or speaking choir.

27   *Spiral* (Spirally) for a soloist with short-wave receiver – 1968
P: Zagreb, 15 May 1969, Heinz Holliger (version for oboe)

28   *Dr. K*, sextet for flute, cello, tubular bells and vibraphone, bass clarinet, viola and piano – 1969
P: London, 22 April 1969, London Sinfonietta, cond. Pierre Boulez

29   *Fresco* for 4 orchestral groups – 1969
P: Bonn, 15 November 1969, Beethovenhalle Orchestra, cond. Volker Wangenheim, Volkmar Fritsche, Bernhard Kontarsky and Georg Földes

30   *Pole* (Poles) for 2 players and 2 short-wave receivers – 1969 and 1970
P: Osaka, 20 March 1970, Michael Vetter (electrically amplified recorder), Johannes Fritsch (viola with contact microphone)

31   *Expo* for 3 players and 3 short-wave receivers – 1969 and 1970
P: Osaka, 21 March 1970, Harald Bojé (electronium), Peter Eötvös (55–chord), Rolf Gehlhaar (tamtam)

32   *Mantra* for 2 pianists and ring-modulated pianos – 1969 and 1970
P: Donaueschingen, 18 October 1970, Alfons Kontarsky and Aloys Kontarsky (pianos)

33   *Für kommende Zeiten* (For times to come), 17 texts of intuitive music – 1968–70
1. *Übereinstimmung* (Unanimity) for ensemble, P: London, 20 May 1970, Gentle Fire (at that time the title was *Annäherung* [Approximation]); 2. *Verlängerung* (Elongation); 3. *Verkürzung* (Shortening); 4. *Über die Grenze* (Across the boundary) for fairly small ensemble; 5. *Kommunikation* (Communication) for small ensemble, P: Shiraz, 4 September 1972, Gentle Fire; 6. *Intervall* (Interval), piano duo, P: London, 5 May 1972, Roger Woodward and Jerzy Romaniuk; 7. *Ausserhalb* (Outside) for small ensemble; 8. *Innerhalb* (Inside) for small ensemble; 9. *Anhalt* (Halt) for small ensemble; 10. *Schwingung* (Vibration) for ensemble; 11. *Spektren* (Spectra) for small ensemble; 12. *Wellen* (Waves) for ensemble; 13. *Zugvogel* (Bird of passage) for ensemble; 14. *Vorahnung* (Presentiment) for 4–7; 15. *Japan* for ensemble; 16. *Wach* (Awake) for ensemble; 17. *Ceylon* for small ensemble, P: Metz, 22 November 1973, Stockhausen Group

34   *Sternklang* (Star-sound), park music for 5 groups – 1971
P: Berlin, 5 June 1971, Gentle Fire, Intermodulation, Collegium Vocale Köln, Stockhausen Group

35   *Trans* for orchestra – 1971
P: Donaueschingen, 16 October 1971, SWF Orchestra, cond. Ernest Bour

36   *Alphabet für Liège* (Alphabet for Liège), 13 musical pictures for soloists and duos – 1972
P: Liège, 23 September 1972; 1. *Am Himmel wandere ich* (Indianerlieder) (In the sky I am walking . . . ; Indian songs), Helga Hamm-Albrecht (mezzo-soprano), Karl O. Barkey (tenor); 2. *Making the vibrations of sound visible in liquids, light beams and flames*, Herbert Henck (synthesizer); 3. *Making sound spectra visible in solid material*, Hans-Alderich Billig (bass); 4. *Shattering glass with sounds*, Hugh Davies (sine-wave generator); 5. *Magnetizing food with sounds. Making the magnetization visible with a pendulum*, Gaby Rodens (soprano), Jill Purce (pendulum); 6. *Massaging a human body with sounds*,

Michael Robinson (electric cello), Rosalind Davies (dancer and singer); 8. *Making love with sounds*, Michael Vetter and Atsuko Iwami (recorders); 9. *Harmonizing the seven corporeal centres with sounds*, Wolfgang Fromme (tenor); 10. *Beating back thoughts and keeping them away with sounds*, Richard Bernas (tamtam); 11. *Continually accelerating and slowing the breathing- and pulse-rhythms of animals (fish) with sounds*, Johannes Kneutgen; 13. *Praying with sounds*, Dagmar von Biel (soprano); Peter Eötvös (musical director)

Not performed: 7. *Extinguishing sounds by oneself*; 12. *Invoking and summoning dead spirits with sounds*

36½   *Am Himmel wandere ich . . .* (Indianerlieder) – 1972
P: see *Alphabet für Liège*

37   *Ylem* for 19 players/singers – 1972
P: London, 9 March 1973, London Sinfonietta

38   *Inori*, adorations for 1 or 2 soloists and orchestra – 1973 and 1974
P: Donaueschingen, 18 October 1974, Alain Louafi, SWF Orchestra, cond. Karlheinz Stockhausen

38½   *Vortrag über Hu* (Lecture on Hu), (Musical analysis of *Inori*) for 1 female or male singer – 1974
P: Donaueschingen, 18 October 1974, Gloria Davy (soprano)

39   *Atmen gibt das Leben . . .* ('Breathing gives life . . .'), choral opera with orchestra (text: Stockhausen, Buson, Issa, Shiki, Socrates, Meister Eckhart, the Gospel according to St Thomas [Apocrypha]) P of the first part (a cappella): Hamburg, 16 May 1975, NDR Chorus; – 1974 and 1976–7
P of the complete work: Nizza, 22 May 1977, NDR Chorus (tape playback: NDR Orchestra)

40   *Herbstmusik* (Autumn music) for 4 players – 1974
P: Bremen, 4 May 1974, Peter Eötvös, Joachim Krist, Suzanne Stephens and Karlheinz Stockhausen

40½   *Laub und Regen* (Leaves and rain), final duet from *Herbstmusik* for clarinet and viola – 1974

41   *Musik im Bauch* (Music in the belly) for 6 percussionists and music boxes – 1974 and 1975
P: Royan, 28 March 1975, Les Percussions de Strasbourg

41½–⁷⁄₈   *Tierkreis* (Zodiac), 12 melodies of the star signs for a melody and/or harmony instrument; further versions for voice (text: Stockhausen) and harmony instrument – 1974–7
1. high soprano or high tenor; 2. soprano or tenor, P: Aix-en-Provence, 27 July 1977, Annette Meriweather (soprano), Majella Stockhausen (piano); 3. mezzo-soprano or contralto or low tenor; 4. baritone; 5. bass; for chamber orchestra (clarinet, horn, bassoon and strings); for clarinet and piano

42   *Harlekin* (Harlequin) for clarinet – 1975
P: Cologne, 7 March 1976, Suzanne Stephens

42½   *Der kleine Harlekin* (The little harlequin) for clarinet – 1975
P: Aix-en-Provence, 3 August 1977, Suzanne Stephens

43   *Sirius* for electronic music and trumpet, soprano, bass clarinet and bass (text: Stockhausen, Lorber) – 1975–7
P of unfinished version: Washington, DC, 15 July 1976, Markus Stockhausen (trum-

pet), Annette Meriweather (soprano), Suzanne Stephens (bass clarinet) and Boris Carmeli (bass); P of the complete work: Aix-en-Provence, 8 August 1977, interpreters as in Washington

44   *Amour*, 5 pieces for clarinet – 1974–6; version for flute, 1981
      P: Stuttgart, 9 January 1978, Suzanne Stephens

45   *Jubiläum* (Jubilee) for orchestra – 1977
      P: Hanover, 10 October 1977, Regional Orchestra of Lower Saxony, cond. George Albrecht

46   *In Freundschaft* (In friendship) for clarinet — 1977–8; further versions for flute, recorder, oboe, bassoon or bass clarinet, violin, cello, saxophone, horn and trombone
      P of version for flute: Aix-en-Provence, 6 August 1977, Lucille Goeres; P of version for clarinet: Paris, 30 November 1978, Suzanne Stephens

47   *Der Jahreslauf* (The course of the years), scene from *Dienstag* from *Licht*, for ballet, actor and orchestra, or for orchestra – 1977
      P: Tokyo, 31 October 1977, Wataro Togi (choreography), Hioaki Togi, Hideaki Ho, Masaru Togi and Hiroharu Sono (dancers), Shigen-Kai (gagaku)

48–50 *Donnerstag* from *Licht* (Thursday from Light) for 14 musical performers (3 solo voices, 8 solo instrumentalists, 3 solo dancers), chorus, orchestra and tapes (libretto: Stockhausen; *Unsichtbare Chöre* [Invisible choirs]: Ascent of Moses and Apocalypse of Baruch) – 1978–81
      Donnerstags-Gruss (Thursday greeting)
      Act 1   *Michaels Jugend* (Michael's youth): *Kindheit; Mondeva; Examen* (Childhood; Moon-Eve; Examination)
      Act 2   *Michaels Reise um die Erde* (Michael's journey around the earth)
      Act 3   *Michaels Heimkehr* (Michael's return home): *Festival; Vision*
      Donnerstags-Abschied (Thursday farewell)
      P: Milan, 3 April 1981, Luca Ronconi (producer), Gae Aulenti (stage design), Robert Gambill (tenor, Act 1), Paul Sperry (tenor, Act 3), Markus Stockhausen (trumpet), Michele Noiret (dancer), Annette Meriweather (soprano), Suzanne Stephens (basset-horn), Elizabeth Clarke (dancer), Matthias Hölle (bass), Mark Tezak (trombone), Alain Louafi (dancer), Majella Stockhausen (piano), Alain Damiens (clarinet), Michel Arrignon (basset-horn), Hugo Read and Simon Stockhausen (soprano saxophones), Elena Pantano and Giovanni Mastino (silent roles), WDR Chorus (tape playback: *Unsichtbare Chöre*), Orchestra and Chorus of La Scala, Milan, cond. Peter Eötvös, Karlheinz Stockhausen (sound projection)

48   *Michaels Reise um die Erde* with trumpet and orchestra – 1978
      P: Donaueschingen, 21 October 1978, Markus Stockhausen (trumpet), Suzanne Stephens (clarinet), Ensemble Intercontemporain, cond. Karlheinz Stockhausen
      from 48: 1. *Eingang und Formel* (Entry and formula) for trumpet; 2. *Halt* for trumpet and double bass, P: Bologna, 20 July 1983, Markus Stockhausen (trumpet), Peter Riegelbauer (double bass); 3. *Kreuzigung* (Crucifixion) for trumpet and 1st basset-horn; clarinet, 2nd basset-horn, 2 horns, 2 trombones, tuba and electronic organ; 4. *Mission und Himmelfahrt* (Mission and ascension) for trumpet and basset-horn, P: Schloss Georghausen, nr Kürten, 22 August 1980, Markus Stockhausen (trumpet), Suzanne Stephens (basset-horn)

48½ *Donnerstags-Gruss* (*Michaels-Gruss*) for 8 brass, piano and 3 percussion
      from 48½: *Michaels-Ruf* (Michael's call) for variable ensemble (8 orchestral parts)

48⅔   *Michaels Reise*, soloist's version for a trumpeter and 9 other players – 1978 and 1984
P: Bremen, 8 May 1986, Markus Stockhausen (trumpet), Suzanne Stephens (1st basset-horn), Kathinka Pasveer (flute), Ian Stuart (clarinet), Lesley Schatzberger (clarinet, 2nd hasset-horn and bass clarinet), Michael Svoboda (trombone and tenor tuba), Andreas Böttcher and Isao Nakamura (percussion), Michael Obst and Simon Stockhausen (synthesizers), Karlheinz Stockhausen (sound projection)

49   *Michaels Jugend* for tenor, soprano, bass; trumpet, basset-horn, trombone, and piano; electronic organ; 3 dancer-mimes, tapes of chorus and instruments – 1978 and 1979
P: Jerusalem, 17 October 1979, interpreters as for *Donnerstag* from *Licht* (Milan, 3 April 1981)
from 49: *Unsichtbare Chöre*

49½   *Kindheit* for tenor, soprano, bass; trumpet, basset-horn, trombone; dancers; tapes
from 49½: 1. *Tanze Luceva!* (Dance, Luceva!) for basset-horn or bass clarinet; 2. *Bijou* for alto flute and bass clarinet

49⅔   *Mondeva* for tenor and basset-horn, ad lib: soprano, bass, trombone, mime; electronic organ; 2 tapes

49¾   *Examen* for tenor, trumpet, dancer; basset-horn, piano, ad lib: 'Jury' (soprano, bass, 2 dancer-mimes); 2 tapes from 49¾: *Klavierstück XII* (Piano piece XII), P: Vernier, 9 June 1983, Majella Stockhausen

50   *Michaels Heimkehr* for tenor, soprano, bass; trumpet, basset-horn, trombone; 2 soprano saxophones; electronic organ; 3 dancer-mimes; old woman; chorus and orchestra; tapes – 1980

50½   *Festival* (instrumentation as for 50)
P: Amsterdam, 14 June 1980, performers as in *Donnerstag* from *Licht* (Milan, 3 April 1981, but with Michael Rosness instead of Paul Sperry, and the Orchestra and Chorus of Radio Hilversum instead of the Orchestra and Chorus of La Scala from 50½: 1. *Drachenkampf* (Dragon fight) for trumpet, trombone, electronic organ or synthesizer, 2 dancers (ad lib); 2. *Knabenduett* (Youths' duet) for 2 soprano saxophones or other instruments; 3. *Argument* for tenor, bass, electronic organ (or synthesizer), ad lib: trumpet, trombone, 1 percussionist
P of *Drachenkampf* and *Argument*: St Paul de Vence, 16 July 1987, Markus Stockhausen (Trumpet), Michael Svoboda (trombone), Simon Stockhausen (synthesizer), Julian Pike (tenor), Nicholas Isherwood (bass), Michèle Noiret and Jean Christian Chalon (dancers), Andreas Boettger (percussion)

50⅔   *Vision* for tenor, trumpet, dancer; Hammond organ; tape, ad lib: shadow plays

50¾   *Donnerstags-Abschied* (*Michaels-Abschied*) for 5 trumpets

51–4   *Samstag* from *Licht* (Saturday from Light), opera for 13 musical performers (1 solo voice, 10 solo instrumentalists, 2 solo dancers), wind orchestra, ballet or mimes; male chorus with organ (libretto: Stockhausen) – 1981–3
Samstags-Gruss (*Luzifer-Gruss*) (Saturday greeting; Lucifer's greeting)
Scene 1 *Luzifers Traum* (Lucifer's dream)
Scene 2 *Kathinkas Gesang als Luzifers Requiem* (Kathinka's chant as Lucifer's requiem)
Scene 3 *Luzifers Tanz* (Lucifer's dance)
Scene 4 *Luzifers Abschied* (Lucifer's farewell)
P: Milan, 25 May 1984, Luca Ronconi and Ugo Tessitore (stage directors), Gae Aulenti (stage design), Matthias Hölle (bass), Adriano Vianello and Sebastiano

Vianello (stilt-dancers), Majella Stockhausen (piano), Kathinka Pasveer (flute), Slagwerkgroep Den Haag, University of Michigan Symphony Band, cond. Robert Reynolds, Kama Dev (dancer), Markus Stockhausen (piccolo), Piero Mazzarella (silent role), Händel Collegium, Günther Hempel (electronic organ), Michael Struck (trombone), Karlheinz Stockhausen (sound projection)

51   *Luzifers Traum* or *Klavierstück XIII* (Piano piece XIII) – 1981
P: Metz, 19 November 1981, Majella Stockhausen (piano), Matthias Hölle (bass)

51½   *Klavierstück XIII* as piano solo – 1981
P: Turin, 10 June 1982, Majella Stockhausen

51⅔   *Traumformel* (Dream formula) for basset-horn – 1981–2
P: Cologne, 29 January 1983, Suzanne Stephens

52   *Kathinkas Gesang als Luzifers Requiem* for flute and 6 percussionists, or as flute solo – 1982–3
P: Donaueschingen, 15 October 1983, Kolberg Percussion Ensemble, Kathinka Pasveer (flute)

52½   *Kathinkas Gesang als Luzifers Requiem*, version for flute and electronic music – 1983
P: Paris, 6 May 1985, Kathinka Pasveer

52⅔   *Kathinkas Gesang als Luzifers Requiem*, version for flute and piano – 1983

53   *Luzifers Tanz* for bass (or trombone or euphonium), piccolo trumpet, piccolo; wind orchestra or symphony orchestra (and stilt-dancer, dancer, ballet or mimes for stage performances) – 1983
P: Ann Arbor, 9 March 1984, University of Michigan Symphony Band, cond. Robert Reynolds
from 53: 1. *Linker Augenbrauentanz* (Left-eyebrow dance) for a percussionist, flutes and basset-horn(s); 2. *Rechter Augenbrauentanz* (Right-eyebrow dance) for a percussionist, clarinets and bass clarinet(s); 3. *Linker Augentanz* (Left-eye dance) for a percussionist and saxophone; 4. *Rechter Augentanz* (Right-eye dance) for a percussionist, oboes, cors anglais and bassoons; 5. *Linker Backentanz* (Left-cheek dance) for a percussionist, trumpets and trombones; 6. *Rechter Backentanz* (Right-cheek dance) for a percussionist, trumpets and trombones; 7. *Nasenflügeltanz* (Nostril dance) for a percussionist, ad lib: electronic keyboard instruments; 8. *Oberlippentanz* (Protest) (Upper-lip dance) for piccolo trumpet; trombones or euphonium, 2 percussionists and horns, or as a solo for piccolo trumpet P: Donaueschingen, 18 October 1985, Markus Stockhausen (piccolo trumpet), Michael Svoboda (euphonium), Marcie McGaughey, Gernot Scheibe, Ralph Warné and Gaby Webster (horns), Mircea Ardeleanu and Robyn Schulkowsky (percussion), Karlheinz Stockhausen (sound projection); P of the version as piccolo trumpet solo: Milan, 16 May 1984, Markus Stockhausen; 9. *Zungenspitzentanz* (Tip-of-the-tongue dance) for piccolo and dancer (ad lib); a percussionist and euphoniums (or electronic keyboard instrument), or as solo for piccolo, P: Bergisch-Gladbach, 27 September 1986, Kathinka Pasveer (piccolo), Kama Dev (dancer), Michael Mulcahy and Michael Svoboda (euphoniums), Andreas Boettger (percussion); 10. *Kinntanz* (Chin dance) for trombone or euphonium; 2 percussionists, euphoniums, alto trombone(s), 'baritone(s)', tenor horn(s) and bass tuba(s)
P: Paris, 23 January 1991, Dodécatuor Saxophone Ensemble, Claude Delangle (percussion), Simon Stockhausen (synthesizer)

53½   *Samstags-Gruss (Luzifer-Gruss)* for brass and 2 percussionists – 1984

54   *Luzifers Abschied* for male chorus, organ and 7 trombones – 1982
P: Assisi, 28 September 1982, Händel Collegium, Helmut Volke (Hammond organ), Michael Struck (trombone), Perugia Wind Society (trombones)

55–9   *Montag* from *Licht* (Monday from Light) for 21 musical performers (14 solo voices, 6 solo instrumentalists and 1 actor), chorus, children's chorus and modern orchestra (libretto: Stockhausen) – 1985–8
Montags-Gruss (Monday greeting)
Act 1   *Evas Erstgeburt* (Eve's first birth)
Act 2   *Evas Zweitgeburt* (Eve's second birth)
Act 3   *Evas Zauber* (Eve's magic)
Montags-Abschied (Monday farewell)
P: Milan, 7 May 1988, Michael Bogdanov (stage director), Chris Dyer (stage design), Marc Thompson (costumes), Annette Meriweather, Donna Sarley and Jana Mrazova (sopranos), Julian Pike, Helmut Clemens and Alistair Thompson (tenors), Nicholas Isherwood (bass), Suzanne Stephens, Nele Langrehr and Rumi Sota (basset-horns), Kathinka Pasveer (flute and voice), Pierre Laurent Aimard (piano), Alain Louafi (actor), Michael Obst, Simon Stockhausen and Michael Svoboda (synthesizers), Andreas Boettger (percussion), WDR Chorus (tape playback), Zaans Kantatekoor, cond. Jan Pasveer, Radio Budapest Children's Chorus, electronic and *concrète* sounds, cond. Peter Eötvös, Karlheinz Stockhausen (sound projection)

55   *Montags-Gruss* (*Eva-Gruss*) for basset-born orchestra and electronic keyboard instruments – 1984–8
from 55: 1. *Xi* for basset-horn; 2. *Xi* for alto flute or flute, P. Sienna, 3 August 1987, Kathinka Pasveer

56   *Evas Erstgeburt* for 3 sopranos, 3 tenors, 1 bass; 1 actor, chorus, children's chorus; modern orchestra – 1987
P: Cologne, 7 April 1988, interpreters as for *Montag* from *Licht* (Milan, 7 May 1988), WDR Chorus live

57   *Evas Zweitgeburt* for 7 solo choirboys; basset-horn with 3 female players; piano; chorus, girls' chorus; modern orchestra – 1984–7
P: Cologne, 7 April 1988, interpreters as for *Montag* from *Licht* (Milan, 7 May 1988)

57½   *Mädchenprozession* (Girls' procession) for girls' chorus, ad lib: chorus, modern orchestra – 1987

57⅔   *Befruchtung mit Klavierstück* (Fertilization with piano piece) for piano; girls' chorus; modern orchestra – 1984–7
from 57⅔: *Klavierstück XIV* (Piano piece XIV) – 1984, P: Baden-Baden, 31 March 1985, Pierre Laurent Aimard

57¾   *Evas Lied* (Eve's song) for 7 solo choirboys; basset-horn with 3 female players; modern orchestra, ad lib: female chorus – 1986
P: Berlin, 3 September 1986, interpreters as for *Montag* from *Licht* (Milan, 7 May 1988)
from 57¾: *Wochenkreis*; *Die sieben Lieder der Tage* (Week-cycle; The seven songs of the days), duet for basset-horn and electronic keyboard instruments

58   *Evas Zauber* for basset-horn, alto flute, piccolo; chorus, children's chorus; modern orchestra – 1984–6
P: Metz, 20 November 1986, interpreters as for *Montag* from *Licht* (Milan, 7 May 1988)

58½   *Botschaft* (Message) for basset-horn, alto flute; chorus; modern orchestra, or for basset-horn, alto flute; chorus, or basset-horn, alto flute; modern orchestra – 1984–5

58½   ossia: *Ave* for basset-horn and alto flute
from 58½: 1. *Evas Spiegel* (Eve's mirror) for basset-horn; 2. *Susani* for basset-horn; 3. *Susanis Echo* for alto flute

58⅔   *Der Kinderfänger* (The Child-catcher) for alto flute and piccolo; children's chorus (may be omitted); modern orchestra, ad lib: basset-horn – 1986
from 58⅔: *Entführung* (Abduction) for piccolo, ad lib: modern orchestra

59   *Montags-Abschied* (*Eva-Abschied*) for children's chorus; piccolo orchestra; electronic keyboard instruments – 1988
1. *Quitt* for 3 players with microtones – 1989; 2. *Ypsilon* for a melody instrument (with microtones) – 1989; 3. *Ypsilon*, version for basset-horn; 4. *Ypsilon*, version for flute

60–62   *Dienstag* from *Licht* (Tuesday from Light) (opera) for 17 musical performers (3 solo voices, 10 solo instrumentalists, 4 dancer-mimes); choir, orchestra and tapes – 1977
Willkommen with *Dienstags-Gruss* (*Friedens-Gruss*) (Welcome with Tuesday's Greeting (Peace Greeting))
Act 1 *Jahreslauf* (Course of the Year)
Act 2 *Invasion – explosion* with *Abschied* (Invasion – Explosion with Farewell)

60   *Dienstags-Gruss* (*Friedens-Gruss*) for soprano (9 trumpets, 9 trombones, 2 synthesizer players), choir, conductor and co-conductor – 1988
P: Cologne, 4 November 1988, Annette Meriweather (soprano), an ad hoc instrumental ensemble with Markus Stockhausen (trumpet), Michel Svoboda (trombone), Simon Stockhausen and Michael Obst (synthesizers), the University Student Choir, conducted by Dieter Gutknecht and Rolf Wiechert

1 ex 60   *Willkommen* for 9 trumpets, 9 trombones, 2 synthesizer players

2 ex 60   *Su-Kat* for basset-horn and alto flute – 1989

61   *Jahreslauf* from *Dienstag* (Act 1 of *Dienstag* from *Licht*) for tenor, bass; 4 dancer-mimes; an actor, 3 mimes, little girl, beautiful woman; modern orchestra, tape; sound projectionist – 1977/91

62   *Invasion – Explosion* with *Abschied* (Act 2 of *Dienstag* from *Licht*) for solo soprano, solo trumpet, solo synthesizer player; tenor, bass, 2 trumpets, 3 trombones, 1 synthesizer player, 2 percussionists; trumpet- and trombone-ensemble (*ad lib.*); choir; 8-track tape (octophonic electronic music); sound projectionist – 1990–91

1 ex 62   *Pieta* for flugelhorn, soprano and tape or as a solo for flugelhorn – 1990

Unpublished and Unnumbered Works

Scherzo (in Hindemith-style) for piano – ?1950

Drei Chöre (Three choruses; text by Stockhausen), in two and three parts – ?1950
1. *Gottes Krippen* (God's crib); 2. *Maria*; 3. *Bei dem Kinde* (With the Child)

Burleska, a musical pantomime (idea and libretto: Stockhausen), joint composition with Detmar Seuthe and Klaus Weiler; for a speaker, 4 solo singers, 4 pantomimes, chamber choir, string quartet, piano and percussion – 1950
P: Steinbach, ?24 July 1950, students from the School-music Department of the Cologne Musikhochschule, Detmar Seuthe (percussion), Karlheinz Stockhausen (piano), cond. Klaus Weiler

6 Studien for piano – ?1950 (destroyed)

Präludium (Prelude) for piano – 1951 – this piece is identical with the piano part of the first movement of the Sonatine, no. ¹⁄₈)

Sonate for piano – 1951 (destroyed)

Ravelle for clarinet, violin, electric guitar, piano and double bass – 1951
P: Freiburg, 14 June 1974, Hans Dietrich Klaus (clarinet), Masufumi Hori (violin), Anton Stingl (electric guitar), Wolfgang Marschner (piano), Michael Erhardt (double bass)

Studie über einen Ton (Study on one sound), in two parts – 1952 (? not realized)

Klavierstück V¹⁄₂, Klavierstuck VI¹⁄₂ (Piano piece V¹⁄₂, VI¹⁄₂ – 1954).
P: Cologne, 18 January 1974, Aloys Kontarsky

Ensemble, studio concert for Karlheinz Stockhausen's Composition Studio – Darmstadt 1967 (Stockhausen composed the overall plan and 8 inserts)
Performance: Darmstadt, 29 August 1967, Hudba Dneska Ensemble, Aloys Kontarsky (Hammond organ), Harald Bojé, Alden Jenks, David Johnson and Petr Kotik (potentiometers)

Musik für ein Haus (Music for a house), studio concert for Karlheinz Stockhausen's Composition Studio – Darmstadt 1968 (process planning by Karlheinz Stockhausen)
Performance: Darmstadt, 1 September 1968, Pierre Thibaud (trumpet), Georg Nothdorf (double bass), Josef Horák (bass clarinet), Eberhard Blum (flute), Georges Barboteu (horn), Vinko Globokar (trombone), Heinz Holliger (oboe), Janos Meszáros (bassoon), Harald Bojé (electronium), Saschko Gawriloff (violin), Othello Liesmann (cello), Aloys Kontarsky (keyboard instruments), Johannes Fritsch (viola), David Johnson (alto flute), Satoshi Nozaki (potentiometers)

Tunnel-Spiral, contribution to a group project for a sound tunnel in the city of Los Angeles – 1969

Singreadfeel for a singer with various instruments (text: Aurobindo) – 1970

Cadenzas for Mozart's Clarinet Concerto – 1978

Cadenzas for Mozart's Flute Concertos in G and D – 1984–5

Cadenza for Leopold Mozart's Trumpet Concerto – 1984

Cadenzas for Haydn's Trumpet Concerto – 1983–5

Unfinished works

Monophonie (Monophony) for orchestra – 1960–

Projektion (Projection) for 9 orchestral groups and film – 1967–

Hinab-Hinauf (Downward-upward), electronic music and *musique concrète* with soloists – ?1968 and 1969

Index

Figures in **bold** type refer to pages with illustrations.

Adam de la Halle, 49
Adieu, 146
Adorno, Theodor Wiesengrund, **120**; at
    Darmstadt, 35–6, 147; *Philosophie der
    neuen Musik*, 26; pupil, 82; relationship
    with Stockhausen, 35–6, 104, 106, 147;
    'Resistance to New Music', 104
Adrion, Alexander, 43–5
Agnello, Baron Francesco, 117
Ahlbom, Pär, 108
Aimard, Pierre Laurent, **225**
Aix-en-Provence Festival, 209
Albertus Magnus, 231
Albrecht, George, 209
Alings, Alfred, 150, **155**, 169, 181
Alphabet für Liège, 192
Amour, 194, **202**
Amy, Gilbert, 96
Andreae, Doris, *see* Stockhausen, Doris
Andreae, Johann Valentin, 23
'Ankunft', 162
Anzengruber, Ludwig, 8
Arroyo, Martina, 119, 128
Arts Laboratory Ensemble, 169
Atmen gibt das Leben . . ., 196, 208
'Aufwärts', 185
Aulenti, Gae, 217
Aurobindo, Sri, 162–4, 169, 172, 185
Aus den sieben Tagen, 160–3, 164, 166, 170,
    172, 173–4, 182, 185, 188, 208
Ay-O (painter), 132

Babbitt, Milton, 95
Bach, Johann Sebastian, 63, 200
Baggiani, Guido, **131**
Bailey, Alice, 4
Bali, 178
Barkey, Karl O., 194

Barlow, Clarence, 194
Bartók, Béla, 22, 26, 28, 30–2, 37, 39, 43
Baruch, Gerth-Wolfgang, **51**
Basle conservatory, 125
Baudelaire, Charles, 31
Bauermeister, Mary **115**; background, 110;
    children, 141, 149; in Ceylon, 180; in
    Cologne, 89, 106, 110; in Corsica, 174;
    Hymnen, 154; in Japan, 144; in Kürten,
    137, 171; *Momente*, 121; *Originale*, 114,
    116, 131; relationship with Stockhausen,
    111–12, 117–18, 135, 141, 148–9, 158,
    160–1, 166, 171, 184; in USA, 123–4,
    128–32, 139, 156; work, 110, 112, **115**,
    117–18, 124, 128, 135
Beatles, 171
Beckett, Samuel, 107
Beethoven, Ludwig van, 49, 153, 174, 176,
    208, 228
Behrmann, David, 96
Bein, Dr, 15
Béjart, Maurice, 197
Benn, Gottfried, 39
Berberian, Cathy, 128
Berg, Alban, 49
Bergisch-Gladbach grammar school, 19–20
Berio, Luciano, 128
Berliner Festwochen, 98, 185
Bernstein, Leonard, 129, 147, 169
Beurle, Jürgen, 152
Beyer, Robert, 39, 52, 58, 61, 63
Biel, Michael von, 112, 139
Bill, Max, 64, 110
Billig, Hans-Alderich, 193
Blake, William, 121
Blavatsky, Helena, 4, 190
Blinken, Judith, 129
Blume, Friedrich, 105

Boehmer, Konrad, 89, 96, 189
Boettger, Andreas, **223**
Bogdanov, Michael, 222, 234
Böhme, Jakob, 190
Bojé, Harald, 149–50, **155**, 169, 172, 186
Bonn, Beethovenhalle, 174–5
Bonn University, 68–72
Bornemann, Fritz, 166
Bose, Hans-Jürgen von, 197
Bosseur, Jean Yves, **131**
Botticelli, Sandro, 217
Böttner, Karlheinz, 178
Boulder, Colorado, 129–30
Boulez, Pierre, **91**, **120**; aleatory music
   debate, 87–8; classes, 126; Club d'Essai,
   53, 55; Cologne Counter-Festival, 110;
   conducts Stockhausen's works, 91, 124;
   Darmstadt, 76; IRCAM, 211; on *Kontakte*,
   104; *Polyphonie X*, 46; relationship with
   Stockhausen, 50, 65, 86–8, 90, 106–7,
   211; *Structures*, 33; texts, 61; passing
   references, 41, 49, 52, 105
Brahms, Johannes, 228
Brandt, Willy, 185
Bratislava, 158
Braun, Hermann, 68
Braunfels, Walter, 22
Brecht, George, 110
Bremen Pro Musica Nova festival, 159, 201
Brimberg, Jack, 112, 123
Brown, Earle, 73, 87, 90, 95, 128
Brown (painter), 132
Brücher, Ernst, 90, 103
Brühl, 185–6
Brün, Herbert, 89, 90
Brussels, 135, 169
Brussels World Fair, 94
Buffalo, 131
Bunje, Harald, 8
Burleska, 29–30, **30**
Bussotti, Sylvano, 96, 110

Caen conservatory, 232
Cage, John, **73**; at Darmstadt, 92–3, 106;
   Imaginary Landscape, 40; influence, 73–5,
   90, 96–8; *Music of Changes*, 74–5;
   relationship with Boulez, 50, 88;
   relationship with Stockhausen, 87, 95, 98,
   106, 110; passing references, 86, 109, 123
Calder, Alexander, 72, 74
California, University of, 147
Cambridge University, 234
Cardew, Cornelius: *Carré*, 107–8; in
   Cologne, 89–90, 110; in London, 106;
   Refrain, 98; relationship with Stockhausen,
   107–8, 189; works, 96
Carmeli, Boris, 208

Carré, 16, 49, **99**, 100, **101**, 106, 107–9, 121,
   183
Caskel, Christoph: Cologne Courses, 128;
   Kontakte, 103, 114; *Mikrophonie I*, 137;
   North American tour, 129; *Originale*, 114;
   Osaka World Fair, 178; Stockhausen
   Group, 181; *Zyklus*, 96
Caspari, Arthur, 114, 116
Cerha, Friedrich, 96
'Ceylon', 180
Chagall, Marc, 173, 208
Champollion, Jean François, 48–9
Choral, 27, 46, 184
Chöre für Doris, 27, 184
Clementi, Aldo, 112
Club d'Essai, 40, 53
Cocteau, Jean, 94
Collegium Vocale, 156, 168, 178, 185, 193
Cologne, Apostel-Gymnasium, 152
Cologne Counter-Festival, 106, 110
Cologne Musikhochschule, 1, 21–3, 26–9,
   39, 194, 230
Cologne New Music Courses, 126–9, 146,
   168
Cologne Philharmonic Hall, 232
Cologne Radio, *see* WDR in Cologne
Cologne, Theater am Dom, 116
Cologne University, 230
Columbia University, 40
Copland, Aaron, 95
Cott, Jonathan, 76, 153, 172, 182, 186
Couraud, Marcel, 184
Cowell, Henry, 74
Craft, Robert, 92
Cullen, Philippa, 196, 200
Cunningham, Merce, 110

Dadelsen, Hans-Christian von, 197
Darius Milhaud Conservatoire, 1
Darmstadt Summer Courses: 1949 series,
   32; 1951 series, 31, 34–7, 60; 1952 series,
   52–3; 1953 series, 61; 1954 series, 66–8;
   1955 series, 76–7; 1956 series, 86–7;
   1957 series, 87; 1958 series, 92–3; 1959
   series, 95–8; 1960 series, 106–7; 1961
   series, 111–14 **120**; 1962 series, 121–2;
   1963 series, 122–3; 1966 series, 146–7;
   1967 series, 150–2; 1968 series, 164–6;
   1969 series, 173–4; 1970 series, 181;
   1972 series, 197–9; 1974 series, 199
Davies, Hugh, 90, 135–7, 139, 169, 185
Davy, Gloria, 121
Debussy, Claude, 49
Deller, Alfred, 168
Delvincourt, Claude, 49
Den Haag, Royal Conservatory, 219
Deutsch, Max, 82
Deutsche Grammophon, 174

Dienstag, 4, 230–1, 235–6
Domaine Musicale, 86
Donaueschingen Festival, **54**; *Gruppen*, 92;
    Inori, 197; *Mantra*, 183; *Momente*, 119,
    121; *Punkte*, 123–4; *Spiel*, 50, 52–3;
    Stockhausen commissions, 43, 45, 50,
    106, 182
Donnerstag, 4–5, 201, 210–16, **212–13, 215**,
    222
Drei Lieder, 27–8, 31, 39, 184
Dudley, Homer, 70
Düsseldorf, 176
Dutschke, Rudi, 160
Dyer, Chris, 222

Eckhart, Meister, 74, 118
Eimert, Herbert, **59**; Cologne Radio, 30, 39,
    52, 56–7, 60; electronic studio, 57, 58,
    62–4, 66, 82, 125; Ligeti contact, 89;
    relationship with Stockhausen, 26, 30–1,
    41–3, 49, 60–1, 111; 'What is Music?'
    debate, 105; works, 66, 72, 111
Einstein, Albert, 118
Eisler, Hanns, 174
Englert, Giuseppe, 96
Ensemble, 150–2, 165, 174
Eötvös, Peter, **179**; *Alphabet*, 193;
    Herbstmusik, 201; Oeldorf Group, 200;
    Osaka World Fair, 178; *Pole*, 185–6;
    Stockhausen Group, 181
Erdmann, Eduard, 22
Ernst, Katharina (*née* Stockhausen), 11, 14,
    16
Ernst, Max, 168, 173, 176, 185
'Es', 169
Etude – *musique concrète*, 55–6
Evangelisti, Franco, 89–90, 93
Expo, 146, 178
Eysler, Edmund, 20

Fairleigh Dickinson University, 128
Fano, Michel, 65
Farah Diba, Empress, 188
Farmer, Paul, 152
Fassbaender, Brigitte, 184
Feedback, 180
Feldman, Morton, 73, 75, 87, 95, 123
Ferrari, Luc, 128
Feussner, Alfred, 116
Fleischer, Herbert, 52
Fleuret, Maurice, 174, 184
Fluxus movement, 114, 117, 131, 132
Formanten, 66
Formel, 43, 184
Fortner, Wolfgang, 31, 87, 105
Foss, Lukas, 129, 171
Francis of Assisi, 219
Frankfurt Festival, 230

Frankfurter Allgemeine Zeitung, 214
Frankfurter Rundschau, 214–15
Free Music Group, 173
'Frei', 27
'Freibrief an die Jugend', 145, 163
Frémy, Gerard, 178
Fresco, 174, **175**
Friedens-Gruss, 231
Frisius, Rudolf, 45, 56, 207
Fritsch, Johannes, **155**; Cologne Courses,
    128; departure from group, 180, 184;
    'Es', 169'; *Mikrophonie I*, 137; on *Hymnen*,
    153; on Stockhausen, 5; *Prozession*,
    149–50; works, 139
Fromme, Wolfgang, 193

Gamsjäger, Michael, 164
Gawriloff, Saschko, 184
Gazzelloni, Severino, 96
'Geburt in Tod', 24–5, 41
Gehlhaar, Rolf, **155, 165**; 'Es', 169; on
    Ensemble performance, 152; Stockhausen
    Group, 150; *Prozession*, 150; relationship
    with Stockhausen, 90, 149, 160, 180, 184
Gentle Fire, 185
Gesang der Jünglinge, 49, 82–4, 86, 87, 89,
    103–4, 121, 171
Gesualdo da Venosa, Don Carlo, 49
Gielen, Michael, 108, 128
Ginsberg, Allen, 131–2
Ginsberg, Louis, 133
Globokar, Vinko, 128, 173–4, 180
Goeyvaerts, Karel, **38**; Darmstadt, 34–7; on
    Cologne Radio concert, 72; relationship
    with Stockhausen, 35–6, 41, 43, 45, 48–9,
    55–6, 60–2, 65; works, 34–5, 72
Goldmann, Friedrich, 96
Goldmann, Marcel, **131**
'Goldstaub', 161–2, 173
Goléa, Antoine, 36, 85
Gorbachev, Mikhail, 233
Götz, Karl Otto, 116
Grabovsky, Leonid, 121
Grange, Henri Louis de la, 174
Grateful Dead, The, 148
Gredinger, Paul, 64, 66, 72, 79
Grimaud, Yvette, 37
Gruppen, 49, 76, 79–80, 84, 86, 89, 90–2,
    95, 108, 123, 149
Günther, Gotthard, 119
Gürzenich Orchestra, 232
Gutenberg, Johannes, 63
Gütersloh, 230

Hackenberg, Kurt, 126
Hambraeus, Bengt, 34
Hamburg opera house, 234
Hamburg Radio, 50, 56, 106, 108

Hamm-Albrecht, Helga, 194
Hanover Opera House, 209
Hansen, Simon, 15
Harlekin, 194, 201, 221
Hartmann, Karl Amadeus, 56
Hauer, Josef Matthias, 27, 35
Haydn, Joseph, 18
Hecker, Anno, 20
Hecker, Rita, 20
Heidegger, Martin, 38–9
Heike, Georg, 72
Heikinheimo, Seppo, 232
Heinemann, Gustav, 185
Heinemann, Hilda, 185
Heisenberg, Werner, 118
Heiss, Hermann, 27, 31, 87
Heissenbüttel, Helmut, 139
Helms, Hans G., 89, 114
Helsinki, 150
Helsinki Biennale, 232
Henck, Herbert, 93, 193
Henius, Carla, 147
Henze, Hans Werner, 34, 111
Herbstmusik, 200–1
Hesse, Hermann, 23, 25, 35, 38, 216
Hessenberg, Kurt, 39
Hessian Radio, 104
Higgins, Dick, 131
'Himmlische Parlament, Das', 192
Hinab-Hinauf, 166–7, 178
Hindemith, Paul, 22, 26–7, 29, 46, 66
Hitler, Adolf, 19, 27
Holland Festival, 155, 171–2
Holliger, Heinz, 149, 168
Hübner, Herbert, 50, 56, 106
Huddersfield Contemporary Music Festival, 230
Humayun, 24–5
Humperdinck, Engelbert, 8
Huxley, Aldous, 74
Hymnen, 142, 145, 152–4, 158, 170–1, 186, 187, 188, 206, 207, 221

In Freundschaft, 202
Indiana, Robert, 123
'Indianerlieder', 193, 199, 200, 208
Ingram, James, 204
Inori, 196–7, 198, 200, 204, 208, 232
Institut de Recherche et de Coordination Acoustique (Musique) (IRCAM), 211, 221, 232
'Intensität', 174
Intermodulation, 185
International Society for Contemporary Music (ISCM), 103, 106, 149
'Intervall', 174
'Invention and Discovery', 112
Isaac, Heinrich, 20

Jacob, Paul, 88
Jahreslauf, Der, 2, 4, 231, 236
'Japan', 180
Japanese Radio, 2, 141
Jefferson Airplane, 148
Jeita caves, 175–6, 177
Jenny, Hans, 193
Johns, Jasper, 123, 153
Johnson, David, 178, 180, 200
Johnson, Dennis Lee, 96
Journal Musical, 163
Journées de Musique Contemporaine, 184
Joyce, James, 90
Jubiläum, 208–9
Judine, Maria, 94

Kagel, Mauricio, 89–90, 93, 96, 103, 108
Kaiser, Hermann-Josef, 96
Kalinowski, Horst Egon, 90
Kaprow, Allan, 131–2
Kassel Musiktage, 105
Kataragama Festival, 219
Kelemen, Milko, 96
Khan, Hazrat Inayat, 189, 196–7
Khan, Imrad, 222
Kiel Opera House, 189
King, Alvin, 129–30
Klaiber, Joachim, 147
Klavierstücke I-IV, 46, 50, 66, 68, 94, 95, 98, 146
Klavierstücke V-VIII, 65, 68, 69, 75, 76–7, 94, 98, 146
Klavierstücke IX-X, 133, 146, 148, 158
Klavierstück XI, 86–7, 88, 92–3, 98, 146
Klee, Paul, 33, 90, 96, 145
Kloth, Franz-Josef, 14, 20
Koch, Karl O., 147
Koenig, Gottfried Michael: Cologne Courses, 128; Cologne studio, 82, 94; Darmstadt, 34; memories of Stockhausen 65, 84; passing references, 90, 103, 106
Kölner Rundschau, 30, 111
Kontakte, 16, 93, 100–4, 107–8, 112, 113, 114, 129, 148, 158, 192
Kontarsky, Alfons, 182–3
Kontarsky, Aloys, 155; Cologne Courses, 128; Ensemble, 151; 'Es', 169; Klavierstücke, 146; Mantra, 182–3; Mikrophonie I, 137, 149; Prozession, 149–50; Sonatine, 184
Kontarsky, Bernhard, 137
'Kontrapunkte', 52
Kontra-Punkte, 56, 58–60, 75, 95
Kopling family, 8
Kotoński, Welodzimierz, 121, 128
Kramer, Harry, 90
Krauss, Else C., 26
Kremer, Gidon, 205
Krenek, Ernst, 87

Kreuzspiel, 37, 40–3, **42**, 52, 98, 99, 124, 184
Krist, Joachim, 90, 181, 194, 200–1
Kruttge, Eigel, 60, 90
Kupković, Ladislav, 151
Kurtág, György, 122
Kürten, 117, 137, **138**, 160, 171, 184, 194, 234–5
Kurzwellen, 146, **158**, 159, 160, 167
Kurzwellen mit Beethoven Opus, 1970, 176

Lachmund, Peter, 22–3
Lauhus, Haro, 110
Le Corbusier, 64
Le Jeune, Claude, 49
Lee, Robert James, 190
Leeuw, Ton de, **71**
Lehmann, Hans Ulrich, 125
Leibowitz, René, 31, 87
Lemacher, Heinrich, 22
Lenin, Vladimir Ilyich, 189
Lennon, John, 171
Lewinski, Wolf-Eberhard von, 147
Licht, 1–2, **4**, 5, 29, 141, 158, 188, 192, 202, 210–36
Lichtenstein, Roy, 123
Liebe der Anderen, Die, 24
Liège, 192–3
Ligeti, György, 33–4, 41, 89–90, 106, 121
Limmer, Joachim, 96
Lindlar, Heinrich, 169
Lisbon, 234
Liszt, Franz, 122
'Litanei', 162
Ljubimow, Alexei, 208
London, 140
London, Covent Garden, 216
Lorber, Jakob, 190, 207
Lorenz, Konrad, 118
Lorimer, Michael, 166–7
Louafi, Alain, 197
Louis Ferdinand, Prince of Prussia, 39
Luening, Otto, 40
Luig, Anton, 15
Lutoselawski, Witold, 121
'Luzifers Tanz', 107

Maas, Walter, **71**
Macerro, Teo, 95
McGuire, John, 194
Machaut, Guillaume de, 49
Maciunas, George, 132
MacLow, Jackson, 131–2
Macnaghten Concerts, 169
Maconie, Robin, 139, 205
Maderna, Bruno, 34, 52, 75, 90, **91**
Madison, Connecticut, 156, 166–7, 170–1
Maeght, Aimé, 172
Mahler, Gustav, 153, 174

Maiguashca, Mesias, **131**, 178, 200
Mann, Thomas, 36, 38, 216
Mantra, 99, 182–4, **183**, 199
Mao Tse-tung, 172, 188
Marcuse, Herbert, 188
Mariétan, Pierre, 129
Markowski, Andrzej, 108
Marks, Jay, 148–9, 159
Marschner, Wolfgang, 31
Martin, Frank, 28
Marx, Karl, 188
Masson, André, 173, 176
Masson, Diego, 171–2
Masson, Gérard, **131**
Melos, 105
Mercenier, Marcelle, 66, 68, 76–7
Meriweather, Annette, 208, 231
Mersmann, Hans, 22, 26
Messiaen, Olivier, **47**; influence, 27, 32, 36, 41, 73, 154; on Stockhausen, 48–9; pupils, 33, 34, 86; teaching, 46–8; works, 27, 32–3, 38, 41, 55, 228
Metzger, Heinz-Klaus: Boulez contact, 50; 'Cologne Manifesto', 106–7, 110; Darmstadt, 34; influence, 82, 90; on *Gesang der Jünglinge*, 84; on *Zeitmasse*, 85
Mexico City, 154
Meyer, Wilhelm, 85, 145
Meyer, Wolfgang Sebastian, 145–6
Meyer-Eppler, Werner **71**; aleatory music, 70, 83; at Darmstadt, 34; death, 108; electronic studio, 39; relationship with Stockhausen, 52, 68, 70, 72; work, 70
Mielke, Georg, 20
Mies, Paul, 22, 26
Mikrophonie I, 135–9, 144, 146, 149, 150, 199
Mikrophonie II, 129, 139, 146
Milan, La Scala, 211, 213, 222, 236
Milhaud, Darius, 36, 38, 46
Miró, Joan, 172–3
'Mitten im Leben', 27
Mixtur, 133–5, **134**, 137, 140, 150
Miyawaki, Aiko, 143
Moles, Abraham, 53, 55
Momente, 5, 16, 49, 117–18, 119–21, 126, 128, 133, 135, 137, 140, 146, 194
Mondrian, Piet, 145–6
Monophonie, 107
Montag, 221–8, **223**, **225**, **226**, 230, 233, 234
Monteverdi, Claudio, 49
Moorman, Charlotte, 114, 131–2
Morton, Lawrence, 94
'Mosaik', 37
Moscow, 232–4
Mosel (policeman), 15
Mothers of Invention, 171
Motte, Manfred de la, 90

Mozart, Wolfgang Amadeus, 18, 49, 72, 230
Müller-Blagovitsch, Rolf, 22
Munich Musica Viva concerts, 56
'Music for the Beethovenhalle', 174–5
Musik für ein Haus, 164–6, 174, 181
Musik im Bauch, 204–5
'Musik im Wald', 181

Neuhaus, Max, 129, 132
Neutra, Richard, 117
New Music Festival, 58, 60
New York, 129, 130–2, 135, 153, 186–8
New York Philharmonic Orchestra, 147–8, 170
New York Times, 186
Nizza, 208
Nono, Luigi, **54**; at Darmstadt, 34, 61, 77; relationship with Stockhausen, 87–8, 90, 98; works, 36, 52
North German Radio, 50
Nostradamus, 190
Novalis, 84
Nuits de la Fondation Maeght, 172

'Oben und Unten', 162, 171, 173
Obst, Michael, **223**, 231
Oeldorf Group, 200
Oldenburg, Claes, 123
Opel, Jean, 18
Orff, Carl, 29
Originale, 114, 117, 131, 192
Orlovsky, Peter, 131
Osaka World Fair, 166, 168, 178–80, **179**

Paik, Nam June, 89, 114, 116, 132–3
Palermo New Music Week, 128
Palm, Siegfried, 128
Paris Conservatoire, 32, **47**
Paris Festival d'Automne, 230
Paris Radio, 40, 168
Paris, Théâtre de Ville, 184
Paris, Théâtre National Populaire, 171
Partch, Harry, 95, 130
Paspels, 79–80, **81**, 106–7
Pasternak, Boris, 94
Pasveer, Kathinka, **203**, 221, 222, **223**
Pees, Ewald, 20
Peixinho, Jorge, 152
Pekarski, Mark, 208
Penderecki, Krzysztof, 108, 121
Pennsylvania University, 129, 130
Petrescu, Christian, 194
Pfrogner, Hermann, 40
Piene, Otto, 166, 178
Platz, Robert H.P., 194
'Pluramon', 154
Plus-Minus, 124, 128–30, 133, 144, 149
Pogačnik, Miha, 200

Pole, 146, 178, 186
Pollock, Jackson, 72, 74
'Polyvalent Form', 107
Portal, Michel, 172
Portmann, Adolf, 118
Pousseur, Henri: relationship with Stockhausen, 65–6, 68, 76, 90; teaching, 87, 128; works, 66, 72, 93
Prague, 158
Projektion, 148–9, 170
Prozession, 99, 146, 150, 158, 162, 164, 167, 232
Punkte, 52, 58, 123–5
Purce, Jill, 189, 193

Rabinowitsch, Alexander, 208
Ranta, Michael, 178
Rauschenberg, Robert, 74, 95, 123
Redel, Kurt, 77
Refrain, 98, 108, 129, 148
'Resistance to New Music' broadcast, 104
Reuge, Jean, 205
Rheinische Musikschule, 126, 169
Richertz, Josef, 20
'Richtige Dauern', 161
Rihm, Wolfgang, 194, 199
Rilke, Rainer Maria, 23
Rio de Janeiro, 230
Rockefeller, Nelson, 208
Rockstroh, Siegfried, 98
Rodens, Gaby, 193
Rognoni, Luigi, 77
Ronconi, Luca, 211, 217
Rosbaud, Hans, 43, 50, 52–3, 107
Rostand, Claude, 77
Royan Festival, 204
Rudesheim Music Weeks, 126
Ruland, Heiner, 40

Saariaho, Kaija, 232
Sacher, Paul, 125
Saint-Phalle, Nicki de, **221**
'Saitenmann, Der', 27–8
Salm, Altgraf, 53
Salzburg, 230
Samstag, 141, 216–21, **218**, **220**, 222
Sartre, Jean-Paul, 231
Satprem, 160, 162–3, 185
Saucedo, Victor, **131**
Schaeffer, Pierre, 34, 39, 50, 53, 55–7
Schat, Peter, 172
Scherchen, Hermann, 36, 58, 60, 76
Schibler, Armin, 61
Schieri, Fritz, 27
Schlagquartett, 50, 56
Schlagtrio, 50
Schlee, Alfred, **54**; *Mikrophonie*, 137; Prague

visit, 158; relationship with Stockhausen, 53, 61, 66, 168, 184
Schmidt, Helmut, 208
Schmidt, Hugo Wolfram, 126, 169
Schmidt, Loki, 208
Schmidt-Görg, Joseph, 72
Schmidt-Neuhaus, Hans Otto, 22–3
Schneider-Wessling, Erich, 117
Schoenberg, Arnold: 'Dance around the Golden Calf', 34, 36–7, 38; Darmstadt, 34–5, 61; death, 36; influence, 32–3, 53; influence on Stockhausen, 26–7, 173; *Moses und Aron*, 34, 153; 'O Du mein Gott', 84; on Cage, 74; performances of works, 26; twelve-note music, 26, 32–3; passing references, 46, 49, 94, 104, 216, 228
Schroeder, Hermann, 22, 27–9, 39
Schröter, Heinz, 194
Schubert, Franz, 39
Schuller, Gunther, 95
Schumacher, Gaby, 200
Schütz, Heinz, 63
Schweinitz, Wolfgang von, 199
Schwenk, Theodor, 189
Schwertsik, Kurt, 96, 112, **120**, 122–3
Seismogramme, 66
Senden, Paul, 23
Senfl, Ludwig, 20
Serocki, Kazimierz, 121
'Setz die Segel', 171
Seuthe, Detmar, 26, 29, **30**, 31
Shakespeare, William, 23
Shearing, George, 137
Shinohara, Makoto, 112, 140
Shiraz-Persepolis Festival of Arts, 188
Shostakovich, Dmitri, 94
Sibelius, Jean, 114
Sil'vestrov, Valentin, 121
Sirius, 1, 190, **206**, 206–9
Sirius Centre, 1, 4
Smalley, Roger, 185
Sokolov, Ivan, 233
Solo, 144, 149
Sonatine, 30, 43, 46, 184
Souster, Tim, 185
Souvtchinsky, Pierre, 168
Spek, Jaap, 135–7
Spiel, 50, 52–3
Spira, Emile, 96
Spiral, 146, 167–8, 172, 178, 189, 208
Stein, Leonard, 94
Steinecke, Wolfgang: Darmstadt Courses, 31, 66, 87, 95–6; death, 112–14, 121; *Klavierstücke*, 66
Steiner, Rudolf, 189, 196
Stephens, Jayne, 204
Stephens, Suzanne, 200–2, **203**, 208, 222

Sternklang, 184–5, 188, 190
Stiebler, Ernst-Albrecht, 96
Stimmung, 156–8, **157**, 168, 172, 176, 185, 197, 199
Stockhausen, Christel, 90, **195**
Stockhausen, Doris (*née* Andreae) **38**; *Carré*, 100; children, 64, 79, 90; *Drei Lieder*, 27; *Klavierstücke*, 47, 77; marriage, 45, 52, 63–4, 66, 79–80, 90, 94, 111, 124; *Mikrophonie*, 137; *Momente*, 117; relationship with Stockhausen, 23, 25, 37, 44–5, 90, 150
Stockhausen, Gert, 18
Stockhausen, Gertrud (*née* Stupp), 7–8, **9**, 13–14, 212
Stockhausen, Hermann-Josef, 11, 13, 212
Stockhausen, Julika, 141, **195**
Stockhausen, Katharina (grandmother), **16**
Stockhausen, Katharina (sister), *see* Ernst, Katharina
Stockhausen, Luzia, 18, 19, 24
Stockhausen, Majella, 90, **195**, 202
Stockhausen, Markus, 90, **195**, 202, 206, 208, 222
Stockhausen, Simon (father), 7–8, **10**, 11–15, **17**, 18–19, 213
Stockhausen, Simon (son), 149, **195**, 202, 222, 231
Stockhausen, Suja, 64, 90, **195**
Stockhausen, Waltraud, 18
Stop, 146, 171
Stour Music Festival, 168
Stravinsky, Igor, 22, 26, 29, 32–3, 46, 49, 92, 104, 168
Strobel, Heinrich: death, 190; Donaueschingen Festival, 43, 106, 123–4; *Melos*, 105; *Monophonie*, 107; *Punkte*, 123–4; relationship with Stockhausen, 43, 46, 50, 124; *Zeitmasse*, 84–5
Stuckenschmidt, Hans Heinz, 58, 77
Studie I, 62–5, 72, 83
Studie II, 65–6, **67**, 72, 83
'Studie für Orchester', 43, 50
Stupp, Gertrud, *see* Stockhausen, Gertrud
Süddeutsche Zeitung, 214
Suzuki, Daisetsu T., 74, 118, 144
Swiss Radio, 230

Tanning, Dorothea, 168
Tarr, Edward, 178
Tawaststjerna, Erik, 114
Tchaplygina, Marina, 233
Telemusik, 142–4, 146, 152–3
Telemusik Festival, 232
Tenney, James, 132
Texte zur Musik, 90
Tezak, Mark, 194

Thernierssen, Theo, 18
Thomas, Ernst, 121, 128, 146–7
Thompson, Marc, 222
Thomson, Virgil, 95
Tibetan Book of the Dead, 190, 216
Tierkreis, 194, 205, 207, 208
Tillmann, Hans Günther, 68, 96
Tinguely, Jean, 90, 123, **221**
Togni, Camillo, 52
Tokyo, 141–4
Tokyo National Theatre, 2
Tomek, Otto, 90, 122, 190
Toop, Richard, 93
Toyama, Yazo, 95
Trans, 107, 190–2, 204
Trautwein, Friedrich, 39
'Treffpunkt', 169
Tudor, David, **88**, **120**; Cage's influence, 73; in Cologne, 110; Darmstadt, 87, 96, 111; *Klavierstück XI*, 87; *Kontakte*, 103; Locust Valley, 123; *Originale*, 114; *Refrain*, 98; relationship with Stockhausen, 75, 87, 129

Uenami, Wataru, 143
'Unbegrenzt', 172–3
Universal Edition, 53, 184
Urantia Book, The, 188, 196, 210, 228
Ussachevsky, Vladimir, 40

Varèse, Edgard, **71**; at Darmstadt, 31; death, 140; *Déserts*, 75; relationship with Stockhausen, 76, 95, 129, 132, 140; Stockhausen on, 130
Venice Bienniale, 174
Verdi, Giuseppe, 37
Verlaine, Paul, 27
Vetter, Michael, 178
Victoria, Queen, 190
Vision, 182
Vivier, Claude, 194
Volans, Kevin, 194

Wagner, Richard, 49, 228
Wangenheim, Volker, 174
Warhol, Andy, 123
Warsaw Autumn, 94
Washington DC, 208
WDR in Cologne (Cologne Radio): Broadcasting Hall, 72, 90, **127**, 139; *Chöre für Doris*, 27; commissions, 79, 110; Eimert's position, 30, 39, 61; electronic studio, 39, 52, 56, 58, **59**, 62–6, 110, 194, **227**, 236; *Hymnen*, 152; *Kontra-Punkte*, 58; *Montag*, 223; Musik der Zeit concerts, 90; New Music Festival, 58–61; Stockhausen broadcasts, 31, 130; Stockhausen's grant, 68
WDR Wind Quintet, 85, 145
Webern, Anton, 26, 32–4, 36, 49, 60–1, 145
Weidemann, Gerhard, 60
Weiler, Klaus, 29, 60
Weizsäcker, Richard von, 231
Welt, Die, 208
Wesselmann, Tom, 123
Wieser, Wolfgang, 124
Wildgans, Friedrich, 52
Wilhelm, Jean-Pierre, 90, 114
Wolff, Christian, 73, 75, 95
Wolpe, Stefan, 132
Wörner, Karl H., 139
Wright, Frank Lloyd, 117
Wyle, Nancy, 148, 154, 158, 196, 205

Xenakis, Iannis, 49

Ylem, 183
Young, La Monte, 96, 110

Zappa, Frank, 171
Zeitmasse, 84–6, **85**, 88, 93–5, 98, 145, 168
Zimmermann, Bernd Alois, 34, 52, 105, 110
Zyklus, 96–8, **97**, 108, 126, 129, 158, 208